Far From Home
When Georgiana Gregory makes the long journey from Hull for New York, she hopes to escape the confines of English life. But once there, Georgiana finds she isn't far from home when she encounters a man she knows – a man who presents dangers almost too much to cope with . . .

The Kitchen Maid
Jenny secures a job as kitchen maid in a grand house in Beverley – but her fortunes fail when scandal forces her to leave. Years later, she is mistress of a hall, but she never forgets the words a gypsy told her: that one day she will return to where she was happy and find her true love . . .

The Songbird
Poppy Mazzini has an ambition – to go on the stage. Her lovely voice and Italian looks lead her to great acclaim. But when her first love from her home town of Hull becomes engaged to someone else, she is devastated. Will Poppy have to choose between fame and true love?

Nobody's Child
Now a prosperous Hull businesswoman, Susannah grew up with the terrible stigma of being nobody's child. When daughter Laura returns to the Holderness village of her mother's childhood, she will discover a story of poverty, heartbreak and a love that never dies . . .

Fallen Angels
After her dastardly husband tries to sell her, Lily Fowler is alone on the streets of Hull. Forced to work in a brothel, she forges friendships with the women there, and together they try to turn their lives around. Can they dare to dream of happy endings?

The Long Walk Home
When Mikey Quinn's mother dies, he is determined to find a better life for his family – so he walks to London from Hull to seek his fortune. There he meets Eleanor, and they gradually make a new life for themselves. Eventually, though, they must make the long walk home to Hull . . .

Rich Girl, Poor Girl
Polly, living in poverty, finds herself alone when her mother dies. Rosalie, brought up in comfort on the other side of Hull, loses her own mother on the same day. When Polly takes a job in Rosalie's house, the two girls form an unlikely friendship. United in tragedy, can they find happiness?

Homecoming Girls
The mysterious Jewel Newmarch turns heads wherever she goes, but she feels a longing to know her own roots. So she decides to return to her birthplace in America, where she learns about family, friendship, love and home. But most importantly, love . . .

The Harbour Girls

Jeannie spends her days at the water's edge waiting for Ethan to come in from fishing. But then she falls for a handsome stranger. When he breaks his word, Jeannie finds herself pregnant and alone in a strange new town. Will she ever find someone to truly love her – and will Ethan ever forgive her?

The Innkeeper's Daughter

Bella's dreams of teaching are dashed when she has to take on the role of mother to her baby brother. Her days are brightened by visits from Jamie Lucan – but when the family is forced to move to Hull, Bella is forced to leave everything behind. Can she ever find her dreams again?

His Brother's Wife

The last thing Harriet expects after her mother dies is to marry a man she barely knows, but her only alternative is the workhouse. And so begins an unhappy marriage to Noah Tuke. The only person who offers her friendship is Noah's brother, Fletcher – the one person she can't possibly be with . . .

Every Mother's Son

Daniel Tuke hopes to share his future with childhood friend Beatrice Hart. But his efforts to find out more about his heritage throw up some shocking truths: is there a connection between the families? Meanwhile, Daniel's mother Harriet could never imagine that discoveries about her own family are also on the horizon . . .

Little Girl Lost

Margriet grew up as a lonely child in the old town of Hull. As she grows into adulthood she forms an unlikely friendship with some of the street children who roam the town. As Margriet acts upon her inspiration to help them, will the troubles of her past break her spirit, or will she be able to overcome them?

No Place for a Woman

Brought up by a kindly uncle after the death of her parents, Lucy grows up inspired to become a doctor, just like her father. But studying in London takes Lucy far from her home in Hull, and she has to battle to be accepted in a man's world. An even greater challenge comes with the onset of the First World War. Will Lucy be able to follow her dreams – and find love – in a world shattered by war?

A Mother's Choice

Delia has had to fend for herself and her son Jack for ten years, and as a young unmarried mother, life has never been easy. With no money, Delia is faced with an impossible, heart-wrenching choice. Can she bear to leave Jack behind, hoping another family will care for him? What else can a mother do to give her son the life he deserves?

NOBODY'S CHILD

Val Wood

CORGI BOOKS

TRANSWORLD PUBLISHERS
61–63 Uxbridge Road, London W5 5SA
www.penguin.co.uk

Transworld is part of the Penguin Random House group of companies
whose addresses can be found at global.penguinrandomhouse.com

Penguin
Random House
UK

First published in Great Britain in 2006 by Bantam Press
an imprint of Transworld Publishers
Corgi edition published 2007
Corgi edition reissued 2018

A CIP catalogue record for this book
is available from the British Library.

ISBN 9780552173643

Typeset in New Baskerville by Kestrel Data, Exeter, Devon
Printed and bound in Great Britain by Clays Ltd, Elcograf S.p.A.

Penguin Random House is committed to a sustainable future
for our business, our readers and our planet. This book is made
from Forest Stewardship Council® certified paper.

1 3 5 7 9 10 8 6 4 2

*To Peter, Catherine, Ruth and Alex for their
constant support and encouragement*

ACKNOWLEDGEMENTS AND AUTHOR'S NOTE

My thanks are due to many people of East Yorkshire who have been generous enough to give me their time and knowledge of Holderness. They include: Larry Malkin, the members of the Hidden Holderness group, and my good friend Chris Buckle who 'walked the fields' of Welwick with me in order that I might find the right place to inspire me for the setting of this book.

Grateful thanks are given to Dr Martin T. Craven for his excellent book, *A New and Complete History of the Borough of HEDON*, which was not only informative but also made most enjoyable reading.

Nobody's Child is a book of fiction, though I must explain that according to *The Victoria History of the County of York East Riding*, volume v, Burstall priory and the manor house Burstall Hall did once exist near the banks of the Humber estuary.

Burstall House, which features in this novel, is a figment of my imagination and the description of it could apply to many moated houses once found in Holderness.

The Hedon Fleet or *creke* was once an ancient waterway and probably served the Hedon Haven, but by the nineteenth century, the period of this book, it had long disappeared or been absorbed into other canals, streams, dykes or drains. The Fleet Inn described in this book is my fictional creation.

Books for general reading:

Martin T. Craven, B.Sc., *A New and Complete History of the Borough of HEDON*, The Ridings Publishing Company, Driffield, 1972

The Victoria History of the County of York East Riding, Volume v, published for the University of London Institute of Historical Research by Oxford University Press, 1984

CHAPTER ONE

1880

Laura stood by the edge of the saltmarsh, gazing over the Humber estuary. She kept very still so as not to disturb the hundreds of wading birds – curlew, shelduck, redshank and oystercatcher – that were probing the mudflats for shrimps, lugworms and sea snails. It was just after midday and the sun glinted sharply on the wet surface of the estuarine silt. Was this the spot where her mother had stood debating her future? Had her grandmother come here to contemplate hers? She looked back over her shoulder. The carriage that had brought her was a good distance away, and beside it her brother, in a caped coat, top hat and warm scarf, was pacing impatiently.

Her feet were cold and wet and she glanced down, ruefully regretting that she hadn't thought to wear more sensible boots than these highly polished ones. Her eyes wandered over the spread of the saltmarsh and were caught by the different species of plants. Some look like Michaelmas daisies, she thought; perhaps they're sea asters. She narrowed her eyes and noticed other plants and fine-leaf grasses. Pink thrift, blue couch grasses, and sea lavender. Some of them were growing in the deep channels and runnels which were filling rapidly as the tide turned, flooding the low-lying marsh. Mother would know what they are, she mused. She was a country girl.

'Laura!' James's voice broke into her meditation. The wind was blowing towards him, off the estuary, carrying the sound away, back towards the village of Welwick, yet it was loud enough to startle the feeding birds, causing them to rise up in a soaring feathered flight to freedom. 'Come on! It's freezing out here and the tide is turning.'

She shivered, the coldness of the wind and his words biting into her. So it was.

'I don't know what on earth you are doing, Laura,' her brother grumbled as she returned. 'What a godforsaken place this is!' She lifted the hem of her wool coat as he helped her into the curricle before seating himself beside her, taking the reins and cracking his whip to urge the roan-coloured pair back towards the village. 'I'm thankful you asked me to drive you and not

Stubbs. He'd have thought you mad, wanting to come out here!'

Not mad but curious, she thought as they drove down the rutted track. She glanced curiously at the village homesteads they passed. Did Mama once live in one of these cottages? She would never say, only that she had been born somewhere round here, and that she knew nothing of her own mother except her name. Mary-Ellen.

'Why do you want to know about the past anyway?' James continued brusquely. 'We know who we are. Mother lived here only briefly. She was widowed when Father died at sea. What more is there to know? Leave it at that!'

I can't, she thought as they drove through the village of Patrington and onto the turnpike road towards the ancient town of Hedon. I have to know. I need to know who I am and where I came from.

Their mother, Susannah, had always been reserved and unwilling to speak of her background. She said she hadn't known her mother or father, only Great-aunt Lol, who had brought her up, Aunt Jane, and Jane's husband Wilfred Topham. Of him she said little.

'And what of our papa?' Laura had asked when she was a child. 'I don't remember him at all and neither does James. I wish that I did.'

He was dead, her mother had told her flatly,

he had died not long after Laura was born, and she had to be satisfied with that, though she had the vague feeling that her mother was being evasive and not telling the whole truth. However, she would not be drawn further.

Her mother was still fair and comely, her hair thick and honey-coloured as James's was, her eyes wide and blue; but she was quiet and self-contained, unlike James who oozed confidence and authority, and totally unlike Laura herself, who was above average height, with a mass of unruly dark hair, and invariably spoke her mind without thinking first. But that, Laura mused, as they rattled on towards Hedon where they were to spend the night, is because Mama has given us the confidence to think for ourselves. She's worked to give us a secure background, to be beholden to no-one.

The Fleet Inn where they were staying was on the outskirts of the medieval town of Hedon. An age-old hostelry, it had been built to serve farm labourers, annual harvesters and seamen using the ancient waterways of the town, and was, in the late 1850s, on the point of collapse, until a new owner had come along and bought it, renewed the stables in the yard, put on a new frontage and rearranged the interior to give a public bar, several small rooms, and bedrooms to accommodate visitors. There were frequent walkers in the area who liked to tramp the country roads on their way to Spurn Point, the headland which stretched betwixt the Humber estuary and the sea, or follow the havenside path to the riverside village of Paull.

Their mother Susannah was the leaseholder of the inn and had been for over twenty years, sub-letting it to a succession of licensees. She was also the owner of an inn in Beverley, two shops in Hull and her own house in the village of Hessle where the three of them lived. How she had achieved this when she was a widow, her son and daughter didn't know, for in answer to their questioning she would simply tap the side of her nose and say 'survival instinct'. They agreed to humour her and together privately agreed that their late father must have left her a considerable amount of money which she had invested wisely, for that she was an astute and shrewd woman they had no doubt.

Up in the bedroom which was kept for her mother when she visited, Laura washed her hands and face, tidied her hair and pinned on a white lace cap. She had already changed her wet boots for a pair of indoor slippers, so when James knocked on the door to tell her he was ready to escort her downstairs for the chop supper they had ordered she did not keep him waiting. She was pleased that their mother had suggested they stayed the night here, for she was quite tired and would not have relished a further journey into

Hull and then out again to Hessle on the western side of the town.

The stairs led down into the front entrance of the inn and they could hear the rumble of male voices in the public bar. 'We're in here, I think,' James began, indicating a half-open door through which Laura saw a table set for supper. There was a sudden gust of wind as the front door opened and the man coming in grabbed it to stop it crashing against the wall.

'I beg your pardon,' he said to Laura, taking off his hat. 'I didn't mean to startle you.'

Laura smiled and nodded at the stranger. 'There's quite a breeze getting up,' she answered.

'Ellis? Edmund Ellis? Is it you?' James stared at the man, who was taller by a head than he was.

'It is!' A small frown appeared above the man's nose. 'And you are?'

'Page. James Page! Perhaps you won't remember me? I was in the year below you at Pocklington school.'

'Great heavens! So you were!' Edmund Ellis extended his hand. 'What are you doing out here?'

'Oh, er – just visiting the area. My sister was keen to see Holderness. May I introduce – Laura, this is Edmund Ellis. Ellis – my sister Laura Page.'

Edmund Ellis gazed openly at Laura and gave

a bow. She inclined her head and dipped her knee. Then, unconventionally, she put out her hand. 'How do you do?'

He raised his eyebrows as he took it. 'I'm well, thank you!' He smiled and she saw admiration in his eyes, which did not daunt her in the least. She was used to such glances for her boldness as much as for her beauty.

'You and James were at school together, Mr Ellis? I don't recall James mentioning your name,' she said.

'Our paths didn't cross all that much,' Edmund Ellis replied, 'and I left when I was sixteen to help my grandfather on the estate. Are you staying here?'

'Yes. We're just going in for supper,' James said. 'Perhaps you'd like to join us?' He turned to Laura for her approval and her heart sank. She really didn't want to hear endless tales of schoolboy pranks or reminiscences.

'I'm afraid I can't,' Ellis said. 'I'm on my way home, but if I might join you for a glass of ale before you eat?' He too glanced at Laura for her consent, which she gave. I suppose a short conversation might be interesting, she considered, for he was a personable-looking man, with thick fair hair and very searching blue eyes. He was dressed in country tweeds and cord breeches with long leather boots.

He was also very confident and self-assured,

she decided as she listened to them talking. Rather like James, so perhaps boarding school instils those traits into schoolboys. Perhaps it's a veneer they cultivate to prove they are superior. He stayed chatting and drinking his ale, and in the short time he was with them they learned that both his father and his mother were dead, and that he and his grandfather ran the considerable family estate in Skeffling. He'd grinned. 'He likes to keep an eye on me – hold the reins, you know!'

James had, at Ellis's questioning, told him of his business interests, banking and property, and where they lived.

'Hessle!' Ellis had exclaimed. 'You're a long way from home! I've never been. Quite civilized out there, so I believe?' He'd grinned and looked at Laura. 'Come to look at the country folk, have you?'

She was saved from answering by the arrival of supper and he took his leave of them, which was just as well, she thought, as she wasn't sure whether she would have told him why they were here: that she was in search of her roots, and that her mother had at last decided to humour her and talk a little of her own childhood in isolated Holderness.

'As I've said before, I can tell you nothing about your grandparents,' her mother had said, and her eyes were wistful. 'When I questioned

Aunt Jane, who was my mother's cousin, or her mother, my great-aunt Lol, about whose child I was, they simply said—' She'd swallowed hard and her eyes had filled with tears as she whispered, 'Nobody's. You are nobody's child.'

CHAPTER TWO

1837

'Mary-Ellen! Mary-Ellen! Where are you?' Jane called, looking first in the falling-down cow shelter, and then behind the dilapidated hen house. 'Where are you?'

A figure in the distance coming across the marshy grassland from the estuary waved to her and called back. She had a bundle under one arm and was carrying a metal pail. She looks like a gypsy with that wild black hair blowing round her face, Jane thought as she walked towards her, and she's barefoot! She isn't even wearing boots!

Since they were children, Jane had been in awe of her cousin. Mary-Ellen had been feisty, daring and mischievous and often even scary to quiet mouse-like Jane who was urged to do things she wouldn't have dreamed of doing on her own, such as jumping over the wide dykes and ditches which were scattered over the Holderness fields and marshes to drain the surplus water off the land and back into the Humber.

Sometimes they would clamber onto the barges moored off the banks of the estuary. 'We'll fall in,' a nervous Jane would cry. 'I don't want to.' But she would be urged on and she didn't drown, as she feared she might, not with Mary-Ellen there to look after her, and she had always felt a sense of triumph and achievement as they ran home for their supper, Jane to the village of Welwick and Mary-Ellen a mile further along the estuary bank to her isolated home at Welwick Thorpe.

'Look.' Mary-Ellen raised the pail. 'Elvers and shrimps for supper.' She held up a wet greeny-coloured bundle. 'And samphire. Food for free! And I've set another trap for rabbits. There's dozens about.'

Jane wrinkled her nose. Though she knew how to skin a rabbit, she hated to do it or see them caught in a trap. 'I've come to tell you summat,' she said, as they turned and walked back to the cottage where Mary-Ellen lived with her widowed father. 'I've got a job! A proper job o' work.'

Mary-Ellen put down the pail and brushed her hair away from her forehead, leaving a muddy streak. 'Where? Who'd have a scrap like you?'

She grinned as she asked and it wasn't meant unkindly, for Jane was small in height, and as thin as if she'd never had a decent meal in her life. In this isolated rural area of Holderness close by the river, they all ate whatever they could grow or catch: potato soup, fish stew or rabbit. Some, like Mary-Ellen, thrived on it; at seventeen she was tall and had the rounded curves and breasts of womanhood, whereas Jane was childlike in appearance.

'I've been took on at Ellis's farm at Skeffling. I'm to help with 'washing and to do 'rough.'

'To do 'rough?' Mary-Ellen laughed. 'You'll not last five minutes! Why you? You've allus stopped at home and helped your ma.'

'I know.' Jane was rueful. 'But Maggie's getting wed soon and will move away, so we won't have her wages, and Ma says I should start work now that I'm thirteen. Our Sally's old enough to help her in 'house and with 'bairns. I don't want to go,' she added.

'You'll be all right, Janey.' Mary-Ellen put her arm round her cousin's shoulder. 'Who got you 'job then? Mr Bennett?'

Mr Bennett was the agent who collected rents from the smallholders, tenant farmers and cottagers on behalf of the various landowners.

'Yes,' Jane replied. 'Ma had asked him during 'summer if he'd put in a word for me at some of 'big houses, cos I was honest and willing 'n' that. And he came round 'other day and said he'd heard that Ellis's cook was wanting somebody, and she didn't want to ask at 'workhouse like last time. She said that 'young lasses from there didn't know one end of a broom handle from t'other. I'm to start at Martinmas,' she added.

'I'll miss you, Janey,' Mary-Ellen said. 'Who'll I talk to when you're gone?'

Jane shrugged. 'Onny my ma,' she said. 'She likes you to come. She still misses your ma, I think.'

Mary-Ellen nodded. Aunt Lol was her mother's sister and had been a surrogate mother to Mary-Ellen after her mother died until she was old enough to look after herself and her father Isaac. Isaac Page, however, was extremely demanding and grumbled if she spent time away from their homestead. 'Lol has plenty of her own kin to blether to. She doesn't need you,' he would say, if ever Mary-Ellen went to visit. 'And you've plenty to occupy you here without gallivanting over to Welwick.' He had never really got on with Aunt Lol, probably because she had a sharp tongue and he had felt its lash from time to time.

A rough, hard-working labouring man, he had felt his wife's loss keenly. He hadn't wanted much, he ruminated into his ale. He liked his food on the table, a good fire in the hearth and a warm bed. Mary-Ellen kept hens, milked the cow, grew vegetables, and washed and cooked for him. For his bed she provided a hot brick wrapped in a piece of flannel, though there were some nights when he stayed overlong at the hostelry in Welwick, drowning his sorrows and occasionally taking comfort from an obliging female.

'November?' Mary-Ellen said now. 'Well, you'll be well settled in before winter comes. You'll be in a warm kitchen; they'll have fires in every room, I should think—'

'Aye, and I'll have to clean 'em,' Jane interrupted.

'But you hate 'winter! You're allus complaining about being cold. And you'll get fattened up with all that good meat that 'toffs eat.'

'But I won't know anybody, Mary-Ellen, and nobody'll talk to me.'

'Well, you don't know anybody round here! And who is there to talk to 'cept me and a few other bairns?' Mary-Ellen patted her on the shoulder. 'It'll be a new life for you, Jane, just you see.'

Do I wish it were me? she wondered later as she filled another pail from the pump. She scooped up the pale gritty shrimps, put them into the fresh water and began to clean them. I could wish I was going from this drudgery, though I wouldn't want to work in the big houses and be at the beck and call of anybody. But it would never happen. Her father wouldn't allow it. He agreed that she could go into the fields at harvest time, but vowed that she'd never go into service, nor work in any of the inns or hostelries.

She must keep house for him. But she also knew that no-one would employ her. She was known to be wild, with a sharp tongue and a will and spirit that couldn't be tamed. The only one who held any sway over her was her father, and he did that with the back of his hand and on occasions with his belt as if she was the son he had never had.

Yet Mary-Ellen was generous of spirit and could be kind and loving, as she was with Jane, of whom she was fiercely protective. Jane was invincible when Mary-Ellen was there. No lad or teasing lass would torment Jane if they thought that her cousin would find out.

Isaac Page came home in the late afternoon. A square-set, heavy man, he worked the farms when they needed him for spring sowing or autumn harvesting; he could dig a ditch and turn a furrow, or fish with the boatmen of Patrington Haven or at the riverside village of Paull. He boasted that he could turn his hand to anything, and he did. He had never refused an offer of work.

Mary-Ellen could smell ale on him as he came into the one-roomed dwelling, but he wasn't drunk, and he sniffed appreciatively. 'Fish pie?' he asked.

'Eel pie,' she said, 'and shrimps! I've been down to 'river, and on 'way back I found some elvers buried in the mud.'

He nodded. 'Was 'tide in? Did you tek 'boat out?'

'No. I thought I might catch flounder, but 'tide was running too fast for me to go out, so I just dipped my net and found a few shrimps. It would have been a poor supper if I hadn't found these elvers.' She'd made a substantial meal, chopping off the heads of the little eels, and then cutting them into small pieces before putting them into a pie dish with onions and potatoes. She covered the mixture with a thick flour and water paste and cooked it in the brick oven at the side of the fire. She'd rinsed the samphire to remove the salt and then heated it over the flame, in a pan with a drop of water and a knob of dripping.

Her father had built the brick oven and fire-place for her mother when he had first brought her here, before Mary-Ellen was born. It was heated by wood, so they wasted nothing. Every twig or fallen branch was kept for fuel, both to keep them warm and for cooking. Sometimes a log or spar was washed up on the estuarine marsh and she would drag it home triumphantly, leaving it to dry in the lee of the cow shelter, ready for use on the winter days when they couldn't go out. The weather could be cruel here in the depths of winter, when the flat marshy land was covered in snow, and there were no indications of hidden drains or ditches.

They scraped up the few fallen leaves in the

autumn, for this was almost a treeless country-side, and piled them in the hen house, leaving them until they settled to a thick matted texture, when a handful would be put on the fire over-night to give a slow burn. Then in the spring they dug the rotted mulch into the area where Mary-Ellen grew potatoes, leeks, onions and carrots.

'You're a good lass,' her father admitted, as he tucked into the pie. 'But you must tek care if you go out on 'river. How would I manage if owt happened to you?'

She reflected that he would only miss her for her skills at keeping him fed and warm. *Is that all women are useful for? Is that why he married my mother? Was he attracted to her when he met her? She was pretty, I remember, more comely than Aunt Lol; at least she was before she became ill.* Her mother had been dragged down by repeated miscarriages. Mary-Ellen, the eldest and sole surviving offspring, had only memories of her mother constantly carrying a child and then losing it.

That's not what I want, she thought, clearing away the dishes and putting them into a tin bowl to wash later. Then she set the kettle over the fire to make a hot drink. *I don't want to be constantly having babies. One would be all right, or maybe two, but no more than that. You're for ever poor when there's a lot of bairns. Look at Aunt Lol and Uncle Ben and their brood.* She gave a deep

27

sigh. But how to stop them from coming, that's the problem. You can keep a cock away from the hens and a ram away from the ewes, but how do you keep a husband out of your bed?

'Mary-Ellen!' Her father's voice broke into her thoughts. 'Tha's lookin' dowly. What 'you pondering on?'

She shrugged. 'Nowt much,' she said, knowing the subject wasn't one to share with her father. 'Just this and that.'

He screwed up one eye and gazed at her with the other, a habit he had if he was concentrating. 'Fed up with your lot, are you?' he asked perceptively. 'Wishing for summat more?'

'Don't know what more there is,' she muttered. 'I haven't seen owt for me to wish for. Our Janey's going into service at Martinmas, at one of 'Skeffling farms,' she added.

'Janey who?' he grunted.

Irritated, she raised her eyebrows. 'Aunt Lol's Jane,' she said testily. *You* know!'

'How am I expected to keep track of all them bairns?' he answered sharply. 'Is she 'skinny lass that's allus coming here? She's got nowt on her. How is it they've tekken her?'

'Cos she's honest and willing, I think,' Mary-Ellen said, 'and their cook needs somebody.'

He humphed, muttering something about gentry and their servants. 'Is that what you want to do?' he asked abruptly. 'Cos if it is, you can

28

forget it! Don't get any fancy ideas. You're wanted here!'

'I didn't say I wanted to go into service,' she said sullenly. 'But I never see anybody from one day to 'next. I've nobody to talk to, Da, not till you come home, and then you're either off out or you fall asleep in front of 'fire.'

'Talk to?' he barked. 'I've told you afore, there's plenty for you to do without spending your time gossiping.' This time he narrowed both eyes. 'Or are you talking about meeting lads?' He pointed a threatening finger. 'Cos I'll not have that! I'll tek 'strap to you first, aye, and them as well.'

She curled a disdainful lip. The village lads from Welwick or Weeton who came larking down to the river held no attraction for her, though they called jokingly to her or showed off in front of her. 'I'm talking about conversation, Da! Somebody to discuss things with.'

'Discuss? What's to discuss apart from 'weather and where 'next meal is coming from?' He chewed on his lip as he deliberated and stretched his legs up onto the hearth. 'When 'time comes – when I can't work any more – then I'll look round for some likely fella for you to marry and he can come here and keep us both.'

She tossed her head. 'I'll be too old then! You forget I'm seventeen! And if I wanted to marry – which I don't – then I'd choose for myself, thank you! And besides,' she added, 'I don't know who you think'd want to come and live here in this rat hole.' She flinched as she spoke and dodged the slap which she had known would come.

'Just watch your mouth, lass,' he threatened, standing up, and picking up his jacket to go out. 'I'll not stand for it.'

'And what'll you do if I decide to leave?' she taunted, unable to leave well alone. 'You just asked how you'd manage if I drowned in 'river!'

'I'd find some poor wench down on her luck.' He pulled on his hat. He glanced at her as he spoke and their eyes met. He grinned and so did she.

'She'd have to be at 'bottom of 'barrel to come out here,' she shouted after him as he went out of the door. 'Really hard pinched. With no hope at all!'

They'd both backed away from confrontation, but it was an argument that raised its head time and again.

Mary-Ellen made a pot of tea and, cradling a cup in her hand, stood in the open doorway looking out. Nightfall was slow in descending on this flat hummocky plain but an orange incandescent sun was sinking towards the horizon and the vast sky was brushed with a rich palette of colours: deep purple, ruby red, saffron yellow and hues of apricot, aquamarine and rose. The few trees in the landscape, ash and sycamore, were etched black against the sky. In the distance was the spire of St Patrick's church in Patrington, and beyond that the church steeple in Ottring- ham village. She took a deep breath and drew in the salty aroma of the estuary, the gathered corn and turned brown earth, the smoke of burning fires. September was a notable time, particularly if there had been a good harvest. It saw the culmination of hard work well done, when the winter corn was gathered in, and pigs, sheep and cattle put to graze on chopped turnips and garnered stubble.

I wouldn't want to leave here, she thought. This is my home. My own place. I'm at one with the landscape and the river. But I could wish for more company, for something exciting to happen in my life, for I have this urge that there should be something more than I have now. She felt a quickening sensation of wanting to run like the hares, to fly like the birds which soared above her as they flew to and from their feeding grounds.

She shrugged into herself, a shadow flitting over her. Life is passing me by. She watched the inky darkness fall, fading out the colour and leaving only blackness and silence pressing in on her.

CHAPTER THREE

When Martinmas came, Jane went away to start work in service. She left home blubbering and sobbing, her eyes swollen and her nose red. 'They'll tek one look at you and send you straight back,' her mother, Lol, scolded her. 'Tell her, Mary-Ellen; tell her they won't want a bawling lass working for 'em.'

'It's true, they won't, Janey,' Mary-Ellen agreed. She had come over to the cottage in Welwick especially to say goodbye to Jane, even though her eventual destination was in the opposite direction. 'Come on, I'll set you on 'road. Have you got everything?'

'Nowt much to take,' Jane sniffled. 'Just my nightshift and a bit o' candle.'

'You'll not need that.' Her mother took the candle stub from her. 'They'll surely give you a candle to light you to bed!'

'And I've got my hairbrush and pins, cos I've got to have my hair pinned under a cap.' Her mouth trembled and she began to cry again. 'I don't want to go!'

Her mother picked up the potato sack which she had washed for Jane's belongings. She had packed a parcel of bread and cheese and a bottle of water, and now she handed it to her. 'Come on now, lass, bear up. Just think on how you're helping us out. Your money'll buy all sorts of things and help towards 'new babby.'

'I'll not be here to see it,' Jane wailed. 'It won't know who I am by 'time I come back.'

'They'll give you a day off at Christmas,' Mary-Ellen coaxed. 'Course they will. You'll see it then. It'll not be more than a week or two old. It won't know anybody but its ma.'

She glanced at her aunt as she spoke. Lol was heavily pregnant, fit and hearty, unlike Mary-Ellen's mother, who had always been tired and worn out by her unsuccessful pregnancies.

'Eat that bread and cheese afore you get there,' Lol called after Jane as, clinging to Mary-Ellen's arm, she set off. 'Don't go wasting good food. It'll give you strength and raise your spirits afore you meet them new folks.'

They walked down the muddy track of Sheep Trod Lane into the village where they were to part company, Jane heading to Skeffling and Mary-Ellen in the other direction to Patrington. Today was Patrington's hiring fair, when servants, agricultural workers and casual workers, such as

33

Isaac Page, gathered in the market place in order to obtain employment for the following year. Migrant workers came here too to join the locals: gypsies, Irishmen and tramps, all looking for work on the farms, from digging ditches in the marshy plain of Holderness to loading grain onto the barges at Patrington Haven.

Mary-Ellen rarely went to Patrington, but she liked to go to the annual hirings to see who was about and listen to the local gossip. 'You'll be glad you don't have to stand at 'hirings, Janey,' she said to her cousin as they reached the road where they must separate. 'I'd never want to do that. It must be like being sold as a sheep, or a sow!'

Jane shook her head miserably. 'If these folk don't tek to me I might have to do that next Martinmas.'

'Then you'd best cheer up,' Mary-Ellen advised, 'and do your work well and then they'll want to keep you.'

'It'll be freezing at Skeffling,' Jane complained. ''Wind really blows out there and 'big house stands near 'river and catches all of 'draughts.'

There was no consoling her, Mary-Ellen decided. Whatever words of comfort she offered, they would be rejected. They waved goodbye and Mary-Ellen turned round once to see Jane walking with her head bent, dragging her feet as if she was going to her doom.

Mary-Ellen wrapped her shawl round her head and shoulders. It was a bitterly cold November day and she knew that this was probably the last day of the winter when she would venture so far abroad. Her outdoor activities until the weather turned again would take her no further than their own garden or down to the estuary. Her father had tenanted the cottage, cowshed and plot of land for nearly twenty years, but there had been rumours since the last hirings fair that the title deeds for the acreage at Welwick Thorpe were to be sold. The present landowner was old, and as there was little or no profit in the often flooded area he wanted rid of it.

I hope they don't put the rent up, Mary Ellen mused as she trudged on, and then turned to look over her shoulder as she heard the clip-clop, rumble and rattle of a horse and waggon coming towards her.

'Want a lift?' the driver called out as he reached her.

'Yes, please.'

He put out a hand to help her and she scrambled up to sit by his side on the wooden seat. 'Mary-Ellen!' he said. 'Dost remember me? Jack Terrison? We both went to school at Welwick.' He grinned. 'Not that I went all that often.'

'Yes,' she said, 'course I do! I didn't go all that often either. We had lessons in Mrs Barnes's cottage sometimes, or else in 'church. I used to set off for school,' she recalled, 'but if it was a nice day I used to go down to 'river instead.'

'By, weren't it cold when we were in 'choch!' he said. 'I couldn't feel my fingers sometimes.' He grinned again, and she remembered that he had been a good-natured lad who didn't tease as some of the others did. "Parish paid for me to go, but 'schoolmaister told 'council it was a waste o' their money cos I was nivver there.'

Mary-Ellen nodded. "Parish paid for me as well, and for my cousins. I don't know of anybody who paid for themselves. Who round here can afford schooling for their bairns?' she scoffed.

'Onny thing I remember larning at school was about 'Wright brothers,' Jack said reminiscently. 'You know, Guy Fawkes and his conspirators 'n' that. 'Maister said them two brothers lived ower at Ploughlands.'

'I knew that afore I went to school!' Mary-Ellen said. 'My da told me about them. He reckoned that Guy Fawkes himself came down 'river from York just to meet up with them. Nobody round here would have known him, you see, so they could plot without any fear.'

'Aye!' Jack puckered his lips and nodded. 'Happen he was right. And do you remember – were you in school that day when they told us that 'owd king had died?'

'Yes, I do,' she said. 'We stood up when 'parson

36

came in and announced it. *'King is dead, God save 'king.* I was ten and didn't understand what he meant at first, then 'teacher explained that King George had died and William 'Fourth was now our king.' She laughed. 'Some of 'bairns on Crown land started to cry cos they thought he might want his land back and they'd have nowhere to live!'

They travelled in silence for a while until Jack asked, 'Are you applying for a job o' work, Mary-Ellen? Going into service, is tha?'

'No!' she said. 'I keep house for my da. I'm just going to have a look round. See who's about and what 'gossip is.' She shrugged. 'And buy a sack o' spuds if 'price is right. Ours haven't done all that well this year. They'll not last us over 'winter.'

'I'll carry 'em back for you, if you like?' he offered. 'I've just a few things to pick up for 'maister. I'm being kept on,' he said. 'Fourth lad I am now; went to 'em as least lad. I'm useful,' he added, but without boasting. 'I can turn me hand to most things. I'll be a waggoner one day.'

'Where do you work?' she asked.

'I'm at Ellis's farm at Skeffling. Been there for ower two years. I heard . . .' He hesitated. 'Well, I don't know if it's right, but rumour has it that 'maister is looking to buy more acreage and he's considering land at Welwick Thorpe, where you are.'

'My cousin Jane is starting work with 'Ellises,'

she told him and he nodded and said he knew her. 'I'd heard that 'title deeds were up for sale. They'll have to put in drains and sluices if they want to farm it.'

'Aye, well, Ellis's son is tekking ower some of 'estate and it must be his idea. Though it seems right daft to even consider that waterlogged land if you ask me.' They were pulling towards Patrington now and the tall church spire stood out proudly against the backdrop of leaden, overcast sky. 'Course, they're not farming folk, not originally anyway,' he offered as an excuse for them. 'Family were in woollens, so I believe, ower in Wakefield or somewhere like that.'

Mary-Ellen made no answer, but smiled to herself. According to people round here, you were a newcomer unless your family had lived in the same area for generation after generation. She was sure that the Ellises had been in Holderness for a very long time.

Jack dropped her off in the market place and asked if he could give her a lift home. 'I'll be here until after dinner,' he said. 'I'll get a bite to eat at 'Three Tuns and then mek my way back.'

'I'll look out for you,' she said, 'but don't wait.'

'What about 'taties? You won't be able to carry 'em all 'way home.' He seemed anxious to oblige but she gave him a withering glance.

'Course I will,' she scoffed. 'Who do you think

fetches and carries all day long when my da's at work?'

He shrugged. 'Just trying to save you 'bother, that's all.'

Mary-Ellen relented. 'Well, if I see your waggon, I'll put 'em in 'back, then you can set 'em down at 'lane end. Don't come down with 'waggon, though, cos you'll get bogged down.'

'Bad, is it?'

She nodded. 'Right clarty. Da says he'll break up some old bricks to fill in 'holes afore winter sets in.'

'Is there no chance of you going to live in 'village? Be better for you than being stuck out in middle o' nowhere.'

'No. Da's settled, and 'rent's cheap. He says there's everything there that he needs.'

She turned away to leave, but he held her attention again when he asked, 'What about you then, Mary-Ellen?' His weathered forehead wrinkled into an embarrassed frown. 'Isn't there owt else that you need?'

She looked up at him for a moment as if considering. Then she shook her head. 'Not at 'minute there isn't. Nowt that I can think of, any road.'

The market place was crowded and in spite of the dull, rainy day, most people were in a holiday mood. Farm foremen were there to choose reliable men and lads for heavy work.

39

Housekeepers were looking to take on spruced and tidy parlour or kitchen maids. But times were changing. Working men and women were beginning to object to being picked over in public places. It was demeaning and humiliating, and it was the pushy ones, those who didn't mind being cross-examined in front of others, who gained employment, whilst the quiet ones, the shy or reserved folk, the ones who stood back, were left without a job of work.

Mary-Ellen stood in a shop doorway out of the rain and watched as a juggler entertained the crowd. A man in a threadbare coat was playing on a whistle and a very young girl, a child almost, was dancing in front of him. Her skirt and bodice were of thin cotton and her hair was straggling in wet rats' tails beneath her bonnet. But she was smiling for all she was worth as with her hands on her hips she hopped, skipped and jigged round the plate on the floor which contained but a few coins.

Poor bairn, Mary-Ellen mused; she'll not make much money. Nobody has any, only rich farmers and they'll not be here; they'll have sent their hinds and foremen to do their bartering for them. Across the street she saw Jack Terrison with a group of farm lads. They were strutting, it seemed to her, with their hands in their pockets and their caps pushed to the backs of their heads. They were laughing gleefully and one elbowed another in a jocular manner. She recognized one or two of them as being from Welwick village, lads who worked on the local farms.

Then she saw Jack say something to them, and they looked at him enquiringly and then over their shoulders across and around the market place. Instinctively she drew back into the doorway. She couldn't hear if Jack was speaking of her, and yet she could tell that he was, by how he pointed with his hand back up the road to Welwick, and the way in which they glanced searchingly about. She had always been an enigma to the young people in the village. Always an outsider from the day she had left Aunt Lol's to live permanently with her father down the muddy rutted track which led to the estuary.

What do I care about them, or what they think of me? She lifted her chin and tossed back her head. Her shawl slipped off, letting her mane of dark hair fly free. They're nothing to me. Peasants, every one of them. Scratching a living day to day, just like my da. Getting up in a morning, going to bed at night, and only the daily grind of work in between. No joy, no real happiness.

Someone else was looking at her from across the street. Joseph Ellis had stabled his horse, visited the gunsmith's, asked the wheelwright to call the next time he was in Skeffling, and made

41

some purchases at the draper's for his mother from the list she had given him.

'Be sure to get what I have written down,' she had said. She was unable to come herself because of a heavy cold, and needed her maid to tend to her. 'Don't be fobbed off with a silk thread which is a near match. It must be exact!'

He had been gazing round at the busy scene and wondering if it was too early to call at one of the hostelries and have a glass of ale and a slice of pie. Oblivious of the rain, he had stood with his arms folded, watching the comings and goings, the bartering and the laughter, and thinking of the relief that would be felt by those who had been taken on today for their yearly work. Bed and food provided, and no anxieties about whether the seed would rot in wet ground, or the harvest be safely gathered in, since they'd get their wages anyway. Not like the farmer or landholder, he pondered, who prays every morning for sun and rain in equal measure, and that the price of corn won't drop, or, worse, be depressed by imports of grain from abroad, as it was beginning to. Once these workers have their contract shilling, they'll go and spend it on drink, lifting their glass to another year's employment or the health of some lissom young woman.

Joseph had seen Jack Terrison in the market place with some other horse lads, and thought that, although he might have a glass of ale, the youth wouldn't get drunk. He was a reliable worker and Joseph had kept him on, as he had some of the other men. He had persuaded his father that this was the preferred way to employ farmhands, apart from the casuals who were hired at harvest time. The hiring fairs were abhorrent to him, even though the custom was an old-established one, and he could not bring himself, or even ask his foreman, to walk up and down the line of workers wearing the badges of their trade. The horse lads with strands of horsehair pinned to their caps, the cowmen with a bit of cow tail, the maids with feather dusters or besoms, all waiting to be chosen. Waiting for someone to nod or tap them on the shoulder, to say, 'Aye, tha'll do.'

But his attention had been caught by a girl standing in a doorway opposite: sheltering from the rain, he supposed, and watching the scene as he was doing. She was raven-haired and held her head high. She was different, in a manner he couldn't quite determine, from most of the other young girls here today. He glanced across to where her gaze was directed and saw that she was watching Terrison and the group of lads horsing about. She didn't seem interested in them, he thought, but appeared to be observing them and their actions with a detached and aloof mien.

How does she know them? he wondered. What

43

is any of them to her? Brother? Sweetheart? Or just village lads that she's known all her life? Why would I be interested? He laughed at himself. But strangely, he was. Was it her long black hair, which was uncovered and blowing about her face, or her shapely figure, partly covered by her shawl? Was it the proud way she held herself, her body alert, like a cat about to spring? He was too far away to see the colour of her eyes or whether her nose was long or her lips were full, but there was something about her which attracted him. He walked slowly across the street to discover what it was.

CHAPTER FOUR

Mary-Ellen saw him coming. Though he walked casually towards the shop where she was standing, she felt his purpose. If he thinks I'm here waiting for custom, then he'll soon find out he's mistaken. She had been accosted before when she had been watching people and minding her own business, and there was many a man with a cut lip or smarting cheek for his insolence.

She timed it just right. As he stepped within a few feet of her, she swiftly moved from the doorway and out into the muddy road, dodging between donkey carts, carriers and horse-drawn waggons. She suppressed a laugh of satisfaction as she saw a confused look on his face. Just who does he think he is?

Gentleman farmer, I'll bet, she surmised. Clean breeches; a good pair of boots, though muddy; an old leather hat which partly covered his eyes, but revealed a generous mouth. As she bent down to examine a box of carrots at a stall, she looked under her arm and saw him watching her and was curious enough to wonder who he was.

He went into the shop and she turned away and continued with her purchases. She bought the carrots and a small sack of potatoes, and then crossed the square to the grocer's where she bought tea and a bag of flour. As she came out of the shop, the rain began in earnest. Pelting, sleeting, icy cold rain which made everyone run for shelter into doorways or under the awnings of the stalls. She was hampered by her purchases and couldn't stay in the shop doorway as she was blocking the entrance, so she began to run, the potato sack banging across her shoulder, towards the archway of the smith's shop.

In his haste to escape the worst of the downpour, Joseph pulled down his hat and ran in the same direction, and crashed right into her. The sack of potatoes fell, scattering the contents on the ground. She managed to keep hold of the tea and the flour, but the paper bag holding the carrots split and spilled those too into a heap.

'Clumsy oaf!' she chided, her head bent, intent on picking up the vegetables. 'Why don't you look where you're going?'

'I beg your pardon,' he said, crouching down to help her. Green, he thought, as, on hearing the timbre of his voice, she turned to look straight at him. Or are they blue? Bluey green,

anyway, or greeny blue. He lifted his hat, showing a head of fair hair, and placed the carrots in
it. And her nose is neither long nor short, but
suits her face perfectly. 'The bag is useless, I
fear.' He crumpled up the paper bag that had
held the carrots and held out his hat. 'It seems
that I must loan you my hat.'

He saw the suggestion of a grin but she
pinched her lips together and took the hat from
him, tipped the carrots in with the potatoes, then
handed it back. 'You'd best give it a shake,' she
said, and her voice was low and rather husky,
with a trace of hidden laughter, 'or you'll get
mud in your hair.'

They both stood up at the same time and he
saw that she was above average height. 'I'm used
to mud.' He grinned. 'We're not strangers to
one another.' As he spoke there was a flurry of
hail and Jack Terrison and others came dashing
inside.

'Hey up, you lot.' The smith came out of his
dark workshop smelling of heat and iron. 'Mek
some room fer my customers.' Then he caught
sight of Joseph Ellis. 'Begging your pardon, Mr
Ellis. Didn't see it was thee.'

'Sorry, Carter,' Joseph said. 'Might we stay
until the rain stops?'

'Mr Ellis, sir,' Jack butted in. 'I didn't know
you were coming in today. I could mebbe have
saved you 'journey.'

'I had to come in,' he answered. 'I'm errand boy for my mother, amongst other things.' He turned to Mary-Ellen and lowered his voice. 'I do beg your pardon for my clumsiness. My name is Joseph Ellis. When the rain stops perhaps I could assist you with your parcels, Miss . . . ?'

'I can manage,' she said boldly. 'I'm used to doing for myself. Thanks,' she added, looking away.

'Mary-Ellen! Did you get them taties?' Jack Terrison called. He had been standing with his hands in his pockets, looking out into the rain. 'I'm going back to 'waggon with some goods. I can tek 'em for you.' He glanced at Joseph Ellis. 'That's all right, isn't it, sir? I told Mary-Ellen I'd carry 'em back for her to her lane end.'

'By all means, if you have the space.' Joseph lifted the potato sack from the ground and handed it to Jack. 'I think the rain is easing.'

Jack tipped his cap, then nodded to Mary-Ellen. 'See you about then, Mary-Ellen,' he said, and departed along with the others.

'You've got very wet,' Joseph murmured to her. 'Would you – erm, would you care for a cup of hot chocolate to warm you?'

'I'm not cold,' she said. 'And a drop o' rain won't hurt me.'

'Is that a no, then?' He grinned.

'It is,' she answered flatly. 'I'm not in 'habit o' supping wi' folks I don't know.'

He was not going to be deterred. 'I have introduced myself,' he said, holding her gaze. 'But I'll remind you again in case you've forgotten. My name is Joseph Ellis—'

'Well, Mr Ellis,' she interrupted, 'so we're halfway to being introduced.' She lifted her chin defiantly. 'You heard Jack Terrison name me Mary-Ellen and as he's an employee of yours you could no doubt find out my surname from him, so I'll save you 'bother. Mary-Ellen Page is my name and I live with my father at Welwick Thorpe.'

She saw his eyebrows, slightly darker than his hair, rise up at the mention of Welwick Thorpe. 'Ah,' he murmured, and then said humorously, 'So now that we know each other, will you come?'

She gave a sudden laugh. 'No, I won't!' she said, but she was amused by his persistence and the merriment in his eyes. 'I told you, I don't dine wi' strangers.'

He nodded his head slowly as he gazed at her. 'But if, by chance, we should meet again one day and I lifted my hat to pass the time of day, as we would no longer be strangers, but acquaintances, would you then consider the invitation?'

Mary-Ellen looked back at him. He was, she thought, the finest specimen of manhood that she had ever seen. Thick fair hair, discerning, confident blue eyes, and a wide mouth which lifted without any effort into a smile. Tall, too, so

49

that he had to bend his head to look at her. 'I think, Mr Ellis,' she said, 'that you should reconsider that question once you're safely back home. Perhaps discuss with your mother whether or not you should invite a low-bred lass to tek a cup o' coffee with you!'

He folded his arms in front of him. 'Chocolate!' he pronounced. 'I said chocolate, not coffee! And I don't ask my mother what I should do any more. I'm too old for that.'

Mary-Ellen shook her head, but there was warmth in her eyes, and, he thought, wistfulness, as she said, 'It's still no!'

The rain was coming down in a steady drizzle as she tramped back on the Welwick road towards home. She was beginning to feel shivery and hoped that the fire which she had banked with a mound of dried moss would still be in. She had bought shin of beef and pig's kidney from the butcher and was thinking of making a stew for their supper, for her father would be back late from his day at the hirings. I'll eat without him, she decided, for he'll be at the Hildyard Arms until they throw him out.

She turned to look over her shoulder as she heard the sound of hoofbeats. A lone rider in hat and rain cape was trotting towards her. She stood back on the grassy verge to let him pass, but the rider slowed and, as he reached her, lifted his hat.

'Miss Page! We meet once again! May I offer you a ride on my sturdy steed?' Joseph looked down at her. 'Or do you not accept rides with mere acquaintances?' His eyes creased in merriment. 'My horse is called Ebony.' He patted the sleek black neck. 'Say how-de-do to Miss Page, Ebony,' he instructed, and his mount obligingly nodded his head and blew through his nostrils.

They both laughed. 'You're very wet,' Joseph said. 'You'll catch your death, as my old nanny used to say. Won't you come up?' he asked, appealing. 'I can have you home in half the time.'

Mary-Ellen hesitated for only a moment. She was very cold and very wet and so far there had been no-one else on the road to offer her a lift. People were obviously still at the hirings, making the most of their day off work in spite of the rain. Jack Terrison must have gone ahead much earlier, she thought, unless he was still in one of the hostelries.

'All right,' she said. 'I can do.'

He leaned down and put out his hand to help her up. He was wearing soft leather gloves. Then he realized that her parcels were bundled under her shawl, and said, 'Just a minute.' He swung himself down. 'Let's put your packages into my bag.' He was wearing a large leather knapsack across his back and he took it off and unfastened it. 'Put your things in here. It will keep them dry.'

51

She put in the tea, the flour and the parcel of meat. At the bottom of the bag was a paper parcel. 'Will they hurt anything?' she asked. ''Meat's a bit bloody.'

'Nothing,' he said, gazing down at the top of her bent head. 'Nothing that matters,' and thought that he would think of some excuse to give his mother if her embroidery silks were spotted with blood.

He mounted again, putting the knapsack in front of him, and again leaned over and put out his hand to help her up. She put her left foot into the free stirrup and sprang so that she was sitting astride behind him. 'All right?' he asked. 'You can hold on to my belt. Here, take my gloves. You must be frozen.'

She was; her hands were red with the cold, and she put on his large gloves and felt the warmth of his fingers as if he was holding her hands.

They trotted on in silence until they reached the lane end at Welwick Thorpe. She thought he would rein in and drop her off to walk the rest of the way, but he turned onto the beaten track and continued.

'You can drop me here,' she began. 'I can walk 'rest.'

'Might as well take you,' he said. 'You're half-way up the lane, aren't you? There's only one cottage there.'

Mary-Ellen thought that if the Ellises were

considering buying the land, as Jack Terrison had said, then perhaps he would have looked it over at some time without their knowledge, for she had never seen anyone around.

He reined in at the cottage and she wondered what he thought of it. In the dank November day, it looked little more than a hovel. But then, she pondered, that is what it is. But it's got a sound roof and we've got a good fire, and, as Da says, what more do we want? But it wasn't enough, she admitted to herself as she slid down from Ebony's back, and waited for Joseph Ellis to unfasten his bag and hand over her parcels. It isn't enough, but it is all I shall get.

He dismounted and made a great show of taking off his knapsack and opening it and handing out her belongings. Then he looked at her. 'Are you not going to ask me in for a moment, before I go on my way?'

He saw a sudden caution in her eyes and anger too and cursed himself for his stupidity. Of course she was vulnerable. There was no-one about in this lonely landscape and she would be completely defenceless, though he guessed that she would put up a fight if she had to.

'Is your father not at home?' He found himself stammering awkwardly. 'I must meet him sometime. My father and I are thinking of buying the title deeds for the land at Welwick Thorpe.'

'I'd heard,' she muttered. 'But he's not at home. He'll be still at Patrington, I expect.'

'Ah! In that case I'll not inconvenience you. Do you have a fire to warm yourself?'

She swallowed but lifted her chin and said defiantly, 'Yes – of course! That is,' she added grudgingly, 'if it's kept in. I banked it up before I left.'

'Then let me collect some kindling for you,' he said, glancing round at the bare landscape. 'It'll only take a minute.'

She smiled and he thought how her face lit up from within when she did so. She doesn't have much to smile about, he mused, and was surprised when she said teasingly, 'It's all right, Mr Ellis. I've got dry kindling inside. We have to be prepared for every situation.' She hesitated for a moment, and then said, 'You can come in for a minute and warm yourself if you like. I don't mind.'

He gazed at her as she stood in front of him. Her soaked shawl clung to her shoulders and her wet bodice to her breasts. Her hair looked blacker than ever because it was so damp and tendrils corkscrewed round her cheeks. He suppressed a sigh that seemed to come from deep within him.

'I think,' he said softly, 'that perhaps I'd better not.'

He mounted again and wheeled round without

looking back, but at the end of the track he raised a hand to Jack Terrison, who looked up from unloading the sack of potatoes from the waggon and watched him as he cantered away.

CHAPTER FIVE

Mary-Ellen stripped off her shawl, bodice and skirt. She was shivering, her teeth chattering with cold. Her cotton shift was damp where the rain had soaked through her skirt. She drew it up above her head and rubbed it over her naked body to dry herself, then reached for the coarse cloth that she used for a towel and dried her dripping hair. She took a blanket from her bed in the corner of the room and, wrapping it round herself, bent to stir the fire.

There was still a red glow beneath the banked-up moss and she carefully fed it with the small dry twigs and dried leaves which were kept at the side of the hearth; then, as the flame grew brighter, she put on bigger pieces of light rotten wood so that the fire soon burned merrily. She sat back on her haunches and considered. What would have happened if she had let Joseph Ellis in? She had wanted him to come in. Not at first. At first she had been startled and afraid of his attentions. She had seen the admiration in his eyes and was wary. But then he seemed to realize that what he had said was improper and had retracted.

But if he had come in, she thought. What would they have talked of? She couldn't have offered him a pot of tea, for the fire would have taken too long to boil the water. And besides, what would her father have said about offering their precious tea to visitors?

No, they would have just stood there in their wet clothes. He would have been embarrassed at their poverty and tried to think of an excuse to leave as quickly as possible. And she, she would have been either tongue-tied in her confusion or curt and scornful as she knew she could sometimes be if she thought she was being belittled.

Yet, she thought of how he had looked at her as he stopped his mount, and of how her heart had hammered as she had ridden behind him. She could smell the wet leather of his hat and the steamy odour of the horse, the two aromas mingling, and as she put her head down to avoid the rain she had felt the warmth from his back and wanted to lay her face against him and let his body heat enfold her.

She stood up from the fire and the blanket slipped down to her waist. She opened it out and let one end drop and ran her hand over her body. She touched her throat, her breasts and flat belly, and felt a quickening of her pulse, a shortness of breath and dryness in her mouth. She ran her tongue round her lips to moisten them. Is this what he wanted? Was it desire she had seen in his eyes? Or was it simply lust for a girl who wouldn't have been able to object? It was not! She drew the blanket tightly about her. It was something more; otherwise he would have come in and not backed away when he saw her wariness.

By choice she was still a virgin. She could have had her pick of village boys or men, but she scorned them all. She had seen and heard their fumbling attempts to attract her, and when she had withered them with a glance or a sharp word their compliments had turned to derision and contempt. But today she had met Jack Terrison again, and to him she had been kinder. He had not attempted to be anything more than a friend, though she had sensed that perhaps he was more interested in her than he had shown.

She had made the stew, eaten and gone to her bed before her father came home. The room was warm now and her wet clothes were steaming in front of the fire. She was almost asleep when she heard the rattle of the sneck. Her father stumbled in, cursing as he fell over the ragged mat that she kept by the door.

'You asleep, Mary-Ellen?' She didn't answer, but he called again. 'Mary-Ellen! You asleep?'

'Yes,' she answered drowsily. 'There's beef stew keeping warm on 'hearth.'

'Nay, I want nowt. I'm full up with ale and mutton.' She heard the rattle of the pan lid as he lifted it. 'Smells good, though. Mebbe I'll have a drop. Just gravy and some bread.'

'Help yourself,' she murmured. 'There's bread on 'table.'

'What sort o' daughter are you?' he snapped. 'Get up and get it for me.' She heard him collapse into a chair and by the firelight saw him struggling to remove his boots.

'I can't,' she said. 'I've got no clothes on. Mine are still wet from when I got back.'

He grunted and heaved off his boots. 'Then wrap a blanket round thee. Don't give me excuses.'

Sighing, she pulled the blanket round her and rolled out of her bed. Since she had come home from Aunt Lol's to live with her father, they had respected each other's privacy. Whenever either of them wanted an all-over wash, the other would go outside. Mary-Ellen was usually the first to bed, after visiting the earth closet at the end of the vegetable plot. When she was in bed on her palliasse on the floor, she would turn her face to the wall while her father undressed and got into the bed he had once shared with her mother. He had never brought another woman home, and for this Mary-Ellen was thankful.

She spooned some of the beef broth into a tin bowl and broke off a chunk of bread, and placed them in front of him. 'Did you get work?' she asked, sitting opposite him. 'I didn't see you in Patrington.'

'Aye, I did. But I went to Patrington Haven. There's nowt much on 'land at 'minute so I thought I'd try for some fishing ower 'winter. Parrotts have tekken me on; they're a bit short-handed on 'shrimp boats.'

The Parrotts were a well-known fishing family who operated out of the small haven a mile or so from Patrington which ran directly into the Humber.

'You'll not make much money,' she said.

'It'll last us for a month or two, then I'll go back on 'land.' He slurped his broth and dipped the bread into it. 'We'll manage.'

She hesitated for a moment, unsure of whether to tell him about meeting Joseph Ellis. But if he found out and she hadn't told him he would want to know why.

'I got a lift into Patrington with Jack Terrison,' she said. 'I don't suppose you remember him. He was at Welwick school when I was.'

'Oh, aye!' he grunted.

'He works for 'Ellises at Skeffling. I met him when I was sheltering from 'rain.'

Her father lifted his eyes to hers, but went on eating. Then he said, 'Met who?'

60

'Joseph Ellis. The son. They're thinking of buying 'title deeds of Welwick Thorpe.'

Her father frowned. 'Did he tell you that?'

'Yes.'

'He'd no right. He should discuss it wi' me, not a lass like you. What would you know about it?'

'He doesn't have to discuss it with you either,' she reminded him. 'They could just send a letter to tell you that they've taken over.'

He burped loudly. 'But they're gentry, aren't they? It's onny common courtesy that they would come and tell folk that there's been a change of ownership. Onny right. Besides, not everybody can read a letter.'

Mary-Ellen got back into bed, wrapping the blanket up about her ears. Perhaps he'll come back, she thought, when they've decided. Or maybe his father will. But no, she reflected. Of course they won't. They'll send their agent, or else Mr Bennett will tell us that we've got new landlords.

It was three days later and her father had left for work at Patrington Haven. It was a dry morning, though cold, and she was coaxing the cow to give milk when she heard someone coming along the track. She moved the half-filled pail so that the cow wouldn't kick it over, and wiped her hands on her apron, then came out of the cow shelter. Joseph Ellis was riding towards the

61

cottage. He was wearing his leather hat and a tweed jacket with cord breeches and riding boots. He had a wool scarf round his neck and carried his knapsack over his shoulder.

He dismounted and removed his hat. 'Good day to you, Miss Page. I trust I find you well and no worse for your soaking?'

'I ail little,' she muttered, staring at him.

He nodded and for a moment seemed lost for words. 'I – er, I hope you will not take offence, but I noticed that—' He swallowed, and she wondered what he was going to say. 'I saw that your shawl had become very wet and wondered if perhaps it had been damaged beyond repair.' He started to fumble with the clasp on his knapsack and brought out a brown paper parcel which he thrust towards her. 'I wondered – if you don't think me forward – if this would be of any use to you.'

Her eyes narrowed, but she took it. 'What is it?' She turned the parcel over.

'It's a shawl – I had reason to visit Patrington again and saw it in the draper's.'

Slowly she opened the package, and saw the colour of a cream shawl. She touched it briefly with her fingers. It was light and as soft as thistledown, yet she knew it would be warmer than anything she had ever possessed. She handed it back to him. 'I don't accept gifts from—'

'Strangers.' He finished for her. 'I realize that.' He flushed slightly. 'It's just that when I saw it—'

She lifted her chin and glared at him. 'You thought, I know a poor lass who'd be grateful for such a splendid thing!'

He looked back at her, his eyes flickering over her face. 'I thought how well it would suit you and how much warmer it would be than the one you'd been wearing.'

She sneered. 'Are you in 'habit of giving out shawls to every village lass you come across?'

'Never! Never in my life have I done such a thing. A mental aberration!' he said abruptly. 'I must have taken leave of my senses.'

'Indeed you did, Mr Ellis.' Her voice was scornful. 'Whatever possessed you to think I could accept something from you? I suggest you take it back to 'shop, or else give it to your mother.'

He pushed it back into his knapsack with an angry jerk. 'I purchased it in good faith,' he snapped. 'There was no ulterior motive!'

'No?' she scoffed. 'My father wouldn't have thought so had he seen me sporting it! He'd have thought I'd got it by shameful means.'

He pressed his lips tightly together to avoid another retort. It had crossed his mind that her father would question her, but then he had reasoned that he and his father never observed whether the female members of their family were wearing something new, or something they had had a long time and had adapted with a different collar or piece of lace. He had hoped that Mr Page wouldn't notice either. Now he realized how foolish he had been. Mary-Ellen quite possibly didn't have any other garments than those she was wearing now.

'I'm sorry,' he said, and took hold of his mount's reins. 'I apologize if I've offended you. That wasn't my intention.'

'Tell me, Mr Ellis, for I don't know about these matters.' Her voice was light and vaguely derisory. 'If you'd given such a gift to a lady of your acquaintance – I mean a lady of . . . *distinction* – what meaning, what understanding would she have put on your giving her such a gift?'

He took a deep breath. He wouldn't, of course, have done any such thing, unless it was to an older married woman, an aunt perhaps, who would have been delighted to receive the acknowledgement.

'A young lady,' he said slowly and emphatically, 'would have thought I had serious intentions towards her, and I would have had, first of all, to ask her mother's permission to offer it.'

Her cheeks coloured and he saw the slight movement in her throat as she swallowed. 'But you didn't think that a lass from a hovel such as

64

this' – she indicated behind her – 'would expect such politeness as that?'

Joseph hesitated. What had been his intentions? He had seen how cold she was and how thin her shawl; and when he had spotted the cream shawl in the draper's where he had gone once again to replace the spoiled and bloodied silks for his mother, he had instantly thought of Mary-Ellen. Indeed, she had never been far from his thoughts. He had seen how the softness of the colour would contrast with her black hair and enhance her green-blue eyes, and knew he had to buy it. He would keep it, he decided now, if she wouldn't accept it, and not give it away. Keep it and think of her each time he opened the drawer where it was hidden and work out some other way that he could maintain a bond with her.

CHAPTER SIX

Burstall House, it was said, was named after the hamlet of Burstall where once stood an ancient priory close to the Humber estuary. Where the boundary between Burstall and the village of Skeffling lay no-one knew, and as for the priory, that had long ago disappeared beneath the turbulent waters of the Humber. Joseph's great-grandfather, when deciding to abandon the family tradition of wool manufacturing in the West Riding of Yorkshire and take up farming, came in the eighteenth century to look at Holderness in the East Riding; he read the history of the area, where the land had once been owned by the Crown, the church and the abbeys, and had subsequently been sold into the hands of farmers and estate owners.

He saw the vast acreage, the mighty waters of the Humber which ran into the German ocean, and the boundless infinite sky. He was captivated by the openness of the countryside, the possibility of river transport for the corn which he would grow and ship, but most of all seduced by the silence, broken only by the bird call and the ripple of the river against the bank of the land which was for sale.

I shall come here to Skeffling, he considered, and found my own succession of farmers. He was young and inclined to be of a romantic nature, and had visited the area when the sun was shining, the corn was golden, and the cottagers from their open doors had greeted him cordially and deferentially as he rode by. He was departing from the home where his family had lived for generations, leaving the hated thud and boom of machinery, the clatter of looms, and the noisy hustle of the busy towns. Besides, he was subservient to his two older brothers, who had already been in the manufacture of wool for many years and did not welcome an upstart with fresh ideas of his own.

He came, married a local farmer's daughter, bought an old farmhouse and converted it into a splendid mansion which he named Burstall House after the said priory, fathered three sons and two daughters, and discovered that the low land he had bought was so close to the Humber that it constantly flooded. He dug drains and ditches and eventually a moat to keep the water out of his house and garden. He died a relatively satisfied man and had achieved most of what he had set out to do. All his sons went into farming, his eldest grandson ran the Skeffling estate and in time his great-grandsons would be expected to keep up the tradition, marry well and father more sons.

Joseph cantered over the moat bridge. He was in a foul temper and behind with his work because of the extra trip into Patrington. His mother had looked at her silks and exclaimed that she couldn't possibly use them as they were so soiled. 'I shall write a note to the draper,' she had said crossly. 'How dare she sell such shabby goods? Janet will return them first thing in the morning with my strongest complaint.'

'I think, Mama, that it was not the draper's fault.' Joseph had attempted to explain. 'The rain was torrential and I dropped my satchel into a pool of water. I rather fear that the leather became wet and soaked the silks. I need to return to Patrington to speak to the wheelwright. I'll take them back myself.'

His father had grumbled when he said that he was going into Patrington again and told him to ask one of the men to go for him. 'I shall be quicker on Ebony,' Joseph had insisted. 'I shan't linger or be tempted to call at one of the inns on the way back.' He didn't want the draper to tell his mother's maid that the silks were stained with blood, for she would most certainly know that that was what it was, unlike his mother who hadn't guessed. His aim had been to find an opportunity to call on Mary-Ellen, and the shawl had been the perfect excuse.

Fat lot of good it did me, he thought now. I've wasted a whole morning on a damned fool's errand. I must have been mad to even think of giving her a present. How crass. How unthinking. She has probably never had anything new in her life, let alone a gift.

He couldn't get her out of his mind. All the rest of the day he thought of her as he went about his normal tasks. He rode across to where the men were repairing the flood bank, for the battle to keep out the river was constant. There were nine or ten farmers in the Skeffling district and all regularly maintained their drains and ditches in the low-lying land.

How can I get to see her without its appearing obvious, he thought, as he stood with his hands in his pockets watching the men. She'll be suspicious now, and of course she would be. Why do I want to see her? What possible motive can I have? There can be no future with her. I can't be seen with her, and yet I want to – to – what? To hold her. He gazed unseeing out at the river. To run my hands through her thick black hair. To dress her in fine clothes, but first to remove the ones that she is wearing, those thin shabby garments which do not hide her beauty, but only reinforce it. He began to sweat at the thought of her being in his arms, of

69

the touch of her skin beneath his fingers, of her rounded body beneath his.

'*Sir!*' The voice was urgent; a shout. 'Tha fayther's just riding up.'

Joseph had climbed up onto the river bank, yet had no recollection of having done so. He turned and looked down at the man who had called him. 'He's shouting at thee to come, sir!' The worker's face was expressionless, yet he must have thought him an idiot.

Joseph jumped down from the bank and un-hitched Ebony from where he had tied him to a stubby hawthorn bush, then mounted and rode towards his father.

'Where the devil have you been? I've been all over looking for you.' His father was red-faced with irritation. 'I wanted to ride over to Welwick Thorpe, but it's too late now. It'll be dark in half an hour. We'll have to go in the morning.'

He glared at Joseph, who looked blankly back at him. 'I've signed the papers,' his father said testily. 'We've acquired the title deeds. We need to tell the allotment holders and cottagers.'

Joseph continued to stare at his father. So he would be able to go legitimately down the track to the cottage where Mary-Ellen lived and which now belonged to them. 'It's a quagmire,' he heard himself say. 'It needs further drainage.'

'I know that!' his father snapped. 'But we shall benefit in the long run, even if it takes twenty years. The accretions on Sunk Island continue, and when the North Channel is warped, as it no doubt will be, we shall gain extra land. Or you will,' he added. 'It's your future I'm thinking of.'

'The saltmarsh will be Crown land,' Joseph said vacantly. 'It won't be ours.'

'As good as,' his father declared. 'Mark my words.'

The fire had gone out overnight. Mary-Ellen and her father had woken to a cold room and therefore a cold breakfast of bread and cheese. Try as she might, Mary-Ellen couldn't get the fire to light and Isaac had been in a bad temper at having to go out without a hot drink. After her father had left for work, she cleaned out the dead ash, laid dry moss and kindling in the hearth and went outside to collect more wood from the rear of the cow shelter. She was coming back with her arms laden with logs when she saw two riders coming up the track towards the house.

She peered curiously. Were they coming here or going on to the river bank? There had been some activity there recently; part of the bank had crumbled away and a gang of Irish labourers had come to rebuild it. But they had walked up the track carrying their picks and spades; they hadn't ridden on horseback as these two men were doing. One of the men was wearing a top hat; the other – and she suddenly held her breath – the other wore a floppy one which partly obscured his face.

It's him! She felt her pulses race. What do they want? Who's the other man – the agent perhaps? Have they bought the title deeds as Jack Terrison said?

'Good morning, miss.' The older man swung down from his horse. 'Is Mr Page at home?'

She looked straight at him. 'Who wants to know?'

Joseph hid a grin. Was she afraid of no-one?

The man took off his top hat. 'I beg your pardon. My name is Ellis. I live at Skeffling. I've recently acquired the title deeds of Welwick Thorpe. I wished to make Mr Page's acquaintance and to inform him of the change of ownership.'

'He's gone to work,' Mary-Ellen said calmly. 'You'd have to be here early to catch him.'

Ellis gave a grunt. He thought it was early. 'What time do you expect his return?'

'When 'fishing's finished. He's working with 'Parrotts over at Haven just now.' She gave a slight shrug. 'There's no knowing what time he'll be back.'

'What about Sunday?' Joseph said, looking down at her. He had stayed astride his mount. 'Would Mr Page be about on Sunday?' He knew his father wouldn't want to come on Sunday; he liked a nap in the afternoon. But he could come.

The thought of coming here alone and seeing her brought a flush to his face.

'He might be,' Mary-Ellen conceded and thought that if he was, it would be the first time in weeks. Her father liked to go to the hostelry in Welwick on a Sunday and usually stayed all day. 'I'll tell him, if you like, that you'll be coming.'

'Thank you.' Joseph's father put on his hat again. 'I'm much obliged to you. Miss Page, is it?' At her assent, he said, 'I trust all is well here? You have no major problems?'

She shook her head. 'None that we could trouble you with, Mr Ellis.' Then she added. 'You'll know that 'land up to 'estuary floods? You'd be as well to put in sluices. It's of no use for livestock.'

'I realize that,' he said, putting his foot into the stirrup. 'We've taken that into account.'

'Will 'rent stay 'same?' she asked boldly. 'Or will it go up?'

Ellis permitted himself a smile at her candour. 'For the time being it will stay the same. We have no plans to increase it.'

'Good.' Mary-Ellen nodded. 'See you on Sunday then.' But though she looked at his father, Joseph knew, with a quickening breath, that she spoke to him.

'Why does he want to see me?' Isaac said to

Mary-Ellen when she told him of the Ellises' intended visit. 'Hasn't he got an agent to attend to such matters?'

'I expect so,' she replied. 'But it's common courtesy – isn't that what you said?'

Her father humphed. 'Well, if 'rent's staying 'same, then I don't see why I should stop in just to see him. It's 'onny day I get off and I've got other plans.'

A shiver ran down Mary-Ellen's spine. She felt light-headed and had hardly slept properly since Joseph Ellis and his father had visited. She had tossed on her bed and hadn't known that she had groaned until her father had shouted at her from his bed to be quiet. 'What's up wi' you, girl? Got a belly ache?'

She had, but not the sort that he meant. Her body had ached and throbbed in a manner which she hadn't experienced before. She had to cross and clench the tops of her thighs to obtain relief and her breasts felt tender. She had put her face into the palliasse and this was when the groan had escaped. Her father, who was usually asleep before her, had heard her.

She had rolled out of her bed. 'I must have eaten summat that disagreed with me,' she'd muttered, going across to the uncurtained window and looking out. There was a flurry of snow blowing across the yard and she thought that if the weather was bad perhaps they might

74

not come, or maybe her father wouldn't go on his jaunt to the hostelry.

She slept no better the following night and woke bleary-eyed on Sunday morning to see a thin covering of snow but bright sunshine; and it seemed as if her father might change his mind and stay at home after all. 'I wouldn't want 'em to think we'd no manners,' he said, and she didn't know whether to be pleased or sorry.

I'll keep out of the way, she decided. They won't want to talk to me. Mr Ellis will want to speak to my father about the land, and maybe Da will ask him if he will fix the cow shelter where the tiles have fallen off.

They hadn't come by midday, and Isaac, who had been clearing and digging in the garden all morning, swilled his face and hands under the pump and came into the house when she called that their dinner was ready. She had made a rabbit pie, and when they had eaten he reached for his coat and hat and said, 'Well, I'll wait no longer. Give 'em my apologies and tell 'em I've had to go out.'

He glared at Mary-Ellen as if it was her fault he had been delayed. 'They must realize I'm not a man of leisure. That my time's precious.'

She made no answer. Perhaps they might not come, or perhaps Mr Ellis senior would come by himself. She only knew she felt sick and jittery at the thought of Joseph Ellis coming alone, and that in her unease she would be offhand and probably rude to him as she had been when he'd brought the shawl. But what did he expect? she thought irritably. How could I have accepted it? Much as I might have wanted to. But what did he expect in return? He wasn't giving it for nothing, and that's a fact. The more she thought about it, the more indignant she became.

'Will you be in for supper?' she shouted after her father as he crossed the yard, taking her frustration out on him. 'Or shall I feed it to 'pig?'

'I'll give you 'back of my hand if you don't mind yourself!' He shook his fist at her. 'I might be back and I might not.'

She knew he would be back sometime, even if it was the middle of the night. He never forgot, no matter how much ale he had drunk, that he still had to get up for work on a Monday morning.

Mary-Ellen cleared away the remains of the pie. Putting a tin plate over it, she went outside and placed it in the metal meat safe that hung high up on the side wall of the house, away from rats and mice. She looked round the room as she came back in. Her father's bed was tidied and her own rolled up and put away in the corner. The dinner plates she put into a bucket of cold water to wash later. She could have done them now, but she suddenly felt dispirited and didn't have the inclination.

Why do I keep thinking of him? she wondered. He's nothing to me and he probably won't come, and if he does, then so what? He's gentry, and I'm nothing. He's very fair, she reflected, her thoughts jumping about. I've never seen anyone quite as fair as him. Most folks round here are brown-haired, mousy or dark. Not blond like him. And besides, he probably thinks I'm just easy game. He probably thinks he can throw me a copper or two and I'll do what he wants. Well I won't!

She threw a log onto the fire. It was still green and it spat and crackled, and then cast out a spume of dense smoke. Unexpectedly she wanted to cry. 'Nowt ever goes right,' she muttered. ''Fire won't burn; and he needn't think he can buy me wi' summat I'd never wear.'

She pressed her hand to her face to hold back the tears, and then turned to open the door to dispel the smoke. She gave a sudden start when she saw Joseph Ellis's broad frame filling the doorway.

He took off his hat. 'I . . . was about to knock – I'm sorry if I startled you.'

She gazed up at him and a tear trickled slowly down her cheek. Her mouth trembled and for a second she was unable to speak, as for once she couldn't think what to say.

'Miss Page? Mary-Ellen?' he said softly. 'Is something amiss? Can I help?'

She swallowed. 'No,' she whispered, and stepped back inside the room.

'Is Mr Page at home?' he asked. 'I'm afraid my father was unable to come.'

Mary-Ellen shook her head. 'He had to go out. He sent his apologies.' She stared up at him and wondered at his expression. She licked her lips, which had suddenly gone dry. 'Would you like to come in?'

CHAPTER SEVEN

Joseph bent his head to come through the low doorway and Mary-Ellen noted that he was a lot taller than her father, who didn't have to duck his head as he came in. He was broad-shouldered, too, and the small room seemed crowded with his presence.

'I beg your pardon if the time isn't convenient,' he murmured. 'But I'm sure our fathers will meet at some future time.'

She shrugged. 'I never once saw 'other land-lord,' she said. 'He allus sent his agent to collect 'rent.'

'We will do the same,' he said, his eyes resting on her. 'But we wanted to meet our new tenants, both here and in Welwick. I've been to see the Smiths, the Browns and the Marstons.'

'My aunt and uncle,' she told him. 'Mrs Marston was my mother's sister. Didn't you meet my father on 'track coming up? He's onny just gone.'

'I came along the river bank after I'd been to the Marstons'.'

'Do you like 'river?' she asked.

'Yes. I like its different moods. It's wild some-times and unpredictable.' He kept his eyes on her, drawn to her in some irresistible way. 'Other times it's calm and gentle.'

'But it's tricky. You can't allus trust it.'

'I've lived here all my life,' he told her. 'I know it well enough.'

'You can never know it completely,' she declared, tossing her head. 'You might think that you do, but it can catch you out.'

'Why have I not seen you before, Mary-Ellen?' he asked softly. 'Where have you been that our paths haven't crossed?'

She gave a derisory grimace. 'I reckon we don't keep 'same company, Mr Ellis! But I've allus been here, except when I was a young bairn and lived with Aunt Lol after my ma died. But I knew about you,' she said, 'even though I'd never seen you.' Her mouth turned up irreverently. 'I knew of 'Ellis family who lived at Burstall House; of course I did! You were away at school for a bit, and you have a sister,' she added. 'I know that as well.'

Of course she would know of them, he con-sidered. She and those like her would know all the landowners round about. But there was no reason why he should have heard of her family;

not unless they were troublemakers and involved in petty crimes. Then they would have been known.

'And now we meet at last,' he murmured.

Why did I ask him in? she thought. There was no need. The agent used to come in sometimes to warm himself and look round. She suddenly felt touchy, peeved. Why should he want to see what we've got? We pay the rent and that should be enough.

'Do you have all you need here?' he was asking.

'Well, as you can see.' She swept her hands in an extravagant motion round the room: at the smoky fire, the low-beamed ceiling, the earth floor and the bucket of dirty crockery which she now wished she had washed. 'We live in 'land of plenty.'

She saw his eyes pause at her father's bed and took in a breath. 'It'd be nice to have another room with a bed, so I didn't have to sleep on 'floor,' she said hastily. 'But then, it's warm by 'fire, so that's a luxury; and besides, we couldn't afford 'extra rent we'd doubtless have to pay for such comfort!'

She didn't know why she was being so antagonistic towards him; perhaps it was to show that she didn't care about him or anybody. But she knew that she was trembling inside; that the emotion she had felt earlier was close to the surface, ready to pour forth and drown her in its forceful power.

'Not necessarily,' he said.

She gazed at him with her lips parted. 'What?' she whispered.

'The rent wouldn't necessarily go up.' His eyes flickered over her. 'I'll speak to my father about it. I noticed that there were some pantiles missing from the roof. I'll see that it's fixed.'

Mary-Ellen nodded. 'Thank you. Will that be all?' She bit on her bottom lip. 'I don't want to detain you.'

'What about the fire?' he asked.

She looked at the hearth where the green log was smouldering. 'What about it?'

'Will it burn? Shall I bring you some wood inside?'

She gave a sudden laugh. 'No. I'll ask 'maid to do it!' She gazed scathingly at him and then showed him her hands. 'Look at these, Mr Ellis—'

'Joseph,' he said quietly.

She ignored him. 'Who do you think brings 'wood in when my da isn't here? I've been lighting fires since I was six. Chopping wood since I was eight. I'm as strong as any man—'

'And yet still womanly,' he said in an undertone.

She caught his words, which were not quite soft enough. She put her hands on her hips, without realizing that the gesture emphasized even more the curve of her hips, the smallness of her waist. 'Beggin' your pardon, Mr Ellis.' She was abrupt and couldn't contain her tenseness. 'If there's nowt else, I think you'd better go.'

He looked sorrowfully at her and turned to leave. 'Please give your father my regards. I'll try to catch him at some other time. I – I trust I've said nothing to offend you? That wasn't my intention.'

There was a pleading in his eyes and in his manner, but she swung back her head and faced him eye to eye. 'I don't know what you mean, Mr Ellis.' Her face was defiant, as was her stance. 'Good day to you.'

He put his hand on the sneck, but still he hesitated. 'Does Jack Terrison come here? To call, I mean?'

Mary-Ellen was bewildered for a moment, and then she said, 'What if he does? He'd onny come in his own time anyway. Not in yours.'

'I was curious, that's all. I wondered – if you and he had an understanding?'

She blinked. Why should he ask about Jack Terrison? A warm feeling spread over her and she felt her breath quicken. 'We might have,' she said, and saw regret in his eyes. 'On 'other hand, we might not. Anyway, he onny works for you. His life's his own!'

Joseph nodded. 'That's true.' He turned again

to leave, and then looked back at her. 'You're a wilful woman, Mary-Ellen,' he murmured. 'I pity any man who becomes entangled with you.'

She leaned against the door jamb and watched him ride away, back up the track towards the river. The sky was darkening with a threat of more snow. She could feel a tingling in her nostrils and a sharpness which cut through her thin bodice and shawl, making her shiver. There's going to be a blizzard. Will he get back in time or will he be caught in it? No matter, he's wearing a heavy cape. But will his horse slip on the bank? It's narrow in places and the tide will be rushing in.

She turned away and banged the door shut in a sudden burst of temper. She was wilful, as he'd said; she was aware of that. But why did she feel frustrated and down-hearted? What had she wanted from him? What had he wanted from her? She took a breath and closed her eyes for a second. There had been nothing spoken, no question asked, no hint of why he was really there, yet she had known that the reason was something other than the courtesy of a new landlord as he had suggested.

'Whatever it was,' she muttered, 'it spells danger. For me and for him. He can't come visiting whenever he feels like it, even if he thinks he can. A gentleman and a poor wench! What would folks say? What would they think?'

And what folks would they be? she argued with herself, when you don't see a soul from one week to the next.

She sat down on the chair by the fire, which at last was throwing out some heat, and put her hands towards it. He was jesting, she thought. That's what some men do, aye and some women too I shouldn't wonder. They call it flirting, I believe, but it means nothing much, though I don't suppose he'd do it with a gentlewoman in case she took him seriously. Mary-Ellen had never had cause to flirt, not ever, mainly because she hadn't met a man who had taken her fancy. No-one whom she had considered remotely attractive enough to egg on with a saucy smile.

'I'd never know how to do that anyway,' she muttered aloud. 'If I was attracted to anybody then he'd have to take me as I am. I'll not pretend to be summat I'm not, just to attract a man's attention. I'll stay an old maid rather than that.'

Yet she had felt a longing. A coursing through her veins of some desire which was strange and unfamiliar to her. A desire that had been kindled by Joseph Ellis; by the interest she had seen in his eyes that first day they had met in Patrington and had done her best to ignore.

He's very handsome, she thought. But that's not all. There aren't that many men who have a pleasing manner that sets them apart from the others. Is it his eyes? Or his bearing? His voice maybe? It's deep, yet soft enough to make a lass drop her guard and be seduced by sweet words. But I'll not be tempted. Not me. 'Only time I'll be persuaded is when some man can offer me something I really want, and what that is I haven't yet discovered.

The snow came down that evening whilst Mary-Ellen and her father slept. She got up once and put more wood on the fire, and then huddled deeper under her blanket. She could hear the wind gusting down the chimney and the hiss of snow as it settled on the burning embers.

The next morning, Isaac got up and opened the door, relieved himself from the doorway, then got back into bed. 'They'll not be fishing today,' he grunted. 'And if they do they'll have to go without me.'

In a few minutes, Mary-Ellen could hear him snoring again. She lay for a while, but she was restless and couldn't settle back to sleep, even though she guessed it was probably very early. She could see a deep layer of white on the windowsill and the snow still coming down in a fast flurry. She rose up from her bed and wrapped her blanket round her. Her toes curled on the cold floor and she put on the thick stockings she had left on the chair the night before.

She stirred the fire and swung a kettle of water

over the heat to make a drink, and thought of how the day would stretch long and dismal in front of her.

Her father got up an hour later, and went outside to chop wood. He brought in a large basket which they normally used for potatoes, but he had filled to the brim with logs, and then went out again to bring in a sack of kindling. 'I'll have to go and look to see if any branches have come down,' he said. 'We're running short of wood. It won't last if this cold weather keeps up.'

They ate a breakfast of gruel and weak tea, and then he put on his hat and jacket and the scarf which his wife had knitted him many years before, and set off. Mary-Ellen cleared away, put water on to boil again and then took out her mending basket. She darned her father's socks, put a button on his other shirt, and mended a rent in his nightshirt.

The next day was much the same; the snow still fell but there was a glimmer of sunshine. Mary-Ellen wrapped herself up in several layers, including a flannel shirt belonging to her father, and put a shawl about her head and another round her shoulders.

'Where 'you going?' Her father was huddled close to the fire.

'I have to go out,' she said. 'I can't stay in any longer. I feel trapped. I'll just walk as far as 'river bank.'

'Put my coat on,' he suggested. 'You'll freeze to death out there. And just watch you don't slip and tummel into 'water. You'll not get out if you do.'

'I'll not fall in,' she said. 'When have I ever?'

He grinned. 'Nay, you never have. But there's allus a first time. You know what you're doing, I realize that.' There was a touch of pride in his voice and Mary Ellen looked at him in surprise. He was never one to give praise or acclaim. If she cooked a good dinner, the fact that he ate it was commendation enough. But this was something more and it disturbed her.

'I know that you could manage if owt should happen to me,' he muttered, his gaze on the flames. 'I've brought you up as if you were a lad, able to fend for yoursen. There's not many lasses can do what you can do. I know it's not allus easy for you, Mary-Ellen, but life's hard and you should expect nowt from it, onny hard knocks. I'm sorry it's this way, but there it is. That's how it's been doled out for us.'

She had never in her life heard such a long speech from him and for a moment she was tongue-tied. She cleared her throat. 'Nowt's going to happen to you, Da,' she said huskily.

'No,' he grunted, and spat into the fire. 'Course it's not.'

The track was rutted but the potholes were hidden by the snow and a few times she almost tripped. But she plodded on, exhilarated by the effort and the sharp crisp air, in spite of the heavy snow which was still falling. She noted where there were some broken branches, poking up from the drifts. Slender sticks which would burn well and start off a fire; she would collect a bundle on the way home.

She took in a deep satisfying breath as she reached the bank and saw the sun rippling on the surface of the river. The best place in the world to live, she breathed, and then smiled to herself at the thought that she neither knew, nor ever would know, any other. There were ships on the estuary, heading out towards Spurn Point and the sea. The breeze was carrying them swiftly and she thought that the snow wouldn't hamper those on the water in the way that those on the land would be obstructed, their everyday work curtailed.

I'll walk as far as Weeton, she decided, and make sure that Da's boat is secure. The saltmarsh wasn't so wide at Weeton, the village to the east of Welwick, and it was there her father moored the old coggy boat which he used for fishing on his own account.

She had walked for about fifteen minutes and was considering turning about and going back, for the path along the bank was slippery and very uneven and she didn't want to take a fall, when she saw a horse and rider coming towards her.

She stopped and waited. One of them would have to give way and it would have to be her. She stepped back into the scrub of hawthorn bushes to make room.

The rider hailed her, lifting a hand in appreciation as he came nearer, and with a start she saw it was Joseph Ellis. He hadn't recognized her. He drew closer and then reined in.

'Mary-Ellen? Is it you beneath all those wrappings?'

She was muffled up to the eyes in shawls and her father's overlarge coat, which had the collar turned up. 'Yes,' she said. 'It is.'

'Whatever are you doing out on a day like this?' He looked down at her in astonishment. Then he grinned. 'You're a regular snow maiden.'

'I came out for some air.' She lowered the shawl from where it had been covering her mouth. 'We've been cooped up in 'house since day before yesterday, and I had to get out. I was going to walk as far as Weeton but I've changed my mind. I shall turn back.'

'What's at Weeton?' he asked. 'Another aunt? Can I carry a message for you?'

Mary-Ellen shook her head. 'I was onny going to check up on my father's boat. Make sure it was safely moored.'

'There are two boats tied up to a stump,' he said. 'I noticed as I came past. Would one be your father's?'

90

'Oh, yes,' she said. 'It will be. Thank you.'

He opened his mouth to say something else, but then closed it and surveyed her. Then he said, 'I too am only taking the air and giving Ebony some exercise. I, er, was going to turn at Welwick Thorpe. Could I offer you a ride or would that be out of order? I do seem to make a habit of doing or saying the wrong thing!'

She caught a hint of amusement in his voice which irked her, and she felt at a disadvantage as he gazed down at her from his mount's back.

'There'd be no point in me taking a walk if I was to accept a ride,' she said contentiously. 'But don't let me detain you. You'll need to get back afore dark.'

He touched his hat and without a word he moved on, his horse making a snickering sound as they passed her. She turned round and followed him, until as he came to a wider part of the track he deftly manoeuvred Ebony and turned him back, facing the way he had come. As they came up close to her she once more moved back into the bushes. He lifted his hat in salutation, but didn't speak, only pursed his lips as if he was hiding a grin.

She walked on without looking back. If he thought I'd dip my knee to him he'd be mistaken, she scoffed. I'll not do that for any gentry, man or woman. She looked out at the estuary. The water was choppy, the surface breaking and surging as the tide turned. I wonder why he was riding from Skeffling to Welwick Thorpe. Why didn't he go the other way towards Kilnsea? He'd have had a much better ride.

An unbidden smile played around her mouth. He was hoping to see me! A deep, powerful elation rushed over her. One that she had experienced before. It wasn't true when she had told her father that she had never fallen in the river. When she was eleven, she had tripped and had felt the waters close over her head. After the initial panic she had held her breath until she rose to the surface. It had been a terrifying ordeal, but also exhilarating. I must be careful, she told herself now. Or I could drown.

CHAPTER EIGHT

'I didn't tell you that I visited the tenants at Welwick and Welwick Thorpe last Sunday,' Joseph told his father during supper that evening. They had dined on cold mutton, roast potatoes, mashed turnip and carrots, and were about to start on marmalade pudding. 'They seem to be reliable. I just missed Page, though. Seemingly he'd had to go out in the afternoon.'

'He was probably having his afternoon nap like your father,' his mother remarked, 'and said he wasn't to be disturbed!'

'Gone down to the hostelry more like,' his father grunted, pouring extra sauce over his pudding. 'Still, it doesn't matter. He knows who we are and that's all that counts.'

Joseph glanced at his mother and sister, Julia. 'I know that he wasn't having a nap, Mother, because I went inside the cottage. It's only one room where they live and sleep, and I was think-ing—'

His father looked up. 'What?'

Joseph shifted uncomfortably. 'Well, there's a daughter, as you know, and I happened to notice that there was only one bed—'

His mother drew in a breath and Julia's mouth opened into a round 'oh', and a pink spot appeared on each side of her face.

'That's enough!' his father barked. 'Not in front of your mother and sister!'

'No. No!' Joseph protested. 'You don't understand! There was a straw mattress rolled up in the corner of the room and the girl sleeps on that in front of the fire. It's an earth floor, and it must be most uncomfortable as well as damp. I wondered if we could perhaps build on an extra room? It wouldn't take much. The present house is boulder and rubble with some ashlar stone—'

'The daughter – she's about seventeen, eighteen, as I recall,' his father interrupted. 'She'll surely be getting married before long and moving out. That'll mean her father has a room he doesn't want and yet has to pay for. The rent will have to go up if we do any building work. No,' he decided. 'Best leave well alone. They've not complained, have they?' and when Joseph shook his head, he added, 'Well, there you are then.'

Later, Joseph's sister took him on one side. 'This young woman you mentioned,' she whispered. 'Does she not have a mother?'

'Seemingly not if she lives with her father,' he answered abruptly. The discussion hadn't gone the way he wanted. But, he reminded himself, I was looking for a means, an excuse, to visit her again.

'Would she, do you know, would she be disposed to accept charity? What I mean is, if we were to give her an extra blanket or a warm gown? I have several that I'm no longer fond of, and I'm sure Mama would not object. Would she be grateful, do you think? I'm assuming that they are poor?'

Joseph looked down at his sister. Though out here in Holderness fashion wasn't predominant, Julia liked to appear at her best. She wore a full prettily patterned gown with a ruched bodice and a wide buckled belt round her small waist. Her brown hair was parted smoothly down the centre and arranged in pretty ringlets over her ears. He pondered that Julia was completely submissive and biddable, adhered faithfully to the pattern of what was expected of her and had not one ounce of the fire and personality of Mary-Ellen. I'm being unkind, he thought. She is obliging and well meaning, yet has no will of her own. She only knows what she has been taught.

'They are certainly poor by our standards, Julia,' he sighed. 'But it's my considered opinion that if you were to give her a charitable gift, then she would either refuse it or give it away to someone else.'

'Not sell it, then?' she exclaimed. 'But give it to someone poorer than herself?'

'Probably.' He nodded and, excusing himself, left the room. More likely throw it in the river, he judged resentfully. I can just see her, scraping and dipping, mealy-mouthed in front of Julia. *Thank you kindly, Miss Ellis. Much obliged, Miss Ellis!* Huh, he grunted beneath his breath. A lick with the rough side of her tongue more likely!

The next morning he strode out across the stack yard. It had been cleared of snow and he went towards one of the cart sheds where the door was propped open. Jack Terrison was inside swinging an axe. A pile of chopped logs was against the wall.

'Where's this come from?' Joseph asked him, indicating the pile of branches.

Jack put down the axe and touched his cap. 'That old ash from 'bottom of West Field, sir. It's lost several branches, all dead wood. I noticed it a week ago and thought as it'd burn well. I reckoned I might as well do this seeing as we can't get out into 'fields. Keep me warm as well.' He grinned, and then added hastily, 'I've seen to 'hosses, sir. Turned 'em out into 'foldyard, but 'hind says there'll be no fieldwork today. Snow's still too thick.'

Joseph considered. The wood shed was full of

logs, all cut for the house. This lot would have to be stacked against the side. He rubbed his chin. 'Tell you what, Terrison. Fill up one of the small carts and take it over to Mr Page at Welwick Thorpe.'

He saw Terrison's eyebrows lift in surprise. 'I noticed they were short of wood when I was there after the hirings.' A small white lie, he conceded, but Jack Terrison had seen him leaving that day when he had given Mary-Ellen a lift back home. But Joseph saw no reason to explain to his employee that he had been there again since Martinmas.

'And then, if the weather worsens,' he added, justifying his generosity, 'we'll perhaps send some over to the Marstons at Welwick.'

Jack Terrison's eyebrows shot up again. 'By heck, sir. They'll think it's Christmas come early. She works here, you know – young Janey,' he said.

'Who?'

'Jane Marston. Mary-Ellen's cousin. She works in 'kitchen. Started at Martinmas.'

'Oh! See to it then.' Joseph turned away. Then he added, half jokingly, 'And don't be spending all morning philandering with Miss Page. There's plenty for you to do here.'

'No chance o' that, sir,' Jack said. 'She'll not entertain me. Send me off wi' sharp words and a flea in me ear more like!'

Good, Joseph breathed. If she's not interested in him, then perhaps there's a chance for me. He was a fool, he knew very well. Nothing could come of it. No relationship between them could flower. There would be no introducing her to his parents or his sister, and neither would her father welcome him. But he couldn't get her out of his mind. Day and night he thought of her. She haunted his dreams as he lay in bed, and pervaded his waking hours with the consciousness of her existence. He was amazed that no-one noticed his preoccupation, for it seemed to him that he walked around in a daze most of the time. Sleepwalking with Mary-Ellen in his arms.

'What's this then? Who's sent this?' Mary-Ellen stared at Jack Terrison, who had arrived at the door with a single horse pulling a cart full of logs.

'Mr Ellis – Mr Joseph, not senior. Where do you want it stacking?'

She viewed him suspiciously. 'Why's he sent it?'

Jack blew out a breath. He'd had to jump down and take the reins and urge the old horse up the track; he was the only one that the foreman would let him bring and it had been a slow journey. The animal was getting past it, he decided. He was ready for putting out to pasture or the knacker's yard. 'I don't know,' he said irritably. 'I onny tek orders, but he said to bring

98

'em. Said he'd noticed you were running short when he was here at Martinmas.'

'Did he?' Mary-Ellen looked at the load of wood. That would last them over the winter. 'That's generous of him.' She glanced at Jack. Would he be curious enough to question why Joseph Ellis would send them fuel?

'He's going to send some over to 'Marstons as well if bad weather keeps up. That's what he said, anyway.' He started to unload. 'Shall I stack 'em for you?'

She gave him a brilliant smile. 'Yes, please. Have you time for a cup o' tea? I'll make it while you're unloading.'

'Aye, that'd be grand,' he said, his spirits cheered by her friendliness. 'He said to me, no phil— no time wasting, but he didn't say I couldn't stop for a cup o' tea.'

'He'll not find out if you don't tell him,' she said, giving him a cheeky wink, and went inside to hide her exhilaration.

'How's our Janey getting on?' she asked, when he had finished stacking the wood and come inside.

He blew on the hot tea that she had poured. 'All right, I reckon, though I don't see much of her. She spends all her time in 'kitchen fetching and carrying for everybody else, I expect. Do you know Wilf Topham? He's a year or two older than us. No? Well, he was took on as fifth lad at

Martinmas, same time as Janey. He's allus hanging round 'kitchen door sweet-talking young maids.' He wrinkled his nose. 'I wouldn't trust 'im with lasses. And if 'maister caught him he'd be in right trouble. Bit of a chancer, he is, in my opinion.'

After Jack had left, Mary-Ellen put an extra log on the fire, a luxury that she decided they could afford now that they had such a plentiful supply. She drew the rag rug away from the hearth so that it wouldn't catch any sparks, put on her shawl, and set off to see Aunt Lol in Welwick.

She hadn't visited her for several days and she knew that her aunt's child was due fairly soon, certainly before Christmas Day, which was just under two weeks away. When Mary-Ellen arrived at her door, however, it was plain to see that her aunt had already begun in labour.

'Can I do owt for you, Aunt Lol? Make you a hot drink or summat?'

'No, nowt.' Lol's forehead was wet with sweat. 'I've just got to get on wi' it. I'll be glad of a cup when it's ower. Though mebbe you could run along to Mrs Brown, next door but two, and tell her I'll be about half an hour if she'd come then to give me an 'and.' She gave a sudden grunt as a spasm stopped her perambulations up and down in front of her fireside. 'If I ask her to come too soon, she'll charge me extra,' she explained in a breathy voice, and leaned heavily over the wooden table. 'Our Sally's tekken 'young bairns out into 'village till it's done. Can't be doing with them about me.'

A bead of perspiration clung to her top lip and she brushed it away with the back of her hand. 'I hope this'll be me last,' she said. 'I'm getting ower old for this malarkey.' She gave Mary-Ellen a grin, revealing missing teeth. 'Time for you young 'uns to have a turn.'

'Not me, Aunt Lol,' Mary-Ellen told her. 'I've yet to find somebody I want to wed.'

Her aunt grimaced with another pain. 'I allus thinks of your ma when I'm about to farrow,' she panted. 'How she suffered, poor lass. I hope to God you don't tek after her.'

A few minutes later Mary-Ellen scooted off to fetch the neighbour when her aunt said suddenly, 'Go fetch Mrs Brown, will you? Tell her to come now!'

Mary-Ellen paced up and down outside the cottage door whilst her aunt with her neighbour's assistance got on with the business of birthing. She saw her young cousins coming towards the cottage and indicated to Sally to stay away a little longer. The girl turned round and shooed her charges back the way they had come, towards the village. Ten minutes later, Mary-Ellen heard a squalling cry and knew that the ordeal was over.

'It's a lad,' Mrs Brown said, on opening the

101

door. 'So that's a blessing. She says for you to come in.'

Mary-Ellen's eyes filled with tears when she saw her aunt propped up in bed with the new babe in her arms. His face was pink and wrinkled and he had a mass of black hair. 'He's lovely,' she choked.

'Aye,' Lol said wearily. 'He's grand. Let's hope he survives 'winter, and then he can look after me in me old age. You can shout our Sally in now,' she added, 'and they can tek a peek at him. I wish I could get word to Janey. She'll be wondering about us.'

Mary-Ellen thought of Jack Terrison, who had left earlier to go back to Skeffling. She wouldn't be able to catch up with him now, even if she ran. 'I'll go,' she said impulsively. 'It's onny just after midday, and I can be there and back in an hour. I've cooked some soup ready for when Da gets home, and built up 'fire.'

'Nay, lass. Tomorrow'll do soon enough.'

'But if I go now, they might let Janey come home tomorrow for an hour or two.' She was filled with the need to go now, to see the house where Jane worked and Joseph Ellis lived.

'Dost think they would?' Her aunt was doubtful, but Mary-Ellen could see that the idea of Jane's coming home was pleasing to her.

Mary-Ellen flung her shawl around her. 'There's onny one way of finding out,' she said. 'I'll go right now.'

It was a dry bright day, and bitingly cold, but she soon became warm as she strode out, occasionally slithering and slipping on icy patches. The snow hadn't yet melted and was piled so high on either side of the narrow road that she couldn't see over the top of it. She saw no traffic and no other person as she walked through the hamlet of Weeton towards Skeffling, and it was as if she was walking through a white tunnel.

The heavy farm gate had the name of Burstall House nailed on it and Mary-Ellen turned up the woodland track. This too was lined on each side with piled-up snow which someone had shovelled aside to make a way through. Sand had been sprinkled over the cleared surface and wheel tracks and hoof prints were embedded in the thick ribbed ice.

It was very quiet and she saw no-one as she approached the three-storey house from the side, which led her to assume that the front of the house faced the river. It was built of grey brick, with a single-storeyed side wing of stone and boulder. She approached this wing, thinking it would lead to the back of the house, and found herself in an enclosed stable courtyard. A young lad was scurrying across the cobbles and he stopped when he saw her.

'I'm looking for 'kitchen door,' she said, and he pointed to where he had just come from.

Mary-Ellen gave the message to the maid who answered her knock, and the girl told her to wait. She stepped into the lobby as she was bid and glanced round. Rubber boots and heavy shoes, walking sticks and water pails were all stacked neatly. Outdoor coats and hats were hanging on brass pegs on the wall.

The inner door opened and Jane came out. Her cap was askew and she wore a coarse grey apron over a black skirt. She was flushed and glad to 'see Mary-Ellen. 'Is Ma all right?' she asked in a whisper, when she was told of her new brother. 'I wish I could see him. If Cook wakes up in a good mood I'm going to ask if I can have tomorrow afternoon off.' She dropped her voice further. 'I'll say Ma's had a bad time and needs to see me.' She glanced over her shoulder. 'I'll have to go. Thank you for coming, Mary-Ellen.' Her eyes flooded with tears. 'I do miss everybody. I don't like being at work. I'd rather be at home.'

'I know.' Mary-Ellen nodded. 'But you've got to make 'best of it, Janey. We'll see you at Christmas, anyway. You'll get 'day off, won't you?'

'I think so, but I'm not sure,' she said. 'Cook won't say yet who can have it off.'

Mary-Ellen closed the door quietly behind her. She was glad that her father wouldn't allow her to go into service. I'd not hold a job down, she thought ruefully. I wouldn't like taking orders the way Janey has to. She walked swiftly across the courtyard, rounded the corner and crashed headlong into Joseph Ellis.

CHAPTER NINE

He had been thinking of her, and there she was. Joseph grasped Mary-Ellen's arms as she cannoned into him. Her shawl had slipped from her head, her cheeks were flushed and her eyes shone green with shades of sea grey and sky blue as she gazed up at him.

His lips parted as he searched for words, but he could find none. In a moment of utter madness, he bent his head and kissed her mouth, warm beneath his. He saw her momentarily close her eyes, but then she pulled away. 'No,' she breathed. 'No!'

'What . . . are you doing here?' His words were stammered like those of a love-sick youth. He still held her by her elbows, which were cold beneath her shawl.

'My cousin – she – I came to tell her . . .' He could barely hear her whispered words.

'Have you walked?' Still he kept his eyes on

her soft moist mouth. His voice was low; he could barely speak.

Mary-Ellen blinked and it was as if she had just woken up, wondering where she was. She pulled away again, but this time more urgently. 'Course I've walked.' Her voice was firmer now and he could hear the cutting edge to it. 'How else would I get here?'

Joseph shook his head. 'I've wanted to see you, Mary-Ellen.' He felt like a jelly turned out of its mould, quaking and quivering in front of her.

She tossed back her hair. 'Well, now you've seen me I'll be on my way.'

He thought he sensed a tremble in her voice and on her lips. 'Don't go,' he pleaded. 'At least . . .' He saw the lift of her eyebrows and the twist of her mouth. 'Let me take you home.'

'In your carriage, Mr Ellis?' she said cynically and he knew he had to seize the moment or she would be gone, out of his life for ever.

'No. Wait. Please! Let me saddle up my horse and I'll ride you back. Please!' Joseph gazed at her imploringly. 'We can ride along the river bank. It's perfectly safe. I've been out this morning.'

She looked at him, and then glanced back at the house as if checking whether they had been observed.

'Go down the drive,' he urged. 'Halfway down

on the right, there's a gate leading into the wood. Go through it and you'll come to a track that takes you to the river bank. It's ours. The villagers don't use it.'

He saw the misgivings written in her expression, the battle that was evidently going on in her head, but he knew no hesitation, no faltering over right or wrong. No matter what the outcome, no matter what fate had in store. 'There's no help for it,' he muttered. He was resolute. He had to be with her. His heart told him he must.

She turned away and disappeared round the side of the house. He had no idea if she would do as he asked or continue to the main road and back towards Welwick Thorpe. She had given no answer to his muttered words, but merely looked at him with her cat-like alluring eyes, her lips parted on a breath.

He ran to the stable and with fumbling hands and shaking fingers saddled up Ebony and sprang up on his back. Will she wait? He was filled with an urgent need, as restless and mettlesome as Ebony, full of fire and ready to burn. She must. He dug his heels into the horse's flanks and cantered out of the yard. She must or I'm destroyed.

She's not here. Joseph dismounted as he reached the river bank. He felt the energy draining out of him in his disappointment as he glanced up and down the bank; then a movement near a thick scrub of hawthorn came into his side vision and he turned sharply. There she was.

He saw how she pulled in her bottom lip with her teeth and chewed on it; saw the tip of her pink tongue and the nervous swallow in her throat. She stared at him but said nothing.

'I thought—' His voice cracked and he cleared his throat. 'I thought you hadn't come. I thought you'd gone back the other way, along the road.'

She slowly shook her head. 'As you see, I didn't. Though I don't know what madness made me come this way. If 'horse should slip we'll all three end up in 'river.' She kept her eyes on his. 'We could ride on 'road just as well.'

Then her head came up in the haughty way he now recognized so well as her particular trait. 'Though p'raps you don't care for folks to see me riding up behind you?'

Joseph came towards her, trailing Ebony's reins. 'I don't really care who sees us, Mary-Ellen,' he said softly. 'But I reasoned that you might. We can go back by the road if you prefer. If you're afraid.'

'Afraid? Who says I'm afraid?' Her eyes glinted tauntingly. 'Of what? Of falling in 'river?'

'No.' He came up close. 'Of me!'

Up came her head again, but she wet her lips with her tongue and glanced away. 'I'm afraid of no man,' she said. 'Unless he's stronger than me and means me harm.'

Joseph reached out to take her hand, which was clutching her shawl. 'I don't mean you any harm,' he whispered, drawing her near. 'Never!' Without taking his eyes from her, he hung Ebony's reins on a shrubby branch and brought his hand to lightly stroke her cheek. 'Never,' he repeated. 'Never would I hurt you.' He bent his head and kissed the other cheek, then turning over her hand he pressed his lips to her palm. He felt her fingers touching his hair and when he looked up he saw a cloud of confusion on her face.

'What then?' she whispered on a breath. 'What is it that you want from me? You're a gentleman and I'm a nobody—'

He put his fingers over her mouth to hush her. 'Don't say that. Don't say that you're a nobody. Of course you are somebody. You're beautiful and vivacious.' He gave a tender smile. 'And you're feisty and spirited and afraid of no-one.' He felt her lips part beneath his fingers and he traced their shape: the slight cupid's bow of her top lip, the fullness of the lower lip, the sensation of moist velvet smoothness as his fingertips gently explored. 'I'm lost, Mary-Ellen,' he murmured and closed his eyes as he was filled with thirsting desire.

She gazed up at him, then bent her head

against his chest. 'You'd best take me home,' she whispered. 'This is no place to be.'

He put his hand to his head. 'Yes,' he said breathlessly. 'You're right. I'm sorry.' He began to shiver. It was so cold and here she was clad in just a thin dress and shawl. He started to unbutton his coat. 'You must put this on,' he muttered. 'You'll freeze.'

Mary-Ellen stopped him. 'No. I'm used to being cold,' she murmured. 'But warm my hands.' She slipped her hands inside his open coat and round his waist. He put his arms about her and held her tight, then she lifted her face to his. 'Kiss me again,' she breathed. 'On my mouth, like you did back there in 'stable yard, when we bumped into each other.'

He looked down at her. They were so close. He could feel the shape of her body folding into his. He lowered his head and this time felt an ardent response as their lips touched and she returned his kiss.

Mary-Ellen raced down the track towards home. She slipped several times and picked herself up, not minding the knocks on her elbows and knees, but anxious to be back before her father came home. Would he notice her agitated state, her flushed cheeks or her tender throbbing mouth where Joseph's urgent lips had sought her fervent consenting ones? She flung through the door and threw a log onto the fire, then seized the pan of soup and placed it over the low heat, spilling it and making the wood sizzle.

It would have been quicker coming along the road for they would have come without stopping for fear of being noticed, but on the river bank he kept drawing up each time there was a wider space where they could jump down, to hold and kiss, touch and cling and kiss again. Her heart had pounded, and still did, at the thought of how he had run his hands over her breasts and waist; but he didn't lift her skirts as she thought he might have done, but pressed her hips hard beneath his fingers and groaned. 'Mary-Ellen,' he'd moaned and closed his eyes tight and she knew how much he wanted her.

As I want him. Her body throbbed and the pulse in her throat pounded. She felt elated, excited, all the things she knew she shouldn't feel. A sweet and aching incautious desire. This is unfamiliar territory, she told herself. Tell him no. Tell him to find somebody of his own kind. She sat down on the chair by the fire and put her head in her hands. But I am his kind, she meditated. I knew that first day I saw him in Patrington that he was the one I wanted. No good will come of it, that I know. She lifted her head and stared into space and it was as if she was listening and looking elsewhere, into the unknown. 'But it can't be helped,' she muttered. 'It's meant to be.'

112

CHAPTER TEN

There were days when the weather was so bad that there was no fishing and Isaac couldn't go out. Mary-Ellen fretted and fumed, was restless and tense, for she knew that Joseph would be waiting on the river bank. It's impossible, she agonized. He must forget me. Find somebody else to whisper endearments to. Not me. How can we meet when I'm shut in here?

Her father frowned at her fidgeting, and, edgy because of his inability to go to work and make money, he would shout at her, telling her that she was ill tempered and useless. She in turn would retaliate, telling him that she was worth more than being a drudge in a hovel. Sometimes after an altercation he put on his hat and coat and slammed out of the door to trudge to the nearest hostelry. But ten minutes later he would come back, apologetic though he wouldn't say so, muttering that the snow was too thick and the cold too bitter to go anywhere.

The hens had stopped laying. Mary-Ellen wrung the neck of one of the older ones to make a meal and some broth to last them a few days. Her father went out one morning to see if there were any rabbits in the traps he had set. He came back empty-handed but told her he had seen Joseph Ellis on the river bank.

'He told me they're going to start work on 'drainage as soon as 'weather clears.' He grunted as he bent to take off his boots. 'I'd have thought he'd have an overseer to look it over, but he must like to tek charge himself.'

Mary-Ellen's heart skipped a beat. 'I suppose there's not much he can do at 'minute,' she murmured. 'With 'weather and that.'

Her father nodded. 'He asked me if I'd much work on. I wondered if he'd had a mind to ask me if I wanted any labouring jobs, but I told him I was set up with fishing until spring.'

The next morning the rain came and the thaw began and her father set off to walk to Patrington Haven. 'I'll have to earn some money soon,' he said. 'We've no grain left for 'hens and they can't scratch till 'snow clears.'

As soon as he'd gone, Mary-Ellen put on her shawl and boots and headed for the river. If what Joseph had told her father was true, that work was to begin on the drainage, then they wouldn't be able to meet. The track would be overrun with working men.

Joseph was waiting. 'I saw your father go out,' he said. 'I hoped that you would come. I don't know how many times I can make excuses for being here.'

'Are you not starting 'labourers on 'drainage yet, then? Was it only a tale?'

He smiled. 'They are starting, but not until spring, so we have until then.'

'Come back with me,' she urged. 'We can't stay here. Da won't be back for hours.'

'Are you sure?'

She saw the hesitation. 'Don't you want to?' she whispered.

'You know that I do.' His eyes searched her face. 'But—'

'What?'

'I can't be responsible for what might happen.' His voice was low. 'I've been longing for you. Wanting you. Desperate for you, Mary-Ellen. I can't guarantee that if I come with you now our lives will ever be the same again.'

She looked up at him. 'I don't want my life to be 'same,' she said. 'It hasn't been anyway, not since that day you brought me home. You've made me want more than I have now. I don't know what it is that I want – at least – yes, I do,' she said softly. 'I want you.'

As soon as they entered the door, he took her in his arms, crushing her with his kisses. 'Stop,' she cried breathlessly. 'Wait. This has

115

to be special. This is 'first time for me, Joseph.'

It was the first time she had said his name. He began to unbutton her bodice, fumbling with the strings, and she removed his clumsy fingers to do it herself. He put his hands round her face as she unfastened it, kissing her lips, cheeks and neck, and finally slipping his fingers through the opened bodice to touch her bare breasts.

She heard his short sharp intake of breath and she began to moan as he bent and clasped his mouth round her nipple.

Mary-Ellen barely knew how they came to be on her father's bed or when he had taken off his coat and shirt and boots, or how she had had the forethought to gather up her own fustian sheet to lay beneath them; but she had surmised that this would be more than sweet and tender kisses. That this would be the beginning and the end, the commencement and the consummation, and that she would bleed.

They were lost to everything but the knowledge of each other's bodies and the joy that it brought. The seductive touch of flesh on flesh, of mouth on mouth, the heart-beating sensation of delectation and rapture, as each provocative touch brought them to a fever pitch of ecstasy and arousal. 'Mary-Ellen,' he breathed. 'Mary-Ellen!' Over and over again he mouthed her name as his hands followed the shape of her breasts, her hips, and the silkiness of her thighs.

And when it seemed that she could take no more, when her yielding throbbing body was not her own, but was melting and on the brink of exploding into a white-hot ball of fire, he ardently and overwhelmingly entered her, calling out her name in a clamorous cry.

Later as he buttoned his shirt and put on his boots and coat, and she fastened up her bodice, they glanced almost shyly at each other. 'What if your father had come back,' he murmured. 'Suppose he'd decided to return.'

She lifted her hair away from her flushed face and tucked it behind her ears. 'He'd have killed you,' she said simply. 'Even though you are who you are.' She heaved a great sigh. 'And then he would've killed me.'

Joseph gave a small smile and said, 'And then he would have hanged, so there's a sorry tale.' He buttoned up his riding coat, then reached out his hand to draw her to him. He kissed the top of her head. 'You're not sorry?'

'About being killed?' She reached up and kissed his lips. 'No. After being with you it would be 'perfect way to die.'

His eyes were tender as he gazed at her. 'I love you, Mary-Ellen. You might think, after I've left, that what has passed between us was just a man's desire. Lust, even. But it wasn't. I love you and always will.'

'Then that's enough,' she said softly. 'No woman could ask for more.'

She stood at the door watching him walk back up the track. He had left Ebony tied to a tree near the river where he could graze. He turned once and looked back but neither of them waved, and as he walked on she came inside and wrapping herself in the sheet lay down again on the bed. She could smell and taste him on her skin and on the bloodstained sheet. She closed her eyes and relived the emotions she had felt. He says he loves me, and I know I love him. But what will become of us?

The fire was almost out when her father came home and he woke her from a deep sleep. 'Sleeping during 'day, girl? Are you sick?'

'No.' She tumbled off the bed, dragging the sheet with her. 'Just 'time of 'month. Sometimes it makes me feel tired.'

'Huh.' He was slightly embarrassed. 'Your ma was 'same. I'll fetch in some more wood, save you 'bother. I'm starting work tomorrow if river's calm. I'll be glad to get back. Can't do with sitting about.'

She suddenly felt guilty about her elation. If her father was out she would be able to see Joseph again.

They met on the river bank a few days later,

but only briefly as Joseph had a meeting with his agent. 'It's Christmas in three days,' he said. 'I don't know if I'll be able to get away. My parents always invite relatives and friends to stay.' Tenderly he stroked her cheek. 'I must see you again soon, Mary-Ellen. It's not going to be easy, and I don't want you to get into trouble with your father, but I miss you, and want you more than I can say.'

'Somebody's coming,' she said urgently. 'Don't look round, just point as if you're showing me something.'

He did as she bid, pointing along the river bank and towards the track.

'Hello, Daniel,' Mary-Ellen called out. One of her young cousins was coming along the bank. 'Where 'you going?'

'Coming to see you.' The boy, who was seven or eight, took off his cap when he came up to them and saw Joseph Ellis. 'Beg pardon, sir. I've got a message for you, Mary-Ellen.' He looked up at Joseph as if undecided whether to say more in front of him, then blurted out, 'Ma says if tha's got a spare rabbit, she'd appreesh— she'd be glad of it, cos she hasn't enough meat for all of us for Christmas dinner.'

'Have you a bird for Christmas?' Joseph asked Mary-Ellen.

She shook her head. 'Onny if I kill one of our own and they're a bit tough, onny fit for soup.'

She turned to her cousin. 'Tell your ma that I'll bring her a rabbit over tomorrow. Da's going out with his gun tonight.'

'Are you one of the Marston children?' Joseph asked, and when the boy nodded he said, 'My compliments to your mother and tell her I'll bring her a bird on Christmas Eve. And take care going back home. It's very muddy on the bank.'

The boy stood open-mouthed, staring at Joseph, then put on his cap and touched it deferentially. 'Yes, sir. Thank you, sir.'

When he was out of earshot Joseph said, 'Is it all right to do that? Your aunt won't take offence? Nor your father? We generally give our tenants a bird at Christmas.'

'Aunt Lol won't refuse it. She's got a brood of bairns to feed and not much money coming in.' There was a touch of pride in her eyes as she looked at him. 'I can't say 'same about my father. He might think it charity – and so might I!'

'Don't! Please don't,' he begged. 'It's just that I thought here is an excuse for me to come and see you.'

She looked away, but her features softened. 'Yes.' She pressed her lips together. 'As you say, it's not going to be easy. Ever.'

He came as promised on Christmas Eve morning, calling first at Welwick at the Marstons' cottage with a fat goose and then riding on through the village to Welwick Thorpe. Isaac

Page wasn't in; he had gone out at dawn to try for duck or widgeon, Mary-Ellen told Joseph, as he had only managed to shoot one rabbit the other night. She had omitted to tell her father that they were to receive a bird from the Ellises, unable to think how to explain that she had seen Joseph again.

Now she was nervous and uneasy. 'Da should've been back by now. He must have gone down to 'Wheatsheaf at Welwick. Come with me,' she said to Joseph. 'And bring 'fowl with you.'

He'd brought a large capon freshly killed and he followed her to the cow shelter where he hung it up high on a beam. Then he turned and put his arms about her. He could feel her heart beating and felt her nervousness.

'Are you afraid your father will come after me with his gun?' he quizzed.

'Don't joke,' she snapped. 'He would!'

'We'll see him coming from here.' He gazed at her. 'This isn't what I want,' he whispered. 'Not hiding away as if this is something sordid or shameful; it isn't just gratification. I need you, Mary-Ellen. Want you. Love you.'

She stopped his mouth with her own. 'I know. I know,' she breathed into him. 'I believe you.' She lifted her eyes to the dilapidated roof. 'We must make believe this is a palace.' She leaned against the wooden stall. 'And imagine this is our bed of fine satins.' But know in our innermost

121

hearts, her head cried out, as gently he tantalized her, that it can't last.

By mid-afternoon, dark cloud had lowered and the rain begun again. Isaac still wasn't back and Mary-Ellen was beginning to worry. She had plucked and cleaned the capon, and scrubbed the potatoes and carrots. She went out onto the track and looked up and down it.

I wonder if he's with Uncle Ben. Sometimes the two men walked to the hostelry together and propped each other up on the way home until their ways parted. She went back inside and decided to put the capon in the oven and partly cook it in readiness for the next day. It was a large bird and would feed them for a week.

Darkness came down and still her father hadn't returned. Mary-Ellen made a decision. She wrapped her shawl round her and set off for Aunt Lol's house.

It was a single-storey dwelling of two rooms in a lane running from the main street, but not as isolated as the cottage where Mary-Ellen and her father lived. She knocked on the door and waited, for she knew that at this time of day the door would be bolted. Her aunt called out, 'Who is it?'

'Mary-Ellen, Aunt Lol. Have you seen Da? Is he with Uncle Ben?'

The door creaked open. Her aunt had the baby at her breast. She looked tired, her face creased with lines. 'Not seen him at all today. Come in. Come in,' she said and Mary-Ellen stepped inside. There was a delicious smell of roasting goose. 'Ben's here by 'fire, where he's been for 'last hour,' Lol added with a slight note of resentment.

Ben took his pipe out of his mouth and yawned. He'd caught her comment. 'Aye. I work hard enough every other day.'

'Da's not come home,' Mary-Ellen said urgently. 'He's been out since early morning. He went to shoot wildfowl but he's not been back.'

Ben looked keenly at her. 'He'd surely have come home afore going to 'hostelry?'

Mary-Ellen nodded. She was beginning to feel sick. What if her father had had an accident? How would they find him in the dark? I should have set out earlier to look for him. I should have gone to the river.

Her uncle got up from his chair. 'I'll tek a lamp and go and look,' he said, and took a scarf from the peg behind the door. 'You'd better stay here, lass, till I get back.'

'I – I can't,' she stammered. 'I've put 'bird in 'oven. Mr Ellis brought us a capon this morning.'

'Aye, he brought us a goose,' her aunt said. 'I'm cooking it now; it'll tek all night.' A frown wrinkled her forehead. 'Why did your da go out shooting when Ellis had promised you a bird?'

'He – Mr Ellis told Daniel he'd bring you one. He'd heard him ask me for a rabbit.' Mary-Ellen felt herself flush. 'I – I wasn't sure if he meant he'd bring one for us as well.' And so the lying begins, she thought. Is this how it's going to be? What if Da finds out? He could have been at home and not on the river bank. 'I'd better get home,' she said. 'In case he comes back. He'll wonder where I am.'

She bent to kiss the baby on his forehead. He smelt of warm milk. 'Will Janey be home tomorrow?' she asked.

'Don't know,' Lol said. 'I thought she might have sent a note to tell me, but she's no great shakes at writing, our Janey. It'll be nice if she is, and she can help us eat this goose.' She gave a grin. 'This'll be 'first Christmas we've had such a feast.'

'Us too,' Mary-Ellen said. 'I hope Da's all right,' she added anxiously. 'He doesn't usually stay out so late on Christmas Eve.'

'He'll be waiting for you at home with 'strap at 'ready,' Lol said. 'He'll be thinking you're out meeting some young fella!' She gazed quizzically at her. 'Which you should be doing,' she added, ''stead of just looking after your fayther.'

When Mary-Ellen got home she sat down by the fire and dropped into a doze. She awoke with a start and could smell the crisp aroma of the cooking capon and got up to take it out of the oven. 'It's nearly ready,' she muttered. 'Whatever time can it be?'

The skin on the bird was browned and crisped and she prodded it with a skewer. The juices ran clear and she realized that she must have slept for longer than she had thought. Wherever has Da got to? she worried. I hope he isn't drunk and has fallen over somewhere, not able to get up.

She heard a sound outside and listened intently. Is that him? Then came a knock and a shout. It was Ben.

'I can't find him,' her uncle said as she opened the door. 'I've been to 'Wheatsheaf and he's not there. Not been in at all today and he won't have gone further than that in this weather. And I've walked along 'river bank, but it's too dark to see owt.'

Ben had a crumpled weather-beaten face most of the time, but now she saw the deep furrows of anxiety. 'Wha – what do you think's happened?' she said. 'Do you think he's had an accident?'

He shook his head. 'Don't look too good, do it? I've asked some of 'men at 'Wheatsheaf if they'll come out at first light and we'll search for him. It's nearly nine o'clock. Can't do more'n that, can we?'

'It's Christmas!' she whispered. 'He'd be sure to come home if he could.'

'You'd best come back wi' me,' he said. 'No sense in you stopping here on your own.' Ben

125

had always had a soft spot for her when she had lived with them, even though he had so many children of his own, but she shook her head. 'He might come home,' she said. 'I have to be here.'

She waited a few minutes after he'd left and then put on her shawl; she put another log on the fire and turned the lamp down to save the oil. Then she went out into the night up the track towards the estuary.

There had been some rain earlier and underfoot was wet and muddy. The cloud still hung low but here and there in the breaks, stars could be seen in the sky. She looked for the brightest one, something she had done since she was a child, when her mother had told her it was the holy star and always appeared on Christmas Eve. She reached the estuary and could hear the swell and lap of the water, the suck and slurp as the tide filled the channels and runnels and covered the hummocks in the saltmarsh. I wonder if he took the boat out? she pondered. He had not known there was no need for him to do so. She cautiously set off in the direction where it was kept, but it was difficult to see the path and after a while she stopped. If I slip in, I shall be here all night or even for ever.

She shivered and turned about. The Humber could be treacherous and had to be treated with respect. If the tide came in high it flooded the banks, washing over into the land below. 'Da!'

126

she shouted. 'Da! Where are you? Hello! Can you hear me?'

There was a croak from the scrubby blackthorn behind her as her call disturbed some nesting bird. She walked on, then stopped. A dark shape lay sprawled over the bank and she thought at first it was a spar or log that had been washed up and wondered how she had missed it as she had walked past. She bent down, then put her hand to her mouth in horror. It was her father.

CHAPTER ELEVEN

Isaac was too heavy to lift but she managed to turn him over. He wasn't drowned as she had thought, but shot; a dark stain had steeped through his clothing in the area near his waist.

She bent over him, cradling him in her arms, and sobbed. 'This is my fault,' she wept. 'If I'd told you we were being given that damned bird you wouldn't have gone out shooting. Da! Da! I'm so sorry! Forgive me. What am I going to do?'

His legs were hanging over the bank but she couldn't pull him out and was afraid that he might slip into the marsh and be carried away. I'll have to run for help. Get Uncle Ben to come back with me. 'I'll not be long, Da,' she whispered. 'I'll be quick as I can.' As she rose to her feet she saw her father's fowling gun lying on the muddy ground and a long skid mark beside it.

Once back on the track she began to run, past

their cottage and towards the road to the village. She could hardly speak by the time she reached the Marstons' house, which was in darkness. She hammered on the door, not caring if she startled anyone or woke the children.

'I've – I've found him,' she gasped as her uncle unbolted the door. She held her hand to her waist, where she had a piercing painful stitch. 'He's – he's . . .' She took a breath and then let out a wail. 'He's dead! Shot. He's lying on 'river bank. I can't move him. Come with me! Please. Or 'river will take him. 'Tide's running fast.'

'Come in, lass, and wait while I get dressed.' Her uncle was in his long johns and vest. He reached for his cord breeches, which were lying over the back of a chair, and put them on. 'You shouldn't have gone down there on your own,' he said, his voice muffled as he pulled on a flannel shirt and a woollen jumper over the top of it. 'You might have tummelled in and we wouldn't have known.'

Her aunt came into the kitchen; the family slept together in the other room. She wore a long grey nightgown and her hair hung down her back. She took in Mary-Ellen's distress and came towards her, putting her arms round her. 'Your uncle Ben will fetch somebody to help him,' she said. 'There's no need for you to go back.'

'No. No. I have to go! They'll not find him. He's halfway between 'village and home. I walked past

129

him once.' She gave a sob. 'It was when I turned back that I saw him. He must have slipped. It's treacherous on 'top of 'bank. I should have told him, Aunt Lol,' she cried. 'I should have said and then he wouldn't have gone!'

'Telled him what, dearie?' Lol asked. 'When could anybody ever tell your da owt?'

Mary-Ellen put her face in her hands. 'That we were getting a fowl,' she whispered. 'I knew that he would bring one.'

'Leave that now,' Lol said. 'You can't go blaming yourself for what might have been, and knowing your da as we do he'd probably have gone out anyway.' She patted Mary-Ellen's mouth with her finger. 'Say no more about that.'

Mary-Ellen trudged back with the men, forcing herself to put one foot in front of the other. Ben had woken two neighbours and they had brought an old door to carry back the body. They agreed, on looking at the skid mark, that as he was aiming his gun he had probably slipped or lost his balance, with tragic consequences.

'I remember it happening once afore,' one of the other men said. 'Dost tha remember that time? A few years back, ower in Holmpton?'

It was of no consolation to Mary-Ellen that it had happened before. She was quite convinced that it was her fault. That she was the one to blame.

He was carried back and laid on his bed and at

midnight the doctor came to pronounce on the death. The next morning the constable was sent for. He came after he had eaten his Christmas dinner, having decided there was no rush when he was told that it was deemed an accident, not suicide and not murder.

Jane arrived home for the day, but after visiting Mary-Ellen and seeing the body of her uncle she returned early to Skeffling as she couldn't bear the sight or sound of Mary-Ellen's weeping, nor eat any of the Christmas goose. She told Jack Terrison what had happened when he saw her sniffling into her handkerchief as she crossed the yard. He told the foreman and the other lads, and by the following morning Joseph and his father had also heard the news of the disaster.

'I'd better go over, Father,' Joseph said, trying to keep calm, for the first he had heard was that there had been a fatal shooting at Welwick Thorpe and he had been horrified to think that it might have been Mary-Ellen. On enquiring further he had discovered that Isaac Page had died in an accident. 'It's only common decency to ask if we can help.'

'Mm,' his father replied. 'I suppose the young woman will go to live with relatives, if she has any. She'll not be able to pay the rent on her own.'

'We can't turn her out!' Joseph said in alarm.

131

'No, she can stay for a while. The rent will be paid in advance anyway, isn't it?'

'I believe so,' Joseph said, determining that it would be. He saddled up Ebony, having told his mother that he would be back as quickly as he could but not to delay the Boxing Day luncheon. The family and their guests should begin without him. 'Miss Page might need some advice,' he explained. 'For the funeral and so on.'

'I fail to see it,' his mother had replied. 'She'll have friends to rally round her. People in that kind of situation always do.'

He approached the cottage cautiously, aware that there might be someone with Mary-Ellen, though his instinct was to rush in and comfort her. Mrs Marston came to the door. She had a child in her arms and a toddler at her skirts.

As Joseph wasn't working today and was expected to help entertain their house guests, he had dressed on rising in formal indoor clothes: a dark green morning coat with matching waistcoat and narrow trousers, and black leather shoes. When he decided to ride to Welwick Thorpe he had changed his footwear for long boots and over his coat had put on his caped mackintosh, which although it stank of rubber would keep him warm and dry. He took off his top hat and greeted Mrs Marston.

'Good morning,' he said. 'I'm so very sorry to hear of Mr Page's demise. I've come to offer Miss

Page my condolences and any assistance that she might need.'

Lol gave a sigh. 'It's good of you, Mr Ellis, but I doubt you can be of any help. My niece is quite bereft.' She looked at him directly and said bluntly, 'I'd ask you in, but there's onny one room and Isaac is laid out in it.'

Joseph took in a sudden breath as he remembered the bed where he had lain with Mary-Ellen. Her father's bed. 'Will she see me, do you think?'

'I'll ask her. I was on my way home. Mr Marston has gone back to work and I've my other bairns to see to.' She gave another sigh. 'A Christmas spoiled,' she said. 'And we didn't do justice to that fine goose you kindly sent us.'

He murmured some platitude and she backed into the cottage and closed the door behind her. Mary-Ellen would agree to see him, he was in no doubt, but surely she wouldn't stay here with only her father's body for company?

After a few moments, Mrs Marston came out again. 'Mary-Ellen said if you'd give her a minute she'll come out and speak to you. If you'll excuse me, Mr Ellis, I'll be on my way home.'

He watched her as she trudged down the track, holding one child by the hand and the other close to her chest. She was unsuitably dressed for the cold weather and he felt guilty, wrapped warmly in his winter clothes.

The door opened and Mary-Ellen came out. He was shocked by her pallor and her red-rimmed eyes. 'My darling,' he whispered, coming towards her. 'I'm so sorry.'

She drew back from him. 'Don't touch me,' she said in a low voice. 'I'm wicked and corrupt.'

'What nonsense is this?' He was alarmed at her demeanour. 'You've had a terrible shock, Mary-Ellen.'

She stared at him with wide tearful eyes. 'I didn't tell him,' she whispered. 'Didn't tell my father that you were bringing a Christmas fowl. If I had, he wouldn't have gone out with his gun. It was my fault that he died.'

'That's foolish talk,' he said. 'This wasn't the first time he'd been out shooting?'

Silently she shook her head and tears trickled down her cheeks. He wanted to take her in his arms and whisper endearments, to soothe her pain. 'Well then,' he said softly. 'It could have happened at any time. He was on the river bank, I understand?'

She didn't answer, but only swallowed, and so he went on. 'I almost fell in the river the other day. The ground is very muddy. Ebony slipped but fortunately recovered.' It was a lie. Ebony was sure-footed, but he wanted to bring Mary-Ellen reassurance. To ease her troubled mind.

'I can't see you again,' she muttered. 'Don't come.'

'What?' He was startled. 'Why not?'

'We're bad for each other. It's not to be. I don't want to see you.'

'You don't mean that, Mary-Ellen. You can't mean it!' Joseph came out in a cold sweat. She didn't know what she was saying. She must be temporarily unhinged with the grief of her father's sudden death.

'I mean it.' She looked straight at him and it was as if he was a stranger. 'It's madness to think of it. We live different lives. Nowt in common.'

'I love you,' he pleaded. 'That's what we have in common. I know we have different lives, but it needn't stop us loving each other.'

She gave a low hard laugh. 'And how do you suggest we continue?' she asked. Her voice was cutting. 'What do you propose? I must leave here now and find work. My father kept me.' Her hand waved towards the cottage. 'Such luxury he kept me in, as you know. But now I must keep myself.'

He opened his mouth to speak, but she cut in and he saw fire flare in her eyes. 'Perhaps you're going to suggest that you keep me? That I become your doxy? That you pay me every time you come to see me, so that I can pay 'rent.'

He shook his head miserably. 'Don't speak like that, Mary-Ellen. Please don't say those things.'

He saw the tremble on her lips as she strove to keep from crying and he took another step towards her. She lifted her arms and in a sudden fury she launched herself at him and hammered her fists against his chest.

'Don't you *see*!' she wailed. 'Don't you *understand*? It's because I wanted you that my father is *dead*! I had to keep you secret from him. Couldn't tell him, couldn't tell anyone about you.'

He locked his arms about her to hold her fast. 'Then the fault is mine as much as yours,' he said softly. 'We're both guilty.'

He felt her go limp in his arms. 'No,' she whispered. 'Only mine.'

'Don't turn me away, Mary-Ellen.' He kissed the top of her head. 'We'll think of some way out of this dilemma. I can't live without you.'

Slowly she shook her head. 'There's no way out of it,' she murmured. 'You can't live with me, and I can't live with you.' She lifted her head and he kissed her wet cheeks. 'Don't come again – at least, not for some time. I have to think about what to do.'

'Don't do anything in haste,' he said urgently. 'Don't go away! Don't do anything without telling me first.' He looked down at her appealingly. 'You owe me that, Mary-Ellen, and you know that you can stay here, don't you? You don't have to leave.'

His mind was working furiously, trying to think of a solution. Perhaps if she was to live in Patrington or Hedon. She could find work there in order to look respectable and they would find somewhere to be together. Or, he thought, if she wanted to stay here he would arrange for the rent to be paid; that would be easy enough to do if she agreed, but it would mean that she lived alone.

She wiped her tears on her sleeve. 'First I must see to my father's funeral. Then I must mourn. And after that – after that . . .' She shook her head and whispered, 'I don't know.'

Because the Ellises had only just taken up the title deeds of Welwick Thorpe, their agent had not yet visited the cottage and so it was easy enough for Joseph to alter in the account book the details of dates and amounts of rent that had been paid by their new tenants. He carefully adjusted the amount so that it appeared that Isaac Page had paid three months in advance. 'Most unusual, I quite agree,' he told the agent when the latter brought it to his attention. 'But there we are. I believe there's been cockfighting in the village. Perhaps Page had a good run of betting and wanted to have security of tenure. Leave it with me. I'll speak to Miss Page at some time in the future. She's within her rights to stay there, anyway.'

He asked his father if he would be present at Page's funeral as a mark of respect, claiming that he himself had other things to see to. I can't bear to be near Mary-Ellen without wanting to take her in my arms, he brooded. Anyone would be able to tell that I desire her.

Jack Terrison had asked the hind if he might have the morning off to attend the service. When it was mentioned to Joseph he was suspicious that Terrison might have an ulterior motive: a wish to see Mary-Ellen.

'Tell him to come straight back after church,' he said brusquely, 'and not go to the wake.'

'That's what I did tell him, sir,' the foreman said, puzzled by his attitude. 'We're clearing out 'foldyards and starting wi' muck spreading. Terrison knows that; he'll not stay away long. Onny pay his due respects.'

Joseph walked away across the stable yard and saw Jane, who he now knew was Mary-Ellen's cousin. She was dressed in her cloak and bonnet and he called to her.

'Are you going to the funeral?'

She dipped her knee. 'Yes, sir. Cook said I could go as he was my uncle. I've to come straight back, though.'

Joseph nodded. 'Would you kindly give my condolences to your cousin,' he said. 'And assure her of our best regard for her future.'

'Yes sir.' She dipped again and he thought how

unlike the cousins were. One so meek and one so full of fire and passion.

I must see Mary-Ellen again soon, he mused as he watched Jane scurry down the drive. My life cannot continue without her. I am *nothing* without her!

CHAPTER TWELVE

I said I never wanted to see him again. When I told him that he should stay away, I meant it. Mary-Ellen viciously struck her gardening fork into the ground. Her father had cleared the vegetable plot and started the digging, but had failed to finish it. But now I want to see him. One of the tines struck a stone and she picked it up and hurled it as far as she could. I want him, I need him, and I know that he's no good for me. We're no good for each other and if he should come I shall tell him so again, in case he wasn't listening the first time.

She stretched her back. The ground was heavy and hard to dig. Why hasn't he been? It's over a week since Da's funeral and I've to make up my mind what to do. She had been into the village and enquired if there was any work at the inn which her father had patronized. She had been told that there was a line of women waiting for work before her. I'll have to go to Patrington, she thought, and ask there. The new agent will be coming for the rent soon.

Perhaps he won't come, she thought, thinking of Joseph. Perhaps he's afraid that I might rely on him now that Da's not here. Well, he's got another think coming! I don't need him or any man. I can survive on my own. She took a breath and went to fetch a spade. The gardening tools were hanging in the cow shelter, except that now there was no cow to shelter. Mary-Ellen couldn't afford to feed her so had sold her, but had kept the hens, which she fed on kitchen scraps and vegetables and the last of the corn.

Her father's old waterproof coat, the one he used for gardening, was hanging on a peg and on seeing it she felt the sudden pang of the guilt that hit her every night as she climbed into bed. The bed that had been her father's.

Uncle Ben had helped her move the iron bedstead to a different position. Now it was against the wall where she had previously slept on her palliasse. She had dragged her father's straw mattress outside and symbolically set fire to it on the vegetable plot. As she watched it burn she had pondered that another part of her life had gone. The dry straw had crackled and fizzed, and spat bright sparks up into the sky before turning into a conflagration. Mary-Ellen thought of the loss of her mother and now her father, who lay with his wife in the churchyard.

141

Isaac had contributed to a scheme which paid for his burial, but the rest of the funeral costs had been met by local people. Men whom Isaac had known or worked with had a whip-round for him. One of the Parrott family had come to see her and told her that they too had made a collection, and had handed over a sum of money to be put towards the cost of a funeral tea.

She put her hand tenderly on her father's coat. Though they hadn't always seen eye to eye – she was too much like him for their relationship ever to be easy – she realized now how he had protected her, even to the extent of keeping her at home where she would be safe. 'Well, I'm on my own now, Da,' she murmured. 'You're not here to look after me any more.'

She picked up the spade and turned to go back into the garden and there was Joseph standing in the entrance of the shelter. 'Am I welcome?' he asked softly. 'Or is it too soon?'

Mary-Ellen held her breath but couldn't hold back the tears. She heard the pleading in his voice, saw the wistfulness in his eyes. She put her hands over her face and sobbed. 'It's no use,' she wept. 'I'll ruin your life. One of us must go away. It can't be you so it must be me.'

In one long stride he was by her side and holding her close, kissing her wet cheeks, stroking her neck and murmuring sweet endearments. 'I love you, Mary-Ellen. If you go away I shall come after you. Wherever you go I shall follow.'

She put her face up to his. 'Love me,' she whispered. 'I'm lost. Hold me close.'

He put Ebony in the shelter so that the horse couldn't be seen from the track and together they went into the cottage. He saw that it looked different. The bed had been moved and there was a rail with a curtain drawn across it so that it was hidden from view.

He slid the bolt across the door and held out his arms to her. She nestled into them and said softly, 'I wasn't ever going to see you again.' She gazed into his tender blue eyes. 'But God help me, for I can't help myself.'

'We were meant for each other, Mary-Ellen.' He stroked her cheek. 'I'm not prepared to give you up. I think of you night and day and I need you.' His voice dropped to a whisper. 'We can't control what will happen in the future. We can only take our happiness now.'

He stayed an hour and then rode away home, promising that he would come back that night. When he arrived at Burstall House, he went into the ironing room and asked the young maid there to fetch him another blanket to put on his bed, saying he had been cold the previous night. He took a bottle of wine from the dresser in the dining room and filched a bunch of grapes from the table. These he secreted in his leather knapsack, and then during the early evening he took the blanket from his bed and placed it inside a horse blanket in the stable.

At eleven o'clock when the house was quiet and the entire household had gone to bed, he slipped out of a side door, locking it behind him and pocketing the key. He saddled up Ebony, putting the blankets on his back, and walked him out of the stable yard, leading him through the wood and onto the track which led to the river. Then he mounted and rode to Mary-Ellen.

He tapped on her door. She had been listening for him and opened it immediately. Joseph put Ebony in the cow shelter with the horse blanket over him and patted the animal's neck, whispering that he would have to get used to the occasional night out of his warm stable, and then went indoors.

There was a good fire burning and the lamp was lit. He threw the blanket onto the bed and opening his bag brought out the bottle of wine, a corkscrew, and the grapes. 'Glasses!' he groaned. 'I didn't bring any glasses!'

'Then we'll have to drink out of cups,' she told him, 'cos I don't possess any.'

'No matter,' he said. 'It will taste all the sweeter.' He poured it into two cups and then kissed her. 'This is to celebrate our love,' he said softly. 'The culmination of our dreams.'

She looked at him with her lips parted; her

dark hair hung below her shoulders and the firelight sent flickering shadows about her.

'You are so beautiful,' he murmured. 'I shall love you for ever, until the end of life.'

He woke during the night and felt the touch of her naked body next to his. He put his arm across her, cupping her breast in his hand, and she murmured in her sleep.

A little later Mary-Ellen woke and turned to look at him. She examined his fair skin. His eyes were closed, dark lashes fringing the lids. Her fingertips fluttered about his firm mouth and then over his cheekbones.

He opened his eyes and gazed sleepily at her. 'This is what I have dreamed of, Mary-Ellen,' he murmured. 'To wake with you beside me.'

'Always wake me before you leave,' she whispered. 'Don't ever go without telling me that you love me, so that I can think of it all day long.'

During the winter days of January and February they had their secret meetings. Sometimes Mary Ellen cooked a rabbit and they ate their supper at midnight, and Joseph left before dawn to be home before the servants stirred. Whether they knew, he cared not, though he realized that they would be curious about the amount of extra wine which was being consumed, and the grapes and melons which disappeared from the table.

His parents suspected nothing, although his

sister sometimes remarked that he was looking tired when he joined them for their midday meal. 'Are you staying out late?' she teased. 'Are you frequenting the hostelries?'

'I don't always sleep well,' was his rejoinder, which was perfectly true. He did very little sleeping when he was with Mary-Ellen.

As winter turned, they both knew it would become more difficult. Dawn was breaking earlier and he had to get home before the stable lads and estate workers were about. Once, when he was late back, he saw Jack Terrison stretching and yawning. Jack slept above the stables and must have got up to relieve himself. Joseph put Ebony into the stable and told Jack, though on reflection he realized he didn't need to, that he'd been out for an early morning ride.

He came to her one night and told her that his parents and sister were going away the following morning for a few days. 'Come and stay with me,' he said eagerly. 'I'll come for you tomorrow night when everyone is in bed and bring you back the next morning.'

Mary-Ellen objected. 'The servants – Jane – they'll see me! How can I?'

'They won't see you. Most of them are abed by nine o'clock, and Jane doesn't come upstairs,' he told her. 'She's in the kitchen or the wash house, I believe.'

'Don't you know?' she asked, wondering what

146

kind of household it was where the son of the house didn't know the duties of the servants.

'Why would I know?' He laughed. 'I have nothing to do with any of that.'

She was curious, she had to admit, about the kind of life he led away from her and so reluctantly she agreed, when he assured her that no-one would see her enter or leave the house.

She rode up behind him until they reached the small wood and then he dismounted and led Ebony through to the drive and the side of the house, where he lifted Mary-Ellen down and hitched the reins to a hook on the wall.

'I'll take you upstairs first and then come down and stable Ebony,' he whispered into her ear. 'Don't worry. Everything will be all right.'

They crept up the stairs and Mary-Ellen jumped as a clock struck ten. He smiled and squeezed her hand but she didn't relax until they reached his room, where a lamp was burning low, a fire was lit in the grate, and she saw that the bed sheet had been turned back in readiness for occupancy.

'I won't be long,' he said quietly. 'There's a dressing room through that door if you should need anything.'

Mary-Ellen gazed round the huge high-ceilinged chamber. This one room would house a whole family. It's bigger even than Aunt Lol's house. And the bed! It could sleep six easily. She looked curiously at a long chair and wondered why it had a back rest only at one end; her eyes were drawn to a wooden carver chair pulled up to a writing desk by the window. She went across to it and saw embossed paper and envelopes, a pen and a bottle of ink. There was also a metal box of lucifers and a stick of what looked like hard wax.

She cautiously opened the door which Joseph had said led to a dressing room, and wondered why he would want a separate room for dressing when he had so much space in the bedroom. It was a small room with a long cupboard and a hanging rail for Joseph's working clothes, his cord breeches and tweed jacket. His shoes and boots stood on a shelf and she marvelled at how many pairs of footwear one man could want. There were dress boots and half-boots and boots with elastic sides, shoes with a loose tongue inside them and another shiny pair which appeared to be hardly worn, that fastened with a broad ribbon.

She opened the cupboard door and saw various top hats, one with a tall crown, others with lower ones, on a shelf above a rail which held a dark green tailcoat and the narrow trousers Joseph had been wearing when he came to see her after her father had died. How odd, she thought, that I should remember that, though in truth every moment that I have been with him is etched in my memory. She turned away and closed the door. Against the other wall was a marble washstand with a flowered jug and bowl standing on it. She put her hand to the jug of water. Warm! One of the maids must have brought it up when she came to turn down the sheets, she reasoned.

Underneath the washstand was a cupboard, and inside, when she opened the small door, was a plain chamber pot. 'Great heavens,' she murmured aloud. 'Does 'maid have to empty that too?'

Joseph returned a few minutes later and found her sitting on the long chair. She had taken off her boots and put her feet up. He smiled at her apparent ease. 'What do you think?' he said. 'Do you like it?'

'This chair?' she said. 'Is it a sofa? Why has it only got one end?'

'It's a *chaise-longue*,' he said. 'French for long chair.'

'Hah!' she scoffed. 'I knew it was a long chair! Why don't they call it that, then, instead of giving it a silly French name?'

He laughed. 'I don't know! Perhaps the French thought of it first.' He put his hands out to her. 'Never mind that. Come here to me.' He pulled her to her feet. 'I want to take you to my bed,' he murmured, 'so that when you are not here I can think of how it was with you in it.'

Slowly he unbuttoned her bodice and the strings on her skirt and let them fall, leaving her naked. 'Sit down again,' he whispered. 'Lean against the back rest and let me look at you.'

She did as she was bid, lifting her hair and draping her arm above her head. He kissed her, his lips traversing her body, and then she watched him as he swiftly removed his garments: his coat and boots, his white shirt and cotton undershift, his trousers and long cotton under-drawers and grey stockings. Naked, he lifted her into his arms and carried her to the bed. She was enfolded in crisp cotton sheets and soft blankets with his warm body next to hers.

'This is what I have wanted so much, Mary-Ellen,' he said softly. 'That one day you would be here in my own bed where you belong.'

Mary-Ellen was the first to open her eyes the next morning, awakened by the cries of geese as they flew over the house. She saw the pale streaks of dawn coming through the gap in the curtains, for they had opened them last night to let in the light of the moon. 'Joseph,' she breathed. 'Joseph, wake up! It's getting light. I have to go home!'

He came to with a start. 'Damn,' he cursed. 'I wanted to savour the moment of waking next to you.' He kissed her mouth and then ran his fingers through his crumpled hair. 'Now we must rush before the horse lads get up.'

It was five o'clock by the timepiece on his bedside table and they both hurried to dress without first washing. 'I'm sorry, my darling,' he said, as he pulled on his boots. She was already dressed, having fewer clothes to put on than he had. 'It won't always be like this, I promise. I'll speak to my parents when they come back.'

'No,' she said quickly. 'Not yet. Wait a bit. It's too soon.' They won't want me, she realized. Why would they want their only son to be with somebody like me? Somebody who doesn't know how to behave, or know what the French is for a long chair! A nobody whose cousin scrubs floors and bleaches the bed sheets below in the wash house. She gazed wistfully and lovingly at him. He's living in a dream and I know that the dream would turn sour.

She waited by the gate in the wood whilst he fetched Ebony. 'Did anybody see you?' she asked, and was relieved when he shook his head. But he didn't tell her that once again he had seen that early riser, Jack Terrison, as he left the stable yard, and that when he looked back before turning into the wood Terrison had been standing with his hands in his pockets watching him.

At the beginning of May, when blackbirds were singing and finches were twittering and the leaves on the trees were a soft new green, he determined that he should declare his love for her to his parents. 'I want to tell them now.

They'll object, I know,' he told Mary-Ellen as he prepared to leave her early one morning and ride home. 'They'll say that this is an obsession and won't last. But I shall tell them that I love you and want you to be with me always.'

Mary-Ellen turned to him. She had been gazing up at the morning sky where the sun was breaking through the soft white clouds which were scudding across the vast expanse of blue and gold. A flock of grey plover flew over, followed by black-headed gulls.

'And carry your bairns?' she asked softly.

'That too.' He smiled, coming towards her and trailing Ebony by his reins. 'Anything you want, I want as well.'

She nodded, gazing at him, preparing for the reaction to what she was about to tell him. 'You know about babbies, do you?' Her voice was nervous, though she had intended it to be sober and unemotional. She had been thinking all the night of how she should tell him and if now she would lose him. 'Know how they're made?'

'What are you saying, Mary-Ellen?' A small frown appeared above his nose. 'Are you telling me – are you saying that – I thought I was so careful!' But not careful enough, he thought. How could I be when I wanted her so much?

She stiffened. 'Well now, there's a dilemma,' she said, her voice flat. She swallowed hard. There was no doubt about it. She had waited until she was sure before telling him, although she had spent anxious days and nights worrying over what would now become of her and whether he would still want her with a child around her skirts, or abandon her.

He grinned. 'Not a dilemma,' he told her. Dropping the reins, he hugged her. 'Now we have no choice. I want to look after you, Mary-Ellen, and our child too.'

CHAPTER THIRTEEN

'So, Mary-Ellen. Who's 'fayther of your bairn?'

Mary-Ellen jumped. She should have realized that Aunt Lol would be perceptive enough to notice. But how? She hadn't put on weight, though she had been sick so perhaps she was looking pale.

'How do you know?' she asked. 'I mean, what makes you think . . .'

Lol slowly shook her head. 'I've had enough childre' to be able to tell 'minute it's conceived.' She took hold of Mary-Ellen's chin and looked deep into her eyes. There was no censure or criticism hidden in her gaze, but perhaps a vestige of disappointment as she said, 'Never thought it'd happen to you, Mary-Ellen! Thought you'd have had more sense than to be caught by some brainless village lad! Now what 'we going to do?'

'It's not a village lad, Aunt Lol, but I don't want to say who it is. Not at 'moment, anyway.'

Lol frowned. 'Will he support you? Have you told him? Will he marry you?'

'Yes, yes, and he would if I wanted. But I don't.'

'Don't want to marry! How will you live?' Lol's voice rose in scorn. 'How will you pay 'rent, and buy food and clothing?'

Mary-Ellen bit her lip. It was a subject she and Joseph had argued about. He had called one morning and found her halfway down the track on the way into Welwick. After much probing he discovered that she was about to apply for parish relief in order to pay the rent which she was sure was in arrears. Then he told her that the rent was paid. He'd said at first that her father had paid it, but she knew that was a lie; her father never had enough money to pay in advance. 'You paid it,' she had accused him. 'That makes me a kept woman!'

'So what?' he'd shouted, and turning her round he'd marched her back to the cottage. 'I intend to marry you and you'll be a kept woman then, so what does it matter if I pay the rent now?'

He had also brought her gifts, though he said they were not gifts but necessities. Bedding, pillows, a new rug for the floor, petticoats, woollen skirts and a warm cloak, things that she found hard to resist and which in any case he refused to take back. She had to either keep

155

them or burn them, he told her. So she kept them.

'Is he married?' Lol asked.

'No. I said he would marry me, didn't I? But I won't marry him.'

'He's gentry then? Gentleman farmer? Did he force you, lass?'

'No.' Mary-Ellen found her lips were trembling as she explained. 'I love him, Aunt Lol. But I'll ruin his life if we marry.'

Joseph had come up with many suggestions when she had told him that she wouldn't marry him and live at Burstall House. He said they would marry and live quietly in Hedon where he was not so well known. He would give up farming and they would go away, to Scarborough or Filey. 'We'll have a little house by the sea, Mary-Ellen. Would you like that?' he'd pleaded. 'Or we could live in Hull. Or go anywhere you want.'

She knew then how much he loved her, to be willing to give up so much. 'Let's wait until 'babby is born,' she'd entreated, and felt a shadow hovering over her. 'I'd like it to be born here in my own home.'

'It's Mr Ellis, isn't it?' Lol said, ''Young 'andsome one, I mean. Our Daniel said he's seen him about a few times.'

Mary-Ellen remained silent for a moment. 'I don't want to talk about it, Aunt Lol. Not just yet, anyway.'

'You can't hide it, Mary-Ellen,' Lol said. 'Tongues'll wag and mebbe some other young blade'll get 'blame.'

'No, they won't,' Mary-Ellen denied hotly. 'I've never been seen with any lad. Nobody will know or even guess. And anyway, who ever sees me in this isolated place?'

She hadn't denied that Joseph Ellis was the father, but she knew that Aunt Lol would keep her counsel and help her when her time came.

'Just think.' Lol pursed her lips. 'You're eighteen now and I'm nearly forty, and my bairn and yourn will mebbe grow up together if you stay round here. When will it be? November? A Christmas babby?'

'I don't know, Aunt Lol,' Mary-Ellen confessed. 'I don't know how to work it out.'

'Christmas then, I should think,' her aunt said, and sighed. 'He won't have told his parents?'

Mary-Ellen took a breath. 'He's telling them today.'

Joseph's parents were furious. At least his father was; livid in his rage. His mother grew extremely pale and Joseph thought she was going to faint. 'We had such plans,' she said quietly, taking out a handkerchief and pressing it to her lips. 'We thought that when you married you and your wife would live here and we would move to a smaller house. But how can a girl without

157

any kind of upbringing run a household like this?'

'You're an idiot,' his father roared. 'Set her up in a house somewhere if you must, but how will you find a wife if you're openly keeping a mistress?'

'You don't understand.' Joseph was baffled by their lack of compassion. 'I love her. I want to be with her. I want Mary-Ellen to be my wife.'

'Well,' his father said testily. 'You're of age to do whatever you want; we can't stop you. But I'll tell you this.' He shook his fist and Joseph had never seen him so angry. 'Don't bring her here, for she's not welcome. And another thing – don't tell your sister! We have her future to think about.'

It was an impasse and it was the thought of his sister which made Joseph hesitate. Julia's own marriage prospects would be ruined if he brought Mary-Ellen into the family.

But at least it was out in the open now and he didn't have to worry about sneaking out of the house to visit Mary-Ellen. 'You are quite right,' he told her as he took her into his arms. 'We'll wait until the infant is born and then decide where we shall live.' He kissed the top of her head. 'Where we shall have our love nest.'

It was a beautiful summer. The sun shone almost constantly and when it rained it came at night, soft gentle rain which renewed the earth. The grain flourished and the peas and beans in Mary-Ellen's vegetable plot grew plump, and the potatoes came up by the bucketful. The hens were laying and Joseph brought a nanny goat and kid, so that Mary-Ellen had plenty of milk. Her skin glowed and her hair became even glossier and she felt fit and well and happy.

The labourers had begun on the river embankment intended to abate the flooding, building it up ready for the winter storms. Joseph had every excuse for coming to inspect their work, and then drop in on Mary-Ellen during the day as well as in the evening. The air was full of the scent of blossom: honeysuckle, dog rose and heady cow parsley; honey bees gathered the nectar, butterflies fluttered in the hedges and frogs hopped about the deep ditches. Curlews and herring gulls flew overhead, whilst kingcups spread a golden carpet beneath their feet.

'I shall remember this for ever,' Joseph said one night as, with his arm round her waist, they stood on the bank looking out across the saltmarsh and the Humber. The men had packed up for the day and gone for their supper and he and Mary-Ellen were quite alone. The tide was swift and a brisk breeze was blowing, catching the white spray and tossing it capriciously.

'I've never been to that place on 'other side,'

she murmured. 'It would be strange to look across 'river from over there.'

'Lincolnshire! Would you like to go?' he asked, anxious to please her. 'I wouldn't think of rowing or even sailing across from here – there are too many shoals and sandbanks, and you're at the mercy of the winds – but we could drive into Hull and cross to New Holland by the steam ferry.'

'One day, mebbe,' she said. 'For now I'm content just to be here with you.' She ran her hand across her belly. 'And with our child.' She lifted her eyes up to Joseph. 'If something should happen to me,' she began, and he turned, a frown creasing his forehead. 'Women do die in childbirth,' she whispered, as she saw anguish written on his face. 'My ma did. You'll take care of it? I don't mean for you to take it home. I know that your ma wouldn't want a bastard child, but would you support it so that it didn't end up in 'poorhouse?'

'Mary-Ellen!' She saw tears glisten in his eyes. 'How can you say such a thing? What would I do if anything happened to you? I wouldn't want to live!' He put both arms round her and held her close. 'I couldn't go on without you.'

'But will you?' she asked again. 'Look after it?' And she wouldn't rest until he had said he would.

Jack Terrison called one day just before the autumn harvest began. He had been to a farm in

Welwick, he said, and thought he would come over and pass the time of day. 'Don't see much of you, Mary-Ellen,' he said. 'I wondered how you were managing without your da. Have you got a job o' work?'

His face was brown and weathered, and he had grown a shaggy brown moustache which made him look a lot older. She felt his eyes on her, and although she didn't think he would notice her thickening body, for she still wasn't large, she dropped her shawl from her shoulders and let it slip about her waist.

'I'm managing,' she said. 'Doing a bit o' this and that.' She had in fact been offered work at the inn in Welwick, but Joseph insisted she refuse it. Submissively, to his amazement she did, as the offer had come at a time when she had felt tired and didn't really want to work there in any case. But she had been gratified to see the pleasure on his face when she had agreed.

''Ellises treating you all right?' Jack asked. 'Good landlords, are they?'

She'd murmured that they were and wondered if perhaps he suspected something for he had kept his eyes on her face as he'd asked.

'I can't offer you a cup o' tea, Jack,' she excused herself. 'I'm right out and was just on my way to Aunt Lol's to beg some from her.'

'I'll give you a lift if you like,' he offered, ''Waggon's just at 'end of 'track.'

'I like to walk by 'river,' she said. 'It's so hot and there's a nice breeze blowing in off 'sea.'

'Aye, there is,' he agreed. 'We're starting to cut corn in 'morning so I hope 'wind keeps up. It'll be all hands on deck. Well, for them as has to work. There's some as can skive off like Mr Joseph. He's nivver there when you need him.' He looked sideways at her. 'You could probably earn a copper or two if you'd a mind to come ower to Skeffling,' he said. 'They're a bit short on women to gather up corn and I can allus give you a ride back.'

'Yes,' she agreed. 'I might do that.' She pondered on what Joseph's mother would think if she saw her out in the fields and knew that she was the woman who was carrying her son's child.

She didn't go to Skeffling, but went instead to help with the harvest in one of the Welwick farms. She valued her independence and felt that she had lost some of it since becoming Joseph's lover. The weather remained blisteringly hot and she was so tired at the end of each day that she fell into bed and slept a dreamless sleep, barely waking even when Joseph slipped in beside her.

'You shouldn't be doing this,' he complained, stroking her brown skin. 'You're carrying a child. My child!'

She smiled and turned over with a sigh. How

different they were. Women like her had to turn their hands to anything. He should know that.

'Jack Terrison suggested I come to Skeffling to help with 'harvest,' she murmured sleepily and made a little laughing sound as she heard his intake of breath. 'But I decided against it.'

'Mary-Ellen!'

She turned back to him and snuggled up close. 'I'm teasing,' she breathed. 'I didn't consider it.' She opened her eyes and gazed at him. 'But I wanted to earn some money of my own,' she said softly. 'I'd have to if you weren't here.'

'But I am here,' he told her. 'I always will be.'

Harvest finished and autumn turned to the cold days of early winter. Joseph sent a waggon-load of wood and a man to repair the cow shelter and put back some tiles that had blown off the roof of the cottage one windy night. Mary-Ellen grew heavier and sluggish and Aunt Lol predicted that the child might be born at the beginning of December and not at Christmas after all.

'Will Mr Ellis pay for a midwife?' Lol asked when she had come one day, with her own child strapped against her like a gypsy woman.

'I don't want one,' Mary-Ellen said. 'Though he's threatened to send a doctor.'

'A doctor!' Lol exclaimed. 'Oh, what it must be like to have enough money to afford a medical man!'

'But I've said I won't have him,' Mary-Ellen told her. 'I'm young and fit. It's a natural occurrence. Why should I want a doctor?'

Aunt Lol nodded. 'Aye! Men are best kept away at a time like that if you ask me.'

Her labour pains began one morning halfway through November. She considered walking to Welwick to tell Lol, but it was a cold wet day and she decided to wait until Joseph came at supper time, as he had been doing every evening. Lol had suggested only the day before that one of her daughters should come and stay with her, so that she could come and fetch her when she was needed, and Mary-Ellen agreed that it was a good idea, but not yet, she said. She didn't think the baby was due so soon, and neither did she want anyone else there when Joseph called.

It was early evening when he arrived. It was dark, wet and blustery and all work was finished at Burstall farm. He brought cold chicken and ham, a loaf of bread and a bottle of wine. He also brought the shawl which he had bought for her, and this time she accepted it, saying tenderly that she would wrap their child in it.

'I don't want any food,' she told him, putting the soft wool to her cheek. 'But I'll have a drop of wine – not a full glass. Then you'll have to fetch Aunt Lol.'

'Will you be all right on your own until I get

back?' he asked, opening the wine and pouring it for her. 'Have you told her about me?'

'She's guessed.' She took a deep breath and her hand was trembling as she took the glass from him and gulped down a mouthful. 'I'm scared, Joseph,' she confessed. 'Bring her back straight away. She'll know what to do.'

He put his mackintosh cape on again. 'And then I'll fetch the doctor.'

'No! I don't need a doctor! Only Aunt Lol.' The fewer people to know about this the better, she thought. The doctor might tell his wife and she might tell their housekeeper and she might pass it on to somebody else and soon the whole neighbourhood would know. Never having had the services of a doctor, Mary-Ellen had no idea of medical professionalism or discretion.

'The doctor we use is very considerate.' Joseph had his hand on the sneck. 'You needn't be embarrassed or—'

'I'm not,' she cried. 'But I don't want him. I onny want Aunt Lol. Now go! Please!' she added fretfully. 'And be quick.'

How do I bring her back? he thought as he swung onto Ebony's back. Will she ride up behind me? I can't expect her to walk all the way here! He reached the road and turned onto it and as he was about to urge Ebony into a canter he heard a shout. He pulled up and saw two figures coming towards him. One was a man

165

carrying a lantern, the other a woman with a bundle draped across her front.

'Mr Ellis, sir!' It was a man's voice.

'Who is it?' It was too dark to recognize them.

'Ben Marston, sir, and Mrs Marston.'

He rode across to them. 'Are you Aunt Lol?' he asked, staring down at her.

'Aye, sir, I am. I was just going up to stop with Mary-Ellen.'

'I was coming to fetch you. Mary-Ellen asked me – she's . . .' Joseph was unsure how to tell her that Mary-Ellen had started in labour. It was different with lambs or calves. No-one thought anything about discussing them, but a woman giving birth was shrouded in secrecy and mystery.

'Aye,' Lol said, squinting up at him. 'I asked Mr Marston if he'd walk me here tonight. I thought when I saw her yesterday she was due any time. Perhaps if you'd be kind enough to come up 'track wi' me, Mr Marston could go back home.'

They trudged back up the track to the cottage, Joseph leading the horse. He realized as they walked that the bundle Mrs Marston was carrying was a child, for he heard it snuffling and Mrs Marston murmuring to it.

When they reached the door, he said, 'How long will it take? Can I stay?'

'You can't come in, sir. Not while she's giving birth!'

166

'But it's my child,' he declared. 'I want to be with her. To help her through it.'

'Never heard of such a thing!' Aunt Lol said firmly. 'Come in and see her now, and then you'll have to make yourself scarce. Beggin' your pardon, sir,' she added.

He looked at her and knew that she wouldn't be moved. It seemed that he would be spending the rest of the night in the cow shelter, with the company of only the goats.

CHAPTER FOURTEEN

Mary-Ellen was pacing the floor. Her cheeks were flushed and the hair curling over her forehead was wet with perspiration. 'Oh, you've come, Aunt Lol!' she breathed. 'How quick you've been.'

She gazed at Joseph, standing there as if uncertain what to do, and said softly, 'Look into my eyes. What do you see?'

'Your heart!' he replied on a breath.

'Kiss me,' she whispered. 'And then you'll have to leave.'

Aunt Lol busied herself putting her child into a chair and making him comfortable whilst Joseph gathered Mary-Ellen into his arms. 'I'm so sorry, my dearest love,' he murmured. 'I don't want you to suffer. This is all my fault.'

Mary-Ellen shook her head. 'Mine too,' she said tenderly. 'I loved you. Wanted you. Never wanted anybody else. Never will,' she said huskily. 'If I'm spared.'

'I beg you, Mary-Ellen,' he pleaded. 'Don't say that! We'll have a good life together, no matter what others think. You and I and our child – children.'

'Go now,' she said, reaching to kiss his lips. 'This is something I must do alone. Go home and come back in 'morning.'

He shook his head and said pensively, 'How can I go home when I know you are here and about to bring our son or daughter into the world? I'll take a blanket and stay in the cow shelter, and Mrs Marston will come and fetch me the minute it's over.' He turned to Aunt Lol. 'You'll fetch me, won't you? I'll be there.'

'It might be a long night, sir,' she said, but her eyes were compassionate. Her husband had always taken himself off to the hostelry whenever she had been in labour. 'You'd be best going home.'

'No,' he said. 'I'll wait!'

It was bitterly cold in the shelter. There were no proper walls and he huddled within the blanket in a corner. The nanny goat wandered over and sniffed and bleated at him and Ebony. I'll stink of goat, he thought, and closed his eyes, trying to snatch some sleep.

It was a cold grey dawn when he felt someone shaking his shoulder and he sat up quickly, his joints aching and stiff.

'Will you come, sir?' Aunt Lol's voice was shaky. 'You've got a daughter.'

169

He scrambled to his feet. 'Mary-Ellen! Is she all right? Is she well?'

'She's had a bad time, sir. Just like her ma allus did.'

'I'll fetch the doctor,' he said. 'I insist. No matter what Mary-Ellen says.'

Aunt Lol led the way and stumbled as she went through the door. 'Here he is, my lovely,' she said, her voice cracking with a false indulgence. 'Just as you asked. Fast asleep with 'nanny goat, he was.'

'Mary-Ellen!' He gave a small gasp when he saw her face, white against her black hair, which streamed across the pillow. He avoided looking at the bundle of bloodstained sheets heaped in a corner, and knelt by the bed. She lifted a frail pale hand and stroked his face.

'We have a little girl,' she whispered. 'Will you love her?'

He pressed his lips to her palm. 'I will,' he said softly. 'Just as I love you. What name shall we give her?'

'Susannah,' she murmured, and tears slid from her eyes. 'My mother's name.'

'I'm going to fetch the doctor.' He put his finger against her lips as she began to demur. 'I want you fit and well, and our daughter too, and then when you're up and feeling better we'll talk of finding a house and—'

'No,' she murmured. 'I think – I think it's too

170

late. I should have done as you said, and had him – here before. I shouldn't have – been so proud. Speak to Aunt Lol,' she said wearily. 'I've no breath left.'

'What?' In stunned bewilderment he turned to Aunt Lol who was standing with her back to them, her hand clutched to her head. 'What does she mean? I'll go for the doctor now. I'll be back within the hour!'

'Yes, sir.' When Lol turned to him, he saw the pain and anguish on her face. 'Tell him to come straight away. She's lost a lot o' blood. It was – complicated,' she stammered. "Babby was 'wrong way on.'

'I don't want you to go,' Mary-Ellen pleaded. 'I want you to stay. And I want – I want to hold my daughter in my arms.'

Joseph gazed at her, the blood gone from his face and his lips parted, and then looked at Lol who was lifting a white bundle from a drawer.

'Here she is, God bless her. Tek a look at your daughter, sir,' and she turned the bundle so that he could see the crumpled face of the child. 'She was early, I think, but that's as well,' she muttered. 'We'd have lost 'em both had she been bigger.'

'What do you mean? What do you mean?' He was angry with tension.

'I mean, sir,' her voice dropped to a whisper, 'that if we're to save Mary-Ellen, you mun go now to fetch 'doctor. She's lost – is still losing – too much blood.'

'Don't – talk about me.' Mary-Ellen's voice was getting weaker. 'I know – what I want.' She stretched out her arms for the child and when she was settled against her breast, she held out a hand to Joseph to come to her. 'Don't leave me,' she whispered. 'Stay with me.'

Joseph dropped to his knees. 'For ever, Mary-Ellen. I'll stay with you for ever, but don't you leave *me*! I can't live without you. Don't *want* to live without you.' He put his hand to his eyes and wept. 'Tell me this isn't true! Tell me it's some nightmare I'm going through!'

'I'm so tired, Joseph,' Mary-Ellen murmured as the life-blood seeped from her. 'I need to rest. We'll talk – when – when I've had a sleep. But don't go. I want to see you here when I wake.'

He half sat, half leaned on the bed, the bed where they had shared such love and passion and their daughter had been conceived, and put his arm round her so that she was nestled in the crook of his elbow. 'Rest then, my darling,' he said softly, and kissed her forehead. 'Everything will be all right. I won't let you go. I'll keep you safe.'

Aunt Lol took the child from Mary-Ellen as her eyes closed, and Joseph gently rested his head against hers, feeling the smoothness of her face, the softness of her thick hair, and heard the sighing of her breath as she fell asleep.

He shivered as he awoke, blinking as Lol spoke to him. She had a child at her breast and he gave a small gasp when he realized that it was the newborn, his own daughter, that she was feeding. He gazed down at Mary-Ellen lying so still in his arms.

'Sir,' Lol said softly. 'She's gone.'

'No!' he said sharply. 'No! She's sleeping. Mary-Ellen!' He gathered her closer to him but she was limp and unresponsive. 'No. Don't leave me! I won't let you go. Never! Never!'

He began to weep, crushing Mary-Ellen's lifeless form against him. 'I can't believe that you'd leave me. You said that you'd always love me,' he cried out accusingly. 'How can you leave me alone?'

'Let her be, sir.' A torrent of tears ran down Lol's cheeks. 'And you're not alone. You have a child. A daughter.'

'I don't want a daughter,' he shouted at her. 'I want Mary-Ellen! She's the only one I've ever wanted. How will I live without her? What will I do?' He laid her back on the pillow and stroked her face. It was cool to his touch. He knelt by the bed and put his hands together. 'God in heaven!' he said vehemently. 'Are you listening to me? Or are you not really there? What did I do to deserve this? Why did you take her from me when I need her so much?'

He got up from his knees and, wrenching open

the door, went outside. Out of control, he ran up the track towards the estuary. Then he suddenly stopped and looked up at the sky. The sun was just risen, a watery sphere of pale gold which spread its glimmering light over the rushing water, heralding a fresh new dawn which he must now spend alone.

Lol put his daughter back into the makeshift crib and had turned to attend Mary-Ellen, just as she had attended her mother, when she heard the clamorous sound which filled the air: the shrill alarm of redshanks, the croak of Brent geese and the cry of a thousand long-legged curlews who rose up to unite in the desperate lamentation of grief.

'Mary-Ellen!' she heard him howl, the heartbreak torn from his core. 'How could you leave me? Mary-Ellen!'

CHAPTER FIFTEEN

1880

'Mama! We're home!'

Laura took off her hat and gloves and handed them to the housekeeper. 'I've ruined my best boots, Smithy,' she told her, slipping off her travelling coat. 'I've put them in a separate bag so that they didn't spoil anything else.'

'Perhaps they'll clean up, Miss Laura,' Mrs Smith replied. 'A bit of spit and polish can work wonders. Tilly can rub them up and you can wear them as second best. Your mother's in 'sitting room,' she added. 'Shall I bring you some tea?'

'Oh, yes please! You're an angel. James will be in in a minute, he's just seeing to his precious curricle. He wasn't very pleased when it got splattered with mud!'

'So have you had much rain, then? It hasn't rained here, not since you left.'

'No, it didn't rain at all, but the roads were

very muddy, especially near the estuary, which is where we've been, and that's where I ruined my boots. I went too close to the saltmarsh. Silly of me. I didn't realize just how boggy it would be.'

Susannah was stitching a gown when Laura went in. She looked up and smiled, and Laura thought, as she often did, how pretty she looked when she smiled, yet how serious when she didn't.

'Oh!' Laura kissed her mother and then flopped into a chair. 'What a journey! I ache all over. What are you doing? Why don't you ask Smithy to repair your gown? She sets a neat stitch.'

'I know.' Her mother bit off a piece of thread. 'But I like to keep my hand in, and besides, she's plenty to do. I'm only restitching 'tapes to make 'skirt narrower and draw up the bustle.'

'Thank goodness we don't have to wear crinolines,' Laura yawned. 'Did you ever, Mama?'

'They were the vogue when I was young and unable to afford them, though I had a cage later,' her mother said vaguely. 'But gowns were not as full then as they had once been, and I've always preferred a trailing skirt. Much more elegant and easier to manage.' She put down the gown and it billowed over the floor. 'But never mind that. Tell me. What did you think of Holderness?'

'Terrible place!' James strode into the room.

176

'Flat, cold and boring. Acres of fields and not much else.'

'It was wonderful, Mama,' Laura interrupted her brother. 'But I'm not going to discuss it whilst James is here. He's done nothing but grumble all the way home!'

'I'll tell you something.' James sat down and stretched his legs. 'The only type of vehicle to be used on those Holderness roads should be a waggon! A curricle is of no use at all. I shall have to get the wheels checked to see if there's been any damage.'

'And get some rubber tyres put on whilst you're about it,' Laura said scathingly. 'I feel like a bag of bones after that shaking about!'

'Children!' Their mother laughed. 'You should have asked Stubbs to take you in 'carriage. It's a long way to travel on two wheels.'

Susannah had bought an old Clarence carriage many years ago when James and Laura were young, and Stubbs, their general handyman cum gardener, drove it for them. It was large enough for four passengers, and well sprung, but not smart or speedy enough for James, who liked to drive his own curricle whenever he could.

Mrs Smith came in with a tray of tea and James jumped up and made room on the small table, which was coved in silk bobbins, scissors and other sewing accessories.

'Thank you, Master James.' The housekeeper nodded to him. 'Most thoughtful of you.'

'There's a motive, Smithy. He's after an extra piece of cake,' Laura said. 'Don't let his charming manners fool you.'

'I know, Miss Laura.' The housekeeper smiled. 'And I brought in extra in case you were hungry.'

'We haven't been to the North Pole, you know.' Laura leaned to pour the tea.

'Just seems like it.' James helped himself to a slice of jam sponge cake and took a huge bite. 'It doesn't compare with Hessle, anyway.'

'Thank you, Smithy,' Susannah said, as the housekeeper went towards the door. She gave a small sigh. 'Indeed it doesn't compare,' she murmured. 'Not with anywhere. It's really rather special.'

'So what made you come here to live,' James asked, 'if Holderness was such a wonderful place? What made you leave?'

'Hessle was more convenient,' she said. 'Easier to get into Hull and Beverley for business. I have always been a working woman, don't forget.'

'James met a former school friend when we were in Hedon,' Laura told her. 'Wasn't that odd?'

'Really?' their mother said. 'From Pocklington? In your year?'

'He was a year above me,' James mumbled, wiping cake crumbs from his mouth. 'I didn't

178

really know him all that well. I just remember him. Some of the fellows used to call him Farmer Ellis, because he said he was going to be a farmer when he'd finished school, and some called him Frenchie Ellis because his mother and grand-mother were French.'

'Is he from Hedon?'

'Mm – no,' James said. 'I can't remember where he said, can you, Laura? It was somewhere I hadn't heard of, anyway.'

'Skeffling,' Laura said. 'It's beyond Welwick which is where we went.'

'Ellis!' Susannah put down her cup and saucer. 'Goodness! The Ellis family owned Aunt Lol's cottage in Welwick. And Aunt Jane worked in their kitchens until she married.' She clasped her hands together and thought back. 'Their agent used to collect 'rent, but sometimes – sometimes old Mr Ellis came himself. I always thought him very grumpy. He used to glower down at us and Thomas and I had to wait outside, but sometimes he'd throw us a penny.' She gave a soft smile. 'Thomas nearly always caught it.'

'Was he your cousin? Thomas, I mean?' Laura asked.

'Well, once removed, I suppose. He was Great-aunt Lol's youngest child, and she was my mother's aunt. I named you after her, Laura. She was like a mother to me, but I didn't know her name was Laura until after she'd died. Thomas

179

and I were brought up like brother and sister. In fact, I thought he was my brother, until—' She suddenly caught her breath. 'Pour me another cup of tea, will you, dear?'

Laura did, and then rang for Smithy to bring more hot water. She could tell, could always tell, when her mother didn't want to discuss her past; when she realized that she had said too much.

'I don't suppose you'd come to Holderness with me, Mama?' she asked later when James had left the room. 'I'd like to go again. I loved it there. I could smell the salty brine so much more strongly on the estuary there than here in Hessle.'

'It's not so far from the sea,' Susannah said. 'Only two or three miles.' She gave a slow smile of remembrance. 'Thomas and I set off once, when we were about six or seven. We thought we'd walk all 'way down 'river bank until we got there. But Daniel, Thomas's older brother, brought us back, and we were given a leathering by Uncle Ben.'

'What happened to Thomas? Do you know where he is?'

Susannah shook her head. 'No,' she said softly. 'I don't.' She bit her lip. 'We lost touch.'

'So would you come? I didn't know which cottage you lived in or I might have knocked on the door. Would they have remembered you, do you think? Who would be there now? Your Aunt Jane? Will she be very old?'

Susannah laughed. 'She'll be in her fifties. Is that old? I suppose it is.' She lost her smile. 'Her husband was quite a lot older than her. And yes, of course she would remember me. I lived with them after Aunt Lol died. Aunt Jane was very loving towards me, and very protective,' she added. 'But I wouldn't go back. Not if he was still there.'

Laura didn't press her any further. There were some things her mother refused to discuss. They sat for a while and Laura glanced over the pages of a magazine, whilst her mother continued with her sewing.

'I had a visit from Freddie whilst you and James were away.' Susannah broke the silence. 'He had some rather disquieting news about his wife.'

'She's not ill again?' Laura asked disparagingly. 'Mrs Cannon seems to enjoy ill health!'

Her mother pressed her lips together. 'I agree, she always has. But this time it seems that she really is ill.'

'Is that why Uncle Freddie called? To tell you about her?'

'No, no! He – he had reason to come to Hessle. One of his clients lives near here, apparently. Freddie and I have known each other for a very long time,' she added. 'He always calls when he's in the vicinity.'

'Mrs Cannon is not so ill that she can't be left?' Laura said. 'I think she's being troublesome again, poor man. She doesn't deserve him. Any other man would have divorced her.'

'Laura! Till death us do part! He married her . . .' Susannah hesitated. 'It's a commitment, and he's had no valid reason to divorce her. You need better grounds than just bad temper and melancholia to end a marriage.'

'I suppose so,' Laura said grudgingly. But I wish you'd met him before she did. He would have made a perfect husband. Still.' She reconsidered. 'Sorry, Mama. I suppose you were already married to my father, were you? Did my father know him?'

'Freddie was always *my* friend,' Susannah said carefully. 'He gave me a great deal of good advice when I started in business; it was Freddie who suggested I bought the Beverley inn, and he showed me how to set up accounts and so on, and of course he helped you and James too, didn't he? With your school lessons, I mean.'

Laura frowned thoughtfully. 'So – did Freddie know you when you had the inn in Hedon?'

'Y-yes. We first met when we were very young and I was living at the Fleet.'

'Before either of you were married, then? Did you ever meet his wife? James and I never have. It seems so odd when we've known Freddie for so long.'

'She doesn't go out very much – her health . . .' Susannah rose from her chair. 'Help me clear this sewing up, will you, dear? It's almost time for supper.'

CHAPTER SIXTEEN

1843

'God in heaven!' Lol jumped at the hammering on her door. 'There's onny one man bangs like that and if he breaks 'door, then he'll have to mend it! Go open it, Susannah.'

The child ran to obey and reached up for the sneck. She raised her head to look up at the thickset man standing by the step and then dipped her knee. 'Gentleman for you, Aunt Lol,' she called out.

Lol came to the door, wiping her hands on her apron. 'Mornin', Mr Ellis.'

'Tell the child to stay outside. I've something to say to you,' he said brusquely.

Lol waved a finger at Susannah and she went out, heading for the horse whose reins were tied up to the iron bar set in the wall. She remembered this ritual from the beginning of the year and from some other times. Mr Ellis came to see

Aunt Lol and she always had to go outside until he had finished speaking to her. Once it had been raining and she'd huddled against the wall waiting for him to come out. When he did, he'd said, 'Is this the child?'

'Is that the child?' Mr Ellis said now to Lol. 'She's growing fast.'

'They do, sir,' Lol answered, and wondered why he was here today. He wasn't due for some time. She recalled the first time he had come. It was three days after Mary-Ellen had died, and they hadn't yet buried her. He hadn't hammered the door quite so hard that time. More of a respectful thud. She'd opened it with both babies in her arms and she saw the widening of his eyes and the way he took a sudden breath.

She had invited him in and put Thomas down on a chair. 'This is your son's bairn,' she'd said quietly, showing him the other child. 'It's a girl.'

Unbidden he had sat down and put his head in his hands. 'This is a fine how-de-do, Mrs Marston,' he'd muttered. 'My son is distraught. I fear for his sanity.'

'Yes, sir. It's a tragedy. Would you – would you like to see her? Mary-Ellen?' She and Ben had brought her here to Welwick, to be with her own kin where they could keep watch.

He'd looked up sharply. 'No! No, I don't think so.' He'd cast his eyes round the room and noticed the curtained-off alcove. He stood up. 'I, erm, I want to make sure you're all right financially. My son will take full responsibility. He says it is his child.'

'There's no doubt of that, Mr Ellis,' Lol said firmly. 'Mary-Ellen was a good girl. Never had any other lad near her.'

Mr Ellis had taken out his pocket book. 'I'll give you some money for the funeral expenses, and then I'll come and see you again about a regular allowance. Joseph might want to make that arrangement himself, but at the moment he's too distressed to see anyone. He won't even speak to his mother.'

Lol didn't tell him that his son had been here or how he had knelt by Mary-Ellen's bedside and sobbed uncontrollably.

'He won't come to the funeral, of course,' Mr Ellis had said. 'It won't do, really, if you understand my meaning. But rest assured, the child will be cared for financially.'

But Joseph had come. Lol had seen him standing at the back of the churchyard. He was leaning on a gravestone and looking as if he was close to death himself.

'The reason I have come today,' Mr Ellis said now, 'is that my son is returning from abroad at the beginning of June. He has, as I'm sure you know, been away for the last four years.' He glanced round the room. It was much the same as always. Mrs Marston, he realized, had spent the allowance on food and clothing for the child and not on extras in the way of furnishings, although she had once asked him if he could supply another bed, which he had.

'I wanted to ask you – that is, we feel, Mrs Ellis and I, that when Joseph returns he might want to see the child.'

'Her name is Susannah, sir,' Aunt Lol interrupted. 'She was baptized with that name. Susannah Page,' she emphasized. 'Her father's name wasn't admitted.'

Ellis nodded. 'Nevertheless, he – what I wanted to say – this is not easy, you understand. He can't bring up a child on his own; so if he should ask you to relinquish her, I would like you to insist that she stays with you and your family.'

'You mean that you don't want him to bring her to Burstall House?' Lol said bluntly.

'That's it exactly,' he replied, equally blunt. 'We understand each other?'

'Oh, yes, sir. Perfectly.'

'Tell him that she'd miss her family, her cousins and so on, and how much better it would be for her to stay with you. We shall finance her, of course, until she's of age to work or marry.'

Better for you, Lol thought. You wouldn't want a bastard child in your household. She'd take some explaining.

'However!' He hummed and hawed for a

moment. 'My wife has declared that she would like to see the child – Susannah – before Joseph comes home. Would that be possible?' He must have noticed Lol's surprise, her raised eyebrows, for he added hastily, 'She's not asked before because, I suspect, she is not over fond of babies, but now that she's grown – she'll be four now, won't she?'

'Four and a half, sir. She was born in the November, if you recall.'

'Indeed!' He sighed. 'So I'll send the trap for you tomorrow if you would be so kind as to get her ready.'

'Very good, Mr Ellis. I'll mek sure she's presentable.' Lol didn't care if he heard the irony in her voice. What she couldn't understand was why Mrs Ellis hadn't wanted to see her only grandchild before. She didn't believe it was because she wasn't fond of young babies. Neither had Mr Joseph's sister asked to see her, even though word in the villages was that she was chock full of good works and benevolence.

Ellis stepped outside. Susannah was holding the reins of his horse, a dark chestnut, and patting its shoulder. 'Would you like a ride?' he asked gruffly.

Susannah looked shyly up at him and then at Aunt Lol, who was standing in the doorway. She saw her shake her head from side to side. 'No thank you, sir,' she murmured. 'He's too big.'

After he had gone, she said to Aunt Lol, 'I would have gone on his horse. Why couldn't I?'

'Best not,' Lol said. 'You might have expected a treat each time he came, and you'd have been disappointed.'

'Why does he come?' Susannah put spoons on the table for their supper. Uncle Ben would be in soon.

'Cos he's a kind, caring man,' Lol answered caustically. 'And tomorrow he wants you to go and meet his kind caring wife.'

The next day, Susannah was washed and dressed in a clean dress with a white apron over the top of it. Her boots were polished and fitted with new laces and her honey-coloured hair was dressed with a ribbon. 'Why are we going?' she asked, after looking out of the door several times to see if the horse and trap were coming. 'Why do we have to?'

Thomas had said that he wanted to go with them until his mother had told him that he would have to get washed and into clean clothes if he came.

'It's a treat,' Lol said. 'We're going to 'big house where our Janey works. She must've told Mrs Ellis all about you, what a good lass you are and that, and Mrs Ellis couldn't believe there was such a perfect bairn and asked to see you for herself.'

189

'Doesn't this lady have any bairns?' Susannah asked.

'Not little 'uns like you and Thomas. They're grown now.'

Susannah thought for a moment and then said, 'She won't want to keep me, will she? Cos if she does, then I'll be naughty so that she sends me away.'

Aunt Lol gave a lopsided smile. 'You don't need to worry on that score,' she said. 'Besides, I can't part wi' you, can I? How would I ever manage without you?'

Susannah put her arms round Aunt Lol's legs. 'I don't ever want to leave you, Aunt Lol. I'll stay with you and Uncle Ben and Thomas and Sally and everybody for ever.'

'I'm to tek you to 'front of 'house,' the driver of the dog cart told Lol. 'Housekeeper'll see to you then.'

Lol didn't answer, but climbed into the cart. She had been prepared to be taken to the kitchen entrance, but then, on reconsidering, realized that Mrs Ellis wouldn't want the servants speculating as to the reason why they were there or questioning Jane, who would be unable to give a coherent answer. Jane was still general dogsbody in the kitchen and likely to remain so. She had no ambition to better herself and since Mary-Ellen's death had become very morose.

'Please come in, Mrs Marston.' The house-keeper opened the door to them. She had obviously been watching out for the dog cart. 'Mrs Ellis is ready to see the child. If you would kindly wait in here.' She opened a door leading into a small sitting room whose walls were lined with books. 'Perhaps you would like a pot of coffee or tea?'

'Aye, I would,' Lol answered. 'Tea if you please. Strong, wi' sugar. Off you go,' she told Susannah, whose eyes were wide and gazing in awe and wonder at the furnishings and large windows and the fire, blazing even though it was a warm day. 'I'll be waiting here when Mrs Ellis is finished wi' you.'

'Can't you come wi' me?' Susannah said.

'No.' The housekeeper took hold of her hand. 'You'll be all right with me. Come along.'

She led a reluctant Susannah along the hall and up the stairs and then along another corridor, and tapped on a door. A voice called 'Come in', and they entered a large airy room with comfortable chairs and a sofa and a writing desk. In front of the window was a table with a vase of flowers on it.

Mrs Ellis was sitting on the sofa. Her hair was a faded gold and she turned to Susannah, putting out her hand and saying, 'Come here, my dear, and let me look at you.'

Susannah turned enquiringly to the woman

who had brought her upstairs, but she had gone, closing the door behind her. She bit on a finger and slowly went towards the golden-haired lady. 'I can't stop,' she whispered. 'Aunt Lol needs me.'

'Aunt Lol? Is that Mrs Marston?' Mrs Ellis asked. 'Does she take care of you?'

Susannah remembered that she hadn't dipped her knee as Aunt Lol had told her to, so she did it now. 'Yes. Cos I haven't got a ma.'

'Where is your mother?' Mrs Ellis said gently.

'She's dead and gone to heaven.'

Mrs Ellis gave a little cough. 'And your father? Where is he?'

Susannah frowned. She hadn't worked that out yet. Uncle Ben was Thomas's father and he was Sally's and Jane's and Daniel's father too, but once when she had called him Da, as the others did, Daniel had laughed and said that he wasn't her father and not even her proper uncle, and he had been given a slap round the ear by Aunt Lol.

'I don't think I've got one,' she said. 'At least I've never seen him. Perhaps he's in heaven with my ma.'

Mrs Ellis put her hand over her mouth and looked as if she was going to cry, but she said in a strangled kind of voice, 'And what name are you known by?'

'Susannah Page.' Susannah wondered why this lady was asking so many questions.

'And how old are you, Susannah?'

'I'm four and a half a year.' Susannah gave a confident smile. She had worked that out for herself. 'My birthday's in November and then I'll be five.'

'Would you like to go to school when you're old enough?'

Susannah considered. She had heard Aunt Lol and Uncle Ben talking about that. Aunt Lol had said she was going to discuss it with somebody. 'Only if Thomas can go as well,' she said. 'I don't want to go without him.'

'And who is Thomas?'

'Erm,' Susannah put her finger to her mouth and nibbled on it. 'I think he's my brother, but I'm not sure.' She gave a deep sigh. It was very complicated. 'Aunt Lol's his ma anyway.'

Mrs Ellis put out her hand to draw her near and gently stroked her cheek. 'We'll see what we can do about school,' she said quietly. 'When the time comes. For you and Thomas.'

Susannah heaved a breath. So that was what all this was about. She dipped her knee again. 'Thank you,' she said shyly. 'I'll tell Aunt Lol.'

Mrs Ellis asked her if she would press the bell at the side of the fireplace and within a few minutes the woman who had brought her upstairs appeared as if by magic at the door. 'Thank you,' Mrs Ellis said to her. 'You may return her to her guardian.' She turned to Susannah.

193

'Goodbye, my dear. It was very nice meeting you.' She took a handkerchief out of her pocket and pressed it to her nose.

She's got a cold, Susannah thought as she took the housekeeper's hand to be led away. Her eyes are all watery.

CHAPTER SEVENTEEN

The barouche trundled across the moat, rattling the two passengers from side to side. 'My God! Wherever are you bringing me, Joseph?' The woman, swathed in fur and wearing a black feathered hat, had a strong French accent.

'Home!' Joseph muttered, knowing that he had made a terrible mistake. He had known it as soon as they reached the small town of Hedon in Holderness; knew by the sinking feeling in the pit of his stomach, and the return of the melancholia which had sent him off to Europe to recuperate, that he shouldn't have come back, and certainly not with a wife, and a French-woman at that.

He had hired a post chaise and pair to bring them from London to Hull. There he had paid the balance owing for the driver's services, stayed the night in a coaching house, and hired a brougham and driver to bring them to Skeffling. His wife, Arlette, whom he had met and married

195

in Paris, had not stopped exclaiming at the emptiness of the landscape, the poor state of the roads and the lack of visible population since they had set out from Hull.

'This is just like rural France,' she had complained. 'Where are ze theatres, ze concert 'alls?' she whimpered. 'Here there is *nossing*. What is there to do all day?'

'There are theatres in Hull,' he contended. 'But we rarely go. We are a working family. I told you that when we met.'

'But you spent so much time in France and Switzerland. You were not working then,' she pouted. 'We should 'ave stayed in Paris.'

'I'm a farmer,' he said testily. 'My father has carried the weight of the farm on his own for over four years. I have to show some responsibility.'

I had to get away, he reflected. I couldn't bear to be in Holderness when Mary-Ellen was gone from me. I was ready to die; didn't want to live without her. It was his parents who had first suggested he went away to recuperate, though they hadn't anticipated that he would leave the country. But he had decided for himself that he would go to Europe.

He went first to France, walking and sleeping under hedges, eating where he could and looking like a tramp with his long hair and rough beard; and then he travelled to Switzerland, where amongst the mountains he didn't feel Mary-Ellen's presence so strongly. He stayed in a monastery, living a sober and simple life. He chopped wood, dug ditches, and did menial jobs which were easy for him and difficult for the elderly monks who were resident there. He was welcomed and given the peace and understanding that he was looking for.

When he thought he was well again, he left the monastery and travelled back to France, where once again he was smitten by loneliness and loss. He frequented bars and hotels, and in Paris he met Arlette. She was elegant, worldly and cultured, all the things that Mary-Ellen was not. She was also amusing, alluring and passionate and he was tempted by her obvious interest in him, and he began to smile again. After only three weeks of knowing her, in a moment of weakness, he had asked her to marry him. To his utter amazement she said yes, and took him to her bed.

They married immediately by special licence and within a month they travelled to England to begin his life again.

He had written to his parents to tell them of his return, but hadn't told them that he was married and bringing a wife. He thought they would be pleased that he was attempting to put the past behind him, but was unsure what they would think of Arlette's cosmopolitan outlook on life or how she would fit in with their lifestyle.

The carriage drew up at the door, and Arlette took his hand as he helped her down. 'So, you are rich, Joseph?' she murmured. 'Such a grand 'ouse.'

'We work for what we have,' he said. 'It doesn't come easily.'

'You 'ave many servants, yes? You won't want me to cook ze dinner?'

'No.' He laughed. She was so amusing sometimes. 'We have a cook to do that.'

'Good,' she said. 'I am pleased to 'ear it.'

'Here are my parents, Arlette.' He saw his mother and father and some of the servants gathered at the door to greet him. Though he knew that they would be surprised to see that he was not alone, their breeding and good manners would not allow their astonishment to show in front of the servants. They came down the steps to greet him.

'Mother, Father,' he said. 'May I present my wife, Arlette?'

CHAPTER EIGHTEEN

Susannah and Thomas were in the small patch of garden at the side of the house where they had been sent to bank up the soil around the potatoes, when a man on a black horse rode up the lane and stopped beside them. He looked down on them, not speaking for a moment. Then he asked if Mrs Marston was at home. Susannah said she would fetch her, but he told Thomas to go instead. Susannah stood shyly in front of him twisting the hem of her apron.

'What is your name?' he said, and she thought he sounded sad.

'Susannah, sir.' She stared right up at him, looking into his blue eyes. She didn't think she had ever seen him before.

'Are you happy, Susannah?' he asked.

She considered. No-one had ever asked her that before. 'I think so,' she said, but before she could say anything else Aunt Lol had come out and put her hand on her shoulder.

'I heard you were back, sir,' she murmured. 'And that you'd brought a wife home.'

'Yes,' he said, and added, 'The little girl looks well.'

Aunt Lol nodded. 'She ails nowt, thank God.' She hesitated for a moment before saying, 'I hope you'll find some peace and be content, sir.'

He glanced towards Susannah. 'I doubt that I'll find peace or contentment ever again, Mrs Marston.'

'You mun try, sir. You've a wife to consider.'

He gave a dry laugh. 'Yes, indeed.'

'You'll not blame 'bairn, sir? It was an act of God.'

'Was it?' he said harshly. 'Then God wasn't thinking of me.' He glanced again at Susannah. 'But no, I don't blame the child. Only myself.' He gathered up the reins in his hand. 'Do you want for anything, Mrs Marston? You only have to ask.'

Lol shook her head. 'We're well provided for,' she said. 'We've all we need.'

His mouth creased crookedly. 'Then you are fortunate indeed,' he muttered, and rode away.

'Who's that?' Susannah asked her. 'I've not seen him afore.'

'Nobody,' Aunt Lol said, gazing after the rider. 'Nobody at all.'

Mr Ellis senior, when he had come in those early days, to make the arrangements for

200

Susannah's welfare, had specifically asked her not to tell the child who her father was; neither should she tell anyone else, if they asked.

'My son will no doubt marry one day and have other children,' he had said. 'And it would be awkward for him if – well, I know how rumours go round in villages; but if there's no flame to fan it, then the fire goes out, if you understand my meaning. And there's no reason for anyone else to know of his unfortunate indiscretion.'

Lol had gazed stonily at him as he fiddled with his pocket book. She understood his meaning, right enough. If word got out about Susannah's father, and if it was thought she had spoken carelessly, then the money would dry up, and God knew, she considered, life was hard enough. Ben wasn't well. His joints creaked and ached, but he had to keep working or they were all for the poorhouse. Susannah, in fate's strange way, had been a blessing to them, and as for the villagers' gossiping, well, it would be a nine day wonder.

'Nobody!' Susannah sang out blithely. 'Mr Nobody.'

Susannah and Thomas, both in new boots, attended the school which was held in the church. Thomas hadn't wanted to go. He complained bitterly that the other lads in the village would make fun of him.

'Not when they hear that you can read,' his mother assured him. 'When they hear that, they'll be spittin' jealous!'

'But what'll I read, Ma?' he grumbled. 'We never gets a letter from 'postie.'

'You'll read books,' she said, 'or else you can read what it says on 'shop windows in Patrington when we go on market day, and you can tell me what it says. Or you can tell your fayther what's in 'newspaper if ever he brings a bit of a page home from 'Wheatsheaf.'

He wasn't convinced, but was told he had to go, no matter what, to look after Susannah who was a year younger than him, and to make sure that no-one bullied her. At the end of their first year he could make out the letters of the alphabet and chalk them on his slate, but couldn't put them together to form words. He could add up numbers in his head, but mixed up his nines and sixes when writing them down.

Susannah sat and listened to the teacher, and although she was often rapped on the knuckles for helping Thomas she absorbed what she was told, and by seven she could read well and was able to add and subtract.

'Susannah does well, Mrs Marston,' Lol was told by the teacher, who was curious as to how such a shabby, poor-looking woman could afford to send to school two children who were not paid for by the parish. She had heard that Mrs

Marston was the child's aunt and that her mother was dead, but that was all she knew. 'But I'm afraid I can't say 'same for Thomas.'

'Aye, well, nivver mind,' Lol said. 'He'll be a farm labourer, I expect, or work at 'brickworks, so he'll not need a great deal o' larnin'. You concentrate on Susannah,' she told her. 'She's 'one who'll need 'schoolin' if she's to get anywhere.'

Susannah became aware of the man who appeared on the black horse from time to time. Occasionally he would arrive at the cottage to see Aunt Lol, but spoke to her too and would ask her how she was getting on at school, did she have friends, and was she happy. She vaguely remembered him asking her that once before, but the best thing was that he called in November when it was her birthday, and had given her small gifts of hair ribbons and once a little doll.

She saw him by the river one day where the men were draining the saltmarsh and embanking. She and Thomas were not supposed to go there, but Thomas had said that it would be all right and that no-one would find out. The man had turned to watch them, but didn't say anything; neither did he tell Aunt Lol.

Once, during the summer holidays when there was no school, they raced along the bank and went right out of Welwick until they could go no further because of a wide dyke. The land they were standing on had been reclaimed from the Humber, Thomas said, and when Susannah asked him how he knew he said that Daniel had told him.

'We're standing in 'river,' he said. 'Just like them Sunk Island folk.' He pointed across the wide drain to the land at the other side. 'All that land over there,' he told her. 'It belongs to Queen Victoria now cos it used to be under water; and,' he gabbled garrulously on, 'they say as some bairns over there are born wi' webbed feet.'

'I don't believe you.' Susannah gave him a push. 'You're mekkin' it up.'

'I'm not, an' I'll tell you summat else,' Thomas said. 'Onny you're not to tell Ma I telled you.'

'What?'

'Down there.' He pointed this time across the field behind them, where an old track showed through the grass and nettle. 'That's 'place where you was born, onny it's not there now cos it got burned down.'

'Where I was born? I was born in our house, same as you.'

Thomas's cheeks flushed. 'Daniel said I hadn't to tell you. He said it was secret and nobody else knew but Ma and Da, onny he knew cos he'd heard 'em talking.'

Susannah chewed on her lip. 'Let's go and see

then,' she said. 'Cos I think that Daniel's telling fibs.'

She never felt wholly comfortable with Daniel. He was fourteen and worked at one of the farms in Welwick. He came home dog tired, and often snapped at her and Thomas when they were rowdy. Sometimes he would pull faces and cross his eyes and call them *peazans* and he always knew what was going on in the villages. 'You're a proper old woman for gossiping,' his mother scolded him. 'You want to watch that tongue o' yourn.'

They clambered down the bank and set off down the track which ran between beds of nettles, drifts of cow parsley, fine whispering grasses and clumps of sea asters, and came eventually to a heap of scorched roof tiles.

'It's not been a house,' Susannah stated. 'There's no bricks or cobbles. It's been a shed or summat.'

'It's been a hen house or—'

'A cow stall!' Susannah interrupted.

'Here's some bricks!' Thomas had been searching about in the long grass. 'And some cobbles as well. Look,' he said. 'There's a whole heap o' them!'

Solemnly they surveyed the pile of bricks. They were swathed in bramble and a small hawthorn tree was growing through the middle of them.

'If it's been a house, where's 'chimney pot?' Susannah said in a sullen voice. If it had been a house, *her* house, how was it that it was burned down?

Thomas eagerly searched around. 'We could build a den wi' all o' these. Look,' he said excitedly. 'Here's a bit o' chimney pot – it's all blackened inside. And here's a hinge! Bet that's off 'door. 'Door would've burned.'

'I want to go home,' Susannah said suddenly. 'I don't want to stay.' She felt frightened. She needed Aunt Lol to tell her that it wasn't true. That Daniel had been making up stories. A dark shadow settled about her head and shoulders and it wasn't just the rain clouds which were gathering above them. It was an obscure feeling of gloom and unhappiness; an awareness of raw emotion which she didn't understand, but which seemed to linger here. There was a sudden agitation and beating of wings and a flock of Brent geese rose quivering from the saltmarsh and flew in across the lonely land, their haunting cry calling, *'Come back. Come back.'*

Thomas got a smack from his mother when she discovered where they had been, and they were told that they were not to go so far out of the village again. Susannah found that she couldn't ask about the burned-down building, for she didn't know what questions to ask, but she did see Aunt Lol take Daniel to one side, and with a

206

pointing finger give him a warning over something.

She and Thomas were given jobs to occupy them for the rest of the summer. Susannah was told to pick beans and peas and shell them, and Thomas to dig up the new potatoes that were ready, and to search for fallen tree branches and chop wood for the coming winter. When autumn came, Susannah went back to school, but Thomas was allowed time off to help with the harvest.

In November they shared their birthday celebrations as the dates were so close, and on the day before Susannah was eleven she made a cake. 'Is it a bothday cake, then?' Thomas asked, poking a finger into the mixture and tasting it. 'Tastes like ginger parkin to me!'

'It is ginger parkin,' Susannah said. 'But it's still a birthday cake, cos we'll eat it on our birthday tomorrow.'

'It's not my bothday till December,' Thomas said. 'But I'm still older than you.'

'I know that, silly,' she replied, giving him a shove with her elbow. 'And get your fingers out of it, or there won't be enough.'

'My last week at school, then,' Thomas said gleefully. 'Da says I don't have to go any more after I'm twelve. Bet you wish it was you!'

'No, I don't,' she said calmly. 'I like going, and Miss says that I can help her teach 'little ones next year.'

Thomas jeered. 'Anyway, I'm off out fer a bit.'

'Don't be long,' his mother called after him. 'Supper's nearly ready and your da will be in any minute.'

'I'll just be larkin' outside.' He opened the door, and then said, 'Somebody's coming. I think it's 'agent coming for 'rent.'

'I hope not,' Lol muttered. 'It's not due yet, or if it is, I haven't got it.'

They were going through a difficult period just now. Ben had taken a good deal of time off work due to his aching bones, and his wages had been reduced. Sometimes when he came home from work he could hardly put one leg in front of the other, and although he had made a stout stick to lean on and help him walk, he was in a great deal of pain.

It wasn't the agent. It was Joseph Ellis. He dismounted and took off his hat as he came to the door, and asked Thomas if he would hold his horse's reins. He glanced at Susannah standing at the table with a wooden spoon in her hand.

'Baking?' he asked, pressing his fingers to his mouth.

'Yes, sir,' she said diffidently. 'It's my birthday tomorrow and Thomas's in three weeks, so I'm making us a cake.'

He nodded, his eyes on her. 'How very grown up you are becoming.' His voice was low and husky. He turned to Aunt Lol. 'I have come, as ever,' he said, sounding tired, and Susannah glanced curiously at him.

'You don't need to, sir,' Lol said quietly. 'In fact, I think it'd be best if you didn't. Years are passing. Everybody has to get on with their lives. It's going to be more awkward as time goes on. We can mek some other arrangements.'

Susannah saw him give a silent sigh which seemed to come from deep within him, and he said softly, speaking to Aunt Lol but looking at her, 'I think you are right, Mrs Marston. You always were wise.'

'Not really, sir.' Lol stood with her back to Susannah, so that her view of Mr Ellis was obscured, and she bent her head to give the mixture a final beat. When she lifted her head, Aunt Lol had moved and had put her hand in her apron pocket.

Joseph gazed down at Susannah and gave her a wistful smile. 'I trust you'll have an enjoyable birthday, Susannah – and a happy life.' He dug his hand into his pocket and took out a gold sovereign which he placed on the corner of the table. 'That's for you to buy yourself a special present,' he said. Then he took out another coin and, going through the door, gave that to Thomas. 'Are you still at school?' he asked the beaming boy.

'Onny till my bothday,' Thomas said. 'Then I can leave and look fer work.'

'Come and see me,' Joseph said. 'I'll see if we can find a place for you on the estate.'

'He's give me a shilling!' Thomas said after he had gone. 'A bob for me to spend!' He caught sight of the shiny sovereign on the table and reached to grab it. 'What's that? Is that worth more'n a bob?'

'No.' His mother scooped it up away from Thomas's grubby hand. 'This is Susannah's and it isn't for spending like a shilling. She'll keep it until such time as she needs it.'

CHAPTER NINETEEN

In June the following year, Uncle Ben died. He came home from work, ate his supper, sat in his chair with a freshly filled clay pipe in his hand, and left them.

'I allus knew he'd make no fuss,' Aunt Lol said, her face drawn but tight-lipped and dry-eyed. 'He was nivver one to be any bother. Allus treated me right. Nivver once hit me. But oh dear me, now what shall we do?'

'I'll soon be able to work, Aunt Lol.' Susannah knew exactly what she meant. Without Uncle Ben's wages, there would be serious shortages. Sally had left home. She had said that she might as well be paid to be a drudge in someone else's house as be an unpaid one at home; but the wages were poor, as were those of Jane, who still worked in the kitchen at Burstall House, and neither of them could send much money home. Daniel worked as a farm labourer, but he flitted from job to job and earned barely enough to keep himself, whilst Thomas had only just started work as least lad, the lowest horse lad on Mr Ellis's estate, and wouldn't be paid wages until the following Martinmas. As for the others of Aunt Lol's large brood, they had all gone their separate ways and came home infrequently.

'I could go to 'new mill in Patrington, Aunt Lol,' Susannah said. 'They're taking some bairns as half-timers.' Enholmes flax mill had opened in 1848. The wages were better than average and workers were flocking there. There were even houses being built to accommodate them.

'I'll mek some enquiries about that,' Lol said, and Susannah assumed she meant that she would ask about a job of work for her. But Lol put on her best bonnet and shawl and took herself off to speak to Mrs Ellis – senior, not the French one; when she came back she told Susannah she was to stay on at school. Lol then found some work in the village, where she hired herself out as a washerwoman in some of the farmhouses where they kept only one servant.

'We'll manage fine now,' she said. 'There's onny 'two of us, after all.'

Two of them, but soon to be three. Jane came home in tears, having been dismissed by the cook at Burstall House.

'She's nivver liked me,' Jane sobbed. 'And now she's got an excuse to get shut o' me.'

'You daft lump,' Lol shouted at her. 'You should've known better than carry on wi' somebody from 'same place o' work.'

'Well how'm I supposed to meet anybody from anywhere else?' Jane retaliated. 'We nivver had a minute to go out and meet other people. Anyway,' she snivelled, 'he says he'll marry me.'

'So who is he?' Lol demanded. 'This darling duck. This honey pot!'

'Wilf Topham.' Jane wiped her eyes. 'He promised me it'd be all right.'

Lol grunted. 'And you believed him! You've less sense than I gave you credit for. What does he do at Ellis's?'

'He works wi' hosses. Wi' Jack Terrison. Our Daniel knows him.'

Lol gave a big sigh. 'He says he'll marry you? Is that what you want?' And at Jane's tearful assent, she said reluctantly, 'I'd better go and see him then.'

'He goes to 'Sun in Skeffling on a night,' Jane said. 'That's where he meets our Daniel and some of 'other lads. I'm sorry, Ma. I nivver thought it'd happen to me, not like—' She glanced at Susannah.

'That's enough said,' her mother barked. 'You're old enough to have known better. It'll not be easy, you know,' she added. 'Having your first bairn at nigh on twenty-six.'

Susannah glanced up from her school books

with interest. She hadn't realized that Jane was so old. She seemed young. Small and thin and quite childlike, and without much to say about anything except what happened in the kitchen at Burstall House. But then, Susannah considered, Jane had never been to school and hadn't been taught how to think. Yet even this puzzled her, for she knew that Aunt Lol hadn't been to school either and she was as sharp as could be and had an opinion on most subjects.

The following night Lol tramped the three miles to Skeffling. Susannah offered to go with her, but it was a cold rainy night, and Lol said there was no use in them both getting wet. She put on Ben's rubber boots, his cap and her two shawls and set off, planning what to say to this man who had seduced her daughter. He would say, she was sure, that Jane was old enough to do as she wanted. She wasn't a child but a grown woman.

'Which she is. But she's not right sharp,' she muttered as she bent her head against the rain. 'And I thought she'd be safe at Burstall.' And if I'm honest, she reflected, I never thought that any man would want her. But there, you can never tell. On the other hand, though, perhaps he took advantage of her. Yes, that's it. That's the route to go. He's taken advantage of her because she's gullible. Well, we'll see what sort of man he is.

She waited, shivering, in the doorway of the Sun Inn and eventually saw Daniel and an older man approach.

'Ma!' Daniel came up, shaking the water from his hat. 'What's up? What 'you doing here? Has summat happened?'

'Aye, you could say that! I'm waitin' on Wilfred Topham. I hear as he's a friend o' yourn.'

'Why – this is him!' Daniel turned to his companion. 'What do you want wi' him?'

Lol was surprised to see how old Topham was; at least ten years older than Jane, she thought, and not a handsome man either. He was short and bow-legged with a mean craggy face. 'Are you 'fellow that's been carryin' on wi' my daughter Jane? 'Chap that's got her into trouble?'

Topham sniffed derisively. 'Why would it be me? What makes you think that? I hardly know her.'

'You know her all right, cos she says so. Got dismissed from work cos of it.'

'Why – you owd devil!' Daniel burst out. 'Wi' our Jane?' He lifted his fist but his mother intervened.

'We'll have no violence,' she said. 'We'll sort this out once and for all. Are you a married man?' she asked Topham. 'You're old enough to be!'

'I'm not,' he said, his voice surly. 'Nor likely to be.'

'That's what you think!' Daniel said. 'If Jane's got caught then you'll marry her.'

'Says who?' Topham snarled. 'It could've been anybody!'

Daniel caught him by his collar. He was taller by far than the older man. 'She doesn't lie.' He glared at him. 'She don't know how to. She's not that bright. You've tekken advantage of her!'

'Put him down, Daniel,' Lol said. 'If he doesn't want to get wed, then that's all right; but I'll mek sure that Mr Ellis knows you've dishonoured an innocent young woman and we'll see how long it teks for you to pack up and leave.'

'He wouldn't do that,' Topham blustered, but Lol noticed that he fidgeted uneasily.

'I think you'll find that he will,' Lol said firmly. 'And don't think that I'll welcome somebody like you into 'family, cos I won't; but our Jane can't support herself wi' a bairn to look after, and I find it hard enough to mek ends meet anyway.'

'Hey, Ma!' A young voice came out of the gloom. 'What 'you doin' here?'

Lol turned in astonishment to see Thomas coming towards the inn. 'What 'you doing, more like?' she answered.

'I said I'd meet Daniel.' He grinned. 'I'm going to have my first pint of ale.'

'You'll have nowt of 'sort!' Lol reached out and smacked Thomas across the side of his head. 'Get yourself back to 'farm and off to bed. Is this

216

what you get up to when I'm not here to watch you?'

'I'm nearly old enough.' Thomas rubbed his smarting ear. 'Dan said it'd be all right.'

'Did he?' Lol glared now at Daniel, who gave a shrug. 'Well I'm telling you it's not! Now get off back like I tell you. You've a job o' work to do in 'mornin' and you'll not be able to do it wi' a skinful o' beer. Time enough for that when you're older and able to handle it.'

Thomas slunk off and Lol folded her arms in front of her chest. She was feeling really cold, but determined to get the matter finished. 'So,' she said. 'We were saying.'

'You said no violence, Ma, but you've just given our Tom a clout,' Daniel commented. 'And that's what I'll give this lover here if he doesn't wed our Janey. Don't think I won't,' he said to Topham, 'just because I know you.'

'Now hold on!' Topham said. 'I didn't say as I wouldn't. It's just come as a bit of a surprise, that's all. Me and Jane have had a bit of a fling and I'll do 'right thing by her if 'bairn is mine.'

'He won't want to lose his job and that's a fact, Ma,' Daniel told her as if Topham wasn't there. 'He was took on as head waggoner last Martinmas. Jack Terrison wanted 'job, but he was given it instead.'

'So you're earning good money?' Lol said. 'Able to keep a wife?'

217

'I suppose so.' Topham grimaced. 'But it's not what I'd planned.'

'Should've kept your breeches buttoned then, shouldn't you?' Lol said bitterly. 'I know it teks two, unless you forced her—'

'I didn't, missus,' he interjected. 'Honest to God, I didn't. She were willing enough.'

'So you'll marry her?' Lol said. 'Mek it legal and pay for 'bairn?'

'Aye,' he said reluctantly. 'If I must. But I live in; what'll we do about that? I've got no house.'

'Jane can live wi' us for 'time being,' Lol said. 'We'll sort summat out later.' She glanced at Daniel. 'You'll mek sure he keeps his promise? He'll not change his mind after a few beers?'

'He'll not, Ma.' Daniel glared menacingly at Topham, and told him, 'You'll not want to mess about wi' Ma. If she says she'll go and see Ellis, she will.'

'That's what I reckoned,' Topham said later, as they sat over their ale. 'Your ma looks 'sort who could stir up trouble if she'd a mind to.' He rubbed his hand across his mouth. 'I hadn't planned to settle down wi' a wife, though. I can't see me livin' wi' your Jane. I mean she's not 'sort you'd want to be tied to, is she?'

'Just watch your mouth!' Daniel said sharply. 'Any road, Ma wouldn't want you to set up house wi' her; they'll just want your name on 'birth certificate. So it's not a bastard like young—' He stopped abruptly and gazed into his tankard. 'It means a lot to Ma,' he said awkwardly. 'Doing things right and proper.'

Topham eyed him curiously. 'Like young who?' he asked.

'Nobody.' Daniel lifted his tankard to his lips. 'Forget it.'

'Oh, I'm so cold!' Lol was soaked to the skin and shivering by the time she arrived home. 'Who would think it was summer? I thought I was nivver going to get here.' Her teeth chattered. ''Road was full o' potholes and I kept cocklin' into 'em. Stoke 'fire up, Susannah. Jane, you fill 'kettle and mek me a drink. I'm going to get into bed to try to get warm. I'll catch me death otherwise.'

Susannah and Jane scurried round and Susannah took a blanket from her own bed and put it round Lol's shoulders. 'Shall I put a brick in 'oven, Aunt Lol? That'll warm you up.'

'Yes, please.' Lol huddled down beneath the bedclothes. 'Anyway, Topham says he'll marry you, Jane. Our Daniel'll see that he sticks to his word. Not that I liked him,' she muttered. 'You can get shut of him as soon as you're wed. Just so long as he gives 'babby a name and meks a contribution towards its keep.'

'Where's 'sense in that?' Jane said, holding the

219

cup of hot tea. 'He's got to help me bring it up. I'll not be able to manage on me own!'

'Give us that tea, you dozy ha'p'orth.' Her mother stretched out her hand for the cup and sipped. 'You can live here wi' 'bairn! We'll help you, me and Susannah. We don't need him. He lives in at Ellis's anyway, which is just as well cos I don't want him here and that's a fact.'

The next morning Lol was sweaty and had a head cold. 'I've caught a chill,' she mumbled. 'Susannah, you go wi' Jane down to 'choch and arrange for 'banns to be read. Tell 'parson it's got to be quick – no hanging about. He'll know what you mean. And if he's not in 'choch,' she added, 'you'll have to walk over to Holmpton cos that's where he lives.'

'I daren't go, Ma,' Jane whined. 'Can't we wait till you're up?'

'No! 'Way I feel I might not be getting up. Though I might sit by 'fire if you'll build it up, Susannah.'

'We'll be as quick as we can, Aunt Lol.' Susannah wrinkled her forehead. She had never known Aunt Lol to be ill. 'Stay in bed and I'll heat some soup for you when we come back.'

Lol didn't answer, but only turned over, groaning slightly.

The parson was in the church when they arrived, which saved them from a long walk to his home in the village of Holmpton close to the sea. 'I'll publish the banns at Welwick and then Holmpton,' he said, on being informed of the circumstances. 'And if there are no objections you can wed the week after the third Sunday. Ask your future husband to come and see me,' he added. 'And I shall expect to see you both in church to hear the banns being read.' He looked down at Susannah. 'I've seen you in school, haven't I?' he asked. 'What's your name? You don't come to church very often. Have you been baptized?'

Susannah bit on her lip. 'I'm not sure, sir,' she whispered. 'My name's Susannah Page.' Aunt Lol wasn't a churchgoer, believing that God's house was meant for weddings, christenings and funerals, and therefore never pressing the children to attend.

'Ah! Your aunt brought you to church for baptism not long after you were born, if I remember correctly.' He nodded sagely. 'Your poor unfortunate mother. Mrs Marston always does the right thing by everybody. Very well,' he said, dismissing them. 'I'll see you in church, Jane, for the banns and the marriage.'

When they arrived back at the cottage they found Lol on the floor. She had turned dizzy and fallen, she said, as she tried to get to the chair by the fire. 'Help me get her back into bed, Jane,' Susannah said. 'I can't lift her by myself.'

'In my condition?' Jane wailed. 'I shouldn't be lifting owt!'

'But she can't stay on 'floor. We have to get her into bed.'

'I can manage,' Lol mumbled. 'Just give me a minute.'

'No,' Susannah said, taking charge when it seemed that Jane didn't know how to. 'Fetch them pillows off my bed, Jane, and prop them round her so she's not in a draught. We'll make you a bed on the floor, Aunt Lol. Just until you can help yourself up or until maybe Daniel or somebody calls.'

'Bless you, Susannah,' Lol murmured, blinking up at her. 'You'll do all right. Even when I'm not here to look after you.'

Susannah sat back on her haunches, tucking her skirt beneath her. She hadn't noticed before, but Aunt Lol seemed older, her face more lined and sunken. She stroked her cheek. 'Won't you always be here to look after me?' she asked, feeling a sudden chill run over her.

Lol took hold of her hand and pressed it, stroking the soft pocket of smooth flesh between Susannah's thumb and forefinger. 'No,' she said. 'One day you'll be on your own.'

CHAPTER TWENTY

Lol managed to walk to Welwick church to see Jane married, but the fever had taken something from her; she had little energy and no inclination to talk. After the brief ceremony, Jane walked home with her mother and Susannah, whilst her new husband went back to work at Ellis's. Daniel had taken the afternoon off to be a witness, and he was the only one out of the five of them to call in at the Wheatsheaf and drink to the health of the newly-weds.

'Well, I'm a married woman now,' Jane commented. 'But I don't feel any different.'

'You're not any different,' her mother groused. 'But at least your bairn will have a name. It can hold its head up.'

Something clicked in Susannah's mind. 'Can I, Aunt Lol? Hold my head up? Have I got a name?'

Lol glanced at her. 'I reckon you will,' she said softly. 'But on your own account, nobody else's.'

Susannah gave a little sigh of despondency. There never seemed to be a straight answer. It was that nobody again.

The rest of the summer was cold and wet and Jane complained bitterly that Wilf hadn't been to see her. Lol told her to think herself lucky; in Lol's opinion he wouldn't make much of a husband anyway. 'He's got a mean streak, if you ask me,' she said. 'You can see it in his face.'

'So why did he marry me then?' Jane scoffed. 'He didn't have to. Some men would have denied 'babby was theirs.'

'Onny because I threatened I'd tell Ellis,' her mother said. 'He didn't want to risk losing his job.'

Jane huffed. 'Well, 'Ellises have no reason to talk! We hardly see hide nor hair of 'em.'

'Well, he doesn't know that, does he? Your husband, I mean. He knows nowt and don't you go tellin' him. We get 'allowance regular and that's that.'

Susannah looked from one to the other. What were they talking about?

In October Aunt Lol was taken ill again. She had been outside chopping wood and caught another chill. She wheezed all night long and coughed throughout the following day. That evening Jane started to miscarry.

'I'll fetch Mrs Davison from South End,' Lol

gasped, hardly able to take a breath. 'She'll be able to help you, Janey. I haven't got 'strength.'

Jane started to blubber and moan. 'He'll not stop wi' me if I lose 'bairn.'

'Then you'll have to mek sure you get caught wi' another,' her mother rasped as she put her shawl over her head. 'Though why you'd bother beats me.'

'Aunt Lol, let me go!' Susannah said. 'I know where Mrs Davison lives.'

'I'll not have you go out on such a night.' Lol unbolted the door. 'Just get them old sheets out of 'cupboard and mek Jane lie still. She might yet keep it; but if she doesn't, then it's God's will.'

She arrived back twenty minutes later, bringing with her Mrs Davison who, Susannah thought, was even older than Aunt Lol. Susannah made a pot of tea for Lol, who was sweating profusely even though she said she felt cold, and also gave a cup to Mrs Davison. The latter had taken off her coat and rolled up her sleeves to her elbows, which frightened Jane rigid.

Susannah sat by the fire, trying not to listen to the sounds from the bedroom of Jane's crying and Mrs Davison's short-tempered admonishments. 'Good heavens, girl,' she heard her say. 'If you think this is a belly ache, you'd not want to go full term! Anyway, you've lost it. Nowt I can do. But I dare say you'll catch on again afore you can blink an eye.'

'I shan't!' Jane wailed. 'I'm done wi' it. He can go to 'other side o' 'world for all I care.'

Lol put her head back against the chair and closed her eyes. 'Doubt he'll do that,' she muttered. 'He'll want his marital rights. Susannah!' she said, with her eyes still shut. 'When you choose a man to be 'fayther o' your bairns, mek sure that he wants 'em as much as you do. That he'll want to tek responsibility for 'em.'

'How will I do that, Aunt Lol?'

Lol opened her eyes. She looked unutterably weary. 'I miss Ben, you know,' she said softly. 'He was a good man. One of 'best. I shan't be sorry to leave here and go and join him.'

Susannah knelt by her feet. 'Please don't,' she begged, tears filling her eyes. 'What'll I do without you?'

Lol put her hand on Susannah's head. 'I promised your ma I'd look after you, just as I promised *her* ma I'd look after Mary-Ellen. And I have. I did. But I'm tired, Susannah. I need somebody to look after me.'

'I will! I will!' Tears ran down Susannah's cheeks. 'I'll look after you, Aunt Lol. I won't go to school. Please don't die. I'll have no-one if you're not here!'

Lol sighed. 'You'll grow up to be strong. And clever too. I know that. Not like Jane. She needs somebody to look out for her, but I'll not mek you promise that; you're too young and besides,

226

she's got a husband who can do that, if he's a mind to. You look out for yourself, Susannah.'

Wilfred Topham put in an appearance when he was sent for after Jane miscarried. Susannah heard raised voices, Jane's mewling one and Wilf's shouting one, but Aunt Lol's could hardly be heard, it was so weak and husky as she implored them to settle their differences.

Lol took to her bed after that. Her chill turned to pneumonia and she put up no resistance to it but simply faded away. Jane was inconsolable after her mother died. 'What'll we do, Susannah?' she wailed. 'It's just me and you now, and I can't manage on me own. You'll have to help me wi' things.'

'But you've got a husband,' Susannah said. 'I expect he'll come when he can.'

Susannah was convinced that Aunt Lol had just given up. 'She'd done what she could for everybody,' she wept to Thomas after the funeral. 'And now she's left us to get on without her as best we can.'

'Aye. Well, I'm all right.' Thomas rubbed his nose on his sleeve. 'I've got a regular job now, so it's just you and Jane; onny you can't really count Jane cos she's got a husband to look after her, so it's onny you. And you'll be able to go to work; you're just about old enough.'

'Aunt Lol wanted me to stay on at school.'

Susannah wiped her eyes. 'How did she manage to pay for us, Thomas?' she said. 'Nearly all 'other bairns are paid for by 'parish.'

Thomas shrugged. 'It were Mrs Ellis who paid for us,' he said. 'I expect it was cos you was a norphan, and you wouldn't go wi'out me.'

Susannah blinked as a distant memory played in her head. 'Oh!' she said. 'Is that what rich folk do? Pay for poor bairns' schooling?'

'Aye, I reckon so. P'raps they've got so much money they have to give it away.'

Wilf Topham didn't go to Lol's funeral, but he came the next evening to tell them he had been to see the agent to arrange to take over the tenancy of the cottage. Jane was relieved for it meant that he would be responsible for the rent. 'I shan't be living here all 'time,' he said. 'Not in 'winter, but in 'summer I'll come when 'mornings and 'nights are light; and I'll expect plenty o' food on 'table,' he added brusquely. 'You'll have to get a job o' work,' he told Jane. 'You can get yoursen off to 'flax mill in Patrington. They pay well there.' He turned to stare at Susannah. 'And tek her wi' you. I'm not keeping her for nowt.'

'She's still at school, Wilf,' Jane interrupted. 'Ma allus said she had to go.'

'Your ma's not here to say what goes on. And I say I'm not paying for her keep!' He scowled. 'She's not one of your kin anyway, is she? Not one of your sisters, I mean?'

'She's my cousin's bairn,' Jane said tearfully. 'Her ma was my best friend. Susannah's allus lived wi' us.'

'Well she can still live here! She'll be company for you when I'm not here; but I'm not working all hours God sends to keep somebody who's not even related! She's old enough to work.' His voice had risen and Susannah cringed. She really didn't like him.

'Any road,' he said to Susannah. 'Get yoursen outside for an hour. I've got things I want to discuss wi' Jane that don't concern you. Go on,' he said, unfastening his breeches belt. 'Afore I give you a taste o' 'strap.'

Susannah saw the scared look on Jane's face and hastily gathered up her books, which had been scattered about the table. She grabbed a shawl and scuttled out of the door.

It was a fine night and not dark as there was a full moon shining. Susannah hesitated for only a moment. She didn't want to sit waiting on the doorstep, so she put her books by the door, weighted them down with a stone and set off to walk the mile to the estuary bank. Sheep Trod Lane was an ancient thoroughfare which it was thought had once been used for animal access to the saltmarsh grazing. Now the low-lying open land was constantly drained by dykes and sluices into the Humber; the silting of the saltmarsh growths was claimed by the Crown though contested by the owners of the adjoining land who wished to eventually use it for agriculture.

Susannah wasn't afraid of the night; rather she enjoyed the solitariness of it. She listened intently to hear the cry of night-time creatures, the rustling of rats, the hoot of owls; and she breathed in a deep breath to catch the aroma of long grass, estuary water and the salty tang of the sea.

She gave a little satisfied smile as she remembered what her teacher had told her. The Humber had once been a valley. A submerged valley. During the melting of the ice sheets, a watery cataract had poured down from the Wolds, plunging into the long depression and rushing to meet up with the watery waste of the sea. 'And then,' she chanted as she sloshed through a deep pocket of mud, 'the great torrent of sea turned about and drove it all the way back to Hessle, where I've never been, and to the Ferriby Sands and beyond.'

Reaching the bank she scrambled up and looked down at the glinting saltmarsh and the rippling shining water of the Humber. 'I never want to leave here,' she murmured. 'Never. Never. Never!' Then she gave a sudden shudder as she thought of Wilf Topham. What was he discussing with Jane that she shouldn't hear? The family had never had secrets from each other; at least she didn't think they had. Except perhaps Daniel, who sometimes made remarks that she didn't understand. So why was Wilf shutting her out now?

As she stared out at the Humber, she heard a snickering snort and the sound of hoofbeats. Startled, she looked up. From out of the darkness a horse and rider were coming fast towards her along the riverside path. She hastily jumped down out of the way, but the rider had seen her. 'Who's there?' a harsh male voice called out. 'What's your business here?'

She got up from where she had fallen on her knees into the grassy delve. 'Nobody, sir,' she stammered nervously. 'Onny me. Susannah Page.'

The rider dismounted and Susannah prepared to run. Who was it? Did he mean her harm?

'Susannah?' The voice had softened. 'Not Susannah from Mrs Marston's house?'

'Y-yes. Onny my aunt is dead now. We've just buried her.'

'Is she? I didn't know!' The man came closer to the edge and looked down. He seemed very tall up there on the bank. She couldn't see his face as it was hidden by his hat. 'I've been away. I'm so sorry to hear that. She was a good woman.'

'Yes, sir,' she murmured. 'I miss her.'

'Why are you out here on your own? You shouldn't be. It's dangerous.'

231

'River doesn't come over 'bank now,' she replied. 'Not since 'embanking.'

'I know.' She heard a tinge of amusement in his voice. 'But you still shouldn't be here. You could slip into the marsh and you wouldn't be able to get out.'

''Tide's out,' she was emboldened to say. 'It's not very deep.'

He came closer. 'Put your head up, Susannah, and let me look at you.'

She took a step back and then lifted her face so that the moon shone on her features. She saw his mouth move though she still couldn't see his eyes. She heard him take a breath, and then he repeated quietly, 'Why did you say you were out here by the river all alone? Do you come here to think, as I do?'

'I came because Wilf Topham, who's married to our Jane, wanted to talk to her privately; so he told me to wait outside.'

'Wilf Topham?'

'He works for Mr Ellis,' she said. 'But he's got Aunt Lol's cottage now.'

'Has he? I see.' His voice had changed again to one of abruptness and she wondered if perhaps she had said too much to this stranger.

'I have to go now,' she said, backing away. 'Jane will be worrying about me.'

'Well, I hope someone is,' he muttered. 'Would you like me to give you a lift back on my horse?'

'Oh, no! Thank you!' She knew better than to accept. He might carry her off and murder her. Thomas said that sometimes happened to girls. She turned away. 'Good night, sir,' she said, poised to run.

'Good night, Susannah,' he said in a low voice. 'Take good care. Go straight home.'

'Yes, sir,' she gasped, starting to run. 'I will.'

Jane was hanging a sheet on the line the next morning and contemplating that she'd never get the stain out. *I can't believe how a man can change. He used to be so saucy and good-natured. Kissed and cuddled me that time in 'Ellises' kitchen garden where he found me when I'd been sent to fetch a bunch of carrots. Though why he was there she didn't know. He must have followed her, she'd worked out at the time.*

He'd teased and tickled her into submission, taking her behind the gardeners' shed where they kept the barrows and spades. And although it had hurt a bit, he'd said how lovely she was and could he see her again. He'd been that eager that she couldn't say no. *But then,* she grimaced, *he never came near after I got caught with 'babby, not even when we'd got married. Not until last night when he came and told Susannah to clear off.* She'd no sooner gone than he shoved me into the bedroom and onto the bed. *Didn't even* have time to get my skirt off before his breeches were down.

She put her hand to her mouth and tried to suppress her tears. He never took no notice when I screamed at how he was hurting me. I told him I was still sore after losing 'babby, but he didn't care. Not one bit, he didn't. He said I'd be even more sore if I didn't stop bawling. And then— She gave a sob. Even after he'd finished, he made me wait on the bed until he'd recovered, and then climbed on top of me all over again. Brutal, he was. No other word for it. He didn't even care when I said I was bleeding and that the sheet would be ruined.

She touched her cheek where it was tender. Walloped me one, he did, and said he wasn't bothered about 'flaming sheet. Well, he doesn't have to wash it, does he? She sniffled back her tears. I could hardly walk when Susannah came back after he'd gone; bent double I was. She must have been waiting outside, poor bairn, but I couldn't tell her what happened. She's too young. I wish my ma was here. She'd have given him a mouthful all right. And he said I've got to look for work. Well, not today I won't. I'd not be able to walk all that way to Patrington, not after what I've suffered. I'll go tomorrow.

'Mrs Topham?'

She jumped at the voice. She hadn't heard

anyone come up behind her. 'Mr Ellis, sir.' She dipped her knee. 'Didn't hear you!'

'Are you all right?' Joseph took off his hat.

'Yes, sir. I'm a bit upset . . .'

'I heard about your mother. I'm so very sorry. I would have come to the funeral if I'd known.'

She gazed at him open-mouthed. He was still handsome, she thought, and polite, and he had a kind face, though he always looked sad. Even though he was married. She gave a small inward sigh. Marriage isn't all that it's cracked up to be.

'I wanted to speak to you about Susannah,' he murmured. 'Have you got a minute?'

'Yes, sir. She's at school today.'

'Yes, I'd guessed that she would be.' His brow creased. 'That's why I came now. Your husband's at work, isn't he?'

She nodded. 'He works for 'Ellises.'

'Yes, I know,' he said patiently. Then he bit on his lip as if considering something. 'He doesn't know about Susannah, does he? Whose child she is, I mean?'

'No, sir.' She looked down at her feet. 'I've never told him, anyway. Ma allus said we hadn't to discuss her wi' anybody.'

'But you do know that she's my child? Look at me, Mrs Topham!'

Jane lifted her head and gazed at the eyes which were studying her face. There was no wonder that Mary-Ellen had loved him so much.

Any woman could. He seemed so strong-willed, yet gentle too. 'Yes, I know that she is. Mary-Ellen was my best friend as well as my cousin.' She swallowed hard. Everybody that she cared for had gone. Except for Susannah. 'I'll . . .' The tears which were so close to the surface began to trickle down her face. 'I'll tek care of her, Mr Ellis,' she blubbered. 'As best I can, anyway.'

'Thank you,' he said huskily. 'I'll make sure the allowance comes to you. And you'll see that she goes to school? I want the best for her.'

She lifted her apron and wiped her eyes. How would she get round that? Wilf said Susannah had to go to work. She'd have to pretend that she was going to work, when she was really setting off for school. But what if he found out? They'd maybe both get a beating from him. She nodded. 'Yes, sir,' she said.

CHAPTER TWENTY-ONE

I don't understand why we have to keep it a secret from Uncle Wilf. Susannah mulled over the dilemma as she trudged home from school. He'd surely be pleased that I'm going to school. He doesn't have to pay for it, and I'll be able to get a better job of work if I can read and write well. And I'm good at arithmetic. The best in school, Miss said.

Nevertheless, Jane had insisted that Wilf mustn't find out. But he probably won't, Susannah thought. He hardly ever comes home. Thank goodness he doesn't, cos when he comes I always have to go outside. He always has something to talk about to Jane that I shouldn't hear. And it's so cold waiting outside. Perhaps if I tell him that I won't listen, he'll let me stay in.

It was her twelfth birthday the following week and she hoped that Thomas would come to see her. He used to sneak home in the evening, but since his mother had died he hadn't come so often. Also, the weather was worsening for the walk from Skeffling. Wilf Topham borrowed a horse and cart when he came, but then he was a waggoner, not a horse lad like Thomas.

Susannah was the oldest girl in the school. Most of the boys had left to apply for work at Patrington's Martinmas hirings fair; the girls who were about her age had also left to look for work, either in domestic service or at Enholmes flax mill.

The teacher had asked Susannah to help teach the younger children to read and write and do their numbers. She had given her extra books to read at home, and had set her tasks in arithmetical knowledge, computation and science, telling her that if she kept up her schooling she might be able to become a teacher herself. Susannah had told this to Jane who had expressed such astonishment that Susannah was sure that she didn't believe her.

She had stayed behind at school to help the teacher clear up, and when she arrived home, later than usual, the horse and waggon were standing outside the cottage. She hesitated, undecided whether or not to go in. Jane had started part time at the mill and told her that Wilf thought Susannah had started work there too. What shall I do? I don't want to lie, but I might have to.

She was saved the trouble of deciding as the

door opened, and Wilf came out, buttoning up his coat. He looked up when he saw Susannah. 'Where've you been?' he barked. 'Working over-time?'

'I – no,' she said. 'I've been somewhere . . .'

He started to question her further about the flax mill and her hours, and she stammered out uncertain replies.

Jane came to the door. She was flushed about her face and neck. Her hair was mussed up and the buttons on her bodice were undone. She looked as if she had been crying. 'She's onny on half time, Wilf,' she told him. 'She's too young for full time.'

'Are you all right, Aunt Jane?' Susannah asked. 'You look feverish.'

Wilf Topham laughed coarsely. 'Aye,' he said. 'I've give her a fever all right. I'll give her summat else 'n' all if she doesn't watch out.'

'Is something wrong?' Susannah was worried. Jane seemed very distressed.

'Is *something* wrong!' Wilf mimicked. 'Where'd you learn to talk like that? Not at 'flax mill, I'll be bound. Been hanging round wi' 'gentry, have you?'

'My teacher says we have to talk properly if we're to go up in 'world,' Susannah said hesitantly.

'Teacher! What teacher?' He frowned and crossed his arms in front of his chest. 'But you've finished at school now. You don't have to do what 'schoolteacher says.' He eyed them narrowly, first Susannah and then Jane, cowering in the door-way. 'Or am I being led up 'garden path?'

He suddenly lunged at Susannah and dragged her towards the cottage door, flinging her inside so that she crashed into Jane. 'Get inside, both o' you. I'll get to 'bottom o' this.' He banged the door behind him. 'Now then,' he said to Susannah. 'Have you been tekken on at 'flax mill or not? Cos if you haven't . . .'

He let the threat hang in the air and Susannah eyed Jane anxiously, not knowing what to say.

'They wouldn't tek her on, Wilf.' Jane began to cry. 'She's not old enough.'

'Course she is! They're tekkin' childre' on half time.' He scowled at Susannah. 'You can still get to school in an afternoon even if you onny work 'mornings.'

'Could I? Should I do that, Aunt Jane?' Susannah said nervously. 'Perhaps they'll take me next week. It's my birthday then, Uncle Wilf. I'll be twelve.'

'Uncle Wilf! I'm not your uncle Wilf!' he roared. 'I'll not be saddled wi' that. You get down to Enholmes' next week and get fixed up or I'll want to know 'reason why.' He scowled again, his brow wrinkled and angry. 'Will 'parish still pay for her schooling if she's working? Find out about that, cos I'll not pay for her.'

Susannah opened her mouth to say that the parish didn't pay for her schooling, but some instinct stopped her and Jane said hurriedly, 'I'll find out, Wilf. I'll do it tomorrow.'

'See you do,' he muttered. Opening the door, he stormed out, leaving the door swinging on its hinges.

'What'll we do, Aunt Jane?' Susannah whispered.

'You'll have to do as he says.' Jane licked her dry lips. 'He'll give me a beating if you don't, and probably you as well.'

'A beating!' Susannah gasped. 'For what?' She had never had a beating. A smack, yes; both she and Thomas when they used to get into mischief, but never by Uncle Ben, always by Aunt Lol and only with the flat of her hand, never the strap. 'Has he hit you, Aunt Jane?'

'Aye.' Jane sat down in a chair and began to sob. 'Every time he comes – he's that rough.'

'Why?' Susannah whispered. 'What do you do that makes him hit you?'

Jane wiped her eyes. 'It's for what I don't do that he hits me.' She took a deep snuffling breath. 'I can't tell you, Susannah. It's not for a bairn's ears. I nivver thought that married life could be like this. My da nivver once hit my ma and when I told Wilf that he gave me another clout; he said it was to show me what to expect.'

Susannah stared at Jane with her lips parted.

241

Why would he do that? Jane was such a quiet woman, and small and thin. It was true that she had rather a whiny sort of voice which could be irritating, but that didn't warrant a beating. Will he hit me if I don't go to work? Who can I tell if he does?

The next day he came back. Jane and Susannah were finishing their supper when they heard the sound of cart wheels outside. Jane stood up and began rubbing her hands together. 'Why has he come?' she whispered. 'Why has he come now?' She put her hand to her face and Susannah saw the yellow bruise on her cheekbone beneath her fingers.

But Wilf Topham was all smiles when he came in. 'Now then,' he crowed. 'Is there a cup o' tea?'

'Yes. Yes.' Jane scurried about getting out crockery and Susannah swung the kettle back over the fire. 'And a bit o' cake if you'd like, Wilf?' Jane said nervously.

'That's more like it.' He sat down in her vacant chair. 'Have you been to school today, Susannah?'

'Yes, Mr Topham.' Susannah stood up. 'We've got tests to do next week.'

'Mr Topham!' he said heartily. 'I'm not your schoolteacher, you know!'

'What am I to call you, then?' Susannah murmured. 'If I'm not to call you uncle?'

He nodded at her, a sly grin on his face. 'Well, it's a bit of a dilemma, isn't it? You could just call me Wilf, I suppose, cos I'm not your proper uncle and not even a proper relation.'

Susannah swallowed and tried to remain calm. Something must have happened to put him in this strange humour.

Jane added more hot water into the teapot and poured him a cup of tea. It was weak but he didn't seem to notice. He blew on it and slurped. 'I've been having a natter wi' Daniel,' he said casually. 'Aye. We get on right well, me and Daniel. Been telling me a thing or two, he has.' He looked up at Susannah. 'About school 'n' that. And who pays for it!'

'It's not a secret,' Susannah said boldly. 'Mrs Ellis pays for it. She paid for Thomas as well. It's cos they're rich that they pay for poor children to go to school.'

Wilf frowned. 'Dan didn't say they'd paid for Thomas. Onny you.'

Susannah shook her head. 'Both of us.'

'Well, that don't matter,' he said, pushing back the chair and getting to his feet. 'What's odd is that 'parish would've paid for you, so why does Mrs Ellis?'

'It's cos Susannah doesn't have no ma or da,' Jane broke in. 'She's a norphan.'

He scowled at Jane. 'All 'more reason for 'parish to pay. And how is this money paid out?

Does it go straight to school? Or . . .' He gave a malicious grin as if he already knew the answer, and grabbed hold of Jane's wrist. 'Does it come 'ere? Does Mrs Ellis send it to you?'

'To my ma,' Jane gasped. 'It was allus sent to my ma. I don't know what'll happen now,' she lied.

'It'll come 'ere!' He wagged a threatening finger at her. 'To you! They'll know your ma's no longer wi' you. And when it does, you'll tell me, do you hear? I'll see that it's paid out to 'school – if I've a mind to, that is.' He tightened his grip on her wrist and twisted it until she shrieked out in pain. 'That's for not telling me,' he snarled into her face. 'For letting me think that 'parish paid for her.'

'Don't do that!' Susannah grasped his hand to shake it off Jane. 'You're hurting her!'

He turned swiftly, dropping Jane's wrist and grabbing Susannah's. 'Hurtin' her, am I?' He squeezed her wrist, nipping her flesh with his fingernails. 'Like that, is it? Does that hurt?'

Susannah screamed. 'Stop it! Stop it!'

He stopped immediately and swung a slap to her face, making her stagger and fall. Then he turned to Jane. 'That's a taste of what you'll both get if I have any bother from either of you. Now listen to me. She goes to 'flax mill next week when she's turned twelve. You both go full time and I want to see your wages. We'll not bother

244

tellin' her up at 'big house that she's finished school; she'll be none 'wiser unless somebody tells.' He glared menacingly. 'And if anybody should . . .'

Jane was speechless and looked completely terrified. Susannah dropped into a chair and wiped her streaming eyes, for the slap had been hard and made her eyes water. What would he do? she wondered. Would he kill them? But then, she pondered, he would lose his job and the money for her schooling. He hasn't got much sense. Doesn't he realize that my teacher will want to know where I am? Then she had the sudden thought that this term would already be paid for. Perhaps her teacher would think that she wasn't coming back for the new term after Christmas. Wilf Topham would be able to keep the money and Mrs Ellis wouldn't know. She never came to the house or the school. Susannah bit on her thumb. I don't even know when she sends it, or who with.

'Is that clear?' he bellowed at Susannah. 'Are you listening to what I say?'

'Yes,' she muttered. 'I heard you.'

Susannah went with Jane to apply for work at the flax mill the following week. The road from Welwick to Patrington was poor, with deep muddy ruts made by waggon wheels, and the rain was sleeting down. They had put on clean white bonnets and aprons, but their boots and shawls were soaking wet by the time they arrived.

'How old are you?' the mill foreman asked Susannah.

'Just turned twelve,' she stated. 'And I'd like to work full time.' Then she added, 'I can read and write. Could I work in the office?'

He grinned. 'A lady clerk? I'll have to ask 'boss about that. Fancy yourself a cut above workin' in 'mill, do you?'

'No,' she hastened to say. 'But it seems a waste if I don't use my education.'

'Ooh!' he said caustically. 'Hark at her! What about you?' he asked Jane. 'Where would *milady* like to work?'

'Anywhere,' Jane said. 'I've signed on for part time already. I don't mind what I do.'

'Well you can go in 'drying room,' he said. 'In summer we dry outside, but in winter, or when it's wet, 'flax has to come inside and somebody has to keep on turning it. When it's dried it goes for dressing – broken and scutched,' he said. ''Men do that usually. You'd not like that. 'Dust gets up your nose.'

'I don't care,' Jane said dully. 'Owt you like.'

'All right.' He glanced at Susannah. 'Start to-morrow, six o'clock sharp, and I'll ask if there's a place in 'office for you. Don't you want to come half time if you're onny twelve?'

She told him no, that she had to work full time

and that she was finished with school. As they tramped back home Susannah reflected how different things were now that Aunt Lol was gone. She remembered last year when, on the day before her birthday, she had made a cake for her and Thomas. This year Thomas hadn't even come to see her. We always shared our birthdays, she mused, and last year young Mr Ellis came to see Aunt Lol, and he gave me a sovereign and Thomas a shilling. Where is it, I wonder? She narrowed her eyes in concentration. Where would Aunt Lol have put it to keep it safe? She said it was mine, for when I needed it.

She asked Jane later if she knew where it was, but Jane knew nothing about it. She was unusually quiet and said little. After they had eaten their supper, Susannah asked if she could look in Jane's room. It had formerly been the family bedroom and then Aunt Lol's and was now Jane's. Susannah still slept in her own bed in the kitchen.

She looked first under the bed; there was a box there which was covered in dust but in it there was only an old fustian sheet to be used for cutting up for dusters, a flannel shirt which had belonged to Ben, and a skirt and worn bonnet which had been Aunt Lol's. Then she lifted the lid of a wooden chest which had been Ben's when he was a farm lad, and underneath a woollen blanket she found a crocheted purse and, in it, the sovereign.

'I've found it, Aunt Jane,' she called excitedly. 'Aunt Lol had been keeping it safe.' Smiling, she went back into the kitchen clutching the precious coin.

'Found what?'

Her smile vanished when she saw Wilf Topham standing there. 'Nothing,' she said, putting her hand behind her back.

He signalled with his finger for her to come near. 'Must be summat,' he said softly. 'You look like 'cat what's got 'cream. Come on! Show me.'

'It's mine,' she said tearfully, reluctantly opening her hand. 'It was a birthday present and Aunt Lol kept it for me.'

'Did she?' He roughly prised her fingers open as she tried to close them over the coin. He felt the weight of the sovereign in his palm and whistled; then, grinning, he tossed it up in the air where it spun, twisting and glistening. He caught it and gently cast it about in his hand. 'Well, I'll keep it for you now.'

CHAPTER TWENTY-TWO

The next morning Susannah and Jane were half-way between Welwick and Patrington when they were caught up by a horse and waggon. 'Want a lift?' the driver called out and eagerly they ran towards it.

'Hey up, Jane! Where 'you off to?'

'Patrington.' Jane climbed into the waggon. 'We're starting work at Enholmes mill. This is Susannah. You know – Mary-Ellen's daughter.'

Susannah climbed in after Jane. 'This is Jack Terrison,' Jane told her. 'He works at Ellis's.'

'Did you know my mother?' Susannah asked. No-one ever really spoke about her. Aunt Lol had said that she was beautiful to look at, with dark hair and bluey-green eyes. But it was as if her life had been forgotten.

'Aye, I did,' he muttered. 'We were at school at 'same time. I used to see her about now and again.'

Susannah examined him surreptitiously. I

wonder if he could be my father. She couldn't see much of his hair beneath his woollen hat, but what she could see was a dull brown colour. He was not very tall and his shoulders were stooped. Susannah's own hair was light in colour, not brown nor blond but somewhere in between, and not dark as her mother's had apparently been. She rather hoped that he wasn't her father. He was a dowly kind of man. Not the sort she imagined her father to be.

'Old enough to work, eh?' Jack said to Jane, nodding towards Susannah. 'Don't know where 'years have gone.'

'I know.' Jane sighed. 'I wish we could turn 'clock back. I'd do some things different, that's for certain.'

'I heard that you lost 'babby you was carrying? Wilf got in a right strop about it.'

'Not because I lost it,' Jane said. 'My ma made him marry me. She told him she'd tell 'Ellises and get him 'sack if he didn't. Then when I lost it he realized he was stuck wi' me for good.' She gave another, deeper sigh. 'Aye, and I'm stuck wi' him.'

'You'd have to have gone on 'parish, though, wouldn't you?' Jack said. 'No man to pay 'rent?'

Jane looked straight ahead. 'Happen so,' she said. 'Who knows?'

'He's in bother though, isn't he? Topham, I

mean?' He shook the reins to urge the horse on. 'That's what I've heard.'

'What sort o' bother? What do you mean?'

'Been given a warning. His work's sloppy, 'maister said. And he's a bully to 'young lads. I doubt he'll be tekken on again at Martinmas, even though he's forever toadying up to Mr Joseph.' Jack cleared his throat and spat onto the road. 'I should've had that job of waggoner,' he muttered. 'Been there as long as him.'

Jane stared at him. 'If he's not tekken on he'll have to find work somewhere else. How'll we manage otherwise?'

'Well, you're working, aren't you? And yon bairn.' He glanced at Susannah.

Jane nodded, but Susannah noticed that she clutched her belly. Jack pulled in at the side of the road in Patrington market place. 'I'll drop you off here,' he said. 'I've to call in at 'wheelwright's. Skeffling one is off sick. Hope work goes all right. They pay well, so I've heard.'

They climbed out of the waggon and joined the stream of mainly women workers heading out of the western outskirts of the village towards the Winestead road where the flax mill was situated. Jane eyed the union workhouse as they passed it and clutched Susannah's arm, whispering, 'That place gives me the creeps. Hope to God I don't finish up there!'

There was good-natured bantering from some

of the women as they trudged down the hill, but others, like Jane discontented with their lot, huddled into their shawls and disregarded anyone else.

The work was arduous, hot and dusty, but at the end of the first week Susannah was paid four shillings and Jane six shillings, better than the average for women workers. Susannah went to speak to the foreman. 'Did you ask if there was a place in the office for me?'

'Aye, I did. But 'manager said no.' He grinned. He was an amiable fellow. 'He asked if I was off me head.' Then he looked sympathetically at her. 'Ask again in a twelvemonth. You'll have learned a bit about 'trade by then, and Mr Marshall is planning on expansion.'

Twelve months! Susannah was cast down. Is this all I've got to look forward to?

When they arrived home, Wilf Topham was waiting for them with his hand outstretched. He'd come over specially, he told them. 'I've walked along 'river bank,' he said. 'Nobody knows I've come so I can't stop.' They handed over their wages and he gave them back barely enough to buy food.

He was about to leave when someone banged on the door. 'Don't let on that I'm here,' he warned and went to hide in the bedroom.

Susannah opened the door and bobbed her knee. 'It's Mr Ellis, Aunt Jane.'

'This is the second time I've been,' Mr Ellis complained. 'You were out!'

'I've started work at 'flax mill, sir,' Jane said. 'We – I don't get home until late.'

'Do you walk in the dark from Patrington?' he asked in an astonished voice.

'Why, yes, sir!' Jane answered, and Susannah wondered how else he thought they would get home.

'Here's the allowance.' He thrust an envelope into Jane's hand. 'I'll call on a Sunday next time.'

'Yes, sir.' Jane dipped her knee. 'Thank you, sir.'

'Make sure it's well spent,' he said brusquely. 'No fripperies.' He turned away and mounted his mare.

Jane looked up at him plaintively and put her arm round Susannah's shoulder. 'I don't know what those are, sir,' she murmured.

He grunted and wheeled away.

'What does he mean?' Susannah asked. 'Fripperies! It's money for school, isn't it?'

Jane blinked. 'Aye,' she muttered. 'Course it is.'

Wilf appeared behind them, keeping within the door. 'So why does Ellis bring 'school money when it's his missus who's supposed to pay for her?'

'She probably doesn't have any money to call her own,' Jane said bitterly. 'Just as I don't!' She flung the envelope at Wilf. 'Women don't have any say about owt.'

He grabbed her roughly and pulled her inside. 'No, that's right, they don't,' he agreed callously, opening the envelope. He gave a soft whistle. 'Phew! This'll come in useful.' He gave a sly grin. 'Didn't know how expensive schooling was! No wonder my ma nivver sent me.'

'What if Mrs Ellis finds out that I'm not at school?' Susannah said nervously. 'Won't she be angry? Won't you have to give 'money back?'

'Nah! Can't if it's spent, can I? Besides, it was your aunt Janey who was given 'money, wasn't it? Not me!' Wilf's eyes slid from Susannah to Jane. 'Such a spendthrift she is. Can't be trusted wi' money, ma'am,' he said in a wheedling voice. 'That's why I keeps her short. Spends it as soon as she gets it. Don't you, little wifey?' he added roughly, giving Jane a slap.

Jane burst into tears. 'I'll get 'blame,' she wept. 'They'll think it's me that's spent it on fripperies!'

'And you'll not tell!' Wilf warned Susannah. 'Or else you'll feel 'leather on your backside.'

Susannah put her hand to her mouth to prevent an outburst of fear and anger. She saw the meanness in his eyes and the way his mouth tightened in a narrow line. She shook her head. 'I won't,' she whispered.

That night after Wilf had gone back to Skeffling, Susannah and Jane prepared for bed.

Susannah washed her hands and face and brushed her long hair. Jane sat in her nightshift gazing into the damped-down fire. She looked up at Susannah.

'Susannah, will you come into my bed tonight? I'm in need o' company and I want to talk to you.'

Susannah put down her hairbrush. She'd never shared Jane's bed, though when she was little she had slept with Aunt Lol, Uncle Ben, Sally and Thomas, until Aunt Lol had had a new bed delivered. 'This is for you, Susannah,' she had said. 'Now that you're growing up to be a big lass. You can sleep in 'corner of 'kitchen and you'll allus be warm.'

Thomas had grumbled that he would have liked his own bed too, but his mother had said no, he could sleep at the bottom of theirs as he always did.

'Yes, course I will,' she said to Jane now. 'We'll be warmer as well if we cuddle up.'

They snuggled up together and Susannah tucked her head under Jane's arm so that their heads were close. Susannah heard Jane's breath in her ear and then Jane whispered, 'Your ma and me used to snuggle up like this, when I was little. We slept in 'same bed when she lived with us. She looked after me, did Mary-Ellen, cos I was allus frightened of me own shadow. Mary-Ellen was frightened of neither nowt nor nobody.'

'Are you frightened now, Aunt Jane?' Susannah murmured. 'Of Wilf?'

'Aye, I am. And I'm frightened for you as well, Susannah.' Jane lay back, looking up at the ceiling, though the room was almost in darkness. 'And I'm more scared for you than I am for myself. I've got summat to tell you.'

Susannah sat up, leaning on one elbow. 'What?'

'I think I'm expecting another babby. I've not told him yet, cos I'm not sure. But I've been sick and I feel as if I am.'

'I'll help you, Aunt Jane,' Susannah said. 'I'll help you to look after it.'

'Ah, but don't you see! You'll still have to go to work and *he'll* tek all your money just 'same. He'll not come round so often, which is a blessing, but he'll come on 'day you bring your wages home.'

'So what can we do?' Susannah cupped her chin in her hands. 'We'll need extra money with a young babby to feed.'

'Aye, we will. I've been thinking about it all week while I've been working. There's onny one thing for it, as far as I can see.'

'What's that?' Susannah leaned her head on Jane's shoulder. 'I'll do whatever you say.'

Jane gave a little laugh which came from the back of her throat, but Susannah thought wasn't a chuckle of happiness, but of bleakness. 'You've allus been a good lass,' Jane said. 'Obedient. A bit like me, I suppose, and not like your ma. She'd have stood up to somebody like Wilf. She'd have shown him 'door, no doubt about that. Though he'd not have got through it in 'first place! But you,' she said. 'I don't see you smile any more and it's not right.'

'We've nothing much to smile about.' Susannah felt tears welling behind her eyes. 'Not since Aunt Lol died and Wilf took over.'

'I know. Well, I've got to do as he says, cos he's my lawful husband. But you . . .' She felt for Susannah's cheek and gently patted it. 'You don't. He's no relation of yours and can have no say ower what you do.'

'But he's taken our money!' Susannah cried. 'Money which should have gone for my schooling, as well as our wages. He'll beat us if we don't give it to him!'

'He can't beat you if you're not here,' Jane whispered. 'Not if you've run away.'

CHAPTER TWENTY-THREE

'Run away! Why would I run away? Where would I go? What would you do? You'd be by yourself!' Susannah got out of bed and opened the thin curtain at the window to let in a ribbon of grey light. 'I couldn't go and leave you.' She sat on the edge of the bed. 'Not with him!'

'You're a clever lass,' Jane said. 'You could go to Hull or anywhere. You'd soon get a job. And if you're not here, he wouldn't come cos there'd be no money – not much, anyway – and he'd have to keep me on his earnings, else I'd go to 'parish and tell 'em that he'd abandoned me and then word'd get back to Ellis's.'

Susannah gazed at her. She seemed to have got a scheme all worked out, but it didn't make a lot of sense. 'Jack Terrison said that Wilf was in some bother,' she said. 'He told you that 'Ellises might not take him on again at Martinmas. So,' she murmured, 'he'd come back here, unless he went away onto another farm.'

'Yes,' Jane said. 'That's why I want you to leave. If you're here and we get money from 'Ellises, as well as our wages from 'flax mill, then he'll not want to try for work. He'll just stop here.'

Susannah started to cry. 'But I've never lived anywhere else. I'll be frightened on my own!'

'You'll be frightened if you stay,' Jane said softly. 'It'll not be easy living wi' an angry man.'

'But what about you, Aunt Jane? He'll be mad at you, and who'll help you with 'new babby?'

'I'll manage,' she said. 'Time I stood on me own two feet; and I'll get Mrs Davison to help me at 'birth like last time – if I can keep it,' she added.

Susannah wiped her eyes on the sleeve of her nightshift. 'When should I go?' she asked miserably.

'Saturday,' Jane said. 'When we collect our wages from 'mill. Instead of coming home you can set off from there. I'll reckon to Wilf that I haven't seen you since 'morning when we went to work.'

'Will he believe you?' She snuffled. 'Suppose he comes to look for me?'

'He won't,' Jane said. 'He won't be suspicious, not straight away. And besides, like I say, you're nowt to do wi' him. He's telled you that already, hasn't he?'

Susannah got back into bed and curled her

knees up to her chest. 'What'll I do then? When I get to Hull? Where will I stay?'

Jane leaned over her. 'You'll have your wages. You'll look for a room for 'night and then – and then . . .'

'Yes?' Susannah felt exhausted and tearful, nervous and worried. 'What then, Aunt Jane?'

There was a silence and then Jane took a heavy breath. 'I've to confess. I've not thought of what might happen next.'

Susannah woke in the early hours of the morning. She was instantly awake and her mind started buzzing with the conversation she and Jane had had. I can't run away, she decided. How can I go on my own? Where would I go? I'd only have my week's wages and they'd have to last me until I found other work. I'd have to say I was older than I was. I suppose I could go into service like Jane did, but who would recommend me? If only I had my sovereign. That would have lasted a long time. I wonder if Wilf's spent it. But where would he have spent it? Innkeeper would be suspicious if he had such a large sum.

She got quietly out of bed so as not to disturb Jane and padded into the kitchen as an idea took hold. Behind the door were shawls and scarves, and a jacket and a coat belonging to Wilf, which he sometimes left here. She patted the pockets but they appeared to be empty. Then she took down the coat from the hook and looked inside in case there was a hidden pocket. Uncle Ben had had a coat with an inside pocket where he used to keep his pipe and a wad of tobacco.

There was! But it was empty. She put her hand inside and found a hole in the lining. She put her fingers further and further down inside the lining until she came to the coat hem where she clutched hold of something hard. She drew it up. Her sovereign! She could take it back and use it.

But suppose Wilf came back during the week and checked to see if it was still there? Susannah pondered uneasily. Come to think of it, the last time he had come, he had fished around in the coat as if he was looking for something. She put the sovereign back in the pocket and shook the coat until the coin fell down to the hem again. I'll leave it there until my last day here, she thought. And then I'll take it out again. He won't be here on Saturday morning when we set off for work.

She climbed back into bed, but she didn't sleep. She felt scared yet excited. She'd never travelled very far, though she remembered going to the sea. Uncle Ben had taken her and Thomas one Sunday when they were little. They'd walked some of the way on the road but had then cut down to the Humber bank at Skeffling and walked alongside the river. Susannah's legs had ached; the bank was narrow and muddy and she had difficulty keeping her feet. Uncle Ben explained that the road leading into the village of

261

Kilnsea was all but washed away and that many of the houses had fallen into the sea.

When they came into the village he saw how tired she was and they stopped at the inn where he'd bought them lemonade and a slice of plum cake and had a glass of ale for himself. Then they'd continued along the sandy promontory towards Spurn Point, where they stood on the very edge of the grassy bank of the peninsula and saw the river on one side and the sea on the other. She and Thomas had rushed down to the seaside and jumped about dodging the waves and throwing pebbles. When they returned home to Welwick, Uncle Ben had had to carry her on his back for she could walk no further. She remembered it as such a happy day.

The furthest she had been inland was to Patrington. She had never visited the market town of Hedon, or Hull which her teacher had told her was a busy port with many foreign ships. Miss will be wondering where I am, she thought. She was relying on me to help with the other bairns. I'll ask Jane to tell her I can't come any more.

At the beginning of the week, whilst going to and from work, Susannah deliberated on her situation. She took particular note of the carriers who went through Patrington, including one from Welwick, and of their destination, and of the farm waggons which stopped at the mill when the workers left and gave some of the women a

262

lift. She asked one young woman whom she had seen climbing into a waggon where she lived.

'Ottringham,' she said, naming a village a few miles further west. 'I've been lucky to get this job. There's nowt much to do in Ottringham unless you want to be in service. And I don't.'

Another girl chipped in that she had even further to come as she lived in Thorngumbald. 'I walk from there to Ottringham and get a lift on 'same waggon as Mary here. We pay 'waggon lad at 'end of 'week when we get our wages.'

'Does he go on to Hedon, do you know?' Susannah asked; she had worked out that she could get another carrier from that town into Hull. 'I need to go at the end of the week. I've to visit a sick auntie,' she added.

'Not after he's dropped us he doesn't,' Mary replied. 'He goes back to 'farm. You'd have to catch carrier from Easington. He comes past here for Hedon, but he doesn't run on a Sat'day. Tuesdays and Fridays he runs, so you'd have to tek 'day off; unless you walk.'

The next morning, Thursday, after she and Jane had parted company for their different jobs, Susannah went into the mill office. 'I need to take some time off,' she told the clerk. 'Tomorrow and Saturday.'

'You'll lose wages,' he told her.

'I know,' she said. 'But it can't be helped. I've to see a sick relative.'

263

'Oh!' He frowned, scrutinizing her. 'Can you come in tomorrow morning? Just for an hour, I mean.'

She hesitated as he winked at her. 'Y-yes,' she said. 'I can.'

'Right,' he murmured. 'Come in as usual, then come and see me at about eight o'clock. I'll have your wages ready.'

'Thank you,' she said. 'Thank you very much.'

That night in bed, she waited until she thought Jane would be asleep. Then she got out of bed and took the sovereign from Wilf's coat pocket and put it in her own cotton purse, which she kept fastened on the strings of her petticoat. She took paper and pencil out of a drawer and began to write two letters, both for Jane.

Dear Aunt Jane,

This is for you to read and then burn before anyone else sees it. I've decided that if I'm going to leave I'd better go on Friday. That way we won't get upset at parting from each other and you won't know where I've gone if anyone should ask. I hope we'll see each other again for I know I'll miss you.

With respect from your loving niece,
Susannah.

PS I know that I am not really your niece, but I've always felt that you were my loving auntie.

The second letter was more formal.

Dear Aunt Jane and Mr Topham,

I've decided to leave home. I hope this is not too upsetting for you, Aunt Jane, though I know that Mr Topham won't care. I'm not happy here any more and don't want to stay. I wanted to keep on at school but Mr Topham said I had to go to work, so I'm running away to try for another life. Please don't try to find me and bring me back because I won't come.

Yours sincerely,
Susannah Page.

This letter she put in an envelope which she addressed to Mr and Mrs Wilfred Topham, and then she put both letters beneath her pillow. She hardly slept that night and it seemed as if she had only just closed her eyes when Jane was waking her and saying that they would be late for work if they didn't hurry.

'We'll talk as we're going, Susannah,' Jane said as they were getting ready to leave. 'About you running away. You don't have to go if you don't want to. I'm just being silly, I expect. But I do worry about you. Goodness,' she said, looking at her. 'Do you need all those clothes on? Are you cold?'

'Yes. I'm freezing.' Susannah gazed at her.

What should she do if Aunt Jane had changed her mind?

Jane closed the door behind them. 'I'm just so afraid of getting into trouble with 'Ellises,' she moaned. 'Wilf'll say it's my fault if Mrs Ellis finds out you've not been going to school. And he'll blame both of us and tell Mr Ellis that we must have spent 'money and that he knew nowt about it. He'll plead ignorance. I know him.' She linked her arm into Susannah's. 'And I'm scared he'll give you a leathering like he does me.'

'Why would he, Aunt Jane? I don't have anything much to do with him.'

'Well, just listen to you,' she said. 'He'd be provoked just to hear you talk. He doesn't need a reason.'

'Oh!' Susannah made an instant decision. 'I've forgotten to pick up my dinner. I've left it on 'table.'

Jane had wrapped up two slices of bread and cold bacon each as always. She had put hers in her pocket and had reminded Susannah to pick hers up from the table.

'You go on,' Susannah said. 'I'll not be a minute.' She turned to race back before Jane could utter a word.

She let herself into the house and saw the parcel of food where she had deliberately left it, collected it and in its place put the letter addressed to Mr and Mrs Topham. 'There,' she said, breathing hard as she ran back to Jane. 'That didn't take long, did it?'

For the rest of the journey Susannah listened to Jane putting forward reasons why she should or should not leave home. 'I'd miss you no end, Susannah,' she told her, as they tramped along the dark uneven road. 'I don't know what I'd do without you; but on 'other hand, there must be more for you out in 'world than what we can offer. Stuck out here wi' no opportunities! My ma thought I'd have better prospects when I went to work at Ellis's, but I didn't, of course.'

Jane chewed her lip as she deliberated on life. 'So mebbe I'd have been better off stopping at home. I'd not have met *him*, at any rate. Mebbe it would best for you to stop where you are. But there again, I don't know.' She was knotted up with indecision. 'I don't want him hitting you an' neither do I want him finding out—' Abruptly she stopped her muttering.

'Finding out? Finding out what, Aunt Jane?'

'Finding – finding *fault*!' she said hastily. 'That's what I meant. Don't want him finding fault wi' us. Not you, anyway. It don't matter too much about me,' she added flatly. 'Folks have allus found fault wi' me. Even my ma.'

When they arrived at the flax mill they hung up their coats and shawls and prepared to go their separate ways, Jane to the drying room and Susannah with the other young girls to the scutching room where they collected the broken straw tow from beneath the rollers.

'Give me a kiss, Aunt Jane,' Susannah said, as Jane turned to go. 'Don't wait for me tonight. I said I'd meet one of 'other lasses and have a chat with her after work.'

'It'll be dark!' Jane said, leaning her cheek towards her. 'I'll wait for you.'

Susannah hesitated. 'Mebbe I'll see you at dinner time,' she said. 'Come back to 'lobby and we'll eat our dinner here. I'll put mine in my pocket. Will you do 'same?' She took Jane's parcel of food from her and pushed it into her coat pocket along with the letter she had written to her. She blinked her eyes and swallowed hard. Now it had come to it, she felt very miserable. Was she doing right? Her lips trembled as she watched Jane walk away. Who'll look after her if I'm not there? she wondered. Would Wilf Topham really ill-treat me if I stay? There was something else, though, she thought, some other reason why Jane wanted her to leave. Wilf is always asking me questions, and questioning Jane about me.

I can always come back, I suppose. She felt suddenly lonely and isolated. I'll have no-one to talk to. There'll be no-one who knows me. I have no mother, no father. Nobody. She squeezed her eyes tight as tears started to fall. *Whose child am I, Aunt Lol?* she recalled saying in a childish whisper. And the answer had always been the same. *Nobody's.*

At eight o'clock she presented herself at the office and asked to speak to the clerk she had seen the day before. He had her wages ready in a brown envelope. 'I can't give you Sat'day's wages,' he told her in a low voice. 'But I've included today's, seeing as you've come in.'

Susannah thanked him, collected her coat and shawls and left the mill. No-one stopped her; there were always people rushing around, coming and going, and without looking back she walked towards the main road. She hesitated there for only a moment and then turned her face away from Patrington and the bumpy road which led to Welwick and what had been home, and set off at a fast pace before she could change her mind. Halfway towards the next village she heard the rattle of wheels. She looked back and saw the carrier's cart coming towards her. She put her hand up and signalled for him to stop.

'Can you take me as far as Hedon, please?' she asked.

'Aye, jump up.' He looked at her and grinned. 'Off on a jaunt, are you?'

'Yes,' she said, close to tears. 'I am.'

CHAPTER TWENTY-FOUR

Jane waited at midday for Susannah to appear, but the time ticked on and she didn't come. The women had little time to eat their dinner and use the privy before they had to be back at their work stations, so she went to take her parcel of food from her coat pocket and found the note. She burst into tears on reading it, blaming herself for suggesting to Susannah that she should run away. 'Poor bairn,' she kept muttering. 'Poor bairn.'

She couldn't eat her food, and because she then felt unwell with hunger and stifled by the heat of the drying room she passed out and had to be taken outside to recover. There was a steady downpour of drizzle and this only increased her misery as she thought of Susannah tramping along some road, cold and wet and alone. She read the note again and then took it to the boiler room and asked one of the men there to put it in the fire.

'You don't want your husband to read it, is that it?' he said saucily.

'Yes,' she said, sniffing away her tears. 'He'd kill me if he found out.'

He took a long iron pole and pushed the note into the flames. 'There you are then,' he said, grinning at her. 'I think I deserve a kiss for that, don't you?'

His face was glistening with sweat and black with coal dust. 'If you like,' she said flatly. 'I don't mind.'

He bent to kiss her cheek. She could feel the heat emanating from him and he pinched her thin bottom with his strong fingers. 'I shan't tell if you won't,' he murmured, and she was reminded that Wilf had said the same thing when he'd first followed her into Ellis's kitchen garden.

'I won't tell,' she said. The man though brawny was short. 'He's a lot bigger than you,' she lied. 'He'd make mincemeat of us both,' and had the satisfaction of seeing him back away.

She tramped home along the long dark road, weeping with misery, saw the addressed envelope on the table, but didn't read it, ate a lonely supper and went to bed. She rose the next morning and prepared for work, leaving the letter on the table for Wilf to find when he came to collect their wages, hers and Susannah's.

He was waiting at the door when she arrived

271

home that night. 'Get inside, you!' he said viciously. 'What's going on? Where is she?'

'Susannah?' She stumbled through the door, Wilf's hand grasping her shoulder. 'She's gone to meet a friend. She said I hadn't to wait for her.'

'So what's this?' He waved the letter at her.

'What?' She pretended ignorance. 'Has 'postie been? Who's it from? We never get letters!'

''Postie hasn't brought this,' he said, thumping the table. '*She's* left it. Telling us she's run off!'

Jane simulated a gasp. 'Never!' she said. 'She never would.' She snatched the letter from him. 'What does it mean? I can't read it properly. I'm not a good reader.'

'Daft bitch!' he spat out. 'She says she's leaving home and we haven't to look for her.'

Jane laboriously spelled out some of the words. 'She says she's not happy and has dec— dec—'

'*Decided*!' he bellowed. 'That's what happens when you give bairns schooling. They start using fancy words.'

'She says that you won't care,' Jane said slowly, lifting her head to face him. 'And I don't suppose you do. Except about 'money she brings in. But I do.' She began to cry, real tears, not false ones. 'She was like a daughter to me. And now I've got nobody.'

'Now listen to me, you.' He pushed her into a chair and stood over her. 'We'll not let on that 'little bastard's gone. We'll not have her wages from 'mill now, but 'Ellises won't find out she's gone unless you tell 'em. So if by chance you should see him, you'll keep your mouth shut.' He glared at her. 'Do you hear?' He shook his fist in her face. 'You'll get this if you don't.'

She was frightened but she had to speak out. 'I'll not lie for you,' she muttered. 'I'll not go and tell him that she's gone; but if he should find out she's not been to school and comes to ask where she is . . .' She was speaking of Joseph Ellis now, not his father, but Wilf didn't know that. 'I'll have to say I don't know.'

The blow he struck across her face shattered a tooth. She could taste the blood and feel gritty pieces of enamel in her mouth. 'Everybody at work'll know I've been hit,' she mumbled.

He hauled her out of the chair and shook her. 'Think I'm bothered about what other folks think?' He punched her in the stomach and she shrieked and bent double in pain. 'They'll not see 'bruise there!' He punched her again. 'Or there.'

She retched and he let her go so that she fell to the floor. 'You've probably killed your babby,' she whimpered. 'But mebbe you don't care about that either.'

He aimed a kick at her. 'I've got bairns all over Holderness,' he yelled. 'One more or less won't make no difference to me.'

He screwed up the letter and aimed it at the

fire, and from her position on the floor she saw it fall from the grate into the hearth.

'Did you fetch your wages?' he asked roughly.

She nodded, hardly able to open her mouth, which had started to puff up. She just wanted him to leave. 'In my pocket,' she mumbled. 'Leave me summat to live on. It's all I've got.'

He gave a humourless laugh and taking the wage packet from her coat he emptied it into his hand. He tossed her a coin which rolled across the floor. 'If there's onny you, you'll not need much. And if that lass comes crawling back, she'll get a leathering. You can tell her that. I've been itching to give her 'strap and now I've got every reason.'

'She's nowt to do wi' you.' Jane struggled to sit up. 'You said that yourself. You've got no rights ower her.' Her head started to swim and she felt a slow wet trickle running down her legs. 'I'm losing 'babby,' she moaned. 'If you've any decency left at all, go fetch Mrs Davison for me. She lives down at South End.'

He walked to the door and took down his coat. 'I'll get wet,' he said. 'And I haven't got time.' He felt in the pockets, patting them, then turned the coat inside out. 'Have you been looking in my coat?' He stared accusingly at Jane, who was writhing on the floor. 'Somebody's pinched my sovereign!'

'You never had a sovereign,' she screamed out

at him, blood trickling from her mouth. 'It wasn't yours in 'first place. Go fetch Mrs Davison!'

He looked down at her, his face creased with fury, and aimed another kick with his boot which caught her on her shoulder. 'Go fetch her yoursen.'

He slammed out of the door and left her. She drew in several gasping breaths and, pulling herself up onto her hands and knees, reached out for the singed letter lying in the hearth and put it in her apron pocket. Then she crawled towards Susannah's bed and dragged herself into it, pulling the blanket over her. 'If I die,' she muttered, 'who'll care?'

CHAPTER TWENTY-FIVE

'Could you drop me in 'middle of Hedon, please?' Susannah asked the carrier.

'Aye, I can, but I'm not going straight there. I've calls to make on 'way. I'm going to 'other villages first. Winestead, Ottringham, then Keyingham and Thorngumbald. I shan't be in Hedon till well after dinner.'

'That's all right,' she said. 'I've brought my dinner with me.'

They travelled in silence and Susannah wished it would stop raining so that she could see the countryside. Everything was dark and bedraggled. The trees were leafless, the branches stark against the overcast sky, and the ditches were deep with water.

'Funny time of year for you to skive off school,' the carrier said. 'Why didn't you wait till summer? Countryside looks lovely then when 'fields are full o' corn and 'birds are singing. It's a real pleasure to come out.'

'I'm not skiving off school,' she answered. 'I'm old enough to work now and that's why I'm going to Hedon.' Then she added, 'I'm going on to Hull then. They say there're some good jobs there.'

'Oh, you don't want to go to Hull! Not a young country lass like you. Not on your own. Do you know anybody there?'

'Yes,' she lied. 'I know somebody who lives there. I thought I'd try for work in 'cotton mill.'

He shook his head. 'They don't pay well. Not as much as at Enholmes. There was a terrible accident a couple o' years back. It happened 'same day I happened to be there. Some of 'mill workers were drowned crossing over 'river Hull to go to work. Ferry tipped over. They were mainly Irish folk,' he added. 'Poor devils.' He looked sideways at her. 'What do your folks think about you going to work in Hull? Or haven't you told them?'

'I'm an orphan,' she said, and looked at him as he gave a fake cough. 'No, really I am! My mother died giving birth to me, and I don't know who my father is.'

'Left you, did he? Worthless so-and-so!' The carrier lashed out with his whip, the leather curling just above the horse's back. 'Folks don't have standards any more. So who's been looking after you? Brought up in 'orphanage, was you?'

'My great-aunt,' she said softly, and thought with tenderness of Aunt Lol. 'But she died.'

'Look,' he said, after they had travelled a few more miles and he had made several deliveries. 'You'll have missed today's carrier to Hull. And I know it's nowt to do wi' me, but if you want somewhere to stop overnight in Hedon, I could show you a place. It's an 'ostelry, but quiet and not ower run wi' drunks. Folks who keep it are very respectable; getting on in years they are, but they keep good ale and don't water it. I know they've got a spare room cos I stopped there a couple o' nights one winter when I couldn't get back to Easington cos of 'snow drifts.'

'I can't pay much,' she said hesitantly. 'I haven't got much money. That's why I've to get work as soon as I can.'

'They'll not charge a lot,' he assured her. 'Not just for a couple o' nights' lodgings. Then if you're set on going to Hull, you can catch 'carrier first thing on Monday morning. It's onny just ower eight miles on 'turnpike road, or you can go on 'old road through Preston village. Carriers go both ways.'

She thanked him for the offer and considered it whilst he was making his calls, dropping off parcels and picking up others to be delivered. She was relieved that he didn't collect any more passengers, for she thought the fewer people she met the better. She didn't want anyone else asking questions and remembering her if Wilf Topham took it into his head to search for her.

Between the hamlet of Thorngumbald and the town of Hedon lay common pasture and meadowland with little habitation, apart from the occasional farm and manor house. Susannah grew more uneasy the nearer they came to the town, worrying about what was in front of her. As they approached the outskirts, the carrier asked her what she wanted to do. 'If you want to stop with these folk I've told you about – Brewster's their name – I'll need to drop you off at 'corner.'

Susannah chewed on her finger as she gazed down the tree-lined road leading into the town. At the end of it, as if guarding the entrance to Hedon, was a noble ancient mansion.

The carrier drew up, calling 'Whoa, fella' to his horse. 'You don't really know anybody in Hull, do you?' he asked. He was an oldish man and had a lined compassionate face. 'You're onny a bairn. I don't like to think o' you wandering about on your own. Let me tek you up to 'hostelry and I'll see if they'll do a special rate for you.'

Susannah nodded. Now that she had arrived she felt frightened and unprotected, exposed to danger. She didn't know Hedon or anyone who lived there, though she had heard that it was a busy place with a town hall and a regular market every Saturday. She had also been told by her schoolteacher that it had once had a profitable haven where ships came up from the Humber, but that it was now silted up to a mere trickle.

'Yes, all right. Thank you,' she said, pressing her lips together in her anxiety. 'But you won't tell them where you picked me up or anything, will you?'

'Are you running from somebody?' he asked kindly. 'Are you in trouble?'

'I'm not in trouble,' she murmured, unsure of how much to tell him. 'But – there's a man – he takes my wages and – he's hit me and he beats Aunt Jane.'

He frowned. 'Thought you said she'd died?'

'No, not her,' she said. 'It was her mother who used to look after me who died; and Jane married this man who takes our wages, and he gives her a thrashing if she does anything he doesn't like.'

'Ah!' He meditated for a moment, and then pulling on the reins he urged the horse off the road and up a rough track which ran alongside a narrow strip of water. 'So this fellow is no relation o' yourn?'

'No!' Susannah said positively. 'So I can do what I want and I'm old enough to work, so I left!'

He whistled tunelessly through his teeth and then murmured, 'Fair enough, I suppose. You're tekking charge o' your own life.'

Her lips trembled as she agreed with him. 'Yes,' she whispered. 'I suppose I am.'

Halfway along the track they came to an old building with a brick archway. Above the arch was a painted sign of an alehouse with the name the Fleet Inn. He pulled through into a cobbled courtyard which was surrounded by dilapidated old buildings. 'Here we are,' he said, climbing down from his seat. 'Come on, I'll introduce you to 'landlady. Don't be scared. She's a grand owd lass.'

Susannah jumped down and followed slowly. Have I done right in telling him? she worried. Suppose he goes back to Patrington and tells the constable or somebody? Though if nobody reports me missing it won't matter. Aunt Jane won't; she wants me to get away from Wilf. And he won't tell – won't dare!

The carrier, who said his name was Bill, led her through a doorway into a low-ceilinged room which had pewter tankards hanging from the beams. It smelled of ale and strong tobacco, and had a fire blazing in the grate which lit up the dark corners. There were benches and wooden tables and along one wall were several ale casks. At the back of the room was a small counter and behind this was a door. The carrier rang a brass bell on the counter, and then turned to the fire, stretching his hands to warm them in front of the flames. 'They've allus got a good fire here,' he told Susannah. 'And good vittles. Come and have a warm. It's cold sitting on 'cart.'

An elderly woman appeared behind the counter in answer to the bell. She was dressed in black and wore a starched white apron over her dress and a buff-coloured pleated bonnet on her grey hair. She was very small and her back was bent. 'Didn't expect you today,' she said to the carrier. 'You don't usually call here on a Friday. Have you got summat for me?'

'No,' he said. 'Well, not exactly. I've given this young lass a lift, but she's missed 'Hull carrier so I suggested she might get a bed here till Monday morning.'

'We don't normally tek folks,' she said, peering at Susannah from dark beady eyes. 'We're not licensed for visitors. She'd best go to 'Sun. They've got more room than us.'

'Aye, but that's a busy inn and not suitable for a young lass on her own,' he persuaded her. 'She'd be safer here wi' you and Mr Brewster.'

'Safer? Is she in trouble?' She came up closer to Susannah, who was taller than she was.

'I'm not in any trouble,' Susannah replied. 'I'm going to try to find a job of work in Hull, but I can't get there until Monday.'

'Hull!' Mrs Brewster exclaimed. 'Why, you're a brave bairn if you're going to Hull on your own! I wouldn't like to do that. Is there nowt you can do in Hedon to save you going all that way?'

'I don't know,' Susannah said, considering that it was Jane who had put the thought of Hull into her head, so as to put a great distance between her and Wilf Topham. 'Perhaps there might be.'

'All right, you can stay,' Mrs Brewster told her. 'But if anybody asks, you tell 'em you're a niece. We've got dozens, so nobody'll be any 'wiser.'

The carrier left and the landlady led Susannah through the door behind the counter into a small room which was furnished with a horsehair sofa and two wooden chairs. A round mahogany table with a fringed chenille cloth and another white cloth over it was set for a meal with two knives and forks, a pewter cruet and two tin plates. A wooden clock ticked on the wall above shelves which held blue and white ware. A shiny black range held a kettle and a roasting jack, and on the floor at the side of it in a wooden box were various other accoutrements: a frying pan, a fish kettle, sieves and meat skewers.

'I'll set another place,' Mrs Brewster said. 'You'll not have had your dinner?'

'Erm.' Susannah could smell roast beef and felt hungry. 'I've had a bit of bread and bacon,' she said.

'Well, no doubt you could eat a bit more, a growing lass like you? Go through yonder and wash your hands,' she told her, nodding towards one of two doors. 'Cleanliness is next to godliness,' she said. 'You'll find 'sink through there and if you need 'privy it's across 'yard.'

Susannah dashed across the yard. She was bursting to use the privy but hadn't liked to ask the carrier to stop so that she could go behind a hedge. She opened the slatted door and saw that the wooden seat had two holes side by side just like the privy they'd had at Welwick.

She came back and pumped water into the stone sink, in a room not much bigger than a small cupboard, and washed her hands and face. She was beginning to feel more at ease now and the prospect of a hot dinner cheered her. She peeped through the other door and saw that the room behind it was slightly larger than the one with the sink in it, and had whitewashed walls and stone ledges with a butter tub, a jug of milk and a cheese dish on one, and on another a ham and a plucked chicken, both covered over with muslin cloths.

'Mr Brewster will be through in a minute,' Mrs Brewster said, when she came back to the kitchen. 'Sit yourself down. He's just rolling another barrel in. We keep 'em in one of 'old stables until we're ready for 'em. We don't use 'stables for hosses these days. Most folks from outside Hedon leave their transport at 'Sun. But I expect they'll come in by train when 'line gets here, as they say it will.'

She took the roasted beef from the side of the

fire where it had been resting, and placed it on a large platter. 'Travelling folks today expect more than we can offer at 'Fleet, though walkers come every summer, them that's walking by 'haven or going towards Spurn Point. They say it's very pleasant at Spurn. Not that I've ever been.' She took up a carving knife and fork and started to slice the meat. 'Never been out of Hedon,' she chatted. 'Lived here all my life and not once been anywhere else.' She reported this with some pride and not with any dissatisfaction. 'Been some changes though,' she went on. 'Why, I remember when I was just a little lass 'town was full o' ditches and streams and becks where us bairns used to go fishing for tiddlers and sticklebacks; but most of 'em have been filled in or rerouted, like the one that runs alongside us.'

'It's lovely at Spurn,' Susannah said. 'I went there when I was a little bairn and paddled in 'sea.'

'Did you?' Mrs Brewer said in astonishment. 'What – do you mean to say you took your boots and stockings off?'

When Susannah said that she had, she exclaimed, 'Well, I never!' in such a startled voice that Susannah laughed out loud.

Mrs Brewster looked at her as she finished carving the joint. 'What a pretty little thing you are when you laugh,' she murmured. 'Am I wrong in thinking you haven't laughed very much lately? You looked such a dowly bairn when you first came in.'

Susannah felt a mixture of emotions all coming together: the worry of leaving home, the indecision, the laughter. Suddenly she burst into tears and sobbed and sobbed.

Mrs Brewster didn't say anything at first, but let her cry whilst she fetched another plate from a cupboard, took a knife and fork from a drawer and set them on the table. Then she drew up a chair and sat beside her. 'There now,' she said softly. 'You'll feel better now that's out. If you want to tell me about it, you can, but if you don't then that's all right. As long as you haven't run off and left your ma worrying about you, you can stop here and no questions asked.'

Susannah was saved from answering by Mr Brewster's coming in. He was tall and thin with a stoop. 'Noo then,' he said in a slow manner. 'Didn't know we had company.'

'We haven't got company, Mr Brewster,' said his wife, screwing up an eye in Susannah's direction. 'This is one of your nieces.'

'Is it?' Mr Brewster took off his cap and scratched his thinning head of hair. 'Don't remember this one. What's your name, m'dear?'

Susannah wiped her eyes and snuffled. 'Susannah,' she croaked. 'Is it all right if I stop for a bit?'

CHAPTER TWENTY-SIX

The next morning Susannah woke to the sound of Mr Brewster whistling. She felt a lurch of nostalgia as she remembered how Uncle Ben used to whistle in a morning.

After they had finished their dinner yesterday, Mrs Brewster had taken her upstairs to show her where she would sleep. It was a tiny room beneath the eaves with a sloping floor and a window which overlooked the narrow strip of water. A fireplace was laid ready for lighting. On a single bed with a patchwork cover over it a black cat was curled up sleeping. It opened one eye as they came into the room and then closed it again. Susannah had squealed in delight.

'You bad cat,' Mrs Brewster exclaimed. 'Off that bed this minute!'

'Oh, please, let it stay!' Susannah pleaded. 'I don't mind at all.'

'She's not supposed to come upstairs,' Mrs

Brewster had said. 'But she allus sneaks up when I'm not looking.'

The cat had stretched and yawned and come to push its nose against Susannah's hand, and then jumped down from the bed and scurried downstairs. Susannah had hoped it would come back, but it didn't and she saw it later running down the bank of the stream.

She rose from her bed. It seemed strange not having to rush to get ready to go to the mill and she thought of Jane going off on her own and then returning later to an empty cottage. But no, it won't be empty. Wilf will be waiting for her – us. I hope he isn't angry with her when he discovers I've gone. I wonder if he will tell anybody, like Daniel or Thomas. But then she surmised that he wasn't likely to, in case Mr Ellis got word of it and wanted the school money back.

Mrs Brewster had said yesterday that she would send Mr Brewster up later to light the fire for her, but Susannah told her that she could do that herself without bothering Mr Brewster. As it got dark, Mrs Brewster had reminded her to go up and put a match to it, and there was soon a warming glow flickering round the room. She had sat back on her heels and contemplated that it was nice to have a bedroom of her own rather than a bed in the kitchen as she had had at Aunt Lol's house. She still thought of it as Aunt

Lol's house, even though strictly speaking it now belonged to Wilf.

A tiled washstand had been placed near the window and on it stood an earthenware jug with water in it, a bowl and a soap dish; underneath was a small cupboard containing a chamber pot and at the side was a rail with a clean towel hanging on it. Susannah washed her hands and face and then dressed. It was a very cosy room, she thought, and she had slept well.

Her boots clattered on the bare wooden stairs as she went down and Mrs Brewster turned from the range where she was stirring something in a saucepan. 'Good morning, m'dear,' she said. 'I hope you slept well.'

'I did, thank you,' Susannah said. 'Mrs Brewster, you haven't said how much I'll have to pay for my board and lodgings.'

'Oh, nor I did!' Mrs Brewster continued stirring the pot. 'Well, let's wait and see how much you eat, shall we? If you onny eat like a sparrow then I'll not charge as much as I will if you eat like a trencherman.' She looked up and smiled at her, her plump cheeks dimpling. 'I quite like having company,' she said. 'We don't get many folks here in 'winter.'

There was crusty bread on the table and a slab of yellow butter. Mrs Brewster set out three bowls and asked Susannah to fetch spoons and knives from the dresser drawer. Then she ladled generous helpings of gruel into the bowls. 'Go and shout Mister in, will you?' she asked. 'He's just out in 'yard.'

As Susannah called, the black cat ran in. Mr Brewster came in and washed his hands and then sat down at the table. Susannah followed suit. She was hungry. The gruel was thick and creamy and quite unlike the thin offering that Aunt Jane made for breakfast. But she was torn between eating a large helping and only eating a little so that the amount she had to pay would be small.

Mrs Brewster saw her hesitation. 'I seem to have made too much this morning,' she said. 'Eat up, m'dear. I can't abide waste and Mr Brewster never has a second helping.'

The cat meowed and jumped onto Susannah's knee. 'I think she's hungry,' she said. 'Can I save her some of my gruel?'

'You'll spoil her,' Mrs Brewster warned. 'She's a madam, that one. Mek her get down and you can give her some when you've finished.'

Susannah stroked the silky fur and lifted the cat down. They had never had a pet at Aunt Lol's. Sometimes she and Thomas fed the wild cats that hung around the garden waiting for scraps, but they were never allowed to entice them into the house.

'After we've finished breakfast' – Mrs Brewster poured honey onto her gruel and handed the jug to Susannah – 'I need to go to 'Market Place and buy a few odds and ends, and Mr Brewster needs his boots mending so I mun call at 'cobbler's.'

'And buy me a newspaper if you will, Mrs Brewster,' the old man said. 'I'd like to know about 'price o' barley. Rumour has it that there's to be an increase.'

'May I come with you?' Susannah asked. 'I could help to carry your shopping and find out what time 'carrier leaves on Monday.'

'Not staying long, then?' Mr Brewster said. 'Where did you say you lived?'

'She didn't say, Mr Brewster,' his wife replied. 'But she's going into Hull on Monday. Yes, you can come, m'dear, and I'll show you our fine town. We have our own mayor, you know, and a town hall! We've got churches and chapels, inns and schools, tanneries and brewers.' She nodded her head. 'We've even got a lamplighter to light 'gas lamps for them as likes to go out at night. Everything any single body would want. No need at all to go anywhere else.' She wrinkled her eyebrows and gazed at Susannah. 'But there we are. If you're set on travelling . . .'

'It's not that I'm set on travelling, Mrs Brewster.' Susannah scraped her bowl clean. 'But I have to find work of some kind or how else will I live?'

Mrs Brewster took the bowl from her and filled it up with more gruel. 'You seem very young to me to be going off on your own. Where will you eat and sleep after a day's work?'

Susannah looked down at her breakfast. Suddenly she had lost her appetite. 'I don't know.' Her mouth trembled. She had never before made such decisions; neither had she ever spent time alone. 'I'll have to try for lodgings, I suppose.'

'Without recommendation!' Mrs Brewster looked aghast. 'Why, you could end up in some terrible place.'

'Shouldn't be going there on your own.' Mr Brewster shook his head. 'What does your ma say about that? Who is your ma?'

'Never mind about that just now, Mr Brewster.' Mrs Brewster poured tea into a large cup and handed it to him. 'We'll have a talk a bit later on. See if we can come up wi' a solution.'

Susannah offered to wash the breakfast dishes whilst Mrs Brewster went outside to feed the hens. Mr Brewster was getting ready to go into the tavern to prepare for the customers. 'Sat'day's a busy day,' he told her. 'We have our regulars on a Sat'day. Some of 'em fetch their newspapers and stay all day. Don't know what their wives mun think.'

'I suppose if they know that they're here, they won't mind so much, Mr Brewster,' Susannah said, recalling that Aunt Lol always knew what time Uncle Ben would be home after visiting the Wheatsheaf.

She finished drying the dishes and looked

round the room to see if there was anything else she could do. But all was neat and tidy, the cushions on the wooden chairs plumped up, the rag rug in front of the fire looking as if it had been freshly shaken. She thought how different it was from home. Aunt Jane wasn't at all house-proud. She said she had scrubbed enough floors at the Ellises' to last her a lifetime. Neither could she cook. After all the years spent in the kitchens at Burstall House, the only thing Jane had learned to do was peel potatoes, scrub carrots or pod peas. Since Aunt Lol had died that was all they had eaten, apart from an occasional burnt chop.

The clock on the wall ticked steadily and Susannah glanced at it. Eight o'clock. Twenty-four hours had passed since she had collected her wages at Enholmes and walked away from all she knew and was familiar with. Suddenly she felt frightened and sat down abruptly, cradling her chin in her hands. What shall I do? I don't know if I'm brave enough to go into Hull on my own. The town will be full of seamen. My teacher said it's a busy port. What if I can't get work? Do I want to work in another mill? What if I can't find anywhere to stay? Aunt Jane, you shouldn't have told me to run away! I wouldn't have thought of it if you hadn't put the idea in my head.

She started to cry. I've got nobody, she wept.

Nobody wants me. Why did my ma have to die? Why didn't I die as well?

'What's this? Tears on a Sat'day!' Mrs Brewster bustled in. 'Most bairns are happy on a Sat'day when there's no school to go to.'

Susannah wiped her eyes with the back of her hand. 'I liked school, Mrs Brewster.' She sniffled. 'I wanted to stay on, onny – only – I wasn't allowed.'

Mrs Brewster sat down opposite and leaned towards her with her elbows on her knees. She had a chicken feather stuck in her bonnet and Susannah gave a trembling smile. 'Do you want to tell me about it?' Mrs Brewster asked gently. 'Or are you not ready yet?'

Susannah shook her head. 'Not yet,' she murmured. 'I can't.'

'All right, m'dear.' Mrs Brewster got up. 'Mebbe later?' She took off her shawl and replaced it with a black cloak from the back of the door. She picked up her umbrella and a wicker basket. 'Let's be off then. We can't sit around worriting. 'Butcher will have sold out of his best if we don't get there soon.'

The rain had eased and the sky was brightening, though a brisk wind sent clouds scudding across the sky as Susannah accompanied Mrs Brewster down the track and onto the tree-lined road which led into the town. They passed the ancient house that Susannah had seen when she'd arrived the day before and Mrs Brewster told her it was called the Old Hall and said that there was another old house called the New Hall at the other end of the street. They came into the main thoroughfare and Mrs Brewster nodded to acquaintances. 'We've got our own mayor,' she told Susannah again. 'We don't have to kowtow to anybody outside o' town. And we had members in parliament to speak for us until a few years back. But that's finished now. Took off us it was,' she said. 'Mr Brewster was most put out about it; he said there was bound to be corruption somewhere. But we've still got all of 'insignia,' she prattled on. 'Maces and seals and silver spoons and wine bowls 'n' what not. Worth a bob or two I shouldn't wonder.

'Here's where you get 'carrier,' she told Susannah as they passed the Sun Inn. 'Busiest inn in Hedon. Coaches stop here. Farmers have their meetings. Samaritans too; and town hall folk eat their dinner here.'

Susannah looked through the archway at the side of the building and saw horses, carts and gigs in the stable yard behind. She felt a fluttering in the pit of her stomach as she thought of what Monday morning might bring.

They called at the cobbler's shop to leave Mr Brewster's boots for repair and then walked across the cobbled Market Place where Mrs Brewster bought a leg of pork, a parcel of mutton chops, and some liver and kidney and brisket of beef from the butcher.

'That's a lot of meat, Mrs Brewster.' Susannah took the basket from her to carry it. She had never seen so much meat before. 'Are you expecting company?'

'Mr Brewster enjoys his meat,' she said. 'But I cook for 'customers sometimes. They like a slice o' pork with homemade pickle to go with their ale.' She tapped the side of her nose with her forefinger. 'And I've noticed that when they eat, they allus drink more.' She wagged the finger at Susannah. 'Remember that if ever you should keep an 'ostelry.

'Now then,' she said, when she had finished her shopping. She had bought a length of material, knitting needles and wool from the haberdasher's, flour and a block of salt from the grocer's. 'Let me just show you 'King.'

'The king!' Susannah gasped. 'Which king has come to Hedon?'

'He lives here,' Mrs Brewster said solemnly. 'He's lived here a long time!'

'Oh, Mrs Brewster! I know what you mean. You mean 'King of Holderness!' Susannah laughed. 'My teacher told me about that. We've got – I mean, Patrington's got 'Queen of Holderness!'

They turned a corner from the Market Place and St Augustine's church stood proudly in front of them. It does look very kingly, Susannah thought as she stared up at the square tower. It's very stately and magnificent. 'It's not at all like the Queen,' she told Mrs Brewster. 'St Patrick's church has a tall spire pointing up to the sky.'

'That must be a fine sight to see,' Mrs Brewster commented, and went on, 'We've got a national school in Hedon, so that even bairns without money can go.' She looked at Susannah. 'You could have gone if you'd been stopping.'

Susannah shook her head. 'I think I'm too old now, Mrs Brewster, but it would have been nice,' she said regretfully. 'We didn't have a national school in – in 'place where I lived.'

'That'd be Patrington, was it?' Mrs Brewster said astutely. 'Is that where you said?'

'No.' Susannah heaved a breath. She didn't like evasion. She liked things to be straight-forward. 'I worked in Patrington for a bit. I lived in one of 'villages nearby.'

'Ah!' The old lady nodded. Then she walked on past the church towards a green rise with chestnut trees set in the middle of it. 'This is where 'young folk gather on a Sunday after church or chapel,' she said. 'Everybody wears their Sunday best and has a bit of a gossip. And we get travelling theatres that put on plays and melodramas.' She pointed to a grassy ringed area. 'When I was a bairn they used to have bull baiting over yonder. But I never did like to watch that.'

They walked back towards the Market Place and Susannah fell silent. Hedon seemed like a good place to live, but what kind of work could she do? She had no experience of anything, having worked for only such a short time at Enholmes. She cast a glance round at the shops. There was everything here that anyone would want to buy, as Mrs Brewster had said. Would they take her on? she wondered. But she would still need to live somewhere and that meant paying rent.

'Drat! I've forgotten Mr Brewster's newspaper.' Mrs Brewster turned abruptly to cross the square again.

'Wait!' Susannah warned, as a horse and cart loomed towards them. Mrs Brewster staggered as her momentum was checked; she fell, dropping her parcels and putting out her hands to stop herself.

'Ooh!' she groaned as she sat in the road, holding her right wrist and with her bonnet askew. 'Oh, my word! I've done some damage here.'

The man driving the cart pulled up and dashed towards them. 'Are you all right, missis? You've took a nasty tumble.'

People began to gather round. 'I shall be all right if somebody'll just help me to my feet,' Mrs Brewster said. 'And then I'll go on my way with 'help of my young friend here. There's no need for a fuss.'

The driver and another man heaved her up, and Susannah put down the basket and brushed her muddied cloak. 'Let me take those parcels, Mrs Brewster,' she said. 'I can carry them.'

Mrs Brewster tottered towards the Dog and Duck Inn, and leaned against the wall. She had gone quite pale. 'I hope nobody thinks I've been drinking in here,' she muttered. 'By!' She winced, holding her wrist and drawing in a breath. 'It don't half hurt.'

'We'd best get back,' Susannah said anxiously. 'Can you manage to walk or would you like to sit down for a bit?'

'Nowt wrong wi' me legs,' she said weakly. 'But I could do wi' a cup o' tea. Help me along to 'Sun, there's a good lass. I know 'landlady in there. She'll mek me a pot, I know.'

Mrs Brewster clutched Susannah's arm as they went back up St Augustine's Gate towards the inn, going through the archway and into the courtyard. The Sun was a long building with several stables and coach houses at the back of it. They stepped inside the door into a dark corridor with several doors leading off it. A woman came out of one of them and greeted them.

'Maggie!' Mrs Brewster panted. 'I've took a fall. Mek us a pot o' tea, will you? This is Susannah,' she added. 'One of Mr Brewster's nieces.'

Maggie acknowledged Susannah and then

gently took hold of Mrs Brewster's wrist, which was set at a crooked angle and starting to swell. 'Well,' she said. 'I reckon it's broke. Come in, come in.'

She led them into a long room and towards the fire at the end of it. 'Sit down, mek yourself comfy and I'll brew you a pot o' strong tea.' She raised her eyebrows at Susannah. 'What a good thing you was here,' she said. 'Your auntie's going to be glad of all 'help she can get. She's not going to be able to use that hand for a bit, that's for sure.'

CHAPTER TWENTY-SEVEN

Mrs Brewster was very shaky when they arrived back at the Fleet Inn and they were both cold and wet for it had started to drizzle with rain as they walked back. Susannah helped her take off her cloak and boots, and brought her a footstool so that she could rest. Then she filled the kettle and hooked it over the fire to make another pot of tea, for the old lady said she was ready for a home brew. 'Just slip into 'taproom and tell Mr Brewster I'll be a bit late with his dinner today,' she said weakly. 'He'll have his nose in 'air expecting to smell his pork cooking.' She gave a great heave of breath. 'I don't think I've 'energy to cook at 'minute.'

'I've never cooked a joint of meat, Mrs Brewster,' Susannah told her, 'but I could cook mutton chops or liver if you tell me where you keep your pans and everything.'

'Could you?' Mrs Brewster grimaced from the pain in her wrist. 'Well, that would be right

301

grand, and it wouldn't matter for once if we didn't have a joint to cut at. We could have pork tomorrow instead.' She sat back, looking more relaxed. 'Yes, that would do very nicely.'

Susannah made the tea and poured her a strong cup, and then went to find Mr Brewster who was in the taproom talking to two customers.

'Who's this fine young lass then?' one of them said. 'This isn't a Hedon bairn.'

'My niece,' Mr Brewster said. 'Come to call on us, she has.'

'Well that's grand,' said the other man. 'How do, miss?'

'I'm well, thank you, sir.' Susannah dipped her knee, and then turned to Mr Brewster. 'Could you just step into 'kitchen for a minute, Mr – Uncle Brewster? You're needed in there for something.'

Mr Brewster shook his head and winked at his companions. 'Never any peace,' he said. 'These women are allus wantin' summat or other.'

'That they are.' The men laughed. 'That's why we're here in 'Fleet, out of 'way.'

Susannah led the way into the kitchen and at the door turned to Mr Brewster with a whisper. 'Mrs Brewster's had a fall. We think she's broken her wrist. She's a bit shaken up.'

'Oh dearie, dearie me! That'll put 'cat among 'pigeons. She'll not like that.' Mr Brewster tutted. 'She'll not like to be put out of her routine.' He followed Susannah into the kitchen and surveyed his wife. 'Now then, me deario, whatever have you been up to?' He tenderly lifted her limp and swollen wrist. 'I'll get you some comfrey for that. Soon have you right as ninepence.'

'It'll take more than comfrey,' Mrs Brewster replied. 'I reckon it's broke. But there, nature'll mend it sooner or later. Susannah,' she said, 'do you know 'willow tree? What it looks like?'

'Yes.' Susannah stood in front of her. 'Would you like me to strip some bark?'

'Aye, I would. Mebbe it'll kill 'pain, for it's hurting no end.'

'Aunt Lol used to wrap our knees with comfrey if ever we fell and hurt ourselves,' Susannah said without thinking. 'And she used to chew willow bark if she had a headache. Where will I find it?'

Mrs Brewster reflectively studied her. 'Alongside 'little stream you'll see some willows, and comfrey grows at 'bottom of 'garden, near to where 'chickens are scratching. You might have to search around to find it cos winter rain will have knocked it back. If you can't find any I've got some dried leaves in 'cupboard, but fresh is best.'

Susannah put on her shawl again, took a sharp knife from the drawer and went outside. The garden at the side of the inn ran alongside the narrow beck. Chickens scratched about in the long grass and a nanny goat was tethered by a thick rope to a stake in the ground. It bleated plaintively at her as she approached and she murmured soothing words to it. The willow trees hung leafless fragile branches over the water and with the knife she carefully peeled a long strip of bark from the trunk of one of them and put it in her pocket. The comfrey was more difficult to find as there were no flowers to identify it, but eventually she found several of the leaves, flattened as Mrs Brewster had said, and lying close to the ground.

She straightened up and looked along the beck. Was this the water that ran into what had once been the port of Hedon? She understood that ships still came into the haven, but that they had to be quick to unload their cargo before the tide turned and left them stranded. It's very narrow, she thought. It seems hardly wide enough to take even a small boat. Perhaps I'll take a walk down there and have a look when the weather is better.

She stopped mid-thought. But I won't be here! She swallowed, feeling miserable. Tomorrow is my last day. I have to leave on Monday.

On returning to the house, Susannah put the comfrey leaves in a basin and poured boiling water over them. Then, taking a pair of wooden tongs which she had found in a drawer where Mrs Brewster had said they would be, she lifted the leaves out, drained them, wrapped them in a clean cloth and carefully placed the dressing round Mrs Brewster's broken wrist. 'There,' she said jubilantly. 'That's what Aunt Lol used to do.' Then she washed the willow bark and gave a piece to Mrs Brewster to chew on.

Mr Brewster went back to tend his customers and the old lady's jaws moved rhythmically as she masticated the bark, watching closely as Susannah prepared the midday meal to her instructions. She put chopped onions in a meat pan with a knob of beef dripping, and then placed the mutton chops on top of them with stems of rosemary scattered over, and put the pan in the oven.

'There's a few apples left over from 'autumn crop in yon stable, if you'd care to fetch 'em,' Mrs Brewster said. 'They'd go real nice with that mutton. You'll have to pick 'em over, for they're all but finished. Then you can put 'rest out for 'hens.'

'All right.' Susannah smiled at her. She was enjoying herself, feeling useful as Mrs Brewster sat nursing her wrist. She ran across the yard and found the box of apples on a shelf in the stable, which was filled with spades and forks and wheelbarrows and all things to do with gardening. The brick walls were cracked and broken, with fat cushions of dark green moss growing through them and ivy spiralling down from the pantiled roof. Lacy cobwebs brushed against her hair.

'Let 'meat cook for a bit,' Mrs Brewster said when she returned with four large bruised apples. 'Then chop up 'apples and add to it. It makes a lovely taste.'

'Does this dish we're cooking have a name?' Susannah asked, as she peeled the fruit.

'Well, I call it squab pie, which is what my mother called it, but don't ask me why, cos I don't know. Now,' Mrs Brewster said. 'Come and sit here by me while 'dinner's cooking. I want to talk to you.'

Susannah pulled up another chair by the fire and gazed wide-eyed at Mrs Brewster. Was she going to tell her how much her bed and board would be, or say that she'd have to leave as she couldn't manage with a visitor, now that she'd broken her wrist?

'Mr Brewster and me have had a little talk,' she began, 'while you were out in 'garden looking for 'comfrey. He said as you'd not be able to find it cos you were just a bairn and wouldn't know one bit o' green from another. And I said that you were a country lass and would know it.' She gave a satisfied smile and added, 'And you did.

'But what we thought,' she continued, 'if you were willing, that is – we would ask you if you'd like to stop on here for a bit, if you're not in too much of a hurry to go into Hull.' A smile lifted Susannah's mouth and her eyes began to sparkle, and Mrs Brewster went on, 'You've proved an asset today, no doubt about it, but there's just one thing I must ask you first.'

'Yes?' Susannah said anxiously.

'I need to know what happened to you. I want you to give me 'reason why you're on your own, just so that I'm sure that there's nobody frettin' over your disappearance.'

Tears started to gather in Susannah's eyes. 'Nobody's fretting over me, Mrs Brewster. I'm an orphan and only Aunt Jane knows I'm gone, and it was her idea. She said I should leave home to get away from Wilf Topham.'

'What! Is this a grown woman who suggested that?' Mrs Brewster appeared horrified at the very idea. 'And who is this Wilf Topham?'

'He's Aunt Jane's husband and he's a bully and hits her. She was afraid that he might start hitting me; he did once.' Susannah paused. 'But Aunt Jane doesn't really know how to look after anybody, especially children,' she explained. 'She's not – not . . .' She hesitated, not wanting to be disloyal to Jane. 'Well, she doesn't really know how to go about things.'

'You mean she's not right sharp, is that it?'

Susannah nodded, pulling a wry mouth. 'Yes. Aunt Lol used to do everything for all of us before she died.' The tears which had been hovering started to cascade down her cheeks. 'And I really do miss her.'

'There, there, m'dear. Don't cry. So you've no

307

ma or da worrying over you? Onny this Aunt Jane who said you ought to run away?'

Susannah nodded again, snuffling away her tears. 'Aunt Jane's got brothers and sisters. Thomas is 'youngest and used to be my best friend, onny now he's a farm lad we don't see him; and Wilf said I had to leave school and go to work cos he wasn't going to keep me.' She didn't mention the school money which Mrs Ellis had paid and which Wilf had kept, because it was all so complicated. 'So nobody will be bothered about me or where I am.' She began to weep again, feeling very sorry for herself.

Mrs Brewster sat silently watching her, shaking her head and pressing her lips together. Then she said gently, 'Well it seems to me that this is very timely. You need somewhere to bide awhile, I need somebody to help me out in 'house now I've got this broken wrist, and Mr Brewster and me are allus glad of a bit o' company. So what do you think; would you like to stop here wi' us? You'd be safe enough, and if this Wilf fellow should come lookin' for you, then Mr Brewster'd tek his shotgun to him.'

Susannah gave a snorting laugh at the thought of old Mr Brewster chasing off Wilf Topham. That she would like to see. She dried her eyes and with a trembling mouth she said, 'Yes please, Mrs Brewster. I would like to stay, but what would I do about paying you? I've only got a bit of money.' She suddenly remembered the sovereign. 'I've got a sovereign!' she said. 'Someone gave it to me last year for my birthday.'

'Somebody gave you a sovereign!' Mrs Brewster said, astonished. 'My word! So there's somebody who cares enough about you to give you such a tidy sum!'

'No!' Susannah gave a watery smile. 'No, he's very rich, I think. He gave Thomas something too, only he spent his and Aunt Lol said she'd keep mine safe for something special.'

'Well, you keep it for a bit longer, m'dear,' the old lady said. 'There might come a time when you really need it. But I don't want any money from you. If you help me out as I suggest, that'll pay for your bed and board, and then, well, we'll see what comes after.' She smiled fondly at Susannah. 'We won't look too far ahead into 'future. We'll let it look after itself. Now then,' she said. 'How do you think them chops are doing?'

CHAPTER TWENTY-EIGHT

As Mrs Marston had suggested last year, Joseph had deliberately stayed away from Welwick on Susannah's birthday; as she had pointed out, his presence every birthday would be awkward to explain as Susannah grew up.

It had been difficult for him. He wanted to see the child, even though it exposed painful old wounds each time he saw her. She was unlike her mother, with fairer skin and light hair. More like me, he had thought each time he had previously visited, though she has a gentler nature than mine. But now he was on his way there, riding through a dark and stormy evening and telling himself that he was only visiting in order to ascertain how she was coping since her great-aunt had died.

Mrs Topham is a poor stick, he mused. I can't think that she has the capability to look after a growing child, and into his head again came the plan, which came so often, that he would at last tell his wife about Susannah and say that he wanted to bring her home to grow up with their three sons, Austin the eldest and twins Philip and Matthew.

Arlette will not agree to her coming, that I know, he mused; yet it should hardly concern her as she spends so little time in Holderness, running across to France on the slightest pretext and taking Austin with her, even though she knows I want him here. How will he ever understand farming when they are forever gallivanting in Paris?

Father will object, of course, as he will not speak of the matter and still has the ridiculous notion that it must be kept from Julia. He pondered on how his sister had been kept in the dark all these years, as his parents had considered the subject of Susannah far too outrageous for her delicate maidenly ears. But it is no longer their concern. I must consider my daughter; her life is what matters, and . . . He paused before dismounting outside the Tophams' cottage. I must confess that I would draw comfort from her presence, and perhaps at last I might accept that my dearest love has gone from me for ever.

He gave a sharp rap on the door and waited. There was no light showing from the window and no sound from inside. He knocked again. Perhaps Mrs Topham is at work. But Susannah should be home from school at this time. He

311

peered in the rain-spattered window but could see nothing. He hit the door harder and thought he heard a shuffling sound inside. 'Mrs Topham,' he called, though not too loudly so as not to disturb the neighbours. 'It's Joseph Ellis.'

He heard the sound of a bolt being drawn back and the door opened a crack. A pale face peered through at him. 'I can't let you in,' a voice rasped. 'I'm sick.'

He stood back a pace. 'Mrs Topham! What's wrong? Do you have an infection?'

'No,' she whispered. 'None that you can catch.'

'Then let me in! Where's Susannah?'

There was no reply. Then the door slowly opened, revealing Jane Topham in an appalling state. Her swollen face was bruised and yellow, her lips were so distended that she could hardly open them, and the clothing beneath her shabby shawl was bloodstained.

'Whatever has happened?' Joseph stared in horror. 'Have you had an accident?' He came inside the room. 'Who's looking after you? Mrs Topham!' he exclaimed as comprehension dawned. 'Who's done this to you? And for God's sake, where is Susannah?'

'Safe,' she mumbled. 'I sent her away.' Her dull eyes looked away from him. 'Sorry. Must sit down.' She held her hands to her ribs as she staggered towards the bed in the corner and he saw the stained bedding, and that there was no fire. He tried not to take a breath for the room stank, more foul and rank than any midden.

'Who's responsible for this? Have you seen a doctor?' She gave him a reproachful glance. No, of course not; people like her didn't use doctors. He recalled with sudden painful clarity Mary-Ellen's refusal of a doctor when she had begun in labour.

'Has your husband done this?' He saw her reluctant nod. 'Has he harmed Susannah?' I'll kill him if he's touched a hair of her head, he silently raged. 'Where is she?'

She lifted her hand and shook it. 'Wait!' she muttered, and he realized that she was having difficulty in speaking because of her sore mouth. 'My teeth are broken.' She tenderly touched her chin. 'And my jaw, I think.' Tears started to flow down her face. 'He kicked me and – I lost 'babby I was carrying. I've been – on my own.' She pointed towards the wall. 'Couldn't mek anybody hear.'

'Will your neighbour come in if I fetch her?'

'Mrs Davison from South End. She'll come.' Jane spoke through swollen lips. 'Don't tell Wilf I told you.' Her voice trembled. 'He'll come back again if you do.'

'Not if he's locked up, he won't!' Joseph retorted. 'I'm going to inform the Welwick constable, and then I'll ask the doctor to call. He'll give evidence on how you've been abused.'

313

'Such shame.' Jane wept. 'What would my ma think?'

Joseph bent towards her. 'She'd think you were better off without him! Don't worry about him coming back. I'll send a locksmith with a new door bolt and chain to keep him out, but he'll be in jail so you'll be quite safe. Now,' he said softly. 'Tell me where Susannah has gone.'

She gave him a garbled account of Susannah's having run away, and showed him the letter she had written, yet somehow he understood that Jane herself had suggested that she should leave. He said angrily that she should have sent for him, but realized after his outburst that she was too afraid of Topham to do that. Then she told him that her husband had taken the money meant for Susannah and had made her go to work at Enholmes mill.

'And you say that she's gone to Hull? But when was this? How long has she been gone?'

She seemed unsure. She had been too ill to notice the time passing. 'It was a Sat'day, I know that,' she pondered. 'No, I think it was a Friday. Yes, it was Friday, cos I pretended to Wilf that she'd gone 'following day when I got home from work.'

Good God, he thought, and today is Thursday! She could be anywhere, and this poor woman could have died in that time.

'Go back to bed, Mrs Topham, and I'll fetch

Mrs Davison,' he said. 'Don't worry about the expense if there is any. I'll see to that, and I'll put the other matters in hand. Ask Mrs Davison to stay with you until the doctor comes.'

He saw the grateful relief on her face and she mouthed 'thank you'.

How do I set about finding Susannah? He worried as he rode home. He'd asked the constable to call on Jane Topham and given him permission to come to the estate and arrest her husband; if he was still there, that was. Joseph had told his father that he didn't want to keep Topham on after Martinmas. Arriving at Burstall House, he sent for Jack Terrison and asked him if he would call on Jane Topham the next day.

'You're a friend of the family, aren't you?' he asked, and when Terrison replied in an uncertain manner that he had known them for some time he said, 'Ascertain if there's anything she requires, will you? She's had some trouble with her husband, but don't tell Topham I said so. Don't let him know that I've asked you to call.'

'Can't do that anyway, sir,' Terrison said. 'I've not seen him all week. I last saw him at Sunday dinner. I've been giving 'horse lads their instructions since then.' He perked up his chin as if to proclaim that it was his right to do so.

'Why the devil didn't you come and tell me?'

Terrison shrugged. 'Mr Ellis knew, sir. Topham had collected his wages from him. He was putting it round to 'other lads that he had summat important to do and was moving on. Said he wasn't stopping in 'district.'

'And I don't suppose he mentioned his wife?'

'I wasn't there, but he told one of 'other lads that he was going to send for her when he was settled on another farm.'

Joseph gave a cynical grunt. He thought it was most unlikely, but at least she was well rid of him. But then what would she do for money?

'Well, I've put the constable on his tail,' he told Terrison. 'He's given his wife a beating which just about damn near killed her.'

Terrison looked alarmed. 'Heck! And what about 'little lass, the one she looks after? Mary-Ellen's daughter?' He looked down at his feet. 'I saw them one day; gave them a lift into Patrington.'

'Apparently she's left home,' Joseph said abruptly. 'To get away from Topham.' He cast a dubious glance at his employee. Did the man guess that he was Susannah's father? 'If you should hear – if anyone says that they've seen her, perhaps you'd let me know? She's very young to go off on her own.'

'Old enough to work, sir. When I saw her and Jane, that's where they were heading. To work at Enholmes.'

Was there scorn in his voice? Joseph wondered. If he did know about Susannah's parentage, did he think that he, Joseph Ellis, had failed in his duty towards his child? Which I have, he considered. No matter that I gave money to cover expenses and material comforts, I most decidedly have failed as a father.

He told his parents what had happened; his mother was very shocked and said he must do what he could to find out what had happened to Susannah. His father nodded and asked if Arlette knew of the child.

'No,' Joseph said. 'She doesn't. I was about to tell her.' He glanced at them both for a second, and said, 'I was on the point of bringing Susannah home – here, I mean. The woman she is with – was with – I did not consider suitable.'

His father's face went very red, and he spluttered, 'Well, just as well the child has gone. It would have been intolerable for her here; what position would she have held? Arlette would never accept her, and nor would Julia. Have you not given thought to your sister's feelings?'

'Frankly, no, I haven't,' Joseph said tersely.

His mother interrupted and spoke to her husband. 'I think, my dear, you underestimate Julia. She would be, would have been, considerate of the child.' She turned to Joseph. 'You must try to find out if she is safe, but be aware also, always supposing that you find her, that she may not want to come and live with you. You are a stranger to her, after all.'

317

That remark really hurt and he spent a sleepless night thinking of it. But the next morning, as he packed an overnight bag, he admitted to himself that his mother was right. Susannah didn't know him. She knew only the people she had lived with for the last twelve years. They were her family; he wasn't. He had left it too late.

Arlette was in France again, though she had gone alone this time and left all the boys behind. He slipped up to the top floor where they and their nursemaid had their rooms, before he left for his journey to Hull.

'Papa!' Austin piped plaintively from his bed. 'I so wanted to go to France with Mama. There's nothing to do here.'

'I want to go the hirings fair, Papa,' Philip said, and Matthew broke in, 'Me too. Me too. Janet said we might.'

'Well, you can't,' Joseph said. 'You're too young; you'll get lost in the crowd. And besides, we're not taking anyone on from the hirings this year.' He looked at his eldest son. The boy was so much like his mother; he even had her way of talking and spoke with a French accent. 'And you, Austin, must work hard at your lessons. In two years' time, when you are nine, you must be ready for school.'

Austin pouted. 'Don't want to go. Shan't go.'

'You will go and that's an end to it. Now, best behaviour, all of you. Do as Janet and Aunt Julia tell you. I have to go away for a couple of days and shall expect a good report on my return.'

Joseph left them all squabbling and then heard the maid's voice chastising them and urging them to wash and dress before breakfast. He had had his breakfast early, and left the house to cross to the stables and saddle up his horse. He could have taken one of the traps or carriages, but he always preferred to ride. He saw Jack Terrison, who seemed to have grown in stature since being told that he was to be head waggoner, and called to him.

'I'll be away for a day or two,' he said. 'There's nothing you need me for, is there?'

'No, sir, everything's fine,' Terrison said. 'I've moved young Marston from being Tommy Owt up to fifth lad. He's good wi' hosses and will make out well now that Topham's left. He allus give him 'worst jobs but he ne'er complained.'

Joseph nodded. 'You'd better get another least lad then. I wasn't going to the hirings this year, but perhaps you could choose somebody? You'll know best who'll be suitable.'

Terrison squared his shoulders. 'Aye, Mr Ellis. Just leave it to me. And I'll slip to see Jane Topham while you're away, and see if she needs owt.'

Joseph mounted his horse. At times like this he wished he still had Ebony. He wasn't usually sentimental over animals, but Ebony had been special. He had sustained some injuries and had been put out to pasture as Joseph couldn't bear to have him shot. Just occasionally he would ride him round the lanes of Holderness or down by the river bank and think of the times when he had ridden with Mary-Ellen behind him. He could swear that sometimes her presence was so close that he could feel her hair blowing against his face and the warmth of her body close to his.

He sighed. But that was then. Now he must try to find their daughter.

CHAPTER TWENTY-NINE

1856

'Aunt Brewster!' Susannah called across the yard. 'Aunt Brewster! There's a letter come for you. It looks like Mr Cannon's hand.'

Mrs Brewster came out of the hen house with a basket of warm eggs. 'Better open it then.' She huffed and puffed as she came across to the house. 'My word, but it's hot this morning.'

'Perhaps we should wash the blankets and winter curtains?' Susannah said. 'They'll soon dry in this heat.'

'Quite right,' Mrs Brewster replied. 'We generally do them in May, don't we? But no reason why we shouldn't wash them now if 'weather's going to hold.'

'It's May already,' Susannah told her. 'You said yourself that the May blossom is out.' The old lady was getting more and more forgetful.

'Aye, so I did,' she agreed. 'Well there we are

321

then. Come along, open 'letter. I know you're wanting to.'

'It's addressed to you,' Susannah said doubtfully. 'It might be private.'

'There's nothing I'll want to hide from you. It'll be from Mr Cannon, like you say. He'll be going walking to Spurn, I expect, it's that time o' year, and staying wi' town clerk.'

Susannah slit open the envelope with a kitchen knife. 'I wonder if Freddie will come with him,' she murmured, opening out the sheet. '"Dear Mrs Brewster,"' she began to read aloud. '"Once again it is the time of year when I shall take a few days' holiday in your delightful district. My son Frederick will journey with me and we shall, as before, reside with my good friend Arthur Iveson but take our supper with you, so as not to inconvenience his household. We shall require a goodly amount of meat: beef, lamb and chicken will be welcome, but not pork as it is now too late in the season. Frederick has also requested that you bake a rice pudding with nutmeg if that is convenient.

'"I trust that you and Mr Brewster are in good health,"' Susannah looked up and grinned, '"Yours sincerely, James Cannon." And Freddie is coming too,' she whooped in delight. 'I'm so pleased! I did so miss seeing him last year when he couldn't come.'

She had met Freddie Cannon in the first

spring she had spent with the Brewsters. He was thirteen and had come walking with his father. After eating their meal at the Fleet Inn, Mr Cannon had walked back to Mr Iveson's house in Hedon and Freddie had stayed behind to talk to Susannah. They'd wandered down by the beck and discussed many subjects: the estuary, the birds and the countryside.

He told her that his mother had died when he was seven, and that her best friend, a widow with a nine-year-old daughter, had come to live near them, so that the children could enjoy companionship and she could assist in his upbringing until he went away to school. 'My father says that we must always be grateful to her for her kind support,' he told her, 'and of course I am. She writes regularly to me, as does Maria.'

When he asked Susannah what relation she was to the Brewsters, she had confessed all. About being an orphan, about running away, and about Mrs Brewster's asking her to stay with them.

'They've never once suggested that I should move on, and I'm always introduced as Mr Brewster's niece,' she had told him.

He had shyly taken her hand. 'They must be really pleased to have you, Susannah,' he said softly. 'They must think of you as a daughter, or perhaps more of a granddaughter, for they are quite elderly. You'll be a great comfort to them.'

She hadn't thought of that, but only of how

grateful and secure she felt being with them. That first winter and spring, she had kept close to the house and only ever ventured into Hedon with Mrs Brewster, carrying her shopping until her broken wrist mended itself. She was afraid, though she confessed it only to herself, that Wilf Topham would come to look for her, and so she rarely went into the inn if there were strangers there, and then only after carefully glancing round to ascertain that all was safe.

The planned journey into Hull was never mentioned, and after that first Easter Mrs Brewster asked her if she would like to go to the national school. She was delighted to, and after an interview with the headmaster in which Mrs Brewster told him that Susannah was an orphan and living with them, he agreed to take her. She proved to be an apt and able scholar and stayed until she was fourteen, walking alone down the avenue of elms into the town and often returning with her school friends via the old haven where they would spend time larking around and tossing stones and chunks of wood over the bridge into the water.

Freddie and his father had come again the following year and he and Susannah picked up their friendship again, falling into it as easily and comfortably as if they had never been apart. Freddie suggested to her that it might be kind to write to her aunt Jane, to let her know that she was safe and well, and said that if she wished he would post a letter for her in Hull as he and his father journeyed back to their home in Anlaby, a village on the west side of that town. She confessed that she had been concerned that Jane might be worried about her, but had been afraid to write and give away her whereabouts with the Hedon postmark. She wrote a short message and sealing it in a brown envelope gave it to Freddie.

He and his father came each year until last year when Mr Cannon came alone, and told her that Freddie was working hard with final examinations before he went to university.

'We might not see so much of him if he's going to university,' Mrs Brewster remarked as she put the eggs into a bowl of water to wash. 'He'll have other interests, I expect, and won't want to be with his father. Young men don't. He'll want to fly his own kite.'

'He doesn't want to go into law, anyway,' Susannah said. 'He told me so. He'd like to set up a business of some kind, but Mr Cannon said it was out of the question that he should go into trade, and he must choose a profession, so Freddie said perhaps he would be a teacher.'

Mrs Brewster pulled a face and said disparagingly that she didn't know why trade was considered to be low. 'Innkeepers especially,' she grumbled. 'We have no standing whatsoever. And yet it's a living that's handed on generation after generation. Mr Brewster's father, grandfather, and great-grandfather too, were innkeepers, and before that his great-great-grandmother kept an alehouse. That's why they're called Brewster. Bet they didn't teach you that at school, did they?'

'No, they didn't!'

'Well, had it been a man, they'd have been called Brewer, but because it was a female it was Brewster, and she never married so the name was kept.'

'You mean – that she had children out of wedlock?' Susannah's voice dropped low.

'Seemingly so.' Mrs Brewster nodded. 'So don't you ever feel shame cos your poor ma didn't marry! There might have been reasons why she didn't, or why your father couldn't marry her. Don't judge what you don't know.'

Susannah thought on this. It was true she had felt some shame, especially when she was at school, and only ever said that she was an orphan, never that she hadn't known who her father was. Not even to Freddie.

She was now turned seventeen and accepted in Hedon as the orphaned niece of Mr Brewster. She felt comfortable and quite at home in this market town, and knew many people. She also worked in the inn, no longer afraid that Wilf Topham would come looking for her. She knew how to draw beer from a cask and what measure of gin to serve, though there was little call for that by the Fleet customers, being too expensive at sixpence a quart. 'It's the excise duty,' she explained, mainly to women, wives of the beer drinkers, when they complained of the price.

'I was thinking, Aunt Brewster,' she said a few days later as they were preparing food for Freddie and his father's arrival. 'Suppose we were to offer coffee or tea to the wives when they come in with the men? They don't all like gin and ale.'

'Well, 'Fleet was allus an alehouse,' Aunt Brewster commented. 'It was safer than water, you see, way back in time. And that's what we served for many a long year, straight from 'cask. Then 'owners had 'counter put in and we started selling gin, and then some of 'men off 'barges would bring in sausages for me to fry, which is why I started cooking a bit o' beef and suchlike to make them sandwiches for their dinner.' She put her fist on her hip. 'I suppose we could ask 'women if they'd like summat else instead, but it'd mean extra doings.'

Susannah pondered. Their customers were few; bargemen, wood workers and other regulars from Hedon who liked the quietness of the inn. At harvest time they were busier, when labouring men from the town went in search of work on the farms and called in on their way home to quench their thirst after a hard day in the fields. The walkers came in at all times of the year, but mostly spring and autumn, whilst the bird-watchers came in the winter, and Susannah felt that these groups of people from out of the area might prefer a pot of hot coffee or tea, rather than a glass of cold ale.

Aunt Brewster commented, 'You'd mek a good innkeeper, Susannah. You've got 'head for it, and men don't seem to mind if it's a woman running an 'ostelry. But this place is falling round our ears and 'owners don't seem to want to spend money on it. There again,' she added, 'you might want to aim higher than just running an inn. 'Schoolmaster said you could teach if you'd a mind to.'

Susannah had only occasionally given thought to the future, and rarely to the past; she had closed her mind to that and was content with her present life, but she conceded that Aunt Brewster, as she always called her now, was right; perhaps she should start thinking about what else she could do. Mr Brewster was very lame and she often helped him with the ale casks, and Mrs Brewster was quite forgetful at times and had to be reminded of tasks to be done. I couldn't think of leaving them, she mused, as she rolled pastry for a meat pie. Not when they've been so kind to me. Perhaps, though, I might discuss my future with Freddie if I get the chance.

When Freddie arrived for supper with his father that evening, she felt a great uplifting of her spirits. He gave her his shy smile, and she thought how tall and handsome he had become. He wore his sideburns long and his dark curly hair was cut to just above his collar. He gave her a polite bow and lowered his dark eyes, murmuring haltingly, 'I've so looked forward to seeing you again, Susannah. It seems such a long time since I was here.'

'I'm glad to see you, too, Freddie,' she said, and wondered if perhaps she should call him Mr Cannon, or Mr Freddie, now that he was grown up.

A table was set for Freddie and his father in a corner of the saloon. She had placed a lamp on a shelf nearby, and a small vase of bud roses in the centre of the white tablecloth. Freddie bent to smell the flowers and smiled appreciatively at Susannah. 'They're very early,' he said. 'The perfume is delightful.'

'Yes.' Susannah was pleased that he had noticed, though she doubted if his father had. He had only briefly acknowledged her. 'They're the first. They came into bloom only yesterday.' She turned to Mr Cannon. 'We managed to get some shrimps from Paull, Mr Cannon,' she said. 'Mrs Brewster has potted some. Would you care to try them? And then steak and kidney pie to follow?'

'And after that?' Freddie quizzed.

'Rice pudding with a browned nutmeg top.'

She smiled. 'Just as you requested, Mr Freddie. Or there's apple pie and custard.'

His eyebrows rose and he opened his mouth to say something, but on glancing at his father seemed to change his mind and thanked her instead.

The Fleet was busy that night, and Mrs Brewster asked Susannah to look after the Cannons whilst she helped her husband to serve the other customers. It was a fine night after a warm day and many local people had come out for a stroll along the waterway. There had also been a meeting of the Holderness Agricultural Society at the Sun Inn, and as the railway line had now come to Hedon, countrymen had arrived by train from Withernsea and surrounding villages and were sampling the ales of the many Hedon establishments.

Susannah looked up from clearing the dishes from the Cannons' table as the door opened and a group of men came in, talking and laughing loudly. Strangers to the Fleet, she thought, not recognizing any of them, and she excused herself as she manoeuvred her way through to go into the house.

One or two doffed their caps and another, younger one winked, but she pretended she hadn't seen him. She had learned when to banter and when not, and she certainly wouldn't with strangers. Another, an older man, stared at her, his mouth slightly open as if drawing a breath.

Later, she and Freddie walked beneath leafy trees on the grassy path by the stream side. He told her of his first year at university, where he was studying law. 'You've decided to follow your father's profession after all,' she said. 'Will you join him when you've finished your studies?'

'No, I don't think so, but I decided that if I studied law it would stand me in good stead for whatever else I might do. And Father thinks that I will join him in his practice, so he's quite happy at the moment.' His fingers touched hers and he grasped her hand. 'I missed seeing you last year, Susannah. It has seemed such a long time that this year I thought I might come again in the summer as well. But there's such a lot of work to do that I might have to forgo another visit.'

'Oh, I'm really sorry.' Susannah was disappointed. 'I do so look forward to seeing you.'

'Do you?' He turned towards her and gently squeezed her fingers. 'I rather hoped you would say that.' He smiled at her. 'Then I shall endeavour to come if I can.'

She gazed up at him, blushing slightly. 'During your summer holidays, could you not stay in one of the inns in Hedon and bring your work with you? Then you could work in a morning and walk in 'afternoon or evening. And,' she added shyly, 'you could eat with us. Mrs Brewster wouldn't mind and neither would she charge you very much.'

'You mean, eat with you and the Brewsters?' His expression lightened. 'In your kitchen?'

'You wouldn't want to do that, of course. I shouldn't have suggested it. I'm sorry.' She was embarrassed at her audacity.

'No. No! I think it's an excellent idea!' He was enthusiastic. 'I'd like to very much.' He pondered for a moment. 'But we won't speak of it just yet. My father is, well, a little old-fashioned, and might not approve. But I'll write and let you know when I'm coming and where I am staying, and perhaps you will ask your Aunt Brewster for her consent?'

'Her consent?' For a moment she was confused. She stared up at him, and saw he was looking at her.

He gently touched her cheek, and, with his eyes soft on hers, bent to kiss her. 'To eat in her kitchen, Susannah,' he murmured. 'Did you think I meant something else?' She lowered her eyes, but he lifted her chin so that she had to look up at him. 'It's too soon for anything else, isn't it?' he asked softly. 'We are too young.'

'Yes,' she breathed. 'We are. Much too young.'

CHAPTER THIRTY

Jack Terrison called at Welwick poorhouse and asked permission to speak to Mrs Jane Topham on a personal matter. He stood waiting in the hall of what was little more than a cottage, and thought that the building was in a dilapidated state of repair. He wouldn't like to think that any relation of his was living here. But Jane had applied to come. She couldn't afford to pay the rent on her own cottage, and neither could she obtain work.

To give Joseph Ellis his due, he pondered, he had tried to help her initially after her husband had disappeared, but she did little to improve her situation, claiming that her health was poor after suffering her last miscarriage and the beating given her by her husband. She was offered a smaller dwelling house and after applying for parish relief for maintenance found that she was still unable to manage. It was suggested that she should apply to Patrington Union workhouse as

333

she was an abandoned wife, but she refused, saying she preferred to stay in Welwick where she had been born and would live in the poorhouse even though it was falling down.

Huddled into her shawl, she tottered towards him now and he reflected that she looked a lot older than she was, with her greying hair, sunken cheeks and sallow complexion. She can't be more than thirty-one or two, he considered; she was younger than me when she started in the kitchens at Burstall House. Years of work left in her if only she would pull herself together. Maybe the news he was bringing would perk her up.

'Noo then, Jane! How 'you doing?'

She frowned at him. 'Do I know you?'

'Course you do! Jack Terrison as works at Ellis's?' He took off his hat. 'You remember me!'

'Well if you say so. From Welwick, are you?' She peered at him, but he felt that she was putting on an act for the matron who was standing behind her, listening.

'Aye. I used to be a friend o' Mary-Ellen, don't you remember?' This wasn't strictly true, but his memory denied the disappointment that he and Mary-Ellen had never been much more than acquaintances.

'That's going back a bit,' she muttered. 'She's been dead these long years.'

'I've called to talk to you about her daughter.'

He carefully spaced out his words as if she was hard of hearing. 'Can we tek a walk outside?'

'She'll not have to be long,' the matron interrupted. 'She's to help wi 'supper.'

'We've got to work, you know,' Jane grumbled as they went out of the door. 'Folks think as you do nowt living here, but it's not true.' She wagged her thumb towards the matron. 'She keeps you at it all day long. We've to earn our keep.' They stood outside the house and Jane looked up and down the quiet road. 'Nowt much happening, is there? Has anybody died or owt?'

'I expect so,' Jack said morosely. 'Folks do. I went into Hedon one day last week,' he told her. 'To a meeting. I thought I saw Mary-Ellen's daughter, Susannah. Some lass, anyway; dead spit of her, she was.'

'Not her,' Jane said. 'She ran off and went to work in Hull. She sent me a note from there some time back. Not heard owt since.'

'Did she say she was working in Hull?'

Jane shook her head. 'Didn't say much at all,' she mumbled. 'Onny that she was well and hoped as I was. Little does she know how I've suffered. I showed it to Mr Joseph,' she said, and then suddenly clamped her mouth shut.

'Why'd you do that?' Jack asked curiously.

'It was just afore I moved here to 'poorhouse. He asked me if I'd heard from Wilf or Susannah,'

335

she said slyly. 'So's he could tell 'authorities that I'd no dependants and that there was nobody to maintain me, I expect. I'm born and bred in Welwick,' she added smugly, 'so Welwick parish has to support me.'

'Well, this lass I saw in Hedon, I'd swear as it was Susannah. Serving in an inn she was, and it was just sheer luck that I happened along there wi' some other fellas.'

'You'd not know her now,' Jane pronounced. 'She'll be grown up. It's ower five years since she left.'

Jack stuck his hands in his pockets. 'Aye – well, I just thought I'd drop by and tell you,' he said. 'She looked right bonny, if it was her. She was smiling, anyway.'

Jane gazed down the road and her eyes became moist. 'Not her then. Poor bairn hardly ever smiled.' She took a breath. 'Nowt much to smile about, is there?'

Jack pondered on whether to inform Joseph Ellis that he had seen Susannah, for he was convinced that it was she, in spite of what Jane maintained. But then, why should I tell him? She's not his concern. At least, I don't think she is. He chewed over the fact that his employer had spent several days away from the farm just after Susannah had disappeared. That was when he had been promoted to waggoner and Ellis had asked him to oversee things whilst he was away. I might just drop it in, casual like, he decided. When 'opportunity is right.

The occasion occurred a week later when Joseph Ellis asked him about the meeting of the Holderness Agricultural Society, and queried if it had been beneficial.

They chatted about farming matters for a while, and then Jack added, 'Odd thing happened when I was in Hedon. After 'meeting was over, I'd time to kill before getting 'train back to Patrington, so I called in at one of 'hostelries. There was a young serving lass in there – a ringer for Susannah Page. You'll happen remember her, sir? Lived with her aunt in Welwick until a few years back? Ran away, cos of Wilf Topham. Anyway, I dropped by to see Jane Topham last week to tell her, but she reckoned it wouldn't be her as she'd gone to work in Hull.'

'Where?' Joseph Ellis said abruptly. 'Which hostelry?'

''Fleet,' Jack said, curious about the sudden change in his employer's manner. 'You'll mebbe not know it. It's tucked away alongside an old track, just off 'Thorngumbald road, near where they say 'owd Hedon Fleet used to flow till they cut Keyingham drain. I was told 'hostelry had good ale, which is why I went. And they did,' he added.

'This girl!' Joseph cleared his throat. 'If it is her, she ought to be told about her aunt.

337

They're going to pull the Welwick poorhouse down before long and she'll be transferred to Patrington.'

'Jane'll not want to go,' Jack said. 'She wants to stop in Welwick.'

'That's as maybe,' Joseph retorted. 'But she won't have any say in the matter. Anyway' – he shrugged dismissively – 'it's nothing to do with us. She's the responsibility of Welwick parish. I noticed that one of the Suffolks was walking lame,' he said, abruptly changing the subject.

'Aye, sir. He is. I've tekken him off heavy work. He's got a corn on one of his front feet. Must have had a stone wedged under his shoe. There's three of 'em due for shoeing so I've asked 'farrier to call.'

Joseph nodded. He couldn't fault Terrison's work, but he always felt uneasy with him. It's a personal thing, he mused. He always seemed to be around when I was seeing Mary-Ellen, and here he is again telling me about Susannah. Once again he wondered if Terrison had guessed at the relationship. And what if he has? he asked himself. Does it matter any more? But it did matter, for he hadn't told Arlette about Mary-Ellen or their child. After Susannah ran away, there seemed to be no point.

He had searched for her. He'd taken time away from the estate, telling his parents that he had to find her and would bring her back.

His father was relieved, he knew, when his search had proved fruitless. He had enquired at the cotton mills in Hull and spoken directly to one of the directors, Martin Newmarch, who personally looked through his list of workers to ascertain if anyone of Susannah's age had joined them. There were several, but none matched her description.

He had stayed in Hull for several days, visiting inns, hostelries and factories, for he couldn't think where else she might be employed. Finally and reluctantly, he informed the police and asked them to keep a lookout for her. They asked what relation she was to him, and when he hesitated he saw the cynicism in their expressions. 'She's an orphan,' he had explained, 'and lives with her aunt, who is worried about her.' But he knew that they would do nothing. There were more pressing matters in this busy town than a runaway girl.

But now! Hedon! Was it possible that she had been in that small market town all the time? Practically under my nose! He often visited the Hedon cattle markets; was a member of the Holderness Agricultural Society and attended the meetings held in the Sun Inn in the town, though he had never had occasion to visit the Fleet.

How can I investigate without her suspecting me? Will she recognize me after five years? She might, for I won't have changed as much as her; still, she didn't see me often, so perhaps she won't remember me. She'll be a young woman now, he thought wistfully, and no longer a child. He decided to wait a while, though instinct urged him to go immediately. He grew a beard, which like his eyebrows grew darker than his hair, and within two weeks was thick and brown and curly.

Arlette grumbled at him. 'You look so much older,' she told him. 'And like a tramp! You must cut it shorter and neater, as Frenchmen do.'

'All the more reason to grow it longer,' he protested. 'I don't want to look like a Frenchie!' He shrugged. 'It's irritating having to shave every day, but if it gets too hot I'll take it off.'

She offered him a wager that it wouldn't last more than a month and he grinned. This was probably the only bet she would ever win from him, for he had no intention of remaining bearded.

The following week he travelled into Hedon for one of the agricultural meetings, but drove in by horse and trap rather than taking the train. He crossed the bridge which ran over the water-way and glanced up it, but continued into Hedon and attended the first half of the meeting. Then he gave his apologies and left before dinner was brought in. He collected his horse from the stables and a lad brought out his trap from the cart shed. The boy hitched up for him and

340

Joseph gave him a coin for his trouble and set off for the Fleet Inn.

The rough track up which it lay was well used by wheeled traffic and by foot, and he surmised that the inn had probably been popular in the past, but had now been left behind in the growth of the town. He mused on whether it was named after the ancient Hedon Fleet, an important water boundary of the town which had flowed into the Haven Basin. He drove beneath an archway, and in a grassy area beyond the yard a young woman with her back to him was hanging washing on a line. She was of medium height and wore a plain cotton gown, and her hair was tied in the nape of her neck.

Is it her? he wondered. He ducked his head as he went through the low doorway and wrinkled his nose appreciatively at the aroma of cooking.

'Good day to you, sir.' An elderly woman greeted him. 'You've brought some good weather with you today.'

'Indeed! It's quite hot. Just the day for a glass of cool ale!' He took off his hat. His hair was long and he ran his fingers through it, glancing round as he did so and noting the polished counter and shining brassware, the scrubbed floorboards and general air of cleanliness in spite of the obvious age of the hostelry.

'You can have that and welcome.' She beamed. 'I've not seen you in here afore, sir?'

'No, you have not, though I'm often in Hedon. It was recommended that I try your excellent ale.'

'Then I'll just fetch Mr Brewster,' she said. 'He knows best how to draw it. He's just brought in a fresh cask.' She went to the door of what he assumed was their kitchen and called his name. 'He'll not be a minute, sir. Won't you tek a seat?'

'Thank you.' He sat down on a bench, with his back to a window. 'Could I by chance have something to eat? A sandwich or a piece of pie?'

'Beef sandwich or meat and tatie pie?' she said. 'Pie's fresh baked this morning.'

'Then that's what I'll have, if you please. Your own home cooking, is it? Or brought in from the baker?'

'All home cooked, sir. My niece made it,' she told him. 'She's got a right good hand for pastry. Got to be kept cool, you know.'

'Ah!' he said. 'That I didn't know.' He stretched out his legs. 'Good cooks are hard to come by, I do believe.'

Mr Brewster pulled him a tankard of ale straight from the cask and Joseph drank appreciatively. 'Excellent!' he said. 'Have you ever brewed your own?'

'Aye, a long time ago,' Mr Brewster said. 'There's no need nowadays. Plenty o' companies making good beer. There's a brewery right here in Hedon. But 'secret is in 'storing and drawing. Got to get that right.'

'Do you keep busy?' Joseph glanced towards the partly open door behind the counter. 'Trade good?'

'Aye, not bad,' Mr Brewster conceded. 'But we're a bit far out o' town and don't have amenities like 'hostelries in Hedon, though folks like to tek a walk on a fine day.'

'So, just you and your wife to manage it?' Joseph nodded. 'Good! That saves on the expense of staff.'

'Oh, we've no staff!' Mr Brewster exclaimed. 'No need of any, now we've got Susannah. She can turn her hand to most things. Even knows how to draw ale.' He grinned.

Mrs Brewster came in with his pie in a brown glazed dish brimming with thick onion gravy. She set it on a nearby table. 'Your Susannah's obviously a pearl if she can bake a pie like this *and* pull a glass of ale,' Joseph said heartily, and licked his lips as the aroma hit his nostrils.

'That she is,' Mrs Brewster said. 'Don't know how we ever managed wi'out her.'

He ate the pie and finished his drink, but the girl didn't appear, and eventually he rose from the table and tapped on the counter to pay. Mrs Brewster bustled in.

'Trust all was in order, sir.'

'It was excellent,' he said. 'My compliments to your niece.'

'I'll tell her, sir.' Mrs Brewster beamed. 'She's busy at 'minute, washing everything she can lay her hands on while 'weather's good.'

He smiled and, complimenting her once more, said goodbye. He put on his hat and went out, disappointed that he hadn't been able to see the girl. But it couldn't be his Susannah, if they said she was a niece. It was just a coincidence. Terrison must have heard her name and mistakenly put two and two together.

The door into the private part of the house gave onto the courtyard. It was propped open and he could hear someone singing. He climbed into the trap and was about to shake the reins to move off when the girl came out of the door. She had a wash basket balanced on her hip and she looked across towards him and smiled.

He put his hand to his head, his arm shielding half of his face. He raised his hat but didn't remove it completely. His heart thudded. It was Susannah.

CHAPTER THIRTY-ONE

Two months later, Mr and Mrs Brewster received a letter from Mr Watson, a Hedon solicitor, asking if they would be good enough to call and see him at their convenience, but suggesting a time and day.

'Why ever does he want to see us, Mr Brewster?' Mrs Brewster said on reading it. 'We've nowt to discuss with any lawyer, and especially not him, for he's not a Hedon man. He's from Preston!'

Mr Brewster shook his head, quite perplexed.

'Perhaps it's something to do with one of your nieces?' Susannah suggested. 'A reference required or something like that.'

'Bless you, child.' Aunt Brewster chuckled. 'We don't have any nieces. It was just a little joke we used to have if anyone wanted to come and stay. At one time, you see, tavern keepers weren't allowed to have guests to stay overnight, but 'licensing laws have been changed since then.

Not that we've got room now that you're living with us.'

'You mean to say that you've no nieces at all?' Susannah said, astonished.

'Onny you, m'dear.' The old lady smiled and Uncle Brewster nodded in agreement.

Susannah laughed. 'But I'm not really your niece!'

'As good as,' Aunt Brewster said. 'We couldn't wish for better.'

'You're so good to me,' Susannah said in a sudden flurry of emotion. 'I really feel as if you are my aunt and uncle.'

Uncle Brewster patted her head as he passed her. 'I thought we were! Anyway, can you cope on your own here if we go to see this lawyer fella? We'd best see what it's about.'

She said she could and a few days later Mr and Mrs Brewster set out for the solicitor's office. Mrs Brewster wore her Sunday bonnet and coat, and Mr Brewster was spruced up in his cord breeches and a tweed jacket which he told Susannah was brand new.

'That it is,' his wife said. 'Thirty years ago. I well remember us choosing 'cloth, and 'tailor cutting it to fit. It's done you proud, Mr Brewster; you must have worn it all of three times.'

'Aye, and this'll be 'fourth,' he said. 'I'll be wearing it out at this rate.'

Freddie called to see her whilst they were out.

He had done as Susannah had suggested, and had come to stay at the Sun Inn where he worked on his books every morning and took a walk every afternoon. Susannah joined him whenever she felt able to without inconveniencing the Brewsters.

'I can't come out today, Freddie,' she told him. 'I'm in sole charge! Uncle and Aunt Brewster have gone out on some kind of legal business.'

'Then I'll stay and talk to you until they come back,' he said. 'Perhaps they're making a will, and leaving everything to you.'

'No,' she said, amused. 'I don't think they have anything much, though I've only just learned that they don't have any nieces after all! They've no living relatives left.'

'So there you are.' He smiled. 'That's what they are doing.'

'No,' she said again. 'Mr Watson wrote to them, asking them to call.'

'Mr Watson? William Watson? He took over Mr Iveson's practice. My father knows him.'

'Aunt Brewster says he's not a Hedon man, he's from 'village of Preston, so she doesn't want to deal with him.' Susannah laughed.

Several farm labourers came in for ale and a plate of beef and bread and Susannah served them whilst Freddie sat in a corner with a book in his hand. She made a pot of coffee and gave a

347

cup to Freddie, and then some people came in who said they were walking down to the Haven and on to the riverside village of Paull. The men asked for ale but the women, smelling the coffee, asked if they might have that and a ham sandwich.

When they had gone and there was just a solitary local man left, Freddie complimented Susannah. 'You would do very well running an inn or an hotel,' he said. 'You're quick and efficient, and it seems that nothing is too much trouble for you.'

'I enjoy it,' she said. 'As a matter of fact, Aunt Brewster said 'same thing: that I'd make an innkeeper. What do you think, Freddie? When the Brewsters leave here – and there'll come a time when they'll be too old to run the Fleet – I shall have to think of my future and what kind of work I should do.'

He gazed at her for a moment, and then anxiously chewed on his lip. 'I – erm, it won't be for ages, though, will it?' He caught hold of her hand, and, conscious of the lone drinker, whispered, 'You wouldn't go far away, would you, Susannah? I couldn't bear to think you would leave the area.'

She too glanced at the other occupant, a regular, steadily drinking from his tankard and reading a newspaper. She gave a little shrug. 'I'd have to go where there was work. I've been so lucky—' She broke off, interrupted by the Brewsters' returning. 'Is everything all right?' she asked.

'Yes. Yes.' They both seemed rather flustered. 'It's, erm, a bit complicated like,' Mr Brewster said. 'We've a few things to think on.'

They both went off to change their clothes, but Mrs Brewster came back within a minute to ask Freddie, 'Will your pa be coming to join you, Mr Freddie?'

'In a day or two, yes, he said he would.'

'Good.' Mrs Brewster looked relieved. 'We might want a word wi' him about summat.'

Later that afternoon, Susannah and Freddie went for a walk. He put his arm round her waist and she did the same with him. 'Susannah,' he said, after a few minutes' silence. 'I shall be at university for a few years yet, and dependent on my father. But I wanted to tell you how much I care for you – have always cared for you.'

She looked up at him, 'I know,' she said, smiling. 'And I care for you too, Freddie.'

He squeezed her closer. 'And when you said about looking for work elsewhere and I thought of losing you—'

'It wouldn't be for ages,' she said softly. 'But I can't depend on 'Brewsters for ever. They're old and I have no-one else. I have to look to my own future – there's no-one else to do it for me. No father, no mother.'

'I'd like to look after you, Susannah,' he said. 'I do love you.'

'Do you?' she said, gazing at him. 'Really?'

'Yes,' he said fondly. 'Really.'

'I don't think anyone's ever loved me before.' Tears sprang unbidden to her eyes. 'At least, no-one has ever said that they did. I suppose my mother would have done, but she died giving birth to me, and perhaps Aunt Lol did, but she wouldn't have said so.'

'What about your father?' he asked. 'Do you remember him? What happened to him?'

She shook her head. 'I don't know who he is or was. He might still be alive for all I know, but if he is, then he doesn't want to know about his daughter.'

'Scoundrel!' Freddie exclaimed. 'How could he be so unfeeling? If I had children I would always cherish and protect them.'

She smiled tenderly. 'I'm sure you would, Freddie, but then you are so kind-hearted.'

'It leads me into trouble sometimes,' he admitted. 'I don't like to hurt anyone, and – well, I'm having a little trouble with Maria. You remember, the daughter of my mother's friend?'

'Yes, I remember you telling me about her.'

'Well, she's very possessive,' he said with a sour expression. 'And she always expects that I'll fall in with her plans. You've no idea what a fuss she made when I said I was coming to Hedon to study. She complained to her mother and then to my *father* and said how inconsiderate I was, and that I should have been spending time with her as she hadn't seen me during term time.'

They stopped to watch a kingfisher on the bank and then continued walking. 'She has this idea that she and I – well, it's her mother's fault really, as she told Maria that when we were small my mother and she used to plan that Maria and I would wed! I've told her that it's nonsense, of course, but she will keep on about it.'

Susannah felt a cold shiver run down her spine. 'So, are you promised to her?' she whispered.

'No!' he said vehemently. 'I am not. But she thinks I am! How can I get out of this position, Susannah? Without hurting her, I mean?'

'I don't know,' she murmured. 'Could you not speak to her mother, or your father – explain to them that you've no wish to marry her?'

'Not to her mother!' he said. 'She frightens me to death! When I was young I was glad to go away to school just to be away from her. She's so domineering, and I'm afraid that Maria will turn out to be the same.'

'You must be strong, Freddie,' Susannah said gently. 'Speak to your father and tell him that you don't want to marry Maria, and perhaps he'll explain it to her mother.'

'What a namby-pamby you must think me,

Susannah,' he said ruefully. 'It's so good to be with you. I feel as if I can be myself, say what is on my mind, and that you won't judge me.'

'I won't,' she assured him. 'But you must stand up for yourself or else you'll only find unhappiness.'

Even as she spoke, she wondered if she would have stood up to Wilf Topham's behaviour if Aunt Jane hadn't suggested she run away. Would I have stayed and been browbeaten – or even beaten in the true sense of the word?

'There's plenty of time,' she said. 'You don't have to make a decision yet. You've to finish at university first, and Maria might transfer her affections elsewhere in the meantime.'

'Pray that she does,' he said fervently.

That evening, after the last of their customers had gone, Susannah cleared away and washed up glasses and tankards, wiped down the counter and tables and generally made everything tidy ready for the next day. She looked up and saw Uncle Brewster watching her, and asked if everything was all right.

'Oh, yes, m'dear,' he said in the slow manner he had. 'I'm sure that it is.'

Aunt Brewster was sitting with her knitting idle on her lap when they went through into the kitchen. 'All done, m'dear?' she asked.

'Yes, all done.' Susannah smiled. 'Aren't you ready for your bed yet? It's gone eleven.'

'I wanted to talk to you. Well, we both wanted to talk to you, didn't we, Mr Brewster?'

'Aye, I suppose we did,' he answered. 'Not sure what we 'going to say, though.'

'No,' his wife agreed. 'Or how we're going to say it.'

'There's nothing wrong, is there?' Susannah asked anxiously. 'Is it something to do with the lawyer?'

'It is.' Aunt Brewster nodded. 'It's a fine how-de-do and no mistake.'

'Do you want to tell me, or is it private? Can I help?'

'Shall I say, Mr Brewster, or will you?' the old lady queried and Susannah glanced from one to the other.

'You'd better say, Mrs Brewster. You've got more words at your disposal than I have.' He picked up his pipe from the shelf at the side of the range and put it between his teeth to chew on.

Aunt Brewster took a deep breath. 'Well, it seems that 'owners of 'Fleet have had an offer from somebody wanting to buy it from them.'

Susannah gasped. Would that mean that the Brewsters would be turned out, and herself as well?

'They've offered a fair bit o' money, seemingly, but there are conditions before they buy.'

'What kind of conditions? Do they want you to

leave? Because if they do that just isn't fair!' Susannah said hotly. 'Not after you've spent your whole life here.'

'Well no, that's just it, you see.' Aunt Brewster wrinkled her forehead as if perplexed. 'The conditions are that we stay here for 'rest of our natural lives, which we would want to do anyway, and that we employ a younger person to help us, who will be given a salary by 'new owners. And if we're not willing, then it won't be sold.'

'Goodness!' Susannah said. 'Well, that's a relief, isn't it? Do you know who 'new owners will be?'

'No. That's 'strange thing,' Uncle Brewster broke in. 'We've to assign somebody to act as our agent. Some legal body. But not Mr Watson, cos he's to act for 'new owners.'

'We thought we'd ask Mr Cannon,' Aunt Brewster said. 'If he's willing; cos he's to lee— lee—'

'Liaise with Mr Watson,' her husband finished for her. 'So can you help us out, Susannah?' he asked awkwardly. 'We don't know any other young person.'

'You mean – for me to help you run 'Fleet? Be the person with a salary?' Susannah was astonished and delighted.

'Aye. 'Present owners are anxious to formalize everything immediately, that's what 'lawyer fellow said,' Uncle Brewster explained. 'Well, they would be, wouldn't they, if 'price is good? I wouldn't have thought they'd get much for it

354

when it needs so much repair. 'Roof needs fixing for a start and I can't climb up any more. So they'll want to shake hands on it, in case these folk change their minds.'

'Oh, yes. Please!' Susannah gave a little whoop of joy and gave them both a kiss. 'I'd love to. I'll do it without a salary if necessary.'

'Oh no,' Aunt Brewster said. 'Mr Watson said that was how it was to be done, and we'll take our profit from 'sale of alcohol as usual.' She shook her head. 'We can't work out what's in it for them: 'new owners, I mean. That's a right mystery and no mistake.'

'They'll be looking to the future,' Freddie said, when Susannah told him. 'When Mr and Mrs Brewster are no longer here. But you'll have experience behind you then, Susannah, and they might keep you on, or else you could run something else. I could be quite envious of you. It sounds so exciting.' He gave a sigh. 'Father keeps on at me about when I'm a lawyer like him. He definitely doesn't want me to go into commercial enterprise, which is a pity, because I'm sure I'd be good at it. I would like the challenge.'

'You'd have the head for it, Freddie,' Susannah said. 'You're so clever and intelligent. But would you have the gift or flair?'

He smiled at her. 'Perhaps not. But you would, Susannah.'

CHAPTER THIRTY-TWO

Mr Cannon joined Freddie at the Sun Inn on the Friday evening and early on Saturday morning they set off on their customary walk to Spurn Point, following the path from the silted-up Hedon haven to the village of Paull on the banks of the Humber estuary. From there they had an approximately twenty-mile walk to reach their destination at the end of the peninsula. It was a bright morning, not too hot, and with a few white clouds, propelled by a brisk breeze, scudding along the wide sky.

Fishermen were returning with their catch of shrimps and Mr Cannon remarked on how much he had enjoyed his last supper of potted shrimps at Mrs Brewster's. 'I understand the Brewsters wish to speak privately to me,' he said. 'I've arranged an hour's meeting for tomorrow morning. We can then take a short walk before I return home by the afternoon train. Perhaps into the countryside rather than by the river?'

Freddie nodded. After spending a whole day with his father today, the notion of enjoying his company for only a short time tomorrow seemed quite appealing. 'I've often thought I'd like to visit Patrington,' he said. 'We've never been and I understand that the church is one of the finest in the country. It will be open for Sunday services, so the vicar will perhaps be willing for us to look round.'

His father pulled a wry face. He had not attended a church service since his wife's funeral, though he had not objected to Freddie's joining the chapel choir whilst at school. 'If we are looking purely at the architecture,' he said, 'then I have no objections. Perhaps we might go by train,' he added. 'There is a limited service running on a Sunday.'

They continued on their trek. Both were well equipped with sturdy boots and rainwear, for they had walked together since Freddie was very young. Though his father was not an imaginative man, he had done his level best to enliven and divert his sad little son who so missed his mother. The problem, Freddie often mused since he had grown into young adulthood, was that his father still considered him to be vulnerable and unable to make his own decisions.

There were a great many ships on the estuary: tug boats, fishing boats, coal barges, and larger steamers and commercial craft coming and going from the port of Hull. Here was one of the biggest whaling and fishing fleets in the country, giving industrial employment to thousands of workers. They continued walking briskly, Freddie's father swinging his stick. They crossed the deep Thorngumbald Drain and noted the isolated farmhouses whose occupants must have barely eked out a living. They didn't talk much but watched the frisky white wave crests and breathed in the sharp salty smells and observed the chimneys and low-lying banks of Lincolnshire on the other side of the Humber.

At midday they approached Cherry Cob Sands – saltmarsh reclaimed from the estuary – and agreed that they must visit again in the winter when the wading birds came to feed. They took a rest and a drink of water and ate a slab of chocolate when they arrived at Stone Creek, and silently watched a sailing vessel approach and then anchor in deep water. This small harbour was used by the farmers of Sunk Island, the land reclaimed from the waters of the Humber, to transport their corn and to import coal and other commodities.

'Do you think the harbour is used by smugglers?' Freddie asked lightly. 'It would be the perfect place.'

'In the old days perhaps,' his father answered seriously. 'But since new roads have been built on Sunk Island I imagine that it is too busy a place for nefarious characters. I understand that the road system is now the best in Holderness.'

Freddie turned to gaze behind him at the flat windswept landscape of rolling corn fields, and the hawthorn and blackthorn hedges where hedge sparrows twittered and water gurgled in the deep ditches. He could hear the cry of curlews and saw a kestrel swooping high in the sky, but not a sign of busy people, though he didn't doubt that they were there, somewhere.

They crossed the bridge at Patrington Haven, which like the haven at Hedon was silting up, and continued along the raised embankment of Welwick and Skeffling, the pathway becoming sandier as they approached the village of Kilnsea. They stopped at the inn there for a glass of ale and a sandwich. Mr Cannon drank thirstily and then said, 'Do you mind if we turn back? I don't think I'm up to walking the last few miles to the Point. Not when it's so very sandy and difficult to walk on.'

Freddie was exceedingly surprised. His father was usually so full of energy. 'Are you all right, Pa? Not unwell?'

'My legs are beginning to ache and I do feel a little tired. I'd prefer to turn back.'

It took them longer to return as his father kept stopping to rest and occasionally stumbling. They reached Patrington Haven at mid-afternoon and Freddie suggested that they walk from there into the market town of Patrington. 'It's only about a mile,' he said. 'And we can hire a conveyance to take us into Hedon.'

His father agreed. 'I'm so sorry to spoil the day,' he said. 'But I'm beginning to feel quite unwell.'

When they arrived in Patrington they were told on enquiring for transport that there would be a train arriving at the railway station in half an hour, which would take them to Hedon in less than thirty minutes. Mr Cannon took Freddie's arm as they walked down the hill to the station and in no time at all the train steamed in; they bought their tickets and were on their way.

'I shall miss supper tonight,' Mr Cannon said as they jolted Hedon-wards, 'and retire to my room for a rest. Perhaps you'd inform Mr and Mrs Brewster that I will meet them as arranged tomorrow morning? I shall depart for home soon after and forgo our walk to Patrington church. I'm sure it is most impressive, but perhaps it can wait for some other time? There is no place more comforting than one's own bed when one is feeling indisposed.'

Freddie agreed and said he hoped the affliction was only temporary. His father assured him that it was.

He told Susannah about his father's being unwell and their walk into Patrington. 'We didn't have a chance to look at the church,' he said, 'because the train was due imminently. I've only ever seen the spire from the river bank.'

Susannah was silent for a while and then spoke in an undertone. 'It's a fine sight. Quite a landmark in Holderness. Aunt Jane and I used to walk from Welwick and pass it on the way to 'flax mill.'

'We passed Welwick,' he said. 'At least, we walked along the Welwick bank. The saltmarsh has grown significantly since I was last there, though it is not so great at Skeffling.'

Susannah grew wistful. 'I used to play on 'Welwick bank with my cousin Thomas. We weren't supposed to in case we fell in 'river, but we never got caught. Water's such an attraction to children. We once went all 'way to . . .' She stopped, frowning, as a distant memory hovered in her consciousness. 'Well, nearly to Sunk Island. Thomas said it was Sunk Island land over the drain. He showed me a burned-out cottage near there at Welwick Thorpe and told me that I'd been born there.' She gave a slight shiver. 'It gave me a funny feeling, though I wasn't sure whether to believe him.'

'How did he know?' Freddie asked softly.

'He said his brother had told him. But Daniel was always making up stories.'

'Would you like to go back?' he asked. 'I would come with you.'

She shook her head. 'No,' she whispered. 'I'd be afraid to. When I reach twenty-one, perhaps I will. When I come of age.'

The following morning, Mr Cannon was closeted in the kitchen with Mr and Mrs Brewster whilst Susannah attended to requirements in the inn. When they had finished their discussion, she was called in. 'Miss Page,' Mr Cannon said. 'You know something of what has transpired through Mr Watson regarding the Fleet Inn. I have agreed to act as the agent for Mr and Mrs Brewster, and before I meet Mr Watson I must ask you if you are willing to stay on at the Fleet as a salaried assistant? I do not wish to prejudice you in any way, but I think you realize that much depends on your answer.'

'I would like to, very much, if Mr and Mrs Brewster would like me to and agree to it,' Susannah said. 'I'm really happy here and would feel secure if I could stay.'

'Very well,' he said. 'I will call at Mr Watson's house and ask if he will oblige me by seeing me today before I journey home. I will hear what he has to say on the subject and then we can make the necessary arrangements.' He looked at Susannah and hesitated before saying, 'It is a most unusual case. There will be more that Mr Watson can tell me, I have no doubt, and I will give my advice' – he turned to the Brewsters – 'accordingly.' He rose from the table and gathered some papers into his hand. 'I wish you all good day.'

'He's an odd sort of gaffer,' Mr Brewster remarked after Mr Cannon had departed. 'But I suppose he knows what he's doing.'

'He's a very proper kind of person,' Mrs Brewster reproved him. 'He'll want to make sure everything's in order.'

Freddie came to see Susannah later in the afternoon to tell her he would be leaving the next day to return to Anlaby. 'Father wanted me to travel with him today but I said I had some work to finish.' He smiled. 'It was a lie, I'm afraid. I wanted to see you. Do you have time to come for a walk?'

'Yes,' she said. 'I can slip out for half an hour.'

They walked into the garden, where runner beans and sweet peas were climbing up tall canes, and white butterflies were hovering over the cabbages. 'I don't suppose your father discussed his meeting with Mr Watson, did he?' she asked. 'I'm most intrigued. I wonder who the buyer can be.'

Freddie frowned. 'Father came back in a very strange frame of mind after the meeting. I don't think he's too well at the moment. Of course he doesn't ever talk about private business with me, but he did say that I mustn't in any circumstances discuss the situation with you or the Brewsters.'

'But I want to, Freddie,' she said, dismayed.

'Who else can I discuss it with? And besides,' she added, 'I'm only going to be an employee, so there's nothing secret about it.'

'I'm sorry, Susannah, but Father was most insistent. He explained that he will be acting for you and the Brewsters and therefore you are his clients. Of course I understand that. His clients must be assured at all times of his probity. Don't be downcast,' he said fervently. 'I'm sure everything will be all right. Father is meticulous in all he does. He'll look after you very well.'

Susannah nodded. 'Yes, I'm sure that he will. It's just that there's a new life ahead of me and I wanted to talk over ideas with you.' She looked up at him. 'I wanted to share it with you.'

He kissed the tip of her nose. 'I want to share my life with you, Susannah,' he said softly. 'Not just ideas.'

She put her head against his chest. 'I want that too, Freddie. I feel now as if my life is just beginning.'

CHAPTER THIRTY-THREE

'I wish to speak very seriously to you, Freddie,' Mr Cannon said, on Freddie's return home. 'It concerns your acquaintance, Miss Page.'

'She's more than an acquaintance, Father,' Freddie protested. 'Much more. She's a very good friend. I'm exceedingly fond of Susannah.'

'Then you must ease yourself out of this friendship before harm is done.' His father had the grace to look embarrassed. 'Discontinue your association with her. I don't mean that you should cold shoulder her, dear me no, you must be polite at all times, but you should keep her at arms' length socially.'

Freddie stared at his father. Had he taken leave of his senses? 'I love her, Pa,' he blurted out. 'I want to marry her when I'm established. I don't understand what you're saying!'

His father looked shocked. 'Come and sit down.' He indicated the chairs placed by the fire.

'I will explain as much as I can without betraying my duty of confidentiality.'

Freddie's head reeled. Whatever had Susannah done? Was it something to do with the business with the Brewsters?

'I have in my possession certain facts appertaining to Miss Page which I cannot disclose, except to say that because of them, it would not be proper for you to continue with your friendship.' His father crossed his legs and laced his fingers together, a habit that Freddie remembered from childhood whenever his father was attempting to explain some complex situation. 'It would not do, you understand, when I am acting on Miss Page's behalf, for my son to have any kind of, erm, relationship with her. There must be no question of any lack of integrity on my part.'

'You're not saying that Susannah is in any kind of trouble, or has done something she shouldn't – something illegal?' Freddie frowned.

'Indeed not! Would I act on her behalf if that were the case?' James Cannon's answer was sharp and to the point. 'No. She is above reproach. But in view of circumstances which will be ongoing for many years, I must advise that your friendship should be terminated.'

'And if I refuse?' Freddie decided that he would refuse, no matter what his father said.

His father heaved a breath and shook his head.

'It would not look good, Freddie. Business and pleasure never mix.'

They stared at each other. They had had a good father–son relationship, but Freddie was aware that he had always deferred to his father's wishes, giving him the respect and esteem that he considered were his due. There had been few occasions so far when they had been in total disagreement. Even the choice of Freddie's future career had been carefully discussed, though he knew how keen his father was to have him join him in his profession.

'Could you explain anything further?' Freddie said. 'I understood that you were acting for the Brewsters, and Susannah is to work for them. That is what she said, anyway.'

'It's a pity that the matter was discussed at all,' Mr Cannon said grimly. 'It is not straightforward, but it does concern Miss Page's future and so I cannot speak of it. When you have finished your studies and join me in the firm, and if Miss Page wishes us to continue acting for her, then all may be revealed.' He gave a thin smile. 'But until then . . .' He shrugged. The subject was closed.

'There is, however, another matter which I must bring up for discussion, in view of your declaration of your partiality to Miss Page!' His father eyed him squarely. 'You cannot have forgotten your attachment to Maria? Surely your affections are not so – forgive me – insubstantial that they are so easily forgotten?'

Freddie was horrified and hurt that his father should say such a thing. But he was also angry that a relationship with Maria should be taken for granted. 'I have no attachment to Maria, Father! I never did have. Affection, if indeed there is any, is on her side only. I view her only as a former childhood companion, nothing more!'

His father frowned. 'I understand differently,' he said. 'Her mother tells me that Maria has been preparing her trousseau for years and often speaks of the plans that she has for when you eventually marry.'

'No!' Freddie got up from his chair in a fury. 'I have never planned anything with her. Any such notions are in Maria's head. Not in mine!' He paced up and down the room. 'Her mother and my mother devised this when we were children,' he said in a low, restrained voice. 'It must have been a kind of amusement or diversion for them to plot our future.'

His father shook his head. 'It wasn't an amusement for your mother,' he said softly. 'A diversion perhaps. She never enjoyed good health. I think she always knew that she wouldn't live to see your future. Perhaps she felt that by planning, she could be part of it.'

Freddie stopped his pacing. He hadn't

thought of that and all the childhood pain of his mother's death came rushing back. 'I'm sorry, Father.' He sat down again, much subdued. 'But it isn't what I want. I remember Mama saying to me that she'd like me to be a doctor or a surgeon when I grew up. Or a man of letters.' He swallowed hard. 'I recall feeling very uneasy. I didn't understand what she meant. I had only just learned to read and write!'

'You were very young,' his father agreed benevolently. 'And your mother was ambitious. But nevertheless,' his tone of voice changed, and Freddie could hear his legal manner clicking in, 'Maria, and her mother, are under the impression that you and she will be married. It would be a good match,' he added. 'She will have a considerable fortune, she is a pleasant enough young woman, and our connections with them are stable.'

'But – I don't love her.' He hasn't been listening, Freddie thought in dismay. 'Didn't you hear me, Father? I don't want to marry Maria, no matter what her fortune.'

'I think you will find it is expected of you,' his father said calmly and rather coldly. 'It is a matter of honour and decency. Only right and proper after all.'

'But I've never suggested to her that we might marry! I have never asked her to be my wife. Never given her the slightest hint or promise . . .' Freddie felt that he was falling into a pit, and the pit was getting deeper and deeper.

'Neither have you given her any indication that you wouldn't fall in with her ideas. By ignoring her when she has suggested that you will have a future together, you have led her to believe that you agreed to it. That was cruel, Freddie,' his father said grimly. 'Maria has expectations and you chose to ignore them. That conduct is not worthy of you.'

Freddie felt battered and bruised and asked to be excused, retiring to his room. His father, always a man of pedantry and exactness, liked matters to be resolved into neat and orderly compartments, and disliked intensely anything that was disorganized or questionable. This Freddie understood and made allowances for, but his father had never spoken to him in such a manner as this before.

He stood with his arms folded, gazing out of the window but not seeing the view of the garden, the neatly manicured lawn, the clipped hedges, and the weedless gravelled drive. What am I to do? What has happened that makes it impossible for me to continue a relationship with Susannah? Father says it is nothing that she has done. There is no slur on her reputation, and he forbids me to discuss the situation with her. But I must! Damn it, I love her, and I'm not a child that must always obey its elders.

There came a soft tap on the door, and he called sharply, 'Yes. What is it?' thinking that it was the housekeeper. His father opened the door and asked, 'May I come in?'

Freddie nodded and his father closed the door behind him. 'I have perhaps been rather unreasonable,' he began. 'I find it quite difficult to shake off my legal role and must apologize if I have also played the part of an overbearing parent.'

As Freddie looked at him in astonishment, he continued, 'I will disclose a little, though I must ask you to swear that you will tell no-one, and certainly not Miss Page.' He clasped his fingers together and fixed his gaze upon them. 'Miss Page, though unaware of the fact, has acquired a benefactor. I do not know who it is, nor does Mr Watson. It is strictly above board, and from being a poor orphan she has the chance of becoming a wealthy one.' He looked at Freddie. 'And that is why I say you must not consider a romantic attachment to her. It might look like collusion on my part and yours.'

'But – I have already spoken of my love for her—' Freddie broke off as his father shook his head.

'It would not do,' he told him. 'You know that it would not be appropriate or proper conduct for a lawyer's son to fall in love with one of his father's clients.' He turned to the door, and with his hand on the knob looked back at his son. 'I'm sorry for you, Freddie,' he said softly. 'I really am. But good marriages are often made without initial love or passion. So marry Maria and keep your feelings for Miss Page strictly professional.'

CHAPTER THIRTY-FOUR

Before Freddie returned to university, he wrote to Susannah to say he would be coming to Hedon as he had something he wished to discuss with her. By the same post a letter from Mr Watson the solicitor came for the Brewsters advising them that a surveyor and an architect would be calling at the Fleet to measure and plan for improvements to the inn.

'I don't know if I can be bothered with all of this,' Mrs Brewster said. 'Can you speak to them, Susannah? Mr Brewster and me are too old for these modern ideas.' She looked down at the letter. 'It says that we are to inform and advise what is required to make this a profitable and well run business.'

'I'd have thought that 'roof needs repairing before they do anything inside,' Susannah said. 'We had a leak the other day when it rained.'

'Tell them that then, will you?' Mrs Brewster asked.

'And tell them that we need a proper place to store 'casks, somewhere a bit closer to 'house,' Mr Brewster added. 'Then we won't have to tramp across 'yard to 'stables.'

'Don't you want to tell them that, Uncle Brewster?' Susannah asked. 'You know best what you want.'

'No,' he said, reaching for his tobacco and pipe. 'You're going to be a sort of manager, so you can tell 'em.'

Susannah pondered. She could think of several things that would improve the running of the inn, but how much money would the new owners want to spend? The roof for one thing would cost quite a lot, though of course I have no real idea. She wondered if Freddie would know and resolved to ask him when he came. She felt a little skip of joy. What did he want to discuss? He would be returning to university soon, but she hoped that he was going to say something about their future, his and hers. Though I dare not think too much on that, she thought. I wouldn't like to build up my hopes only to be disappointed.

She appeared always to be serene and calm, her feelings well under control. But in fact she was so afraid of being hurt or unwanted that at times she dared not show that she was capable of passion or emotion. The Brewsters, though, had made her happy. They had been kind and considerate and treated her as if she were family, and she in turn couldn't do enough for them, so grateful was she that they had given her a home and security.

When the architect and surveyor came, they seemed to take it for granted that she would discuss the essentials with them and didn't ask to meet Mr or Mrs Brewster, though Susannah called in Mr Brewster when they started asking her what kind and size of storage would be needed for the casks and barrels.

'This was an ancient beerhouse, I would think,' the architect said. 'The casks would be delivered by barge along the Fleet stream, or maybe the ale was brewed here on the premises.' He gazed round thoughtfully. 'Once a taproom,' he said, 'and then extended into a saloon. Room for improvement, though. What if we extend the saloon again . . .'

'Could we have a room added on for people who might like to eat?' Susannah asked. She was thinking of the times when Freddie and his father had come and they had put a table in the corner for them. Mr Cannon, and others, she was sure, would prefer to eat out of sight of those drinking ale.

'Indeed,' the architect said agreeably. 'And there could also be a quiet room. There are several ideas I'd like to suggest to you, Miss Page. Perhaps if I draw up some plans for your approval?'

'Oh! But . . . you must ask the owners!' Susannah exclaimed. 'It's not for me to say. Or perhaps you'd consult Mr and Mrs Brewster? I'm only the – the . . .' She couldn't think how to explain her position, but the architect didn't seem too concerned over her status, merely said he would come back with drawings and discuss them with her and the Brewsters.

'What am I exactly, Aunt Brewster?' she asked the old lady later. 'The architect kept asking what I required. Why doesn't he ask the owners? And who are they, anyway? Don't they want to see the place first, or have they been already?'

'I know as little as you, m'dear,' Aunt Brewster said. 'I've racked my brains to think who they could be or when they've been to visit, but I can't think that we've had any strangers here. As for their name, Mr Watson only refers to a Mr Smith, the agent.' She nodded benignly at Susannah. 'And he said that you were to be paid a salary starting in November, so, as Mr Brewster said, you're a sort of manager.'

'There was a stranger come a while back,' Mr Brewster said thoughtfully. 'A right hot day it was and he had a tankard of ale and a meat pie; don't you recall, Mrs Brewster? I remember him asking if trade were good.'

Mrs Brewster paused in the act of raking the fire. She held the fire iron against the bar of the grate. 'Aye! Come to think on it, there was somebody,' she agreed. 'He asked who'd cooked 'pie and I said as it was my niece.' She glanced towards Susannah. 'You were outside hanging 'washing.'

Susannah shook her head. 'I don't remember anyone,' she said.

'He were a bit scruffy,' Mrs Brewster said. 'I don't mean like a tramp or owt, but his hair was long and he wore a beard that needed trimming. Talked proper though,' she added, continuing what she was doing and adding coal to the fire. 'But he didn't look as if he was made o' money.'

'It's rather a mystery,' Susannah said to Freddie when he called a few days later. 'We don't know who the new owners are or anything about them. I'm a bit worried about it because the architect said he was going to come back with plans and suggestions, and the Brewsters said they want me to attend to it.'

Freddie hesitated. 'Father says I haven't to discuss it, Susannah,' he said quietly, 'because of his professional involvement. But he did say that everything was above board, so I don't think you need worry. But what I will say,' he spoke determinedly, 'is that it's a wonderful opportunity and you should tell them what you think. Give them your views.'

'But Freddie,' she said, 'I've not had 'experience. How do I know what will work or if we're wasting money? Somebody else's money!'

'You're very sensible, Susannah, and you have flair,' he said. 'I think the owners would put a stop to it if they thought something wasn't feasible. But I've said too much already. I'm not supposed to talk about it.'

He seemed very gloomy today, she thought. She smiled up at him, hoping to cheer him. 'You're getting taller, Freddie,' she said. 'Each time I see you I think you've grown!'

'They say that men don't stop growing until they're in their late twenties,' he said ruefully. 'I've time to stretch several inches yet.'

She put her hand into his. They had walked alongside the stream. 'So what was it you wanted to discuss, if you can't talk about the Fleet?'

There was a fallen log where they sat sometimes. It wasn't far from the inn: within calling distance if Susannah was needed by the Brewsters. He led her towards it and they sat down.

'Three things,' he said in a low voice. 'And they all concern you, and me,' he added in a mutter.

She gazed at him, hopefully, brightly, yet she felt there was something wrong. He didn't seem at all happy. In fact he looked downright miserable. 'Has something happened?' she asked softly. 'You're upset.'

'I am upset,' he told her. 'I had such plans. For us both. But . . .' He took his hand away from hers and put it over his eyes.

'Freddie?' she whispered. 'Tell me. I'll try to understand. It can't be so very bad – can it?' Her lips parted as she saw the look of distress on his face. 'Is it something that I've done?'

'No. No!' He put his arm round her and lifting her hand he kissed her fingers. 'It's circumstances, and I've been a fool. A young fool who didn't think and didn't know.' He swallowed hard. 'What I'm going to say, Susannah, will affect our future; but the first thing I want to say is that I love you. Will always love you.'

'But . . . ?' she questioned, frightened by his pallor and his obvious wretchedness. 'What of our future?'

'There will be none,' he groaned. 'Not together. I have to marry Maria. My father advises me that it would be dishonourable and unkind not to.' He saw the horrified expression on her face. 'I have never given her cause to think I will marry her, Susannah. I swear to God that I haven't! It was a scheme, a joke possibly, thought up by our mothers when we were children; but Maria was under the misapprehension that it was true and won't give up on the idea. I've been to see her and her mother,' he added, 'and they are so full of plans and arrangements that they wouldn't listen to me when I expressed my doubts.' He squeezed her hand so tightly that she gave a little cry of pain. 'What am I to do? I can't bear to think I shall be tied to her for life when I love you.'

'What would it mean if you were to defy them?' she whispered.

'My father says it would mean that Maria and her mother would be humiliated; they'd become a laughing stock. And they would lose face socially if I don't go through with the marriage as seemingly all their friends and acquaintances have been made aware and accept that we are affianced.'

'But I thought that your mother and Maria's mother had been such good friends! Surely she wouldn't do anything to spoil the memory of that relationship?'

Freddie groaned. 'You don't know Aunt Bertha! If she's set her mind on something there's no budging her! But it's my father I'm thinking of. He's built up a good practice and, what's more, he's invested a lot of money in my education: going to university alone has cost him dear. I feel,' he said miserably, 'I feel that I would be letting him down; that I'm being unworthy.'

'So it is a question of honour. Tell me,' she said, 'for I don't know about these things. Is it normal to marry someone you don't love just because it's expected?'

'In some circles, yes, I believe so.' Freddie blew his nose. 'My father has risen socially,' he explained. 'He was first of all a clerk, though he doesn't tell people that. But Bertha married a rich man and I do believe it might have been difficult for my parents to keep pace with them. But Father is very clever and intelligent and has been successful in his field, and I understand that Aunt Bertha's husband put quite a lot of business his way in the early days; and that's why – that's why it's so difficult for me when Father has worked so hard to achieve all that he has.'

'Yes,' Susannah murmured. 'I understand. At least I think I do.' I have always dreamed, she pondered, about how wonderful it must be to belong to a close-knit family. To have the comfort of loving relatives and caring friends around me. But perhaps it isn't, after all. Perhaps it's better to be independent and not have to consider others' views or feelings that are at odds with one's own.

'Do you, Susannah?' Freddie asked anxiously. 'Do you understand?'

Slowly she nodded. 'But I'm very sad,' she said wistfully. 'I have such tender feelings for you, Freddie, and – and although I didn't allow myself to hope that one day we might share a future together, I confess . . .' Her voice dropped low and he bent his head to hear her. 'I must confess that it was my dearest wish that it might be so.'

'What else can I do? Tell me if you think there is a way out of this tangle.' He gazed at her imploringly. 'I can only hope that whilst I'm away studying Maria will find someone else to care for and will then release me.'

'Yes,' Susannah whispered. 'We must pin our hopes on that.' But she won't, she thought practically. If Maria has held on to this obsessive pipe-dream since she was a child, she isn't ever going to transfer that desire to someone else. I must plan my life without Freddie, she decided. Much as I care for him, I know that he can't, won't ever, be mine. I shall fill my life with work. She brooded that the new owners of the Fleet Inn had come along at the most opportune time. If I can make a success of this perhaps I won't have time to miss him so much.

'What was the third thing?' she asked softly, her voice trembling. 'Can it be any worse than what I've just heard?'

'What?' Freddie said in a dazed manner.

'You said you had three things to tell me.'

He heaved a breath. 'Yes. I have decided that, after I have finished at university, I will join my father after all. I will become a lawyer.'

'But you didn't want to,' she protested. 'Why have you changed your mind?'

Freddie pressed his lips together. 'There are good reasons. Very good reasons, but I'm not at liberty to discuss them. It's my decision, mine alone. I have thought long and hard about it and in the long run this is the only means I have to make up to you for this crushing blow. Susannah!' he exclaimed, his voice thick with emotion. 'This is breaking my heart!'

'I know,' she answered. 'And mine!' She put her head on his shoulder and wept.

CHAPTER THIRTY-FIVE

1880

'Laura!' James had come home from the bank, collected his post from the hall table, opened an envelope addressed in handwriting he didn't recognize, and, after reading the signature, called to his sister. 'Are you in?'

'There's no need to bellow, James.' Laura came out of the sitting room. 'I'm in here.'

'Mm.' James followed her into the room, still reading the letter. 'Where's Mother?'

'Out. She had an appointment with Uncle Freddie and hasn't returned yet. What's the letter? Something important?'

'Erm, no.' He looked across at her. 'We've got an invitation to spend a weekend at Burstall House. Ellis's place. You remember, we met him when we were in Hedon?'

'Yes, I do. And I'm invited? What is the occasion?'

'"Dear Page,"' James read aloud, '"I was pleased to meet you again the other week and thought perhaps we could renew our acquaintance. My sister Amy has suggested that we have a few friends over for a house party this coming weekend, and I wondered if you and your sister would care to join us. The Holderness roads are clear just now, and the weather at the moment is reasonable for November.

'"It might seem to be an odd time for a social event but we have to fit in with the farming schedule. Do hope it appeals to you. There will be one or two other fellows whom you might know.

'"Hope you can come. With sincere good wishes,"' James looked up, '"Edmund Ellis." How can we get out of that?' he said.

'Why would you want to?' Laura asked. 'I'd like to go.'

'Oh!' James said in exasperation. 'It took ages to clean up the curricle. All that mud!'

'We could ask Stubbs to drive us. I'd rather anyway. I feel safer with him than when you're driving.'

'Oh, thanks!' he muttered. 'I suppose we could go,' he said thoughtfully. 'It might be good for business. All those rich farmers.' He grinned. 'You might even find yourself a husband. Would you fancy living in Holderness? In the middle of nowhere?'

Laura shrugged. 'I might. I liked it, as a matter of fact.'

'What did you like?' Their mother came into the room. She had removed her coat but sat down now and took off her outdoor shoes. Their housekeeper entered, bringing her a pair of indoor slippers. 'Thank you, Smithy,' she said softly. 'Could I have a cup of tea, please? I know it's nearly supper time, but . . .'

'Holderness,' Laura said. 'James has had an invitation to a house party this weekend and I'm invited too. Are you all right, Mama? You look strained.'

'I'm rather – unsettled,' she said. 'I was with Freddie when he received a message to return home immediately.'

Laura and James both groaned simultaneously. 'Mrs Cannon isn't ill yet again?' Laura asked.

'It was the doctor who sent for Freddie this time. He said it was most urgent.'

She didn't add that Freddie almost didn't go. 'I can't continue with this, Susannah,' he had said on opening the note, and threw it onto his desk. 'She'll drive me into an early grave.'

Susannah had picked up the message and read it. 'You must go, Freddie,' she said in a low voice. 'The doctor says that your wife is in a fatal collapse.'

'I don't believe it,' Freddie said stubbornly. 'Maria has convinced him that she's sick. She is sick,' he'd added bitterly. 'Sick in the head!'

She had persuaded him that he must return home and that they would complete their business on another day. 'It will give me another reason to come again,' she said softly. They had been so careful over the years. Susannah had always made appointments with his secretary, and Freddie had always called her in at some point during their meeting, either to bring in a file or a document or to make another appointment for Mrs Page.

He had kissed Susannah tenderly before she left and said softly, 'One day, Susannah. One day!'

'So who invited you?' she asked James now. 'One of your business associates?'

'No, the farmer fellow that Laura and I met when we were in Hedon. Edmund Ellis.'

'Ah, yes.' Susannah's eyes flickered. 'From Skeffling. So will you accept?'

'I'd like to,' Laura said. 'But James is bothered about getting his curricle mucked up.'

'Ask Stubbs to take you,' her mother said. 'The curricle won't be safe at this time of year. If there's rain, 'roads will flood. It's such low-lying land.'

'Won't you need the carriage?' Laura asked.

Her mother shook her head. 'I can manage without it for a day or two. I'm not planning on going anywhere.'

James replied to the letter, accepting the invitation, and on the following Saturday morning they set off. Edmund Ellis had written again giving them directions to the house and they had given these to Stubbs.

'Middle o' nowhere, looks like,' he grumbled. He was a lugubrious character, but both James and Laura had an idea that he was quite looking forward to the adventure of going out of their usual area. 'It's to be hoped we don't get bogged down and have to stay all winter.'

'So who are you inviting to this supper party?' Joseph Ellis asked Edmund. 'Usual crowd of young people?'

'Most of them you'll know, Gramps,' Edmund said. 'Some of Amy's friends and some of mine; and Cousin Mark is coming too. You're sure you don't mind? We'll try not to make too much noise.'

'I shan't mind the noise,' Joseph said. 'Though your aunt Julia might. We'll have to send her to bed early. Any young women coming? Any I haven't met, I mean?' He raised his eyebrows at Edmund.

His grandson grinned. 'Yes, as a matter of fact. A real corker, Gramps. Met her a few weeks ago along with her brother. He and I were at school together, though I can't say I really remember him. But that's why I invited him.'

'Well don't forget you need a wife who'll settle in Holderness, or she'll always be scooting off elsewhere.'

'Like Grandmother, you mean,' Edmund said pointedly.

'Exactly!' Joseph said, but privately thought that it was just as well that Arlette spent so much time in her native France, for otherwise neither of them would have any peace.

'Yes, that just might be a difficulty. She lives in Hessle and strikes me as being an independent young woman, used to a lively social gathering.' Edmund pursed his lips. 'Don't think she'd be the type to like a quiet life in Holderness. She seemed very spirited.'

'Where did you meet her?' his grandfather asked.

'At the Fleet in Hedon. She and her brother were touring the area and were staying the night there.'

His grandfather's eyes glazed over. 'Indeed?' he said and gave a small sigh. 'I haven't been there for a long time.'

'Are we nearly there, Stubbs?' James called irritably.

'Can't say, Mr James,' Stubbs called back. 'I

think it's somewhere hereabouts. We've just passed a sign which says Skeffling.'

'Don't be so impatient, James,' Laura said. 'We'll be there when we're there.'

'Here it is, sir,' Stubbs called through the roof hatch. 'Burstall House.'

He slowed to let the horses through the gated entrance and up the long drive, which ran between thick woodland. Laura peered out. It must be lovely in the spring, she mused. There'll be bluebells and primroses in there, I should think. She saw a track leading through it and wondered where it led.

They crossed over a moat and the drive divided, the left hand side going, she assumed, to the back of the house and the right to the front. This Stubbs took, driving round a wing of the grey brick building to arrive at the main entrance, facing the estuary.

'Hope we're not the first to arrive,' James muttered. 'Though he did say come any time.'

'It's lovely!' Laura breathed. 'And look, James. The moat goes all the way round. The river must have burst its banks at some time so it was dug to keep the water out.'

'Mm,' James murmured and drew in his breath. 'Bet the house is draughty.'

The door opened and a maid came hurrying down the wide steps. She dipped her knee. 'Mr and Miss Page? Mr Edmund sends his apologies for not being here to greet you, but he's had to go over to one of 'farms. He'll be back by three o'clock. If you'd come this way, sir, miss, I'll show you to your rooms. I'll get a lad to help 'coachie with your luggage.'

Good. Laura was pleased that Edmund Ellis wasn't there. It will give me a chance to look round without appearing nosy. It's so grand, she thought as she followed the maid up a wide staircase, yet it's homely too. There were walking sticks and rubber boots in the hall and a faint smell of wet dog, but the floor was richly polished and scattered with Indian rugs, and there were some fine pieces of furniture – French, she thought.

Her room, which was next to James's, faced the estuary and from the window she could see the buffeting waves, the progress of ships and barges and the low-lying banks of Lincolnshire across the water.

'It's wonderful,' she said, thinking it was James and turning as the door opened. But it was the maid bringing in clean towels.

'Beg pardon, miss,' she said. 'Trust everything is to your satisfaction?'

'Oh yes, it is,' Laura enthused. 'What a fine view!'

The girl nodded agreeably. 'I'll be serving afternoon tea in half an hour, Miss Page,' she said. 'Miss Julia likes it at that time. She said if you'd like to join her.'

'Thank you,' Laura said. 'I'll just change and be down in fifteen minutes.'

The maid took the towels into a small dressing room and then withdrew, and Laura reluctantly gave up her position by the window. She took off her hat and then looked candidly at herself in a long free-standing mirror. She had dressed warmly, knowing that she was coming to a country house which might be cold. She had on her cotton embroidered combinations, the shaped chemise and wide drawers fitting snugly beneath her pale blue day dress. This had a separate tunic top, buttoned to the neck, and a low, draped bustle. I'll take off the tunic, she decided. The bodice is plain and will be perfectly suitable for afternoon tea if I wear a string of beads. They surely won't be formal out here in the country! And then I'll change later for supper.

James knocked on her door. 'I'm going down,' he said. 'I'll take a walk outside until it's time for tea.'

'Don't be long,' she called after him. 'And mind you don't get your boots dirty!' she added with some sarcasm.

She brushed out her unruly hair and tied it in a loose chignon at the back of her neck, and then searched in her leather bag for a lace cap. Miss Julia? Who is she? she wondered. If she's elderly she'll expect me to wear a cap.

392

Or is she perhaps another sister of Edmund Ellis?

She found a cap, pinned it on her hair and opened the door to go down. There was a low murmur of voices, male and female, though she couldn't hear any actual words. She glanced along the corridor and to the landing. There were several doors, including one at the end which she guessed led to a second staircase. She went towards the main staircase and stood with her hand on the banister. A grandfather clock ticked in the hall below, and as she stood there one of the doors downstairs opened and a man came out.

She saw that he was elderly; his hair had probably been fair and was streaked with white. The grandfather, she thought. He was tall, but had a slight stoop as if he was used to bending his head. He didn't look up and Laura began a quiet descent, her hand lying lightly on the rail and her gown rustling slightly.

He glanced upwards as if sensing her presence and she saw the sudden shift of his head and the abrupt movement as he grasped the banister finial. His lips parted and she saw them form unspoken words.

'Good afternoon,' she said softly, for she thought she had startled him, although surely he was expecting guests. 'Is it Mr Ellis?'

He stared at her for a second, then blinked

and put his hand first to his forehead and then to his mouth. 'Yes.' His voice came out in a husky croak. 'Forgive me.' He transferred his hand to his chest and she saw his fingers shake. 'Wh – whom have I the pleasure of addressing?'

'My name is Laura,' she said. 'Laura Page.'

CHAPTER THIRTY-SIX

My God! Joseph gazed upwards. *Mary-Ellen!* He mouthed her name. Am I dying or hallucinating? He put his hand on the banister, which felt solid and substantial beneath his fingers as he clasped it. Then the apparition spoke.

'Mr Ellis?'

He hardly knew what he said; only that he blurted out something. But as she came closer, he saw that there was a difference. She was perhaps taller; her hair was not quite as dark as Mary-Ellen's had been, and she displayed an air of cultured confidence as she swept down the stairs. Yet there was an undefined similarity. She wore the same aura of boldness, a challenge almost, as Mary-Ellen always carried.

He asked her name and was again thrown into a state of shock when she gave it. It cannot be, he thought. Pull yourself together. It is a common enough name.

'Joseph Ellis.' He gave her a slight bow and extended his hand to her as she stepped off the stairs. 'You must be my grandson's guest?'

She dipped her knee graciously as she took his hand. 'My brother James was at school with Edmund.' She smiled, and his heart turned over. 'Though I don't think they were friends. We met recently and he was kind enough to invite James for the weekend in order to renew their acquaintance.' She smiled again and leaned forward. 'Perhaps I'm here to make up numbers,' she whispered conspiratorially.

'I'm sure you are not,' he murmured. 'I cannot think that that would ever happen to you, Miss Page.'

The front door opened and James and Edmund came in together, chatting animatedly and laughing over something.

'Miss Page!' Edmund hurried towards her and gave a bow. 'How very nice to see you again. You've met Grandfather already, I see.' He beamed at her. 'Do forgive my attire,' he said, displaying his shabby tweed jacket and muddy cord breeches. 'We've had a bit of an emergency. A pregnant cow became stuck in a ditch and it was all hands to get her out.'

'Did you manage it?' his grandfather asked. 'Is she damaged?'

'No, she's fine,' Edmund said heartily. 'But we've put her into the top barn so we can keep an eye on her. I beg your pardon, Miss Page. I'm sure you don't want to hear this.'

'Well,' Laura said, 'it's preferable to discussing embroidery stitches!'

There was a second's silence and then they all laughed. James pulled a wry face and, turning to Joseph Ellis, introduced himself, saying, 'James Page, sir. How do you do? Please excuse my sister, Mr Ellis. She has an odd sense of humour and is quite unconventional.'

Joseph nodded. 'Glad to hear it. Where are you from? Not from round here?'

'No, sir, from Hessle. Lived there since we were children.'

'Your parents from Hessle, are they?'

'Our father died when we were young,' James said. 'We don't remember him. He was a naval officer and spent a good deal of time abroad. He was originally from Southampton.' He glanced at Laura for confirmation.

'Somewhere near Portsmouth, I think,' Laura countered. 'Though I don't know how they met.' A small frown creased her forehead as if she had just remembered or thought of something. 'Possibly he came into the port of Hull.'

'Shall we go in?' Joseph held his hand towards a half-open door. 'Julia and Amy will be wondering what we're doing out here in the hall.' He held the door open for Laura, covertly scrutinizing her as she passed in front of him.

Introductions were made to Joseph Ellis's sister, Miss Julia, who was dressed for afternoon tea, wearing a grey silk gown and a black lace cap on her head, and to Edmund's sister Amy, who was capless but wore a pretty muslin dress and had a piece of embroidery on her knee. 'Come and sit by me, my dear,' Miss Julia said to Laura, 'and tell me all about yourself.'

She looked up and dimpled at Edmund, who dropped a kiss on the top of her head. 'Aunt Julia, don't be asking Miss Page if she does good works,' he said, and added softly to Laura, 'Great-aunt Julia is known for her benevolence all over Holderness. But she will try to draw everyone into her schemes. Where have you been today, Aunt?'

'Oh, I haven't been out at all,' she said. 'I've been getting things ready for the Christmas bazaar. There's such a lot to do,' she told Laura. 'And so many people who need help. But you, Edmund,' she said sternly, 'had better get changed immediately. Whatever will Miss Page think of your coming in to tea in your working clothes?'

Edmund raised a quizzical eyebrow at Laura who gave a slight shrug of unconcern. It is nothing to me how he behaves, she thought. It's his home; he can do whatever he wants. Contrarily she was flattered that he apparently didn't feel that he had to behave in a formal manner because they had invited guests, or hide the fact that he was a working farmer. She had become disillusioned with young men who always did and said the right thing, yet left her unsure whether they really meant it.

'I will go and change right now, Aunt Julia,' Edmund said with a disarming grin. 'Only please save me a slice of cake.'

'That boy!' Julia murmured as he went out of the room. 'Perhaps Joseph should have sent him off to France with Amy, instead of to school in Pocklington.'

'He wouldn't have settled, Aunt Julia,' Amy said. 'He would have been bored by the constant round of balls and soirées that Grandmama loves so much. Our grandmother is French,' she told Laura. 'She spends a great deal of time in Paris, and I often travel with her.'

Laura glanced at Joseph Ellis, who was regarding her, yet seemingly not listening to the conversation.

'Do you know France at all, Miss Page?' Amy asked. 'Are you familiar with that country?'

'I have been to Paris twice,' Laura answered. 'The first time was when I was very young and I barely remember it.' A flash of awakened memory came to mind, carrying her thoughts back. 'And when I was about twelve my mother took me again.' Why didn't James go with us? she thought. Mama generally took us both wherever she went. Perhaps – oh, of course! He would have been away at school the second time. But the first? Again the tug of memory returned. She wore a white dress and bonnet and was laughing as she was lifted high into someone's arms. My feet ached, she remembered. My kidskin boots were new and pinching my toes. I could see so much up there, even over the top of Mama's head.

'Miss Page?' Amy was speaking to her. 'Do you take milk?' Amy had poured the tea and was hovering with a milk jug.

'I'm so sorry.' Laura blushed, something she rarely did. 'Yes please. I was reminded of something as we were speaking of France,' she said. 'Something that I had completely forgotten about. Do you visit France often, Mr Ellis?'

'Never,' he said brusquely. 'Not since I was a young man. That's where I met my wife. I've had no wish to go back. My home, my memories are here.' He took a breath. 'My wife likes to go back to Paris. She never settled in Holderness, even though our sons were born here.'

'How many sons have you, Mr Ellis? Are they all farmers?'

Joseph shook his head. 'My eldest son and his wife, Edmund and Amy's parents, both died of typhoid whilst they were living in France; but Austin wasn't a farmer. He hadn't settled on what he wanted to do, even though he had married and had two young children.' There was a note of bitterness in his voice. 'After they died I insisted that both children should be raised in Holderness.'

'Even though Grandmama wanted us to live in France,' Amy interrupted.

'And my two other sons are twins. One is in banking in London, and the other married a farmer's daughter and inherited her father's property on the other side of Beverley.'

'So you must be relieved that your grandson took to farming?' Laura said. 'To carry on the family estate.'

'Yes,' he said. 'I am. Burstall will be Edmund's one day.'

After they had finished tea, Miss Julia excused herself and went to her room. Joseph Ellis took himself off somewhere and Edmund asked Laura and James if they would like to take a look round the garden and some of the grounds.

'I think I'll stay and keep Miss Amy company if she has no objection,' James said. 'I'd like to know more about Paris, seeing as I have never been.'

Laura smiled. James did not like gardens, mud, or being out in the cold, and there was a keen breeze blowing. She could see tree branches dipping and dancing outside the window. 'I'd like to,' she said. 'Have we time to walk to the estuary before dark?'

'Yes, it isn't far, though I must find you some suitable footwear. It'll be rather muddy,' Edmund said.

'I've brought some,' she said. 'I'm prepared.'

'Really? I'm astonished.' He grinned.

'Oh, Laura is always pottering in the garden at home,' James said, stretching out his legs towards the fire.

'Hardly pottering,' she objected, rising from her chair. 'I plant trees, cultivate fruit and grow vegetables. Some of which you eat!'

Edmund opened the door for her and she said she would take only a moment to change into something suitable. In a very short time she came down into the hall wearing a woollen cloak over her dress and rubber boots on her feet.

'I'm impressed,' Edmund said admiringly. 'I had you down as a lady of elegance and leisure!' He had changed back into his boots whilst she was upstairs and put on a rubber mackintosh over his frock coat.

She gazed squarely at him. 'Perhaps I am that too,' she said. 'But I hate to sit around doing nothing. My mother is very industrious and I suppose I've inherited some of her traits.'

'We can walk down to the river,' he said. 'Or – do you ride?'

She confessed that she didn't. 'Though sometimes I wish that I did,' she said. 'We can see the river from our house in Hessle and I often think that it would be nice to ride along the foreshore.'

'Then we'll walk this time,' he said. 'But perhaps if you come again, I'll find you a steady mount and teach you to ride.'

She lowered her head. His gaze was intense, rather as his grandfather's had been. She had caught the older man looking at her several times during the afternoon. 'Perhaps,' she said softly, and then asked, 'When do your other guests arrive?'

'Later,' he said, 'before supper.'

He led her round the side of the house and towards the track through the woods which she'd noticed on their arrival. 'It's rather overgrown,' he said. 'My grandfather and I are the only ones to use it, but it's a short cut to the estuary. We both like to ride there. There's a good path along the embankment.' He took her arm as her feet became entangled by bramble, and again as she stepped over a fallen log.

'Are there bluebells?' she asked. 'In the spring, I mean.'

'Yes, and primroses and wild garlic, and the snowdrops and aconites will be up at Christmas.'

'We came to the estuary,' she told him. 'That day we met you in Hedon. We'd been to Welwick, and I saw flowers that looked like Michaelmas daisies.'

'Sea asters, probably,' he said. 'Though I'm not

very good with names of plants. But there's a great variety on the Welwick marshes.' He turned his head to gaze at her. 'Why did you go to Welwick? What was there that you wanted to see?'

She hesitated. She wanted so many answers, and yet she hadn't yet formulated the questions. 'I . . . was just interested,' she hedged. 'I've been to Hedon often, but never further than that. Never even been to Spurn Point. My mother has spoken of it, but never got round to taking us when we were children, though we went up the coast to Bridlington and Scarborough.'

She refrained from telling him that their mother was born in Holderness. Something held her back. There were many things her mother hadn't told her about her former life or her marriage to their father; and again came the memory of the first time in Paris. I must have been about three, and James – yes, James remained behind because he had been invited to stay at a friend's house. There was a grey mental mist hovering over the visit and yet she could remember laughing. They had all laughed. The three of them. Her mother, herself, and whoever it was who had lifted her up into his arms. But not my father, she mused. My mother said he died not long after I was born.

* * *

Some of the supper guests had to return home that night; others, like Laura and James, were staying until after tea on Sunday. 'I'd like to get off in good time tomorrow,' James told Laura as they went down to meet the new arrivals. 'Don't want Stubbs driving along these roads in the dark.'

'It will be dark before we get home anyway,' Laura objected. 'The light's already gone by six o'clock.' But she knew he would insist, and make the excuse that he had a busy day on Monday.

There were twelve of them sitting down at table, not including Miss Julia, who excused herself to have supper in her room. Mr Ellis sat at the head of the table and Edmund at the foot. Edmund wanted to have Laura at his side, but his grandfather forestalled him, insisting that she sit on his right.

Joseph carved the meat and a maid served the vegetables. They were a chatty crowd of people and quite informal, obviously used to coming to the house. The young men were farmers; some were with their wives, but the single ones, both men and women, were obviously not intentionally paired, but had been invited for their camaraderie. Edmund's cousin Mark, son of the Beverley farmer, was there. He was tall and fair like Edmund, and as their grandfather had been.

'So, Miss Page,' Joseph began. 'What is your

impression of Holderness?' His gaze lingered on her and she thought he seemed pensive. 'Do you think it flat and boring?'

'No, indeed not,' she said softly. 'I love the openness and the wide skies, and I saw a magnificent sunset tonight.'

He nodded. 'You went down to the estuary?'

'Yes. Edmund took me. It's quite different at this lower end from where we live in Hessle.'

'That's because there are more mud flats,' he said. 'It's also more saline; Spurn Point is constantly changing because of the coastal sediments and with the reclamation of Sunk Island and Cherry Cob Sands, so the tidal channel is narrower.' He continued to gaze at her as they waited for the next course. 'You must forgive me for monopolizing your time, and I know my grandson is angry with me because he wanted you to sit next to him, but you remind me very much of someone I once knew.' He put his hand over hers where it rested on the table. She didn't object, for there was nothing suggestive or secretive about the action. 'Someone I cared for when I was young,' he said quietly. 'She was very beautiful, as you are.'

'Did you love her?' she whispered, for this conversation, she realized, was meant only for her ears.

'I did,' he said. 'Very much.' Then he patted her hand and withdrew his. 'I'm sorry.' He sighed softly. 'Just an old man's memories. My grandson is rather taken with you, I think?'

She smiled. Edmund had been most attentive, and she also found him very appealing.

Joseph was about to say something more, but a sudden guffaw came from the other end of the table. 'Yes, but Edmund, you've got the best waggoner in the district,' Harry Fowler proclaimed. 'I'd give anything to have Tom Marston leading my lads.'

'How very odd!' Laura turned to Joseph Ellis and said, without thinking, 'My mother had a cousin called Thomas Marston. He worked with horses.'

Joseph became very still. 'Did she?' He faltered, his words husky. 'What – was your mother's name?'

Laura hesitated. Had she ever known? Marston? Not Brewster! Why had she never asked? Why had her mother never said? She swallowed, suddenly unsure of herself. 'Her name is Susannah.'

CHAPTER THIRTY-SEVEN

Laura and James arrived home late on Sunday evening. Edmund had insisted that they stay and have an early supper. Only two other guests stayed on, so there were just six of them at the table, as Aunt Julia said she would take a light meal in her room, and Edmund's grandfather, who had appeared only briefly at breakfast, looking red-eyed and tired as if he hadn't slept, didn't come down for supper.

After his grandfather had left the room the previous evening, Edmund had come to sit next to Laura. 'Grandfather is an old devil,' he'd said in a low voice. 'He knew I wanted you next to me. I hope you weren't bored?'

'Not at all. He's charming – but . . .'

'What?' There had been a note of anxiety in his voice.

'Well – he seemed upset, and I'm not sure if it was because of something I said.'

'Miss Page! I don't believe it. Whatever

could *you* have said to upset him?'

She'd shaken her head. 'I don't know. But I think there was something.'

They'd left with Edmund eagerly asking if they would come again. He'd pressed Laura's hand. 'Please do,' he'd urged. 'I would so much like you to.'

She had thanked him, but hadn't promised even though he seemed so ardent. However, she knew that she would like to.

Joseph Ellis came to see them off. He'd given her a courtly bow and said they must come again, but there was a constraint, and Laura thought that he was only being polite to his grandchildren's friends and would relish the quiet of the house once they had gone.

'Mama! Where are you?' Laura called upstairs. 'Where's my mother, Smithy? Has she gone to bed already?'

'Yes, Miss Laura, she has. I think she's sickening for something. She's been off colour all day.'

'Oh! She was all right when we left. Will she be asleep? Should I go up?'

'She isn't asleep. I've just taken her a cup of hot milk.' The housekeeper folded Laura's cloak over her arm. 'She was all right yesterday morning. It was in the afternoon, after Mr Cannon called, that she came over giddy.'

'Mr Cannon called?'

'Yes, Miss Laura, though he didn't stay long.'

Laura climbed the stairs and quietly knocked on her mother's door. Her mother was rarely ill and hardly ever went to bed before eleven. 'It's me, Mama,' she said, going into the room. 'Smithy said you were unwell.'

'I'm perfectly well, Laura. Smithy does fuss so!' Her mother was sitting up in bed, sipping from a cup. 'I was rather tired, that's all, and decided to come to bed early.' She glanced at the bedside clock. 'Though it's not so very early – ten o'clock. Have you had a pleasant time?'

'Yes, lovely.' Laura sat on the edge of the bed. 'Though I don't think James likes the country. He wanted to leave earlier but Edmund insisted we stayed for supper.'

'Edmund?' her mother quizzed her. 'So familiar so soon?'

Laura smiled. 'They're not at all stuffy, but then everyone knew everyone else. James and I were the only strangers.'

'What kind of house was it?' her mother asked. 'When I was a child . . .' She paused. 'Well, I think I went once, but I don't know why I did. I can remember going up some steps and into a large hall and then up a staircase.' She took another sip of milk. 'But there again, I'm not sure. Perhaps I imagined it.'

'I didn't tell them that you were from Holderness,' Laura said. 'I thought they might ask questions, and I wouldn't know the answers.

410

Mama, there are some things I'd like to ask you.'

'Not tonight, Laura,' her mother said, and then, with a slight hesitation, added, 'Freddie called in yesterday. He – that is – he came with bad news. His wife died early on Saturday morning.'

'Oh! Oh, dear,' Laura breathed. 'So she was ill after all?'

'When Freddie was sent for – I told you, didn't I, that I was there when he received the summons from the doctor? Well, when he arrived home, seemingly Mrs Cannon had sustained a fall, but the servants hadn't thought at first that the matter was urgent. Eventually they sent for the doctor, who didn't come immediately; perhaps he too thought she was overstating her symptoms as usual. But when he arrived she had deteriorated and he could do nothing for her, and so he sent for Freddie,' she ended faintly.

'I am sorry,' Laura said. 'Poor Uncle Freddie. Will you go to the funeral service?'

'I don't think so,' Susannah said softly. 'Unless I am asked. I never met Mrs Cannon, but I will send Freddie a letter of condolence.'

Laura rose to her feet. 'I'll tell James, shall I? He won't have gone to bed yet.'

'Yes, please, if you would, dear.'

'And can we speak tomorrow, Mama? There are several things I want to ask you. Things that

I've been puzzling over.' She halted, her hand on the brass bed rail. 'Edmund Ellis's sister, Amy, spends a lot of time in France – their grandmother is French. I told her that I'd been to Paris twice; once when I was very young, and once when I was twelve. Do you remember?' Her gaze took in her mother's startled expression. 'And we bumped into Uncle Freddie, didn't we? We were all amazed at the coincidence of our being there at the same time.'

'Yes, I do remember,' her mother murmured. 'I really am tired, Laura. We'll talk tomorrow. Good night, dear.'

After Laura had closed the door behind her, Susannah closed her eyes and put her head back against the pillows, cradling the cup in her hands. So has the time come? she thought. Is this my time of reckoning? What do I tell the children – except they are no longer children, but adults. Even so, will they understand?

She took another sip of milk. How and where do I begin? Do I tell them bluntly that their dead father didn't exist? That I have lived a lie all these years? Or do I start at the time when Uncle Brewster died and Aunt Brewster was so bereft that she couldn't cope?

'You see, m'dear,' Aunt Brewster had wept, 'we'd been together for such a long time. We never had children – well, just the one and she died within hours – so we onny had each other to care for.' She'd managed a wistful smile. 'So when you came along it was as if we'd been given a granddaughter, for our girl would have been old enough, had she lived, to have had a daughter of your age.'

Susannah was effectively running the Fleet by that time. The alterations and renovations were finished and people were flocking there to take a look. It was a pleasant walk from Hedon, so the locals came; and the inn was now able to accommodate visitors. There were three extra bedrooms, simple but adequate, and an ample breakfast was provided in a small dining room; but when Uncle Brewster had gone and Aunt Brewster wasn't able to help her, Susannah felt she had to take on more staff. She'd discussed it with Freddie, who had almost finished at university and always came to stay during the summer.

'Employ a woman who can cook,' he'd advised. 'And a cellar man. That will leave you free to be with the customers and supervise the running of the place.'

She'd been relieved at his words. She had felt as if she was needed in half a dozen places at once, cooking and serving and looking after Aunt Brewster, with only a young girl to help her. The inn was making money; she could afford to take on staff.

'You're so wise, Freddie,' she'd said. 'I don't know what I'd do without you.'

He'd put his chin in his hand and closed his eyes. 'I have to marry Maria, Susannah,' he muttered. 'Father says he can't afford a scandal. It would ruin him.'

She said nothing, though her mind was in turmoil. Did he really love her? Where did his loyalties lie?

'Father was lost without my mother,' Freddie said quietly. 'That's why he lavished so much on me. My education, my chance of a partnership with him. But I love you, Susannah. I thought that Maria would have given up this obsession. I've told her that I don't wish to marry for years, but she's already planning the wedding; she and her mother. I don't know what to do.' He gazed at her. 'What can I do?'

I can't help him, she thought unhappily. I cannot sway him one way or another. He's promised to Maria whether he likes it or not. She thinks it is a binding contract. She must be desperate to want to marry a man who doesn't want her. She must love him so much that she won't give him up. Susannah took in a deep searing breath. So I must.

'If there is no way out,' she said quietly, 'then you must marry her.'

He'd put his arms round her. 'I won't consummate the marriage,' he murmured into her ear. 'I can't bear to think of it. I will not share her bed!' He looked into her eyes. 'Do you understand what I'm saying, Susannah?'

She looked away. Yes, she did. But she couldn't believe it. Once he was married, she would lose him. He would stop coming to Hedon and she would be alone again.

'I will live in hope that she'll eventually lose patience with me and file for a divorce,' he said. 'It might take a few years, Susannah, but by then my father will probably have retired; he's not all that well, and I shall be running the practice and will have everything at my disposal. She will do it quietly, for I will advise her that the scandal will fall on her head.'

But she didn't. Maria seemed to be content that she had Freddie's name, so he told Susannah, for contrary to her expectations he still came to see her. He had a legitimate reason for visiting, for after the firm of Cannon and Cannon was set up his father handed over to him the file detailing the leasing of the Fleet Inn, which, he said, had to be conducted to the absolute letter of the original contract held by them and Mr Watson.

Freddie read it and realized that he had done the right thing after all in joining his father, for now he could look after Susannah in ways he hadn't envisaged.

Aunt Brewster died in the winter just before Susannah's twenty-first birthday. She was very old and had been in failing health since her husband died. Susannah wrote to Freddie to tell him and asking for advice on the lease of the Fleet. He came to visit her a few days after receiving her letter.

'Everything is in place,' he said. 'The agreement is in your name.'

'So soon?' she exclaimed. 'How is that?'

He explained. 'The owners are quite happy with the way the inn is being run. In fact, there is to be an extra sum of money deposited during November for you to make other changes if you should so wish.'

'I don't understand,' she said. 'Do they not want to come and look?'

'They see the accounts,' he told her. 'That's all they seem to be interested in. But then,' he added, 'perhaps they have been to visit. There are so many customers now, perhaps they have been and you didn't know.'

It was a strange way of doing business, she thought, but she surmised that as Mr Watson lived in Hedon he would hear if something was amiss and would report back to the agent.

'Susannah!' Freddie collected up the papers from the table in the new parlour where they were sitting, and placed them in his brown leather briefcase. 'The Fleet is doing so very well that I wondered if you'd ever thought of taking on another run-down inn and making it a success as you have done with this one?'

'And leave here?' She was astonished at the suggestion. 'No, I hadn't. This is my home. Even though I'm very sad because Aunt Brewster isn't here with me.'

Indeed, she was as low-spirited as she had ever been. She would be twenty-one in just over two weeks, and had been twelve years old when Aunt Brewster had taken her in, giving her a home and the love and care that she longed for; and now she was gone. After everyone had left at night, and if there were no visitors staying, the inn was very quiet; all she could hear was the trickle of water in the stream and the occasional hoot of an owl or bark of a fox, and she felt very alone.

'I thought not.' Freddie deliberated for a moment and then explained his reason for asking the question. 'It's just that I've come across a landlord in Beverley who is struggling and desperately wants to sell. It's only a small place, but I feel it could be a successful business with the right person in charge.' He looked at her and stroked his dark sideburns. 'It would be a big challenge, but if you were interested I'm sure I could speak to the right people for you to raise a mortgage.'

'Oh!' She stared at him, her lips apart. 'To own it! Not to be a tenant?'

'Yes.' He got up from the table. 'Must go or I'll miss my train. Forget I mentioned it,' he told her. 'It was just an idea.' He kissed her. 'I have such faith in you. You're such a clever young woman,' he said. Then he kissed her again. 'I love you,' he whispered. 'For ever.'

She had acted on Freddie's previous suggestion and employed Ruby Cross, a plump and jolly young woman, to work in the kitchen and Jack Howard to look after the beer. There wasn't strictly a cellar, but a brick extension had been built at the back of the house at a slightly lower level than the main building, with an hydraulic beer engine to draw up the ale into the inn. The cook and the cellar man worked well together and Susannah saw that there was a mutual attraction between them. I hope they don't leave, she'd mused, and take a hostelry together, though she doubted that they would as they had no money apart from the wages she gave them.

When her birthday came, there was a letter from Freddie wishing her a happy day and wishing too that he could spend it with her, but as it wasn't long since his last visit there was no reason or excuse to validate another.

She pondered on a few things, and when she saw the large amount of money which had been entered into the inn's account book, and strangely enough on her birthday, she thought again of Freddie's suggestion regarding the inn in Beverley and decided to write to him.

'Dear Mr Cannon,' she wrote, always aware

that his father, or their secretary, might also see the letter.

I have given some thought to the particulars of the business venture in Beverley which you mentioned on your last visit and might be interested to hear more details. The sum of money intended for changes or renewal to the Fleet has been deposited, and I wondered if there were any stipulations on how this should be spent? Perhaps you would inform me by letter or call on me to discuss it. Alternatively I will call on you if that is more convenient.

She finished the letter, signed it and addressed the envelope clearly to Mr Frederick Cannon. She had never called at his office, nor did she intend to, not whilst his father was still there, but she liked to suggest that she might, in case his father read his correspondence.

Freddie's secretary wrote back to inform her that he would call to see her within the week, and when he came she could tell he was brimming with enthusiasm. 'The man is ready to sell,' he told her. 'Are you really interested?'

'Only if I can have a manager here,' she said. 'The Fleet is so important to me. Would I be able to use the extra money to pay someone? Or even use some of it towards the place in Beverley? I'd pay it back, of course.'

'As far as I am aware,' he told her, 'you can do whatever you wish with it. There are no stipulations on its use.'

'Then if that is the case, I'll look at this place in Beverley,' she said. 'And ask Jack if he'd like to be manager here. He's very efficient and he told me last week that he and Ruby would get married if they could only afford it. They could have Aunt Brewster's old room and I'd keep mine. I wouldn't forsake the Fleet entirely.'

Susannah put her empty cup onto the saucer on the bedside table and slid down into bed, pulling the sheets up to her chin. So that is how it began. But it doesn't tell Laura and James about their father. How will they react when they find out how shamefully their mother acted?

I remember the day so well. I was considered to be very successful, a young woman on her own achieving so much without the help of a husband. The inn in Beverley was transformed and I was spending most of my time there, while the Fleet was flourishing under the managership of Jack and Ruby. I'd rented a flower shop in Hull and on Freddie's advice I was about to buy another. Yet I was still unfulfilled. There was something missing from my life.

I'd gone back to Hedon for a few days. Freddie knew I was there for I had written to him to say I needed a quiet time. The fact was I felt very alone, even though by now I knew many people and was responsible for some of them. I walked one day along the beck towards the old Hedon haven and came to the log where Freddie and I used to sit. I was suddenly overcome with grief: for what I had lost and for what I had never had.

Freddie just appeared. It was as if he knew I was at a low ebb, and indeed he said afterwards that he could tell by my letter that something was amiss.

Susannah wiped away a tear with the bed sheet. I don't know how I plucked up the courage to say it, she thought. I'm not the kind of woman to allow my emotions to come to the surface. But I was nearly twenty-four years old, successful, with enough money, thanks to Freddie's advice on how to invest, yet alone and without anyone of my own to love.

'What is it, Susannah?' Freddie had asked tenderly. 'What is it that's troubling you? It's me, isn't it? You think that I don't love you enough. And I understand that you would think that, after the way I've treated you. But I do love you, my darling. I want to prove it, more than anything in the world.' He held her close. 'I've even thought – oh, so many terrible thoughts, about how to remove Maria from my life. But I can't. I should have been brave enough at the start to stand up to my father and to Maria and her mother. I'm not worthy of you, my dearest.' He looked into her eyes. 'But if I didn't have you in my life, then it would be worth nothing.'

Susannah gazed up at him. Was he willing to prove his love? If she was, then so should he be.

'Freddie,' she had whispered, 'I want a child. Your child.'

CHAPTER THIRTY-EIGHT

Joseph Ellis had excused himself from the supper table and paced his bedroom floor. He could hear the voices of the young people below, some laughter, and then music as someone, probably Amy, played the piano. What am I to do? They must be Susannah's son and daughter. Have to be! There couldn't be such a coincidence. Edmund said that he met them at the Fleet Inn! Where Susannah once lived and which is in her name, though she doesn't realize it, if the solicitors have acted as I insisted they must.

After seeing Susannah at the Fleet on that day all those years ago, he had made numerous discreet enquiries about the two old people who ran the inn. He discovered that they were born and bred Hedon people and had been tenants there since their marriage, and was told that they had taken Susannah in to live with them. They claimed that she was their niece, but everyone knew that she wasn't.

He thought of the exorbitant amount of money he had been pleased to pay to buy the inn from the owners, and of the complicated arrangement which he had devised with the two solicitors and his agent to ensure that Susannah would take on the lease after the old people had passed away. He recalled how surprised he was, after depositing the large sum of money on her twenty-first birthday, that she chose to employ a manager for the Fleet and then bought another inn. Some of the money was taken out of the account, but later put back in and used to up-grade the Fleet even further. He felt proud of her success and wished that he could have shared it with her.

But then she had moved out of his sphere. The solicitor who handled her affairs told his agent that she was to be married and that he couldn't disclose her whereabouts, but that the Fleet would remain her responsibility. Joseph had felt cut off and downcast that he was no longer able to play a part in Susannah's life, yet relieved that she had found someone to love and care for her.

'But now,' he muttered, 'here are her son and daughter. My grandchildren! And—' Realization hit him and he felt sick with dismay. Edmund! His grandson had invited them purely because he was attracted to Laura!

I understand how he feels, he thought. I felt

the same for Mary-Ellen. The moment I saw her I knew she was the only one for me. But I must put a stop to this before it's too late! But how? Do I confess? Arlette doesn't know. I never told her. I should have, but there never seemed to be a right time.

He sat down on his bed, leaning his head on his hand. The lamp was dim, the room shadowy. 'Mary-Ellen,' he breathed. 'We never thought, never imagined that our love would come to this.' He recalled the memorable night she had stayed here. His parents were away and he had persuaded her to come back with him. She had gazed round the room, unused to such luxuries, and asking questions. He looked across at his battered *chaise-longue* and remembered, hearing a faint echo of her voice. 'Hah!' she had muttered scornfully. 'I knew it was a long chair. Why don't they call it that, then, instead of giving it a silly French name?'

Wistfully he reminisced. How lovely she was, how wild and unpredictable. I loved her so much. And now I must shatter my grandson's dreams. Just as mine were shattered. He put his head in his hands and wept.

Laura lay sleepless in her bed. She wasn't tired, nor restless, but quite content to lie and think about the weekend. Her mind flitted from the company she had met to the conversations they

425

had had, the walk by the estuary, the laughter; but at each and every shift and turn her thoughts returned to Edmund Ellis. She liked him, liked him a lot, and he had made it quite obvious that he was attracted to her. He was different from most men she had met. Handsome – not that that mattered, she thought. Strength of character was more important, and he had that all right. He seemed strong and positive and knew what he wanted in life. Inherited that from his grandfather, I imagine. I could see Joseph Ellis as being strong-willed and decisive when he was young.

James, too, she pondered, thinking of her brother. He's very positive now that he's older and doing well at the bank. But when he was young he seemed aimless and resentful. Perhaps he missed having a father; it wasn't until Freddie put him on the right track and suggested to Mama that he went away to Pocklington school that he became resolute and ambitious. I wonder how well they knew each other, James and Edmund. I don't recall James ever mentioning him.

Her thoughts meandered back to Burstall House. Such a comfortable house; full of character and echoes of previous generations. I wonder why Edmund's grandmother wasn't there. Why would she spend so much time in Paris, away from her family? Does Joseph Ellis

426

miss her, I wonder. And who was the woman he once loved?

She began to feel drowsy. There were many things she would like to know about the Ellis family. She turned her lamp down, and snuggled into her pillows. I must brush up on my French, she mused. Perhaps Mama and I might go again. Last time we were there— Her mind, inert and somnolent, abruptly awoke. Last time – no, not the last time! The time before! Her heart began to pound. When I was lifted into someone's arms. It was Uncle Freddie! She sat up and clutched her arms about herself. It was Uncle Freddie! He swung me high in the air and my skirts flew up, showing my drawers. We all laughed and my mother – she wore a blue crinoline and a white bonnet trimmed with blue ribbons – admonished him, tapping him playfully on his arm, saying, 'Freddie!'

Sleep deserted her and she rose from her bed and walked the floor. Has Uncle Freddie been my mother's lover all these years? Since my father died? So many things slipped into place. Freddie had always appeared on their birthdays and their mother's birthday, and then that time we met him in Paris, on our second visit. Was it really a coincidence or did they arrange to meet? Mama said she had known Freddie since they were both young. Were they childhood sweethearts? And if they were, why didn't they

427

marry? Will they marry now that Mrs Cannon has died?

She resolved that the next day, after James came home from the bank, she would ask him his opinion. I don't want to jump to conclusions, and I suppose, she reflected reluctantly, it has nothing to do with us. Perhaps it would be better if we didn't know. Mama will be so embarrassed if she thinks I have found out her secret. She will expect me to be shocked and I suppose I am. Poor Mrs Cannon! Did she ever guess that her husband might have been unfaithful? Perhaps that is why she was always ill, with the worry of it.

The following morning she changed her mind. She wouldn't after all mention it to James. He could fly off in a temper sometimes, and he might think she had been ferreting amongst issues which didn't concern her. And she wouldn't ask her mother the pressing questions either. She was obviously under some strain since Freddie had told her of his wife's death. I mustn't meddle, she thought. There are sure to be changes sometime soon. Mama will tell us when she is ready.

Susannah wrote a formal letter of commiseration to Freddie on the sudden death of his wife. She couched it in such a way as to give no hint that he had given her the news in person, and stressed that he should find comfort in the fact that his wife hadn't suffered and that the end had been swift. Then she wrote another note which she marked private and personal, in which she requested a visit as soon as was convenient as she wished to discuss a matter relating to her son and daughter.

He called a few days after the funeral. It was a bitterly cold evening and he said he had come straight from his office. He was wrapped warmly in overcoat and wool scarf, and when he removed his top hat he shook off a flurry of snowflakes.

Susannah greeted him when he was shown into the sitting room. 'Will you stay for supper, Freddie? James isn't coming in until later, so Laura and I will eat early.'

'No, thank you, Susannah,' he said. 'I still have much to do, sorting out Maria's affairs. Good evening, Laura.' He bent to kiss Laura's cheek. 'You're looking well.'

'Good evening, Uncle Freddie.' Laura's cheeks flushed, and she felt rather embarrassed over what she thought she knew. 'I hope you are well, in the circumstances?'

'I am.' He sighed. 'Though it's been a difficult time. A shock, you know.' He glanced at Susannah and Laura turned her eyes away.

'Laura, would you mind asking Smithy to ask Cook to hold supper back for half an hour?' her mother asked.

Laura rose from her chair, musing that her

mother could easily have rung the bell and told Smithy herself. She wants to speak to Uncle Freddie alone. Do I stay out of the way? Do I let them discuss whatever it is Uncle Freddie has called for? 'Yes, of course,' she said. 'And would you excuse me, Uncle Freddie? There's something I need to do before supper.'

She left the room and heard her mother say, 'Freddie dear, won't you come and spend Christmas with us? You mustn't stay alone at this time.'

Laura didn't hear Freddie's reply, for the front doorbell rang, making her jump. 'I'll go, Smithy,' she called out. 'Perhaps it's James after all.'

She opened the door, prepared to deliver a sardonic quip to James for his unreliability, but swallowed her words when she saw Edmund Ellis standing on the doorstep. He wore a heavy caped coat and on his head a bowler hat, which made her smile. It seemed incongruous on him. When they had walked by the estuary he had worn a soft leather one more suited to him.

'Mr Ellis!' she murmured.

He took off the bowler and held it awkwardly in both hands. 'Miss Page. Laura. How – how are you? I called in the hope of seeing your brother.'

'James didn't mention that you were calling. Don't tell me he has forgotten you were coming! That's too bad of him. Please come in.' She opened the door wider to admit him.

He stepped inside the hall. 'I beg your pardon.

He, erm, he wasn't expecting me. I, erm, I was in the vicinity and I'm – so sorry.' Edmund ran his finger round the collar of his coat. 'I – it was on impulse, Miss Page. Not the thing to do at all, I realize. I forget that town and country manners are quite different.'

She stood watching him flounder for a moment, then, raising her eyebrows, said loftily, 'Hessle is hardly town, Mr Ellis.' She saw a slight flush touch his cheeks. Then she laughed. 'Please come and meet my mother. James isn't here. He won't be in until late.'

'I don't wish to intrude,' he said awkwardly. 'Perhaps you are in the middle of supper? No? Well then, if it isn't inconvenient.'

She paused with her hand on the knob of the sitting room door. 'Not inconvenient,' she said. 'As a matter of fact, a friend has also just called to see my mother.' She suddenly remembered that she hadn't passed on her mother's message to the housekeeper. 'Would you care to stay for supper? James won't be back and Freddie can't stay.'

'Thank you, no. It's unthinkable. I will be pleased to be introduced to your mother, but then I'll take my leave of you. It was thoughtless of me to call without an invitation.'

She gave a slight smile and thought that she would be happy for him to call whenever he wished. With a flutter of disbelief, she sensed that James was not the reason for his visit.

'Mama, we have a visitor,' she announced. Her mother was standing by the fireplace, one hand on the mantelpiece, and Freddie was still in the same position as before. 'May I introduce Mr Edmund Ellis? He was in the vicinity and came to call on James.'

Edmund gave a slight bow, but Susannah moved towards him, her hand outstretched. 'I'm pleased to meet you, Mr Ellis,' she said, and Edmund bowed again over her fingers. 'You were most kind to invite James and Laura to your home.' She turned towards Freddie. 'I must introduce you to our good friend Frederick Cannon.'

The two men shook hands. 'Have you come far, Mr Ellis?' Freddie gave Edmund a searching glance. 'It's a cold evening for travelling.'

'Only from Hull. I – I've been visiting the Corn Exchange. My home is in Holderness.'

'Oh!' Freddie looked startled, but, recovering quickly, said, 'I trust you won't travel back to-night?'

'No,' Edmund said. 'I've found lodgings in Hull and will leave early in the morning.' He turned to Susannah. 'Mrs Page, I do apologize for calling unannounced, but I wished to invite James and Miss Page to visit us again. We generally have a few friends to dine with us shortly before Christmas. We haven't decided on the exact date as yet, but' – he looked at Laura –

'if there is a particular day that would be convenient . . . ?' He again addressed her mother. 'And perhaps you would give us the pleasure of your company also?'

Susannah's eyes gleamed as she glanced at Laura. 'That is most kind of you,' she said. 'But I'm afraid we couldn't possibly consider coming to Holderness until winter is over.' Edmund's face fell at her words and he twisted his hat in his hands. 'But in the early spring perhaps,' she added. 'If you would care to invite us then?' Her expression became pensive. 'It's a long long time since I was in your part of Holderness, though I come to Hedon several times a year.'

'Skeffling is not so far from Hedon,' Edmund said eagerly. 'I could meet you there and show you the way.'

Susannah gave a wistful smile. 'I think perhaps I might remember it.'

He departed then and Laura showed him out, opening the front door to see a sprinkling of snow. 'Have you come by hackney?' She peered out into the night.

'No, the brougham,' he said, gazing at her profile, her fine eyes and high cheekbones. 'We use it when the weather is bad. It's old but reliable.'

'And you have your very fashionable bowler to keep you warm and dry!' she said banteringly, turning towards him.

433

He looked at her teasing eyes and laughing mouth, then down at the bowler hat which he spun round and round in his hands. 'I thought it would impress you,' he admitted. 'But I feel I might have been mistaken.'

'I didn't consider you to be a modish man, Mr Ellis,' she said wryly, 'and if you are, and if my opinion is worth a trifle, I must tell you that fashionable attire doesn't impress me in the least!'

He nodded his head slowly as he gazed into her eyes, then turning to the open door he reached out his hand holding the bowler and flung it, sending it spinning into the night.

Laura let out a peal of laughter. 'There was no need to take such drastic action!'

He smiled with her and clasped her hand. 'I bought it only today. You know, don't you, that I came to see you and not James?'

Slowly she released her hand from his grasp. 'You are impetuous, I think, Mr Ellis.'

'Edmund, Laura, and I'm not usually so.' His eyes searched her face for approval. 'May I call on you? May I ask your mother for her permission? Must I wait until spring before I see you again?'

She swallowed. 'I don't know,' she whispered. 'It's too soon. We have only just met.'

'It's not too soon.' He took her hand again and, turning it over, he kissed the palm.

'Forgive me,' he said. 'I'm nothing but a fool since I met you. I may seem hasty but that's not my nature, or at least it wasn't until I first saw you. Did you not find it odd that James should receive an invitation so soon after our meeting at the Fleet?' He stroked her hand, which she hadn't withdrawn. 'I barely remember James from school,' he said. 'But I knew I had to see you again.'

There was the sound of the sitting room door's being opened and he dropped her hand. 'Let me write to you at least,' he whispered urgently. 'Please!'

'Yes,' she breathed. 'But I must show your letters to my mother. Be circumspect above all else.'

'I will.' He grinned with delight. 'Be sure that I will.'

Freddie took his hat and coat from the housekeeper, who bade him goodnight. A worried frown creased his forehead. 'Don't go to Holderness just yet, Susannah, will you?' he said as she stood with him by the door. Laura had said a swift goodnight to him and run upstairs. 'These young people don't know each other.'

She smiled. 'I said that we wouldn't. 'Roads will be bad. I know how hazardous they can be. But we'll go in 'spring,' she said softly. 'I'd like to go back. I'm ready, I think, to see all the old places again. Mr Ellis seemed a pleasant young man, didn't he?' she added.

Freddie gave a soft non-committal grunt. 'He patently didn't come to see James,' he said. 'That was obvious.' He paused. 'Don't let him call on Laura,' he murmured. 'We know nothing of him. I'll make enquiries about his family.'

Susannah's eyes gazed softly into his. 'Very well, *Papa*!' she breathed, smiling gently. 'If that is what you wish. But we do know of his family,' she added in the same low tone. 'The Ellises are well known Holderness people.'

CHAPTER THIRTY-NINE

Laura received the first letter from Edmund a few days after his visit. It was formal and polite, addressed her as Miss Page and apologized to her and her mother for calling without an invitation. 'I regret that time and my manners did not dictate to me that I should send a card to James before calling,' he wrote, 'but quite often out here in rural Holderness if friends, ladies as well as gentlemen, are in the vicinity of one another's houses, then we are apt to visit and enquire after each other's well-being. Perhaps we would be considered socially inferior by some, but we are busy working people and I make no apology for that.'

He went on to tell of his journey home, and remarked that winter was coming with a vengeance.

She showed the letter to her mother, for it had obviously been written for her to see. Susannah smiled and said, 'He knows nothing of our life,

Laura. Perhaps he thinks that we sit at home every day waiting for morning or afternoon callers! If he does think that, then I suggest you write and tell him otherwise. Let him know that you are an emancipated young woman with interests, opinions and views of your own.'

'Oh, I think he realizes that already, Mama,' Laura replied dryly. 'We had animated conversations when James and I visited Skeffling.'

'He came to see you, of course,' her mother commented. 'James was only an excuse. Had James been here, I wonder what they would have talked about?'

'Well, not farming, of that I'm quite sure!' Laura laughed. 'And not the weather. Banking, perhaps? That seems to be James's sole interest!'

'Freddie thinks that we should be circumspect, Laura,' her mother said cautiously. 'We both saw that Mr Ellis is obviously taken with you. It wouldn't do to let events move too fast too soon.'

Laura, unreasonably provoked by Freddie's well-meaning concern, answered abruptly, 'I realize that Freddie has always taken an interest in us and given sound advice, Mama, but I'm quite able to make up my own mind about who shall be my friends!'

'That I realize,' her mother said, equally briskly, 'but Freddie seemed unduly anxious, so perhaps it's as well that winter is here and that your friendship with Mr Ellis is confined to letter writing!'

During supper Laura thought that her mother seemed preoccupied, but she often was for she was always busy. She supervised the accounts of the Hedon and Beverley inns, sometimes calling on the managers unexpectedly, and did the same with the two shops in Hull. Laura and James too were often called on to discuss the businesses and their opinions asked on the running of them.

Over coffee, Susannah said quietly, 'I've asked Freddie to come to us for Christmas, Laura. It is quite fitting that he comes. Widows must stay at home during the mourning period, but it is not the same for widowers, who must of course go about their business as usual.'

Her cheeks had flushed slightly and she lowered her eyes as she spoke. 'I did not like to think he would spend the holiday alone in his house with only the servants for company. Besides which, he – he has things to think about, and discuss with us.'

'With *us*?' Laura said. 'Why with us?'

'He has no-one else. He's always considered us as his family.' Her mother's voice was not only quiet, but tearful too, Laura recognized, so she didn't question her further but merely said warmly, 'Of course he mustn't be alone. And I suppose it is a large house too, too big for a single person?'

Her mother said she believed that it was, though she had never visited it, but didn't give any hint, which was what Laura was waiting for, that perhaps she and Freddie might marry when his mourning was over. It's too soon, Laura told herself. Freddie would want to wait. He wouldn't want to invite any scandal by marrying too quickly after his bereavement.

Laura wrote back to Edmund Ellis, as her mother had suggested, and told him that they were not in the least conventional and rarely went calling; nor did anyone leave cards on them. 'Not now,' she wrote, 'though I believe they once did. My mother is far too busy for such things and so am I. I am like your great-aunt Julia in that respect, though I don't knit or sew for charity but aim to organize others. I am not a blue-stocking, but I have an interest in politics and philosophy and like to read on both subjects.' She paused in her writing as she recalled that it was Freddie who had encouraged her in this.

'I do like feminine things,' she continued, 'but tend to disregard anything too frivolous, and as you will already have gathered I do express my own opinions. I shall quite understand, therefore, if after hearing of my improper and unladylike disposition you do not wish to continue our correspondence.'

She sent off the letter after giving it first to her

mother to read, who told her that she thought she had been rather severe with the young man.

'Not at all, Mama,' Laura exclaimed. 'If he wishes to know me, then know me he will, for I shall tell him myself of my headstrong character and rebellious nature!'

Nevertheless she waited anxiously for an answer, hoping that she had not been too discouraging, and one came just three days later. There were the usual polite enquiries after her health and that of her mother and brother, and then a wry comment on her lifestyle. 'I had thought of you as a young lady who would like to embroider, or play the piano, with perhaps a gentle game of cards for amusement, and for exercise a short walk in the garden or around the drawing room if the weather were inclement.' She smiled widely as she continued reading. 'That is the impression you gave on visiting us here at Burstall House, so I must say how disappointed I am to hear that that is not the case.'

Within the letter was another sheet of writing paper, intended for her eyes only, and containing a pressed red rosebud. 'Dear Laura,' it said, when the other had addressed her as Miss Page.

It is bitterly cold here. There are icicles a foot long hanging from the barn doors and gutters, and sparkling white frost covers the trees and bushes. The robins' breasts are vivid scarlet as is my nose from being outside all day, and yet when I cut through the garden this morning I spied this pristine precious rose still clinging tenaciously to the bush. How it has survived I know not, but I picked it thinking of you, and send it with my admiration.

Edmund.

She was touched by his sentiments. She hadn't considered him romantic and yet he clearly was. She felt a flutter of excitement. We do not know each other, she reflected. And I am wishing that we did.

Freddie arrived on Christmas Eve. He wore a black armband over his coat sleeve and his shirt cuffs were linked with black jet, but he displayed no other sign of mourning. He was laden with parcels and had a hint of suppressed nervousness about him. Laura and James were coming downstairs as Mrs Smith opened the door to him. He kissed Laura and shook hands with James and wished the housekeeper the season's greetings, giving her a small parcel as he did so. 'Just a little something for Boxing Day, Mrs Smith.' He fumbled in his pocket and brought out another. 'And one for Cook in appreciation of the excellent suppers she has given me.'

When she had gone, taking his coat and hat, he followed Laura into the sitting room where Susannah was waiting. She rose from her chair to greet him. 'My dear,' he said, 'it's so good to see you.' He gave her a kiss on her cheek. 'Thank you for inviting me.'

Laura felt that the last few words were for the benefit of her and James, and she saw the flush on her mother's cheeks and the nervous swallow in her throat as she spoke. 'We would have been saddened to think of you spending Christmas alone, Freddie. Isn't that so?' she said, turning to Laura and James.

James nodded vigorously and said, 'Do you know, I can remember when I was young asking Mama why you couldn't come and spend Christmas with us, and she had to explain that you had a home of your own. I cried, I think,' he admitted sheepishly; and then apologized profusely to Freddie for his inane blunder when he had only just lost his wife. 'I'm so sorry, Uncle Freddie,' he said. 'It was tactless of me to remind you of happier times.'

Freddie glanced at Susannah and was about to speak when Mrs Smith came in with a tray set with glasses and a sherry decanter. 'Cook says to thank you very much, Mr Cannon,' she said, before leaving the room, 'and that she will thank you personally on Boxing Day.'

James got up and poured them each a glass of

sherry, then lifted his glass in a toast. He glanced at Freddie. 'Should we drink to absent friends?' he asked. 'Though I never met Mrs Cannon, I'm sure she is sorely missed.'

Freddie hesitated, holding the rim of the glass close to his lips. He gave a deep sigh and said, 'I'd rather we drank to present company, James. My wife never drank, nor to my knowledge or in my presence ever gave a toast in honour of anyone. If she had a good life, then I would be pleased to know that it wasn't wasted.' He looked from an astonished James to an equally startled Laura. 'But I wasn't privy to it.' He drank half of his sherry like a man whose life depended on it, then put the glass down on a side table and got to his feet.

'It wasn't meant to be announced like this, Susannah,' he said to her as she sat with her fingers clasped tightly beneath her chin and a tremble on her lips. 'But now is as good a time as any, I think?'

Laura saw her mother give Freddie an almost imperceptible look of pleading, as if she was asking him something, and he strode across to her. 'They have to know, Susannah,' he said softly, leaning over her. 'They are a grown man and woman. We cannot protect them any longer, and we owe it to ourselves.'

'You're going to be married?' Laura said in a shaky voice. 'I guessed as much. You just have to wait until your mourning is over?'

Freddie gently fingered Susannah's hair as he spoke to Laura. 'Yes, that is true. Your mother has waited a very long time. We have both waited. And although we would not have wished for my wife's death and might have been prepared to wait even longer, that is not the only thing we have to divulge.'

'I was going to tell you,' Susannah said in a low voice. 'But I couldn't seem to find 'courage. I was so afraid of what you'd think. That you would judge us.'

'Mama!' James rose to his feet. 'We would only wish you happiness. There is no-one I'd rather have as a stepfather, and I'm sure that Laura will say the same.'

He turned to Laura for confirmation but she sat still as stone. There is more, she thought, as the memories of Paris came flooding back again. Much more.

Freddie licked his lips and glanced down at Susannah. She straightened her back and lifted her chin and Laura saw a look of determination steal across her face. For all her mother's quiet and gentle manner, she was always purposeful and resolute.

Susannah took hold of Freddie's hand and, holding it by her shoulder, rubbed her cheek against it. 'I have loved Freddie since I was just a girl.' She smiled tremulously up at him. 'And he has loved me. Circumstances decreed that we couldn't marry.' She hesitated. 'When I realized that I might have to wait a long time for him to be free, I asked him something.' She took a deep breath as if she was about to dive into unfathomable water. 'We had never been lovers in the real sense; he had always been an honourable man and I a virtuous woman; but I asked him to give me a child. That was you, James. And then we had another; that was you, Laura. Freddie is your father.'

She stopped and gazed at her children, and Freddie did the same, both waiting for one of them to speak.

James found his voice first. 'But you told us – you said that our father was dead! You said that he was in the Navy. You said he came from Southampton—'

'Portsmouth,' his mother and sister said on the same breath. 'I'm afraid it was a lie, James,' Susannah went on. 'I had to invent a father for you, and his being in the Navy was the obvious excuse for him to be away and for me to claim that I was visiting him in other ports. That is also the real reason why I came to live in Hessle, where no-one knew me. Three months after Laura was born, I said he had died and been buried at sea. I thus became a respectable widow.'

'And our name?' Laura murmured. 'Is it a real name or a made-up one?'

Susannah blinked, but a trickle of tears ran down her face. 'It's my own name,' she said, her voice catching. 'As it was my mother's name. I was happy enough to keep it. If anyone had asked I would have said that I had married a man with the same surname, but no-one ever did.'

'Your mother's name?' James said in a low voice. 'You mean your father's name.'

'No. I don't mean that. I never knew who my father was. At least, by my lie of inventing a father for you, I have spared you that cruel indignity.'

Laura got up and went across to her mother. She bent down and kissed her. 'Thank you for telling us, Mama.' Then she kissed Freddie on the cheek. 'I'd thought that you and Mama might have been lovers,' she said softly. 'Memories have been coming back to me over the last few weeks which have told me that you've always been in our lives. But I never dreamed that you could have been our father.'

Freddie glanced anxiously at James, who was standing as if stunned. 'James,' he said. 'I'm sorry if this has come as a shock to you.'

'I can't take it in.' James's tone was sharp and intense. 'Why didn't you tell us before? Heavens above, it isn't as if we're children who might blurt it out. Would you have told us if your wife hadn't died?'

'Yes,' Freddie said. 'I was about to leave my

447

wife, who – forgive me, Laura, for speaking so frankly – has only ever been my wife in name. It has all been very complicated and we will discuss everything – the whys and wherefores – in good time. Sufficient to say now that I was influenced by *my* father and forced into an unwelcome marriage.'

'I'm going out.' James suddenly headed for the door. 'I need some air. Need to think!'

Susannah looked alarmed, but Laura reassured her as James crashed out. 'He'll be back, Mama,' she said. 'He just needs time to adjust to the news.'

'But you do not?' Freddie asked gently. 'Are you not shocked, Laura, as James so obviously is?'

She shook her head. 'No. I'm astounded that you kept the secret for so long, but I'm not shocked. I remember you saying once that I could do anything I wanted, and shouldn't be held back by convention because I was a woman. You said . . .' She pressed her lips together as she thought back. 'You said, as long as no-one was hurt by our actions we must follow our own path.' She looked at her mother. 'And Mama wanted children.'

'But only Freddie's,' her mother broke in. 'I only wanted his. If I couldn't have Freddie, then I wanted his children.'

They heard a sound by the door. James, with his coat half on, had come back into the room.

He was biting his fingers, as he used to when he was a child, and was obviously trying to control his emotions. 'The thing is, Uncle Freddie.' His voice was thick and choked. 'The thing is – when I was little, I wanted you to be my father! I used to ask God when I said my prayers at night to send your wife away so that you could marry our mother and live with us.'

He came slowly into the room and Freddie moved towards him. 'And now . . .' James couldn't control the tears which coursed down his face. 'Now it has happened.' He gave a sudden sob, somewhere between a cry and a laugh. 'I don't know whether to feel guilty or jubilant!'

Freddie put his arms round him and hugged him. 'Don't feel guilty,' he said softly. 'I'm the one who should feel remorse, and I do, for not being here for so much of your lives, yours and Laura's, but especially your mother's. Especially Susannah's.'

CHAPTER FORTY

The invitation to visit Burstall House came at the beginning of March. Laura had had a regular correspondence with Edmund throughout the winter, but no longer showed the letters to her mother.

'I'm not sure if you should go,' Freddie said to Susannah. 'Can you not wait until I'm free to go with you?'

'Why?' she had asked, laughing at him. 'Do you wish to go as the dutiful father to ascertain whether the young man is good enough for your daughter?'

'You know that is not the case at all, Susannah. Your judgement is as good as anyone's, better probably. No.' He seemed distinctly uncomfortable. 'I just think it's too soon.'

But she disagreed with him and said that they would visit, just she and Laura, there was no need for James to go, and that they would travel by train to Hedon.

'Perhaps then I'll follow on a later train and wait for you at the Fleet,' he said. 'You'll be calling there on the way home, presumably?'

She told him that they would, and that Edmund Ellis had said that he would collect them from there on the outward journey and drive them to Skeffling. 'We could have gone on to Patrington, which is nearer, but I'm overdue a visit to the Fleet.'

Susannah was apprehensive about going further into Holderness. It has been such a long time, she reflected. When I lived in Hedon I was fearful of returning to Welwick; always afraid of meeting up with Wilf Topham. Yet I should have done, she thought, if only to see Aunt Jane. She had sent postcards to Jane over the years, telling her that she was well, but no more than that.

She and Laura waited now at the Fleet Inn for Edmund Ellis to collect them. They had caught an early train so that she could ask questions of the tenants, and make sure that all was in order. Jack and Ruby Howard had moved on several years before and a Hedon couple now ran the inn very satisfactorily. Susannah and Laura had walked from the station and through the Market Place, stopping to look in shop windows and occasionally so that Susannah could greet people who had hesitantly waved or nodded, unsure whether or not they knew her.

They had been given coffee at the Fleet, and

whilst her mother was chatting to the tenants Laura had gone outside into the garden and wandered beside the stream.

'Hello!'

She turned at the voice. Edmund Ellis stood smiling at her. 'Hello!' she replied. 'You're early. We didn't expect you just yet.'

'I couldn't wait to see you,' he said. 'I've thought of nothing and no-one else since receiving your mother's letter. I'm sorry though that it's to be such a short visit. I had hoped you'd be able to stay longer.'

'Mama thought it would be best.' She gazed frankly at him. 'She said it was best not to stay overlong on a first visit. At least that was what she was advised.'

'Advised? By a family friend?'

'Yes.' She looked down and watched the ripples on the water's surface. Now wasn't the time for explanations of Freddie's role. For some reason he didn't want them to come; he said he had to make further enquiries about Edmund and his family.

'Of course.' He gave a little shrug. 'Convention and all that.' Then he gave an appealing grin. 'But you said that you were not at all conventional. And besides, this isn't your first visit!'

'You're being obtuse,' she rebuked dryly. 'You know perfectly well what I mean by a first visit!' But to her annoyance she could feel her cheeks flushing. 'You've invited us for a purpose, and if the visit goes well, then we must invite you back!'

'What bosh!' He bent and whispered, 'I wanted you to come so I could show you how I live, and to ask if you could live here too, with me, as my wife.'

She swallowed hard. She was emancipated, it was true, but he was going too fast. She needed more time.

'I love you, Laura,' he said, taking her hand. 'Say that you care, or could care, for me, and never mind the niceties of how we should behave.'

'You don't know me,' she murmured. 'A few letters cannot tell you what I am like. I'm impatient. I have a sharp tongue. I speak my mind.'

'I know,' he said. 'That's what I love about you. You're not pretentious, you don't flirt or flatter. You speak as you think.'

'Sometimes I speak without thinking,' she said ruefully, and then laughed. 'Perhaps you do know me!'

Her mother called to them. She had seen the brougham in the yard and had come to look for them. 'Mr Ellis,' she said. 'There you are.'

'I beg your pardon, Mrs Page.' He bowed over her hand. 'I spotted Miss Page in the garden and went to speak to her.'

She raised her eyebrows. 'So I see. Shall we go?'

He led them towards the carriage. 'I've brought a driver so that I can sit with you and point out various landmarks on the way,' he said. 'It's not too far to Skeffling, and we have a dry day.'

As they drove on the long road towards Patrington, Susannah recalled the dank, dark November day when she had travelled towards Hedon in the carrier's cart. The trees had been black against the sky and the deep ditches full with winter rain. Now there was a faint greening on the branches, and here and there she spotted clumps of cowslips, celandine and early primroses growing along the drain banks. They passed the villages of Thorngumbald and Keyingham and now she saw the spire of Ottringham church in the distance and a sign showing Sunk Island, and she remembered Thomas telling her tall tales of children born with webbed feet. She smiled at the memory. Dear Thomas. How lovely it would be to see him once more. She gazed out at the rolling warm brown earth, the widespread greening fields and endless infinite sky, and pondered that it was good to be back.

'Mama! Mr Ellis is speaking to you!' Laura leaned towards her. 'You were miles away!'

'I beg your pardon, Mr Ellis. So I was. I was remembering my childhood.'

Edmund gave her a questioning glance. 'I

was only pointing out Patrington steeple. We're coming into Patrington now. St Patrick's is considered to be one of the finest churches in the country.'

'Oh, yes,' she said, looking out of the window. 'I remember it very well, and we've passed Enholmes mill. I see it is still in production.'

Again he gave her a puzzled look. 'Yes, thriving, I understand. We regularly lose farm workers to them as their wages are higher than ours.'

Susannah nodded vaguely. 'Indeed.' I wonder if Wilf still lives with Aunt Jane, she mused. I hope he treats her better now than he did.

'Mrs Page! I was saying that you seem well informed about the area.'

'I am, Mr Ellis.' Susannah gathered her wits about her. 'I lived here when I was a child. I was born in Welwick. My mother died in childbirth and I lived with my great-aunt.'

Edmund cast a bewildered look at her and then at Laura. 'I didn't know,' he said. 'I don't recall Miss Page's mentioning it.'

'I didn't,' Laura said abstractedly. 'Mama never talked of it.'

'I ran away.' Susannah's voice was constrained, her manner inhibited. 'When I was twelve. I've never been back, until now.'

Laura stared at her mother. She had never mentioned that. Why hadn't she? She opened her mouth to put the question, but her mother's

455

face was closed and Laura knew her well enough to recognize that now wasn't the right time; but by admitting what she had, her mother had left an opening for the subject for when it was. It will be up to me to decide when that moment is, Laura thought. Something went very wrong and Mama couldn't speak of it.

'We're coming into Welwick now,' Edmund said. 'You'll know the story of the gunpowder plotters, of course?' He smiled at Susannah. 'We've passed the site of the old Ploughlands farm.'

'What?' Laura asked eagerly. 'What?'

'Guy Fawkes's co-conspirators,' her mother explained. 'All 'local schoolchildren knew about them. Their parents' grave is in Welwick churchyard.'

They passed through the village and Susannah cast a glance up the lane where Aunt Lol's cottage had been. But the driver urged on the horses and they picked up speed and she couldn't be quite sure if her memories were correct. But what I do remember, she thought, is the vast acreage, the openness and the sensation of unlimited space.

'We must take you on a visit, Mrs Page,' Edmund was saying. 'Or perhaps my grandfather might. He knows the villagers better than I do, and *his* father bought land here, and at Welwick Thorpe, many years ago.'

456

'Perhaps on another occasion,' Susannah said evasively. 'You must be busy at this time of the growing season.'

'We are,' he answered. 'But we have some good men. They don't always need us. It's a pity though that you are able to stay only for luncheon – dinner we still call it.' He smiled impishly. 'Aunt Julia will be there, and my grandfather.'

He could have wished that his grandfather had been in a better humour about the visit. Edmund had spent hours convincing him that he wanted him to meet Laura again, and her mother also, but his grandfather had been curiously unwilling, saying that if Edmund wanted a wife he'd be better choosing a farmer's daughter. They had had some sharp words and a few long silences, until his grandfather had finally agreed.

'I regret my grandmother is still in France,' Edmund said, 'and won't be able to meet you. She spends every winter in Paris. She says she cannot abide the cold in Holderness, but she does not spend much time here in summer either.'

'I understand you lost both your parents?' Susannah asked. 'That must have been very hard for you.'

'I hardly remember them,' he said. 'Amy and I were very young. Grandfather brought us up, helped by Great-aunt Julia, as our grandmother was away so much. She's very kind,' he added. 'Aunt Julia, I mean, though she's slightly dotty!'

457

They came into Skeffling and turned through an open gate and up a long track. Susannah felt a thudding in her temple. Did she remember it? She recalled sitting with Aunt Lol in a dog cart with leather seats and being driven somewhere, and yes, there had been a large grey house with wide steps up to the front door. And then what? Her mind was a blank, until they turned a corner of the building and she saw the façade of Burstall House in front of her. There were the steps, though not as high or as wide as she recalled. I must have been very young, she thought, as Edmund came to hand her and then Laura down.

A housekeeper stood on the steps and dipped her knee as they approached. 'Good day, ma'am,' she said. 'Miss Page. Mr Ellis will be in shortly, Mr Edmund. Miss Julia is in the morning room.'

Susannah walked slowly into the hall and looked up the stairs. Yes, now she remembered. She had been taken upstairs to see an elderly lady who had talked to her about something – was it school? That would be it. Mrs Ellis paid for her schooling and for Thomas's too. Mr Ellis used to bring the money to Aunt Lol, but then Wilf Topham stole it when it was given to Jane. Memories which she had buried deep came rushing back up to confront her.

'Mama!' Laura's voice seemed to come from far away. 'We are to go in.'

'I'm so sorry,' Susannah said, coming back to the present. 'But' – she glanced at Edmund who was looking at her anxiously – 'I've been here before.'

'Have you?' He seemed astonished. 'So – do you know my grandfather?'

'No. I think I might have met his mother. I'm not sure. It's so long ago.'

'Come and meet Aunt Julia,' he said. 'Perhaps she can shed light on it. My sister, Amy, is away visiting friends. But she asked me to give you her regards.'

He led them into the morning room, which was lit by bright sunshine; a fire blazed in the hearth and again Susannah's memories stirred as she recalled another room with a fire, where Aunt Lol had sat and waited for her. But she gathered herself together when the older woman greeted her and they sat down as coffee was brought in.

'Mrs Page thinks she has been here before, Aunt Julia,' Edmund said. 'She lived in Welwick when she was a child.'

'Did you, my dear?' Aunt Julia said. 'Did we meet?'

Susannah shook her head. 'I think perhaps I might have met your mother. Did she have a sitting room upstairs?'

'Yes, she did! How remarkable! I use the room now as a sewing room and for writing letters. My

459

own room becomes so cluttered otherwise. I'm not terribly tidy, I'm afraid. I take on too much, I suppose. At least that's what everyone tells me.' She gave a gentle smile, creasing her otherwise smooth face. 'But it is important, don't you think, Mrs Page, to do what we can for others?'

They talked of various subjects and then Julia said, 'I can't think what's keeping Joseph. He said he would be in directly. He has been a little unwell lately, I fear. Would you care for more coffee? Though we shall be going in for dinner in half an hour.' She chatted on as Susannah refused more coffee. 'Do you dine late, Mrs Page? We always eat at midday. We are not at all fashionable. The men need it, you see, when they have had a hard morning. Edmund and his grandfather start very early and do a busy day's work.'

'We usually have a light luncheon,' Susannah explained. 'I'm often out attending to business matters, so we eat together in the evening, when my son James comes home from the bank.'

There was a brief pause, and then the door opened. 'There you are, Joseph,' Julia said. 'We thought you were lost.'

I know him, Susannah thought. He looks familiar. Perhaps Edmund has his stamp; yet there is something more. He reminds me of – whom?

Joseph came towards them. 'I beg your pardon

460

for my lateness. I – I was unavoidably detained. How do you do, Mrs Page? Miss Page.' He bowed stiffly and spoke in a breathless manner. 'I trust I find you well?'

Susannah and Laura had both risen to their feet and inclined their heads. 'I'm pleased to make your acquaintance, Mr Ellis,' Susannah said, and was taken aback at the paleness of his cheeks and the anxiety so obvious in his eyes.

Joseph swallowed hard. How do I recover from this? What can I say to my daughter? He felt dizzy as he stood there in front of her. In front of Susannah.

CHAPTER FORTY-ONE

At the table the conversation was stilted and awkward. Joseph Ellis had little to say, and Susannah, glancing up from time to time, found him watching her intensely, whereupon, seeing he was observed, he would look away. Julia was the only one who seemed to be at ease and she chatted happily to Laura and Susannah, mainly about the weather and the social uncertainties of the times, whilst Edmund, when he could get a word in, gave Laura a brief history of the house.

After they had finished their meal they adjourned once more to the morning room. Joseph Ellis stood by the door for a moment, and then said, 'Julia, could I ask you to entertain Miss Page? There's something important I wish to discuss with Mrs Page.'

They all looked at him. There was a nervous intent in his eyes. Laura glanced at her mother. Edmund stared at his grandfather and Julia raised her eyebrows enquiringly, but with a gracious smile said, 'Of course, my dear.'

Joseph led Susannah into a room at the end of the hall. It wasn't large, but it was comfortably furnished with a sofa and armchairs and a number of small tables, all of which were strewn with books and farming catalogues. Heavy velvet curtains hung at the long windows, and a few pictures of country scenes on the walls, but there were no ornaments or other paraphernalia. Susannah assumed that this was where Joseph Ellis and his grandson came to relax at the end of a working day. A fire was burning in the grate and several logs and a brass hod of coal stood at the side of the hearth.

'Please sit down,' he said politely, indicating an armchair. 'I hope you don't mind, but I've brought you in here where we won't be disturbed. I'd like to talk to you.' His voice was gruff and he cleared his throat. 'You were born in Welwick,' he said. It wasn't so much a question as a statement.

'I was,' she said, and sat down as she was bid, glancing up at him in some concern. There was something familiar about him. He *did* remind her of someone.

'Your mother died?'

She didn't answer. The palms of her hand became hot and sticky and she rubbed them together.

'You lived with your aunt, Mrs Marston?'

'Aunt Lol,' she murmured, and her heart began to hammer as if trying to jump out of her body. 'Yes, I did.'

'Susannah,' he said in a whisper.

She kept her eyes on his. She had looked up at him before. Her lips barely moved as she formed the words which were echoing in her head. Are you happy? He always asked her that. Each time he came he asked her if she was happy. His eyes always looked sad, his expression wistful. He gave her a sovereign, which she had kept.

'Who are you?'

Her words were soft and hesitant. He remembered that she had always been a quiet child, softly spoken and polite. She was nothing like Mary-Ellen. But he realized that she was like someone. His mother and his sister. As gentle as they were.

'Who are you?' she repeated. 'I know you. We've met before. When I was a child. You gave me a sovereign. You used to come to see Aunt Lol.'

He shook his head. 'Not Aunt Lol.' His voice was low. 'I came to see you.'

'Why?'

He saw her tremble. Her eyes were wide as she gazed at him and she barely blinked. He put his hand over his mouth and closed his eyes for a second. He had always wanted to tell her. She

464

must have had the question in her head all her life. And yet he had never dared. But now he must. For the sake of his grandson and her daughter, if not for himself.

'Susannah, I am your father.'

Her face drained of colour and she began to shake. He bent over her. 'I'm sorry. I didn't want to upset you. But I had to tell you.'

'Why?' The word was barely audible. 'Why didn't I know? Why didn't someone tell me? I never heard . . . Why didn't Aunt Lol tell me?'

'Mistakes were made. My father . . .' He swallowed. He wouldn't tell her of the harsh words which were said. 'I don't want to blame him,' he said. 'He thought he was doing the right thing. He asked me how I could look after a child. A single man.' He gazed sadly at her. 'I should have tried. But I was ill after Mary-Ellen died. Bereft at her loss. There were times when I wanted to die too and I think my father knew that, though he wasn't a man to show his emotions – except his temper,' he added. 'Mrs Marston knows best, he told me. She'll bring her up with her family. And he was probably right. And . . .' His eyes became moist and he kept swallowing as if he had something in his throat. 'And each time I looked at you – I was reminded of her.'

'Did – you love her?' she asked. Her words

465

seemed to be forced from her mouth. 'Or was it guilt that you felt when you looked at me?'

'I loved her more than life itself.' He straightened up and walked to the window. 'She lit up the dark by her presence – and when she died the light went out of my life. There's barely a day goes by but I think of her.' He turned round to look at her. 'And of you,' he said softly. 'Don't think, Susannah, that you were ever abandoned, for you were not.'

'You paid Aunt Lol to look after me?'

'Yes, but I didn't mean just that. I meant that you were always in my thoughts, and,' he added, 'especially so after you ran away. I searched for you. I trawled the streets of Hull looking for you, but you had gone. Disappeared.'

Her eyes flickered. 'I ran away because of Wilf Topham,' she said vaguely. 'Aunt Jane's husband.' She shuddered. 'He stole the money which your mother sent for my schooling and he said I must go to work or he would give me a leathering. But before that, I remember now, when Aunt Lol was alive, sometimes you came. You used to come on a black horse, and – you asked me if I was happy.'

He nodded. 'Old Ebony. I asked you if you were happy because if you hadn't been I would have brought you home – here. And then, when you were eleven, Mrs Marston said it would be best if I stopped going to see you. She said that you would start asking questions about why I came. And I had married by then.' He gave a sigh which came from deep within him. 'But I saw you again just after your aunt died.'

'On the river bank,' she interrupted. 'I remember. Wilf Topham had sent me out of the house. I was frightened when I saw you. I didn't know who you were.'

'I was always there,' he said. 'Reliving memories of when I used to meet Mary-Ellen.'

'What was she like?' Her voice shook. 'To look at, I mean? Hardly anyone talked about her. I only ever knew her name.' Her mouth trembled. 'Nothing else. And I so wanted a picture of her in my head.'

He gave a wistful smile. 'She was like your daughter. Laura. When I saw Laura for the first time I thought I was seeing a ghost.' His voice dropped. 'I thought I was dying and that she had come for me at last. What are we going to do about them?' he said. 'About Edmund and Laura?'

Susannah raised her eyes to his; she seemed bewildered. 'Do about them?' she whispered. 'What do you—' Then realization dawned. 'They have the same bloodline!' He thought she was going to faint she went so white. 'Put your head down,' he told her. 'Against your knees.' He rushed to a cupboard and brought out a bottle of brandy and poured a little into a glass which was standing on a tray, then added some water from a covered jug and brought it to her. 'Drink this,' he said softly, putting his hand beneath her chin and raising her head. 'It won't help our dilemma but it might make you feel better.' Then, with a trembling hand, he poured himself a larger measure, and sat down in a chair across from her.

She took a swallow. 'They can't marry,' she whispered. 'I won't allow it. They are related. Laura is – is—'

'My granddaughter, as Edmund is my grandson,' he finished for her. 'Fate couldn't be more unkind. I saw how Edmund cared for her, but I hoped that over the winter when he didn't see her, his passion would die. But it didn't – it hasn't. I tried to put off this visit; told him he should look for a wife amongst the farmers' daughters we know.' He shook his head. 'But he is as stubborn as I always was.' He gazed sadly at her. 'I've done what I always longed to do, to claim my daughter; but Edmund will want to marry Laura and I am uneasy. I cannot, *will not* give my blessing, though he is of age and can do as he pleases.'

'He hasn't asked for her. At least – he hasn't asked my permission.' Susannah took another sip. Cognac. It was a good one, smooth not fiery, her innkeeper's head told her. 'But he might have asked Laura. They are too close,' she said. 'I would be so afraid.' She gave a deep shuddering breath and her eyes were full of tears. 'I've heard of such terrible things that can happen to children born in a marriage where there is a common ancestor. I can't let it happen.'

'I agree,' he said. 'But Edmund will argue.'

'He can't argue with me!' She blinked fiercely. 'Laura is not of age and I will not agree to it, even though . . .' Her mouth trembled. 'Even though I believe it to be a love match.'

'Why didn't you change *your* name?' he said suddenly. 'Or did you marry someone with the same name?'

Susannah put her chin up defiantly, and in that simple gesture he saw her mother. 'I'm not a widow,' she stated flatly. 'I've never had a husband.'

Joseph gave an exclamation. 'Never? But I understood that you went away to be married. The solicitor that you employ would never tell my agent where you were or what your name was.'

Her forehead creased. 'Your agent? My solicitor? Mr Cannon, you mean? Mr Frederick Cannon?'

'Yes.' He nodded vigorously. 'He guards you well. When his father ran the firm we were able to talk to him, through Watson of course, but when the son took over we could find out nothing except what he said was strictly our business.'

'I don't understand,' she said, puzzled. 'What are you talking about, Mr Ellis?'

He drew in a breath. What else could she call him? She was hardly going to call him Father, when she didn't even know him. 'The Fleet Inn,' he explained. 'I bought that for you, as security in case anything happened to me.' He spoke quietly. 'As I said, I searched for you after you ran away from Welwick, and couldn't find you. It wasn't until some years later that someone said he thought he'd seen you at the Fleet. So I came to look. And I saw you. You were spring cleaning, Mrs Brewster said. And I heard you singing!' He took another drink from his glass. 'I knew then that you were all right.' His voice was husky. 'That you were cared for. So I bought the inn. And then I deposited money for your twenty-first birthday.'

'Which I used towards paying a manager, and bought the inn in Beverley,' she said slowly. 'I put the money back into the Fleet when the Beverley inn was making a profit. But I'm the leaseholder,' she said abruptly. 'I don't own it.'

'You do.' He nodded. 'It's in your name. Mr Cannon has the documents.'

Dearest Freddie, she thought. This is the reason he went into law. He did it so that he could look after me and my future. A sudden rush of emotion swept over her. He couldn't marry me, so this was the next best thing, and now – Laura and Edmund. She started to weep. Her head ached. It was all too much to bear.

'Please don't cry, Susannah.' Joseph got up from his chair and bent over her again. 'I want to weep with joy that I've found you after all these years. Confessing to you that I'm your father has lifted a huge weight from my mind.' He took the empty glass from her and placed it on a table and then put his large hand over hers. 'I want to love you as my daughter, to tell you about your mother. But first of all we must break the news to Laura and Edmund and, in doing so, shatter their lives as ours were shattered.'

He gazed at her as she sat weeping copious tears. 'You said you were never married. Do *your* children know who their father is? Have you told them?'

She wiped her eyes. 'Yes,' she said with a sob. 'But only recently. Their father's love has sustained me since I was just a girl. But he was pledged to someone else, and as he is a good and honourable man he wouldn't break that bond. Now he's widowed and we'll marry after his mourning period is over.' She raised her eyes to his. 'It's Mr Cannon. I've always loved him and he has always cared for our children. He has always been there when they needed him, though they thought he was a friend, not that he was their father. But now . . .' She drew in a shuddering breath, and a sudden thought came to her that Freddie had tried to put off this visit to the Ellises. Had he guessed or did he know that Joseph Ellis was her father? 'We must tell Edmund and Laura. Shall we tell them together, or separately?'

He put out his hand to her and gently raised her to her feet. 'We'll tell them together, Susannah,' he said softly. 'We must act as one in this.' He bent and kissed her wet cheek. 'Be brave,' he said, his voice tender. 'As I know you can be.'

CHAPTER FORTY-TWO

Edmund stood for a moment as if stunned. Then he began to rant and rave at his grandfather, telling him that he had ruined his life and that he would never forgive him. 'How could you keep this a secret for so long?' he shouted. 'Your conduct has been appalling!'

Joseph said nothing. He just stood at Susannah's side and waited for Edmund's shock to subside. It was like history repeating itself. He could recall very clearly shouting at his father when he had said that he shouldn't marry Mary-Ellen.

Laura seemed bewildered and her face had paled at the news, but she braced herself and kissed her mother, and then, turning to Joseph, dipped her knee and reached up to kiss him too. She saw him start and take a sudden breath, and then he murmured, 'Thank you, Laura.'

'You're not simply accepting this?' Edmund

asked her bitterly. 'They say we can't marry. Our lives are ruined and yet you kiss him!'

'Please don't raise your voice to me,' she said coldly, though her voice trembled. 'We are not promised to each other. We have merely exchanged letters. You have not asked me to marry you; you simply assumed that I would. And if Mama says we cannot – that she won't give her permission, and I understand why – then we must accept the facts.'

But I would have consented, she thought miserably. I would have made him wait, of course, had he asked me. I would have kept him in suspense so that he wouldn't have been too sure of me. But I would have married him. I wanted to.

'I'm sorry!' He was immediately penitent. 'I should not have taken your consent for granted. But you know that I love you.' Tears were in his eyes and he reached for her hand, but she drew it away. 'I've told you that I do. Told you that I want you to be my wife.' He looked desperately at Susannah. 'I was going to ask today for your permission; I wanted you to come and meet Grandfather and Aunt Julia and know how we lived, and . . .' He pressed his hand across his forehead, trying not to weep. 'And now you say it's impossible.' He looked across at his grandfather, and dashed away his tears. 'You knew,' he said accusingly. 'You knew all the time!'

474

Joseph shook his head. 'I didn't,' he said softly. 'Not until I saw Laura.' He gave a deep sigh. 'You are so much like your grandmother, my dear,' he said to her. 'Your mother's mother. It was when I saw you and you told me your mother's name. Then I knew.'

'Joseph!' Julia had sat very quietly as Joseph had broken the news, but now she spoke. 'Why did I not know of this? Why was I never told?'

'Because our parents considered that your fine sensibilities were too delicate to hear it.' Joseph's voice was flinty. 'You were to be protected from the unseemly knowledge of your brother's wrongdoings. The fact that I had fathered a child!'

'What nonsense,' she murmured. 'I know many young mothers who have no husbands. They come to me for advice, even though I am a single woman myself.' She looked at Susannah and put out her hand. 'Come here, my dear, and let me look at you in a different light now that I know you are my niece.'

Susannah, with fresh tears streaming down her face, did as she asked and stood in front of her. 'May I give you a kiss, Aunt Julia?' she said brokenly.

'I wish that you would,' Julia said softly. 'And I wish that I had known you before. I would have taken care of you. I always longed for a child to love, but I never met a man whom I wished to marry.'

Joseph's temple throbbed. Had it all been in vain, this secrecy? Would Susannah have been accepted had he insisted on bringing her home? She had told Julia before dinner that she had been brought to the house when she was a child, and had met his mother. It must have been whilst he was still away in France. Would his mother have accepted her? Looking back now, he thought that perhaps she would have, had she been allowed. And then my life would have been very different; I would have had my daughter, but not my sons.

'I think, Mama, that perhaps we had better leave.' Laura's voice was calm and controlled, but inside she was aching with a desperate need to weep. 'We – we both have much to consider. We need time to absorb what has happened.' She looked at Joseph, deliberately directing her gaze away from Edmund. 'Perhaps you'd be so kind as to ask someone to drive us back to Hedon?'

'I'll take you,' Edmund broke in. 'I must speak to you, Laura!'

'I think it would be best if you didn't.' She looked at him at last, raising her eyes to his, and her resolve almost gave way when she saw the grief on his face. 'At the moment there is nothing that we need to say to each other.'

'You are so cold,' he said angrily. 'How can you

476

claim that we have nothing to talk about?' He was about to say more, but there was something, some hint of pleading in her eyes, a tremor on her lips, that stopped him.

Joseph decided to drive them himself when he discovered that Frederick Cannon was waiting for them at the Fleet. Laura kissed Aunt Julia, but when Edmund grasped her hand imploringly she pulled it away and wouldn't look at him.

Freddie was waiting for them. He had been there for over an hour, pacing up and down the waterway, unable to sit for long in the crowded inn. He came towards the brougham in the courtyard and Susannah introduced him to Joseph Ellis.

'Freddie,' she said quietly, 'did you know who Mr Ellis was?'

Freddie looked from Joseph Ellis to Susannah and saw the enlightenment. 'I didn't know,' he said. 'But I guessed. Though I couldn't be absolutely sure. I was very worried about Laura.'

He looked back towards the inn, where Laura had retreated after briefly greeting him. 'Very worried indeed. Has it been resolved?' When Susannah nodded, he said, 'It would be an unwise connection, I fear. I confess, Mr Ellis, that I began some sleuthing work after I became Susannah's adviser, which was many years ago. I wanted to be sure that everything was as it purported to be, even though my father was always very particular and meticulous when dealing with his clients. Then quite by chance I met your agent. I'd arrived early for a meeting at Mr Watson's rooms, and your man came out of his office. When I left later I called in at the Sun Inn as my train wasn't due for an hour, and he was there.' Freddie ran his hand over his chin. 'I knew he had something to do with Susannah's benefactor, and most unprofessionally I began to talk to him. He knew nothing of the history, of course,' he assured Joseph, who was surveying him anxiously. 'He was simply the messenger. But he mentioned that his employer owned a large farm estate in Holderness, and I knew of course that Susannah came from that area. Then, all these years later, when Laura and James came to visit your grandson at Skeffling, I began to put two and two together and hoped that it wouldn't make four. I hope, sir, that you do not think I have overstepped the mark in my professional capacity. It is only because I have always had Susannah's best interests at heart, and I was aiming to protect her.'

'I understand that,' Joseph said. 'I'm glad to hear that someone was looking after her.'

Freddie took hold of Susannah's hand and said softly, 'She is of course perfectly capable of looking after herself. But soon I hope that I shall be able to do more than I do now to safeguard and support her.'

'You are to be married, I understand,' Joseph said. 'May I – may I come to the wedding?'

Susannah looked up at him. She had felt very shy of him whilst at Skeffling, apprehensive as to what her role would be or how to behave. Now she said, 'I'll need someone to stand by my side, to give me in marriage. I was going to ask James, but it didn't seem quite appropriate. Would you perhaps be willing to do it?'

He put his hand to his mouth, pressing his fist hard to his lips. 'Thank you.' His words were choked. 'I would consider it an honour.'

Laura had dashed upstairs to her mother's old room and flung herself on the bed. At last, she let the tears flow.

I have acquired a father and a grandfather in a matter of weeks, she thought. But I've lost the only man that I've ever felt I could love and allow to share my life. How can we ever meet again? We cannot! It will be impossible. I can't go to a house where my grandfather and great-aunt live. I cannot even improve my acquaintance with Amy – how could I, when *he* will be there?

There came a soft tap on the door and she sat up as her mother came in. 'Joseph Ellis has gone,' she said quietly. 'He asked me to say goodbye for him.'

Laura nodded and blew her nose and her mother came to sit on the bed beside her. She put her arm round her and said, 'I'm so very sorry, my dearest. So terribly sorry. But you do realize it's for the best? There could be such worse heartache ahead of you if I were to agree to such a match.'

Laura leaned her head against her. 'It's as well that we found out in time,' she said, sniffling. 'Before harm was done. It was true when I said that Edmund hadn't asked me to marry him. But he would have done. He wanted me to be his wife. Oh, Mama,' she cried, 'I wanted to be. What am I to do?'

Edmund wrote to her. Bombarded her with letters which she didn't open. James, on being told the news, arranged to meet Edmund on neutral territory in Hull and listen to his anguish.

'I told him there's nothing to be done,' he whispered to his mother out of Laura's hearing. 'That you won't change your mind as you consider it too risky. But he's bereft, poor fellow. I hope I never feel so badly over a woman.'

Susannah had patted his hand. 'I hope that you do, James,' she said. 'But with a happier outcome.'

She and Freddie had decided to wait a little while longer before their own marriage. 'It would be so unfair,' she said to him, 'when there is so much unhappiness. We can wait a little longer.'

There were other letters from Skeffling, for Joseph wrote to Susannah, telling her of things he had never confessed to anyone before. His love for her mother; what kind of person she was, full of fire and passion, defiance and independence. He told her too of his retreat to France after Mary-Ellen's death to try to escape from the misery of his loss. 'I understand how Edmund is feeling, though he doesn't think that I do; but I remember clearly how empty my life was.' He explained to her his first meeting with Arlette, who had made him laugh and reminded him that he was still alive, and of their subsequent marriage. 'We are totally incompatible,' he wrote, 'but we had three sons to compensate us for an unsatisfactory life together.'

And then their eldest son died, Susannah mused, as she sat reading his letters. That had surely been heartbreaking, and it must have widened the gap between them even further. But she read on and felt a warm rush of joy as he added, 'Now my daughter from my first and only love has been returned to me, which restores my faith that life isn't totally cruel, even though Edmund would not agree with me.'

He went on to say that his wife was returning from France and that he would tell her about Susannah and ask her forgiveness for not having spoken of her before.

Susannah returned the letters to their envelopes

481

and thought of her daughter. Laura had thrown herself into a reckless round of engagements: charity meetings and indiscriminate social events filled each day and evening. She refused to discuss her inner feelings, putting on a façade of wilful indifference which fooled no-one.

Her heart is broken, Susannah thought, though she won't admit it, and yet what am I to do? I should blame myself if something dreadful happened. She sighed. I wish to see my father again. He's asked me to. I'd like to go back to Welwick and see the place where I was born, and perhaps meet Aunt Jane and Thomas if they are still there, for I didn't get the chance to ask after them. But how can I when Laura is so unhappy? Freddie would go with me, but he knows little of the life I led as a child. No – if I return, I must do so alone.

CHAPTER FORTY-THREE

'I can't help you, Edmund. I would if I could.'
Joseph ran his fingers through his hair. 'I know
how you feel. Believe me, I've suffered as you are
suffering now.'

'Laura is only a cousin!' Edmund exploded.
'It's not illegal for cousins to marry. And if we
didn't have children then it would be all right!'

'You know that it wouldn't be,' Joseph said
quietly. 'Your father and Susannah were brother
and sister. Yes, half-brother and sister, I know,'
he said, when he saw the objection on Edmund's
face. 'But I was father to them both. And a
marriage between you and Laura would be not
so much wrong as not right. It would be un-
acceptable in our society, and no clergyman
would condone a marriage entered into with
the stated intention of avoiding having children,
which would be nigh on impossible in any case.
But her mother will not consent; she will not give
her permission so there's an end to it!'

I'll be glad when Arlette comes home, Joseph thought as Edmund crashed out of the door. She's always had a soft spot for Edmund; perhaps she can make him see sense. Usually when his wife came back from France he viewed her return with mixed feelings. Routine was disrupted and within hours they were arguing over something. But now he wanted his confession over, he wanted to make his peace with her, and more than anything he needed her to console Edmund.

Arlette had written to him that she was unsure of her travel arrangements and that she didn't want him to meet her. 'We will come by train from London, though I may do some shopping first and visit the theatre, and then I will travel north. Perhaps I will hire a chaise to bring me to Holderness or maybe continue by train. Gena is good with porters and drivers so there is no need for you to come.'

Poor Gena, he thought, thinking of Arlette's maid. She won't be pleased to be back, any more than Arlette will. I wonder how long she will stay this time.

A hired chaise rolled up to the door a week later. Julia was just pouring tea for herself and Amy. 'Oh!' she murmured, glancing out of the window. 'Here is your grandmother, my dear.' Hurriedly she got to her feet. 'I'll take tea in my room if you don't mind, Amy. Arlette will have much to discuss, I expect, and I'll catch up with the news later.'

'Don't go, Aunt Julia,' Amy said. 'She doesn't bite, you know.'

'I know she doesn't, dear, but she does make me very nervous. All that energy!'

She scurried out of the room trailing her cottons and embroidery silks after her. Julia always kept out of the way whenever Arlette arrived home. And no wonder, Amy thought; it was as if the air was changed when her grandmother whirled in: a charge of exotic French perfume, of wine and crushed spices and mellow cheese, seemed to follow her wherever she went.

Amy went to the front door to greet her as the housekeeper and a maid went down the steps to help the driver with the luggage. There was no maid accompanying Arlette, however. She was quite alone.

'Grandmama! How lovely to see you.' Amy kissed her. She was very fond of her grandmother. 'Where's Gena? You've never travelled alone?'

'Only from London.' Arlette took Amy's arm as they went up the steps. 'The silly girl decided she wanted to go 'ome. She did not want to come back 'ere. She says it is too cold. But it ees all right. I manage very well.' They entered the hall and Arlette looked round. 'Everything is the same, yes.' She gave a sigh. 'Well, that is good! I am so very tired, my darling. Where is your grandfather? And Edmund?'

'Out somewhere. They should be in soon. We were just about to have tea,' Amy said, leading her into the drawing room. 'Would you like some?'

Arlette pulled a wry face. 'Tea? Ah yes, everything stays the same, does it not?' She sank into a chair, not even taking off her coat. 'But yes, I will have a cup, but weak with lemon, not strong as your grandpapa likes it.'

'I'll ring for more hot water,' Amy said, reaching to press the bell on the wall. 'You look very tired, Grandmama. Was the journey horrendous?'

'It was long,' Arlette said. 'I am getting too old for travelling.' Her eyes alighted on the tray set with two cups and saucers. 'Aunt Julia fled, did she, when she saw me arrive?' She gave a wicked grin that brightened up her face. She had always been a striking woman and maturity hadn't lessened her attraction; her bone structure was good, and her hair was fashionably dressed beneath her large velvet hat, which was trimmed with ostrich feathers.

'I told her you didn't bite.' Amy smiled. 'But she says you make her nervous.'

Arlette gave the little shrug which Amy loved to see; it was so Gallic, and a gesture she had practised herself, but not with the same success.

'I don't mean to,' Arlette murmured. 'I admire

her. Where is your grandfather?' she asked again. 'Why was he not 'ere to greet me?'

'We didn't know when you were coming,' Amy said. 'You said you didn't know yourself when you would arrive.'

'Did I? Ah, perhaps so.'

A maid brought in fresh tea and a jug of hot water. 'Mr Ellis is just coming, ma'am,' she said. 'Beg pardon, I mean *madame*,' she apologized, dipping her knee. 'He's just crossing 'yard now.'

Arlette raised a languid hand. 'Thank you.' She turned to Amy. 'She is new, I think?'

'Yes,' Amy said. 'Someone in the kitchen must have told her to call you madame, knowing that you prefer it.'

Arlette shrugged again. 'It ees not important.'

Joseph breezed in a few minutes later. 'Arlette!' He bent to kiss her cheek. 'I've just heard that you travelled alone. Are you exhausted?'

'I am a leetle tired, Joseph. It is a long way to come without a companion. But when we got to London, Gena insisted that she did not want to come back, and I couldn't make her.'

'But she's been with you for so long.' He frowned. 'She knows how it is here . . . and summer is coming.'

'I know,' she said vaguely. 'But she would not come this time.'

Arlette went upstairs to rest and change before supper. She and Joseph had separate rooms, but as Joseph washed and changed out of his working clothes he could hear Arlette moving around next door. He knocked on her door. 'Are you not resting, my dear?' he called to her. 'Would you rather take supper in your room?'

She opened the door to him. She had changed out of her travelling clothes and into a blue silk peignoir and had let down her thick, now fading, fair hair. 'Come in, Joseph. I am too restless to sleep,' she said. 'My mind is in a jumble.'

She is still very beautiful, he thought, remembering how he had been attracted to her vitality and love of life. He came towards her and, putting his arms round her, kissed her cheek. 'You always smell so nice,' he murmured into her hair. He looked at her. 'And you are still lovely.'

She gazed at him and gave what he thought was a rather wistful smile. 'And you are still 'andsome,' she said softly. 'Just as you were all that long time ago.'

He released her. 'I want to talk to you, Arlette. But not now. Later, after supper.'

She nodded slowly and said huskily, 'And I want to talk to you too, Joseph; about many things.'

He kept glancing at Arlette across the supper table. She was talking to Julia and Amy about Paris, and trying to bring Edmund into the conversation, but although he had greeted his grandmother warmly he made little contribution to the general discourse and spoke not at all to Joseph. Arlette noticed and asked jokingly if he and his grandfather had had a disagreement. Edmund said tersely that they had and, excusing himself, left the table.

'He has had an upset, Grandmama,' Amy began, but saw her grandfather's hand raised to stop her and fell silent, her face colouring with embarrassment.

'We 'ave much to discuss, I can see,' Arlette said lightly. 'So many things 'appen when I am away for even five minutes.'

'It's been longer than that,' Joseph said sharply. 'You've been away all winter.'

'Yes,' she agreed, and to his surprise didn't say that she couldn't stand the winters here, as she usually did. 'It 'as been too long.'

After supper Julia asked to be excused and went to her room, and Amy, sensing something in the atmosphere, did the same.

'I've brought you some cognac, Joseph,' Arlette said. 'Shall we 'ave some with our coffee?'

'Yes,' he said. 'But we'll take it in the drawing room. The fire has been lit all day so you'll be warm. I know how you hate the cold.'

'Am I so difficult, Joseph?' she asked, when she was seated on the sofa by the fire. 'Do I disrupt the 'ousehold so much?'

'Only when you try to change our English habits for French ones,' he said, but he gave a smile as he said it, and handed her a glass of cognac.

'I will try 'arder,' she said, and then, 'So what did you wish to discuss? You 'ave been under a strain. I can see it in your face.'

He took a sip from his glass and then held it up towards the fire so that he could see the amber liquid glow. 'This is good,' he murmured. 'Thank you.'

'Ze best,' she answered, pouting her full lips.

'I've something to tell you, Arlette.' He didn't sit down but stood by the fire, his feet apart. 'I should have told you years ago, but I couldn't bring myself to talk about it. It was much too painful.' He looked down at her; her face was serene, but her brown eyes were wide open and gazing at him intently. 'But now . . .' He hesitated. 'Now, my actions when I was a young man have come home to haunt me, and affect not only me but others who are dear to me; and I am distraught!'

He put his hand to his forehead, pressing his temples. When he removed it she saw that his eyes were moist with tears. 'I never meant to hurt anyone,' he said in a choked voice. 'But even if I could undo what went before – I wouldn't. Couldn't! What happened then I will never be sorry for. Never!'

'Come 'ere, my darling.' She reached out a hand to him. 'Come. Tell Arlette.'

And as he sat by her side and she drew him towards her, he remembered that that was what she had done all those years ago, when he had first met her.

When he had finished telling her his story they sat silently for a moment, both gazing into the flames of the fire. Then Arlette took a deep breath and said, 'And now you have seen your daughter again, and she accepts you?' He nodded, and she continued, 'But she will not allow Edmund to marry her daughter zat 'e loves because *she* is your granddaughter? What is she like? Is she suitable for Edmund?'

'It's irrelevant now, isn't it?' he said harshly. 'But suitable! Young men don't look for suitability. They look for love! And he fell in love with Laura – is still in love with Laura, and that's why he isn't speaking to me. He says I have ruined his life.'

She gave a chuckle. 'Young people!' she said throatily. 'They think they are the only ones to feel passion. But they are not!'

'Will you speak to him?' he begged. 'He always listened to you when he was young. Perhaps he'll listen now.'

'You remember when his father and mother died?' she said softly. 'You insisted that Edmund and Amy should come and live 'ere with you?'

'Of course I remember!' he said in a crabbed

491

tone. 'I wanted Edmund to learn farming, not play around in France as Austin did.'

'Ah!' she said, her expression sad. 'Austin would never have made a farmer; but his son, Edmund – yes, I wanted that for him.'

He frowned. 'But you made such a fuss about his coming here.'

'Only because I knew that if I said no, you would insist.' She glanced at him, a triumphant gleam in her eyes. 'And you did. You wanted Edmund to be your heir in place of Austin, and I wanted that too. The twins had made other plans for their lives, and there was no-one else to take over from you.'

'What are you getting at, Arlette?' he said tetchily. 'This has nothing to do with what I've told you.'

'But it has, my darling.' She took hold of his hand. 'Now I 'ave something to tell you.'

CHAPTER FORTY-FOUR

Arlette licked her lips. 'When I met you that night in Paris, I guessed that you were recovering from a broken love affair. But I soon realized that it was more than that, and that you had lost the love of your life.' She looked at him with tenderness. 'I 'ave always known, throughout our life together, that there was a shadow between us. No,' she said, as he began to speak, 'I must finish what I 'ave to say. There is so much more. I knew,' she went on, 'that I couldn't ever compete with a ghost.' She gently touched his arm. 'I 'ave seen you when you were back with her, when your thoughts 'ave returned to the past.'

Joseph buried his head in his hands. 'I'm so sorry, Arlette. So very sorry.'

'*Joseph*,' she murmured, and he looked up. He had always been charmed by the way she pronounced his name; the breathy softness which made it sound so endearing. 'I am ze one who should be sorry. I 'ave lived a lie for all of our life together, and I should ask for your forgiveness.'

'What?' he said. 'For what?'

'When I met you, it was as if fate 'ad sent you to me. I was desperate too, just as you were.'

'Desperate?' he said. 'No! You were so spirited, so vivacious. That is what attracted me to you. You were so alive, and I was living with death.'

She shook her head. 'No, my darling, I was not. I too was trapped by love. The man I loved was married to somebody else. I am sorry to tell you this, Joseph, but that is why I 'ave spent so much time in France over the years.'

'You still see him!' He was astounded. He had thought that perhaps she had had love affairs when she was young, but now – after so long!

She gesticulated with her hands several times, indicating that it was finished. 'Not now. It ees over. The reason I 'ave been away so long this time is because Marcel was dying. At first I visited him, but then 'is wife, she banned me from seeing him.' Her voice broke. 'She 'as always known about me, but finally she refused to allow me to visit. I wrote to her begging to see 'im one last time. I waited outside his door, but she would not open it to me. I was not allowed to say goodbye or attend his funeral.' A slow tear trickled down her cheek. 'It was so very cruel.'

Joseph was silent. How could two people be

married for so long and know so little about each other? He put his arm round her and drew her close. 'I'm sorry, Arlette. We have both known unhappiness.'

'Yes.' She swallowed, and sniffled, and wiped her face with a handkerchief. 'But there is one thing more that I must tell you, and then we will know if we can spend ze last years of our life together.'

We can, he thought. We must. Perhaps we can both find some comfort.

'When I said I was desperate,' she said, 'it was true. I didn't know which way to turn.' She lifted brimming brown eyes to his. 'Then you came into the 'otel, just as I was contemplating ending my life. You looked lonely. As lonely as I was.' She gave a watery smile. 'And you were 'andsome, though morose, and I was always attracted to 'andsome men! And you were tall and fair as Marcel was.'

He nodded. He remembered their meeting well. 'He wouldn't leave his wife? Was that it? You wanted to be married and he was already married to someone else?'

She put her head on one side and looked at him, her face troubled. 'Do you not understand me, Joseph? I was expecting a child. His child. And he could not marry me.'

He stared at her, comprehension dawning. He drew back and watched her as she bit her lip and

495

turned away from him. 'What are you saying?' His words were almost a whisper.

Her face creased as she squeezed her eyes closed but tears still trickled through her lashes. 'I am saying, Joseph . . .' She opened her eyes and looked at him. 'I am saying that Austin was not your child. He was Marcel's.'

Joseph got up and went to the table and with shaking hands poured them both another cognac. He swallowed his down in one gulp and poured another.

Arlette tutted. 'Such a waste of good cognac,' she murmured, and sipped at hers. 'I am sorry, Joseph. I never thought that you would ever need to know.' She gave a wistful smile. 'After Austin died, I thought . . .' She shook her head. 'There seemed no point in telling you. And you adored Edmund and Amy, I knew that.'

'But that's why you took Austin with you to France so often? When he was a child? To see his father!' His voice was bitter.

'Yes,' she said simply. 'And for 'is father to see 'im. Marcel had no other sons. But Austin never knew,' she added hastily. 'He only knew that Marcel was a friend.'

'And the twins?' he questioned harshly. 'Philip and Matthew? Whom do they belong to?'

'*Please*, Joseph!' she implored. 'Do not be angry wiz me. They are your sons. Of course they

496

are. I was expecting Marcel's child before I met you. As you 'ad a daughter before you met me,' she reminded him. 'We each had a life before.' She put out her hand to him. 'When Austin died, I wanted so much for Edmund and Amy to come and live wiz you. To make up for Austin's loss. I bore my grief alone. I couldn't tell you what it meant to me, to lose my son.'

He came to her, holding her close as she cried, and wept with her. 'As I couldn't tell you of my daughter.'

They sat close together, not speaking for some time. Presently Joseph gave a little grunt in his throat. 'So Edmund can marry his lady after all, if she will have him,' he said softly.

Arlette looked at him. Her eyes were red with weeping. 'You will not disown him, Joseph? Because he is not your blood?'

He shook his head. 'He *is* my own, as Amy is. Nothing will change that. They are *our* grandchildren. Yours and mine. But they must be told about their father. I've confessed about Mary-Ellen and Susannah, and now they must know the truth about Austin. It won't be easy for you, Arlette. They've always idolized you.'

She nodded and said ruefully, 'And now they will discover that their grandmother has 'uman frailties just as everyone else.' She shrugged and then chuckled. 'They will say it ees because I am French. The French – zey are so decadent!'

He kissed the top of her head and saw the silver strands in her hair. 'We'll tell them in the morning,' he said softly. 'Then we can all begin again.'

'Can we, Joseph?' she beseeched. 'I would like that very much.'

He kissed her again. 'So would I.'

Amy looked troubled. Her eyes flickered from her grandfather to her grandmother, to Edmund and Aunt Julia who had also been asked to come down to the morning room. 'Does it mean that we have to go and live in France, as we are French after all? Because,' she said in a sudden rush, 'though I love you dearly, Grandmama, I don't want to. I want to stay here.' Her lips began to tremble. 'This is my home. Though I'm not saying that I won't come to see you.' She looked at Joseph. 'We can stay, can't we?'

'You pudding! Of course you can.' He beamed at her, absurdly relieved that she wasn't shocked at this fresh revelation, but only anxious that life would continue as it always had. 'We perhaps wouldn't have told you but for Edmund.'

'And I didn't say that I was going back to France,' Arlette said softly, and smiled at Joseph and then at Julia. 'I will probably stay 'ere and annoy Aunt Julia!'

Joseph smiled back at her. She had shared his bed last night and when he had woken early, as he always did, he had looked down at her as she lay still sleeping. She had seemed fragile and vulnerable, not spirited and strong as she usually did. She had opened her eyes and gazed at him and he had bent to kiss her.

Edmund sat still as stone, as he absorbed the latest news. 'You're saying . . .' He cleared his throat. 'You're saying that I'm not an Ellis after all, but some other name?'

'No!' Joseph barked. 'We're not saying that. You were baptized and registered as Edmund Ellis, just as your father was baptized and registered as Austin Ellis, but – your grandmother has just explained! What's the matter with you, man?' he bellowed suddenly. 'Can't you work it out? You're a farmer. You should know about reproduction, for heaven's sake! You're making your sister and Aunt Julia blush!'

Julia gave a little smile and shook her head. 'Not me,' she murmured. 'I am aware of more than any of you might think.'

Edmund's chair crashed back as he stood up. 'It means – it means that I can ask Laura! Oh!' He put his head back and banged the heel of his hand against his forehead. 'Will she have me?' He looked wildly about him, then planted a kiss on his grandmother's cheek, and came to shake hands with Joseph.

'I'm sorry,' he said. 'I know I said some awful things to you. Blaming you. I—' He suddenly put his hand to his mouth. 'It doesn't change anything, does it? I mean, I'm still your grandson? Because I—' His voice was choked and he swallowed hard. 'Because I wouldn't want to be anybody else's.'

Joseph hugged him. 'No,' he said. 'Nothing changes, except that now you may pay your addresses to Laura.' He gave a sudden grin. 'Of course, you'll have to ask *her* father first.'

'Mama.' Laura and her mother sat alone in the sitting room. They had finished their supper, though lately their appetites had been poor. 'I'd like to go away for a while.'

Her mother looked up from the book she was reading. 'Away? Where and with whom?'

'I don't know yet, but somewhere; and I'll easily find someone to go with me. It's so unfair,' she burst out. 'I'm making you unhappy by my moods, and this should be a happy time for you preparing for your marriage. I think,' she went on, 'that you and Uncle Freddie should start making arrangements now. I know that you have waited because of me, but there's no need. I'm perfectly all right. All I need is a change of scenery and some different company.'

'But Freddie and I want you at our wedding, Laura. We couldn't think of it otherwise.'

'But you said that Mr Ellis – your father –

wishes to give you away. Would you also invite his wife and – and his grandchildren?'

'His wife, of course, if she's in England. But I don't think there is any need to invite his grandchildren. It will be a quiet wedding. There will only be a few guests.'

'But if I went away for a time you could visit your father in Skeffling and not feel guilty about me.'

'I have no plans to visit Skeffling at present,' Susannah said calmly. 'And neither do I feel guilty about you. I'm sorry that you've received such a blow, Laura.' She folded her hands over her book. 'Life is often unfair, I'm afraid. I remember thinking that myself when I thought I'd lost Freddie.' She gave a deep sigh. 'But you will survive.' She looked at Laura's lowered eyes and tense expression. 'You'll learn that life has to go on no matter how you are hurting. But perhaps it would do you good to go away for a while. We'll consider it, and perhaps talk it over with Freddie.'

'Yes,' Laura murmured. 'He's always so wise.' She gave her mother a quivering smile. 'I'm so pleased for you and Uncle Freddie, Mama, and I think – I think that one day I'll be able to call him Papa.'

'He'd like that, Laura,' her mother said gently. 'It's what he's always wanted.'

They were interrupted by a loud peal of the

front door bell. They looked at each other. 'Who can that be at this time?' Susannah wondered. 'Not Freddie; he said he was working late at the office and then going straight home.'

'And not James, as he's staying in Hull and going to the theatre.'

Mrs Smith tapped on the door. 'Excuse me, Mrs Page. Mr Ellis apologizes for the lateness of the hour, but asks if he might see you.'

Susannah mouthed a round 'oh'. She couldn't yet think of Joseph Ellis as her father, and wondered what it was he needed to see her about. Perhaps he had told his wife about her. Maybe she didn't want him to have any further contact with her. 'Please ask him to come in,' she said.

'Shall I leave you, Mama?' Laura rose from her chair. 'Will it be something private do you think?'

'I doubt it. No, please stay, Laura.'

But it wasn't Joseph Ellis. It was Edmund. And he was all done up in a formal tailcoat and narrow trousers and a white shirt with a high collar. He held a top hat in his hand and his hair was neatly trimmed. He looked so personable and dashing that Laura wanted to weep.

He bowed. 'Forgive me for calling so late, Mrs Page. Good evening, Miss Page.'

Laura, her lips clenched, barely acknowledged him as her mother bade the visitor be seated.

502

'Is all well at home, Mr Ellis?' Susannah asked. 'Is your grandfather in good health?'

'Indeed yes,' he enthused. 'As is my grandmother, who has just returned from France.'

'And your great-aunt and sister?' she asked after a suitable pause.

'Yes.' He beamed. 'We are all in excellent health!'

'I'm very pleased to hear it,' she replied politely, and waited.

Laura felt herself growing angry. Why had he come? How dare he come! A flush of red touched her cheeks. He has no sensitivity! Did his previous apparent anguish mean nothing after all? In a moment, she thought, I'll get up and walk out of the room, manners or not!

Edmund cleared his throat. 'I – erm.' He coughed again. 'I travelled into Hull for an express purpose; and with the advice I've been given I came immediately to see you, Mrs Page – and you also, Miss Page.'

'Advice?' Susannah said. 'Whose advice?'

'An eminent lawyer's, ma'am.' His eyes began to sparkle. 'I called on him to ask his permission to address his daughter.'

'Mr Cannon?' Susannah asked on a breath.

'How dare you!' Laura said in a tight, furious voice. 'How could you?'

'That's what Mr Cannon said you would say.' Edmund turned to Laura. 'He said that you'd

503

make up your own mind as to whether or not I might address you.'

'Not that!' she said angrily. 'How dare you suggest it when you know that Mama won't – why would Freddie—' She stopped. Why *would* Freddie concur with such a proposal? He wouldn't, she realized. He had been so anxious about her; so protective.

'You're beautiful when you're angry, Laura,' Edmund murmured, gazing at her. Then he turned to Susannah. 'I've done this all wrong, Mrs Page. My grandfather said I had to conduct myself in a proper manner and not behave like a country oaf, as I did before, and that's why I went to see Mr Cannon first; but when he said it was all right and that he had no objections I couldn't help rushing straight here.'

He went towards Laura and took hold of her hand. 'If you'll accept me,' he said softly, 'we are free to marry. Joseph Ellis isn't my grandfather after all. He wasn't my father's father, though he thought he was. He and my grandmother, it seems, have been confessing their sins – except that I don't think they were sins. They just happened to have loved other people before they met each other.'

Laura felt she was going to faint; which is ridiculous, she told herself, before sinking into a chair. She looked at her mother, who was quietly smiling, although her eyes were moist.

'Well, Laura.' There was a tremble in Susannah's voice. 'Are you going to put the young man out of his misery?'

The doorbell rang again and she got up. 'I'll leave you for a moment,' she said hurriedly. 'Perhaps this might be Freddie after all.'

She closed the door behind her and Edmund drew Laura up to him. 'You heard what your mama said,' he murmured. 'Are you going to put me out of my misery? You know that I love you?'

'You hardly know me,' she prevaricated. 'We have only met a few times.'

He gazed tenderly into her eyes. 'Then I'll wait,' he said. 'And I'll pay my addresses to you as polite society decrees that I should.'

'How long will you wait?' she teased, and then laughed as he drew out a pocket watch from his waistcoat and looked at it.

'A quarter of an hour,' he said. 'May I be permitted to sit down?'

Susannah and Freddie returned to the sitting room fifteen minutes later and found Laura and Edmund standing side by side.

'Well?' Susannah asked. 'What is it to be?' Though she could tell already by Edmund's expression of sheer joy.

'Yes,' Laura said, her face alight. 'I've put Edmund out of his misery and said yes.'

CHAPTER FORTY-FIVE

Susannah walked with Joseph along the Humber embankment towards Welwick Thorpe where he told her she had been born. She was wearing a shawl which had been bought for her mother, and had felt sad and emotional when Joseph had told her how Mary-Ellen had at first refused it, but had later said she would wrap their child in it. He asked Susannah if she would accept it, for her aunt Lol had given it back to him as a keepsake. She had been glad to, for she had nothing else belonging to her mother.

It was a fine autumn day and the tide was running high. Joseph had said that he would drive her in the trap into Welwick village from Skeffling and they could walk from there, but she told him she would rather walk all the way so that they could talk. She had been staying with him and Arlette at Burstall House for the last few days. Freddie hadn't come with her as he was

506

trying to finish off some urgent work before their wedding in October.

Laura and Edmund were holidaying in France after their wedding. France was chosen because Edmund wanted to brush up on his accent now that he was a *bona fide* Frenchman. Laura chose to go because she wanted to recall some memories of her own.

In their time together, Joseph wondered how it was that Susannah, with her sweet, gentle nature and serenity, could have been born from such a passionate relationship as his and Mary-Ellen's. She is nothing like her mother, he had mused; but her daughter Laura, she has fire, just like her grandmother. She will lead Edmund a merry dance. He won't get everything his own way with such a wife. But he obviously totally adores her.

'This is it,' he said, as they came to a gap in the hedge. 'It's very wild and overgrown. Mind you don't slip. No-one ever comes here.'

Once they did, she thought, recalling that she had come with Thomas when they were children and they had searched amongst the rubble and bricks of an old cow stall. Joseph had taken her to meet Thomas, who was the Ellises' waggoner. He was a short man, but strapping, with a broad back and hard muscles. 'How do, Susannah,' he'd grinned, and the years had rolled back for both of them.

'I'd have come to see you,' he explained, 'but when Wilf Topham was waggoner he'd never give me enough time off. He allus found me some job or other that I had to finish. Then, when he married our Jane, I didn't want to come. Didn't want to see him at home as well as at work.' He bit his lip and glanced at her. 'After you left, he gave Jane a right beating; nearly killed her and she lost 'bairn she was carrying.'

She was shocked. 'I didn't know. What happened to him? Where did he go?'

Thomas had looked about him. Joseph Ellis had gone back to the house, leaving them to reminisce.

'Mr Ellis told Jack Terrison what had happened to Jane and he told me. I asked for time off and went to look for him, but first of all I searched out Daniel. I hadn't seen him for a bit – he was working over at Halsham – but I thought he might know where Topham was. And I wanted to ask him about all 'things he used to hint at when we were bairns: you know, about you being born down at Welwick Thorpe in that burned-out house and not having a da and that. But when I told him about Topham giving Jane a hiding, and how you'd run away, he fetched his coat and said, come on, we've a score or two to settle; nobody treats anybody belonging 'us like that. And when I said, but what about Susannah, he said there was nowt to tell. That he'd just been stirring things up.' He'd grinned. 'But seemingly there was, after all, but whether he knew 'truth I can't say.'

'But what happened?' she insisted. 'Did you find Topham?'

Thomas's cheeks flushed. 'Oh, aye, we found him all right. Down on Hull docks. Going to board a ship, he was.' He screwed up his mouth. 'Missed it, though,' he added wryly. 'I mean – really missed it. Tripped over a bollard and fell in 'dock.'

Susannah drew in a breath. 'You didn't—'

'Push him?' He gazed stolidly at her. 'Well, mebbe it was just a little push. That was after we'd told him what we'd do if he ever set foot back in Holderness again; but he was walking back'ards at 'time and not looking where he was going!' He laughed. 'No need to be afeared, Susannah. We whistled on somebody and they fished him out. Like a drowned dog, he was.'

'And Daniel?' she asked. 'Where's he?'

He rubbed his chin. 'Well, seeing as Topham had missed his ship, Daniel said that he'd allus had a mind to travel, so he took his place and sailed off to London docks. Last I heard he was taking a ship to America. Lots o' cheap land for settlers over there. He sent me a postcard asking if I wanted to join him, but I didn't. I'm all right here.'

He'd grinned again and she knew that he was.

509

She had gone also to see Aunt Jane. Jane had refused to move out of Welwick when the poorhouse fell down, and Joseph, wanting to keep the link with the family, had put her into one of their tied cottages. She had whispered to Susannah that she was charged only a peppercorn rent and the parish paid that. 'I manage all right,' she'd said, with a nod and a wink. 'Jack comes to see me and brings me a few eggs 'n' that from time to time.' When asked who Jack was, she'd said, 'Jack Terrison, o' course. He used to be sweet on your ma.'

When she told Joseph this he'd laughed and said he knew. He'd also asked Terrison years ago to keep an eye on Jane, and he still did, even though he didn't need to.

They slithered down the grassy bank and Joseph caught hold of Susannah's arm to save her from falling. 'The cottage was well down this track,' he said, 'but Mary-Ellen – your mother – used to come to the estuary. She told me that sometimes she would take her father's boat out and catch fish; and she caught shrimps and eels and trapped rabbits. Her mother had died in childbirth, but Mrs Marston, your aunt Lol, had raised Mary-Ellen until she was old enough to come here and look after her father, Isaac.'

'It must have been a lonely kind of life for a young girl,' Susannah murmured.

'Yes,' he agreed. 'And I think that's why she

was as she was. Fiercely independent. Contrary and quite untamed.' He sighed. 'I said I would love her for ever, and I have. Her life was so short. I knew her for only a year, and I often wonder if our love would have survived had she lived. Or would our differences have made a difference?' He took a wistful breath. 'I'll never know, of course. I only know that I have carried the image of her and our love within me all my life.' He turned to Susannah, and, as if she was the older and wiser, asked, 'Can love conquer all?'

'Yes,' she answered simply. 'It can, if it's strong enough.'

They came to a clearing where the grass was flattened. 'Someone has been here.' He frowned.

'Village children,' she said, remembering. 'Playing games.' She looked round the open space. There was nothing there, no spar or piece of wood to show that the area had once been inhabited. 'There's a fine view of Patrington church,' she commented. 'You can see 'spire from here. There's nothing left of the house though. I was told that it had burned down.'

'Yes. I set fire to it.' He stared around. 'But this is where it was. See the hawthorn?' A large hawthorn tree, covered in berries, cast a shade. 'Roughly there. I came back after Mary-Ellen's funeral.' There was pain in his eyes as he spoke. 'I was distraught. I didn't know what to do or who to speak to. I came back here and saw where – saw where she had been so alive, and where she had given birth to our child.' His voice was choked, his memories still raw as he told her.

'So I made a fire and set it alight: everything. The house – well, it was little more than a hovel, so it didn't take much burning. The cow stall, where I'd waited all night because I wasn't allowed indoors when she was giving birth. It all went up in smoke. A funeral pyre. A testimony to my grief.' He took a breath. 'I didn't want anyone else living in it. I knew if it remained empty somebody would move in, tramps or gypsies, and I wasn't having that. I wanted my memories left intact.'

The air was still. There was hardly a breath of wind, just a slight swaying of the grasses. 'I can't feel anything,' Susannah murmured. 'I thought that I'd be able to sense her presence. But I can't.'

'That's because you didn't know her,' Joseph said.

'And that is my sadness,' she said, looking up at him. 'One I have to bear.'

'But you have *your* daughter,' he said. 'You've seen her grow up and marry.' He clasped Susannah's hand. 'I told Mary-Ellen that I would love her for ever and I shall. I promised too that I would love our child, *you*, and I will. I do.'

He put his arm round her as they walked back

to the estuary, and she leaned her head against him, her skirts trailing in the mud and becoming caught amongst the brambles. When they reached the top of the embankment she looked back down the grassy slope.

'Why don't you build a house here?' she suggested. 'For Mary-Ellen's granddaughter and Edmund? Young people need a house of their own – not to live side by side with their grandparents.'

Joseph thought of Arlette, who had said she would stay with him. They had agreed to try to make a life together, and they would, he believed. I remember now how she used to make me laugh, how spirited she was, even though I now know that she was suffering too. And he thought of his sister Julia who had asked him if she might have a house of her own. Just a small one, she had said, where I can take in one or two waifs or strays. Which left Amy, who would live with them until she too married.

He looked back down the slope. Swifts and swallows darted overhead, preparing for the long flight south. By next week they would be gone. A skein of geese flying in short formation were flying in off the estuary, calling their croaking anxious cry. A salty breeze was beginning to rise, causing tree branches to sway, rustling and whispering the grasses. An owl, awakened early, hooted, and he thought he could hear laughter.

Was it an echo from the past or the sound of the future? Susannah was right. He should build a house there so that the voices of young people and children could be heard. His mouth turned up. Great-grandchildren! Now that was something to think about.

'But I still miss her,' he murmured, hardly aware that he had spoken aloud.

'She lives on, Father,' Susannah said softly, and his throat tightened at the loving name. 'She lives on through me, and through Laura and James, and whoever might come after.' She tucked her arm into his. 'Come,' she said. 'Don't let's look back. We must now look forward.'

THE END

I was born in the mining town of Castleford, spending my formative years there before coming to live in East Yorkshire as a young girl, and just like a stick of Scarborough rock I'm Yorkshire through and through.

I was such a dreaming child, living in my imagination and through books. My education was dire, and I had the distinction of failing my Eleven Plus – twice. My saving grace was my writing and reading ability; given an essay to write I was in my element, and as for books, I couldn't get enough of them.

In my adult life I took myself off for Further Education to achieve for myself what my teachers couldn't teach me. But, rather than go on to take a university degree which had been my original intention and because I had re-discovered my love of writing, I joined a writers' workshop to polish and hone my writing skills and importantly be with like-minded people.

Prior to this I had in the meantime worked in fashion, trod the catwalk, danced ballroom competitions, married Peter and had two daughters and a grandson. I had lived a full life before taking my writing seriously, but once I did it became my passion. This was the time too when I became a hands-on volunteer and a supporter of various charities, some of which I still support today.

I began my first novel, *The Hungry Tide*, in about 1988 and in the several years of writing it I became completely absorbed in the nineteenth century and the way of life. That novel became the catalyst of what was to come; in 1993 I entered and won the Catherine Cookson Prize for Fiction and was propelled into becoming an author of regional historical novels.

Having lived in the country district of Holderness for most of my married life, I now live in the lovely old market town of Beverley. It featured in my book *The Kitchen Maid*; I've always had a soft spot for Beverley and I have the advantage of both town and country on my doorstep. I have a small gravel garden where I can sit and ponder or retreat to my summerhouse, and I always have a book with me. Old habits die hard.

What was your favourite book growing up?

Louisa May Alcott was my most favoured author when I was growing up and *Little Women* my favourite book. I didn't realize then that I was reading Literature, nor that I would be inspired to write books with similar themes, including that of a family and a mother coping at home without a husband. Another strong woman.

How do you research your novels?

Research is very important to me and we're lucky enough in this area to have good libraries and two excellent venues to gather information, the Hull History Centre and the Carnegie library. Both have archives of local and national interest. For researching places abroad, like America or Europe, the internet is a great source of information, especially for detail of the nineteenth century.

What themes are important to you when you write?

Poverty and injustice are my pet hates and these were prevalent in the nineteenth century. I also like to write about strong women. They had to be strong in order to survive.

Do you have any favourite characters you'd love to write about again?

Sometimes a character stays with me long after I have finished a book, and not always the chief protagonist. This happened in *The Hungry Tide* and the character

Annie, who I felt that, despite appearing to be weak and a hopeless case, had more to offer given the chance – and in her own book in her own name, Annie became strong, warm and with a great humour that hadn't been apparent in the first book. In *His Brother's Wife* there is a child, Daniel, whose forebears were unknown. I had to write about him in order to find out just who he was and what had gone before. This became *Every Mother's Son*.

What advice would you give an aspiring writer?

To anyone aspiring to write, I'd say take a pen and paper or a blank page on your computer screen and start to put ideas down. Write about what is important to you, what stretches your imagination, choose a period in which you feel comfortable and is of interest to you, be it the present, the past or the future, and fill it with characters. Give them a name and they'll come alive. Recently, I have promoted two short story competitions in my local area in order to encourage creative writing, and I provided a sentence to be included in the story, for would-be or first-time writers don't always know how to start. The winner and runner-up had never written before and were thrilled to receive their prizes.

Dear Reader,

I am absolutely thrilled that my much loved book, *Nobody's Child*, has been re-issued. It is one of my most favourite books amongst the ones I have written, having taken the characters to my heart; it is a book that I wept over and yet smiled over too.

It brings back many reminders and memories of friendship and of the many times when I wandered along the lanes and fields of Welwick as I placed my characters where I thought they might belong, and gazed too at the Humber from its banks; I also thought about and still visit the market town of Hedon, close to my former home where I shopped in the butcher's and greengrocer's and almost lived in the local library as I researched the history of this ancient town.

My characters are of course, fictional, but that is not to say that I didn't believe in them, I did, an author has to otherwise they don't come alive to the reader. Holderness people of long ago are like no other that I know of, with a wit and humour and stoicism which comes from living in an isolated area and although today there are good roads to drive on and the many villages and communities are larger than they once were, in some aspects Holderness remains much the same today as it was one hundred and fifty or so years ago.

Many readers might sigh when my many characters in my books comment on the wide skies of Holderness, but it is true that sunset is indeed a sight to behold.

I do hope that you enjoy reading *Nobody's Child* and that it brings you as much joy and pleasure as it did to me in writing it.

With good wishes,
Val

A Mother's Choice

For ten years, Delia has had to fend for herself
and her son Jack, and as a young unmarried mother,
life has never been easy. Every new coat and pair
of shoes was bought with what little money she
could scrape together as a singer on the stage.

But when the theatre jobs dry up, Delia faces
a dilemma: continue the search for paid work
with no knowing whether she'll find the stability
and security her son needs, or return to the place
that should be home . . . where only spite and
hatred await them.

Desperate now, a chance encounter suddenly
presents a lifeline. But Delia is faced with an
impossible, heart-wrenching choice. Can she
bear to leave Jack behind, hoping another family
will care for him? Will they ever be reunited?

**What else can a mother do to give her son
the life he deserves?**

A Mother's Choice is out now
in paperback

Fallen Angels

After her devious husband Billy tries to sell
her at a wife sale, Lily Fowler finds herself
alone, frightened and heavily pregnant
on the streets of Hull.

Running out of options when even the
workhouse turns her away, Lily is forced to
swallow what little pride she has left and accept
work in a once-grand mansion in Leadenhall
Square – now a brothel.

Unexpectedly, she soon forges a strong
bond with the group of people she finds there,
all good-hearted women who have simply fallen
on hard times. Seeing potential where others see
only destitution, Lily and her 'fallen angels' join
forces to outwit the low-life brothel-keeper.

In working to transform the house in
Leadenhall Square into something more
respectable, doors to new opportunities are
opened and lost loves are rekindled.

**Can the happy endings the fallen angels never
dared to dream of finally come true?**

Fallen Angels is out now in paperback

No Place for a Woman

When Lucy's parents are killed in a train
crash, her kindly uncle steps in to look after
the little girl – to the initial apprehension of his
wife and her son. However, Lucy's sweet, spirited
charm slowly wins over her new family, and as
she overcomes the trauma of her childhood,
she grows up inspired to become a doctor,
just like her father.

But studying medicine in London takes Lucy
far from her home in Hull and the people she
loves, and she has to battle to be accepted
in a man's world.

**With the dark clouds of the First World
War gathering on the horizon, an even greater
challenge approaches. Can a woman find her
place on the front line of battle? Will Lucy be
able to follow her dreams – and find love – in
a world shattered by war?**

No Place for a Woman is out now
in paperback

The Kitchen Maid

Jenny is determined to make her own way in the
world, and she secures a job as the kitchen maid in
a grand house in Yorkshire. Gradually, she gains
the attention of the young master of the house, and
they fall in love. But slowly their dreams turn to
nightmares, culminating in a scandal that will force
Jenny to leave behind everything she knows.

Cast aside by her own family, Jenny faces many
difficulties until an unusual promise changes the
course of her life: Jenny the kitchen maid becomes
mistress of her own grand house. Although she
tries to fit in with this new world, however, she
never forgets the words a gypsy once told her:
that one day she will return to where she
was happy – and discover her true love . . .

**But will the tragedy of her past stand
in the way of her happiness?**

The Kitchen Maid is out now
in paperback

Little Girl Lost

Will the troubles in her past break her spirit?

Margriet grew up as a lonely child in the old town of Hull. Her adored father often travelled by sea to the Netherlands, leaving her with an unaffectionate mother and only her imagination of a little Dutch girl, Annelise, to keep her company. When devastation ravages her tiny family, Annelise becomes the comforting friend Margriet needs for a long time to come.

A few years later, Margriet is blossoming into a kind young lady. Keen to escape her mother and strike out on her own, she forms an unlikely friendship with some of the street children who roam the town.

As Margriet acts upon her inspiration to help them, will the troubles of her past break her spirit, or will she be able to overcome them?

Little Girl Lost is out now in paperback

Far From Home

**Can she make a new life away
from everything she knows?**

When Georgiana Gregory and her maid, Kitty,
make the long sea journey from their native Hull
for New York, they hope to escape the confines of
English life and savour a land of opportunity.

But in New York, Georgiana finds she isn't far from
home when she encounters a man passing himself
off as a local mill-owner's son, Edward, who has
fled to America. Georgiana recognizes the man
standing before her as Edward's valet Robert –
Edward himself appears to have vanished.

As Georgiana and Kitty pursue the adventures
of the frontier, and Edward tries to flee his
enemies, are the dangers of this new
country too much to cope with?

Far From Home is out now in paperback

Every Mother's Son

Harriet and Fletcher Tuke have worked hard
to raise their children well. Daniel, the eldest
son, has always accepted that his birth father
died soon after he was born, and Fletcher
has raised Daniel as his own.

But as Daniel comes of age and begins to
fall in love with childhood friend Beatrice Hart,
he can't help but wonder about his heritage – his
olive skin and dark eyes reminding him daily of
the difference between him and his siblings, and
between his and Beatrice's families. Meanwhile,
shocking truths about Fletcher's own family line
are suddenly brought to the surface, revealing
a connection between the two families.

Daniel's wish to learn about his bloodline
takes him to Europe, where decisions about his
future take shape. But will it be one he can share
with Beatrice? And as Harriet hopefully awaits
his return back home on the farm, she could
never imagine that answers to questions about
her own family are also just on the horizon.

Every Mother's Son is out now
in paperback

Join
Val Wood
online

Find out more about Val and her novels at

www.valeriewood.co.uk

Since winning the Catherine Cookson Prize for Fiction for her first novel, *The Hungry Tide*, **Val Wood** has published over twenty novels and become one of the most popular authors in the UK.

Born in the mining town of Castleford, Val came to East Yorkshire as a child and has lived in Hull and rural Holderness where many of her novels are set. She now lives in the market town of Beverley.

When she is not writing, Val is busy promoting libraries and supporting many charities.

Find out more about Val Wood's novels by visiting her website: www.valeriewood.co.uk

Have you read all of Val Wood's novels?

The Hungry Tide
Sarah Foster's parents fight a constant battle with poverty – until wealthy John Rayner provides them with work and a home on the coast. But when he falls for their daughter, Sarah, can their love overcome the gulf of wealth and social standing dividing them?

Annie
Annie Swinburn has killed a man. The man was evil in every possible way, but she knows that her only fate if she stays in Hull is a hanging. So she runs as far away as she can – to a new life that could offer her the chance of love, in spite of the tragedy that has gone before . . .

Children of the Tide
A tired woman holding a baby knocks at the door of one of the big houses in Anlaby. She shoves the baby at young James Rayner, then she vanishes. The Rayner family is shattered – born into poverty, will a baby unite or divide the family?

The Gypsy Girl
Polly Anna's mother died when she was just three years old. Alone in the world, the workhouse was the only place for her. But with the help of a young misfit she manages to escape, running away with the fairground folk. But will Polly Anna ever find somewhere she truly belongs?

Emily
A loving and hard-working child, Emily goes into service at just twelve years old. But when an employer's son dishonours and betrays her, her fortunes seem to be at their lowest ebb. Can she journey from shame and imprisonment to a new life and fulfilment?

Going Home
For Amelia and her siblings, the grim past their mother Emily endured seems far away. But when a gentleman travels from Australia to meet Amelia's family, she discovers the past casts a long shadow and that her tangled family history is inextricably bound up with his . . .

Rosa's Island
Taken in as a child, orphaned Rosa grew up on an island off the coast of Yorkshire. Her mother, before she died, promised that one day Rosa's father would return. But when two mysterious Irishmen come back to the island after many years, they threaten everything Rosa holds dear . . .

The Doorstep Girls
Ruby and Grace have grown up in the poorest slums of Hull. Friends since childhood, they have supported each other in bad times and good. As times grow harder, and money scarcer, the girls search for something that could take them far away . . . But what price will they pay to find it?